Kilian

A Broken Prophecies Story

SA McClure

Not all heroes were meant to save the world.

Kilian
A Broken Prophecies Story

Written by SA McClure

Edited by Linda Sullivan
Front Cover Design by Shayne K.
Graphic Design by Katelin Kinney
Character Art by Stephanie Brown

Lunameed Publishing
lunameed@gmail.com
Indianapolis, Indiana
ISBN 13: 9780692871676
ISBN 10: 0692871675

Printed in the United States of America.

First Edition.

For my father, who always encouraged me to pursue my own adventures.
Thank you for going on this one with me.

Special Acknowledgments

Thank you for your super special support on Kickstarter. You helped make this story happen.

Chris Howe
Vicki McClure
Michael Bishop
And all my Kickstarter backers

Special Thanks

I would have never written Kilian without the prompt from my father. Thank you for encouraging me to tell his backstory. What started out as a brief outline that I was going to weave into the Broken Prophecies series turned into something so much bigger. This one's for you.

Thank you to my partner, Michael. Thank you for always being willing to process my story lines, provide feedback on my battle scenes, and listen me to read passages over and over again. Thank you for your unwavering support and love. I couldn't do any of this without you.

Kilian

Bluebeard

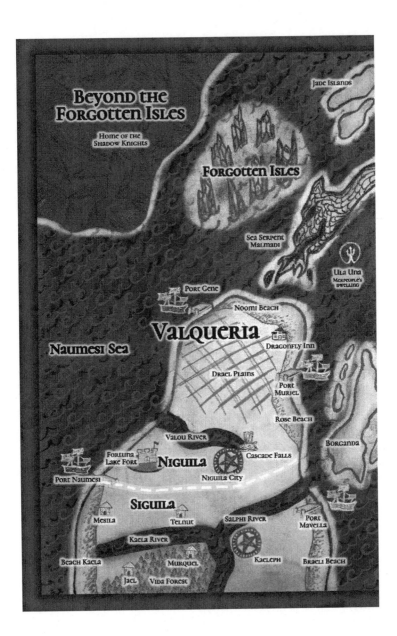

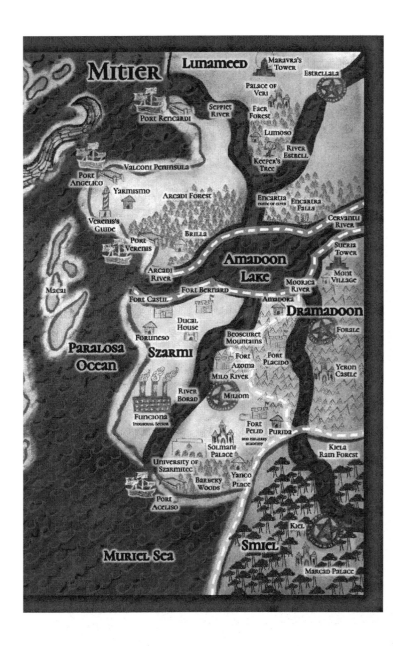

Part One
Chapter One
A small village on the outskirts of the Arcadi Forest, Lunameed

The boy's shoulders shook as he brought down his ax upon the wood with a satisfying thunk. He smiled as the wood split apart and fell to the ground on opposite sides of the chopping block. *I'm getting better at this,* he thought as he set another log into place and brought his ax down once again. His muscles ached in the steady, tired way that indicated it was almost time for him to return home for the day. He wiped the sweat dripping down his brow with the back of his hand and admired the piles of wood that littered the ground before him. Winter was coming, and Kilian had no desire to freeze the way they had last year. The year his father had died. Shaking his head as if to remove the memories that haunted him, Kilian hoisted another log onto the block and readied himself to bring his ax down once more.

The sound of twigs snapping beneath the weight of something heavy drew his attention away from the waiting log. Crouching low and tucking his ax in tight, Kilian did what his father had always taught him to do. He hid. Waited. Breathed in. For one long, awful moment, Kilian listened for the sound of crunching twigs and horses' neighing. This would mean danger. If he heard children laughing, he would know that his younger brother and sister had come to collect him. His lungs burned as he continued to hold his breath. *Just a few seconds more,* he told himself as his eyes began to water, *just a few seconds more.*

Kilian let out the breath he had been holding in a great whoosh. Panting, he clutched his chest as he leaned forward and gulped in the cool, refreshing forest air. He could hear his blood pumping through his body with a loud thumping noise. Kilian froze. *I'm making too much sound,* he realized as he clamped his hand over his mouth and waited for a split second more. The sound of crunching twigs did not happen again. Despite his young age—he was only fifteen—Kilian's body moaned the way an old man's does after sitting for too long as he slowly made his way back to the chopping block.

"Why were you hiding from me, boy?" a gruff voice asked from somewhere behind him. Kilian spun around in a single motion, swinging his ax out as he went. The voice laughed a hearty, almost meaty, laugh. "Come now, me boy, did you really think that little ax would be the end of me?"

Kilian stopped mid-swing and looked at the man standing before him.

He was a tall man with wide shoulders and a narrow waist. He stood at least two hands higher than Kilian did, which was astonishing in and of itself considering Kilian towered over all the other men in his village. A giant sword was buckled to the man's belt, and he wore an oversized, double-breasted coat that reminded Kilian of the soldiers he'd seen marching through his village just the day before. Unlike the soldiers, though, the stranger wore his long hair in braids with metallic beads woven into them. The man's hair was the color of fresh seaweed, and Kilian found himself wondering if the man was a pirate.

He knew this was silly, of course. Kilian lived too far inland for there to be pirates roaming about the countryside. Still, there was an air about the man that gave Kilian the distinct impression that he had explored the Mitierian realm and, potentially, beyond. The idea burned inside Kilian's chest. There was nothing he wanted more than to travel the world and go on adventures.

But he couldn't. Not while his ma had to raise his younger brother and sister on her own. The three of them were all she had left.

"What's yer name, boy?" the man asked. Kilian looked up at the man in surprise. It took him a moment to realize that the man had been speaking to him. His cheeks burned as he realized he hadn't answered the man's first set of questions either. *He must think I'm either deaf or a dolt. Hopefully the first and not the latter*, Kilian thought.

"Kilian, sir, Kilian Clearwater," his voice shook faintly as he spoke and Kilian sent a prayer to the Light that the man wouldn't take his hesitation to talk to him as fear.

The man eyed him for several moments before saying, "And where do ya live, Kilian Clearwater?"

Kilian raised one shaking hand and pointed in the direction of his village, "With my ma, sir. Down by the village. My sister, May, and brother, Willis, live with us."

Kilian clapped his hand over his mouth and stared at the man. He hadn't intended to tell the stranger about his siblings, but when he started talking about his family, he found that he couldn't stop. *Magic,* Kilian realized, *the man was using magic.* He felt the warmth drain from his face.

The man's smile stretched across his face the way a wolf's does when it's about to pounce. Kilian took a small, half-step back from where the man stood.

"There's no reason to be afraid," the man said. "I'm not going to hurt you."

The man took a step forward, and Kilian caught a whiff of his scent. He smelled of smoke and salt water. Kilian wrinkled his nose in disgust.

"Who are you?" Kilian asked in a faltering voice.

The man bowed, "Sir Reginald Bluebeard at your service."

"Never heard of ya," Kilian narrowed his eyes at 'Sir Reginald Bluebeard' and waited for the man to explain himself.

"That's a mighty shame, it is. If ya had, you would have realized how famous I truly am."

"Is that so?" Kilian asked, his voice held the measure of the disbelief he felt. He hoped the man wouldn't be able to detect it.

"'Course it is," Sir Bluebeard bellowed, "I ain't but sailed the Forgotten Isles and met with the dragons."

Kilian snorted, "Everyone knows that dragons aren't real. They're just baby stories mothers tell their children to get them to mind them."

The man laughed a big, hearty laugh. It was the kind of laugh that had the power to make everyone who heard it laugh too.

And that's just what Kilian did.

He laughed until his sides hurt and his breath caught in his lungs. He laughed until his throat ached and his eyes watered with tears. He laughed until the man stopped laughing.

When he stopped, Kilian wasn't even sure why he'd been laughing in the first place.

"If dragons ain't real, then what is this?" the man asked as he pulled a large, sparkling piece of metal from the inside of his shirt. It was a dark golden color that seemed to suck in the sun's light.

Kilian stared at the hunk of metal. To him, it looked like nothing more than a large rock that had been polished to a smooth sheen. He shrugged at the man.

"No? You really don't know?" the man's voice held a note of disbelief as he regarded Kilian.

Kilian shook his head.

The larger man lunged towards him and clapped Kilian on the shoulder so quickly that Kilian barely saw the man move. The man's pungent odor filled his nostrils as he leaned in close to Kilian's ear and whispered, "Would you like to find out?"

Bluebeard's breath reeked of mureechi and apple ale. Kilian gagged a little as he breathed in. He hated the scent of mureechi. It reminded him too much of his father.

Bluebeard leaned away from Kilian and looked him straight in the eyes. They seemed to swim in a swirl of blues, grays, and greens. Kilian almost believed that he could get lost in them.

"Listen to me, boy," Bluebeard's voice came out in a low growl, "I'm in need of a new assistant, and you look like just the sort of whelp who needs a little adventure in his life."

"No, sir. I don't think that's me," Kilian's voice quivered slightly. He couldn't leave home. Not now. He wasn't sure if ever.

Bluebeard looked Kilian up and down. Kilian shifted his eyes away from the man. He did not like how Bluebeard's penetrating look made him feel as if he held no secrets. They stood like that for several moments in silence.

Finally, Bluebeard sighed heavily and said, "Tonight," before leaving Kilian to stand dumbfounded in the middle of the woods.

Kilian waited for several moments before picking up the pieces of chopped wood and dumping them into the small wheelbarrow. They had sold their horse, Nillie, at the end of the winter to purchase cornmeal and dried fruits from the smarmy tradesman his father had always told him to avoid. Kilian had wanted to wait until they could travel to the local market to do business with their neighbors. But his siblings had been hungry. Starving. Kilian still remembered how their bellies had swelled and their eyes had become dull and listless. He had vowed then that he would never let them go hungry again.

The rough handles of the wheelbarrow cut into Kilian's hands as he lugged the heavy load down the hill. He groaned a little but didn't let himself stop. His ma and siblings would be waiting for him, and Kilian knew that they would worry about him if he didn't return before dark. The sun was already setting as Kilian walked the last of the way home. The twin moons of Mitier rose into the pink sky as the sun slipped behind the dark outline of trees in the distance. Tendrils of smoke curled up from the small cottage Kilian shared with his family. He could see where the patch he had put on the roof was beginning to crumble again. *I'll need to fix that again before the next rainfall,* he thought. His siblings, May and Willis, flung the door open before Kilian had even opened their gate.

"Kilian! Kilian!" they shouted.

"You'll never believe who we met today!" May said in her high-pitched voice.

"He gave me this!" Willis exclaimed as he stuck out a long wooden sword for Kilian to inspect.

Knots wound their way around his belly like a noose around a criminal's neck. Still, he grasped the toy sword and waved it in the air a bit before returning it, hilt first, into his brother's hand. "That will do quite nicely, Will." He smiled half-heartedly as he stalked into the house.

The first thing Kilian noticed when he walked into the small cottage was the smell of pipe smoke. It filled the air with a hazy glow. His eyes instantly began burning, and he felt the need to sneeze. He didn't, thankfully.

The second thing Kilian noticed was the roasting goose hung across a bright fire in the hearth. His mother stood, her back to him at the long kitchen table his father had crafted. She moved her arms forward and backward in the natural motion of kneading bread. Kilian's stomach immediately tightened even more. They had not been able to afford the flour and salt necessary to make fresh-baked bread for the past six months.

He opened his mouth to speak when he noticed the third irregular thing: a man sitting in his father's chair.

Kilian raked his hand through his hair and stared at Sir Reginald Bluebeard. *How did he know where I lived?* Kilian thought as he stared at the man. He felt his jaw drop open but could do nothing to wipe the dumbfounded look off his face.

Bluebeard puffed on his pipe, seemingly ignorant of the fact that Kilian stood before him. He was reading one of the many books Kilian's father had collected. Despite being a highly-sought after blacksmith, his father had always taken the time to invest in his learning, and that of his children. *A man only has one life, Kilian. It's important that he understand all there is to know about it. Never forget that,* his father's voice rang in his thoughts.

Finally, Kilian stuttered, "H-how did you get here?"

"Well, the same as you, I suspect. I walked," Bluebeard spoke nonchalantly, and Kilian had the distinct impression that the man had been expecting Kilian to say those exact words.

At the sound of Kilian's voice, his mother turned; a brilliant smile stretched across her face.

"Kilian, isn't it wonderful?" she exclaimed as she held up a small quantity of dough for him to inspect. She beamed at him, and Kilian knew at that moment that he couldn't tell her exactly what he was thinking. He couldn't take away this moment of happiness from her.

"It is, Ma. It is." He smiled as he spoke, yet there was a tremor to his voice that seemed to belay his feelings of hesitation. She didn't seem to notice. She just turned around and began kneading the bread once more. Kilian sighed softly, but the sound was drowned out by his mother's joyful humming.

"We're going to eat bread tonight, Kilian!" May chirped as she rushed past him into the cottage. She danced around Bluebeard's—his father's—chair as she spoke. "Look, he's a pirate," she said as she flung her hands up in the air.

Willis followed behind May until they were both dancing around Bluebeard. They laughed and chanted old songs as they twirled around the man. Willis flung his toy sword around, occasionally bashing it into the stones of the hearth.

Bluebeard ignored them both. Instead, he stared straight into Kilian's eyes with such concentration that Kilian felt his cheeks burn. He had never had someone pay as much attention to him as the man was now.

Without breaking eye contact with the man, Kilian said, "Why are you here, Bluebeard?"

The man took one long drag from his pipe and blew and a ring of smoke towards Kilian's siblings. "Why, to collect you, of course."

Kilian rushed forward and placed himself between his siblings and Bluebeard. He held his arms out to stop them from dancing past him. They whimpered quietly but stayed behind their brother.

"I'm only going to tell you this once, Sir Reginald Bluebeard," Kilian attempted to infuse his words with as much contempt as possible to mask the fear caught in each syllable, "Leave us be."

Before Bluebeard could respond, Kilian's mother turned to face her children. She wiped sweat from her brow but left a smear of flour across her forehead. Tendrils of her gray hair had escaped the tight braid that hung behind her back and clung to her face where the sweat was the most prominent. Her large, soiled apron hugged her body tightly. Even months of starvation hadn't lessened her girth. Still, she was as beautiful to Kilian as the mermaids he had seen drawn in his father's books.

"You listen here, Kilian Clearwater, this man has brought us food, he's given your siblings toys, and he's been nothin' but kind to us. Whatever it is you're about to say to him, I suggest you don't. As far as I'm concerned, this man is welcome and we will listen to anything he has to say."

She stomped her foot for emphasis. Kilian hadn't been scolded by her like this since he'd been a child. He gulped. She pointed one long, thick finger at him and continued, "And if you can't accept that, then you'd better take your supper in the forge tonight." She placed her hands on her hips and stared at him.

Her cheeks were flushed a ruddy red and Kilian found that he couldn't deny her. No matter how much he disagreed with her decisions, she was still his mother.

Kilian stood motionless for several moments as he listened to his mother's words. His sense of unease didn't lessen, but he knew that pushing this matter would be futile. In all his life, he had never seen his ma change her mind once she'd made her decision. And, apparently, she had made up her mind about Sir Reginald Bluebeard.

He nodded once, and his mother wiped her dirty hands on the already dirty apron before turning to push the unbaked bread into a small oven his father had crafted next to the hearth.

Kilian regarded Bluebeard. The man's lips were turned upward as he considered the interaction between mother and son. His expression did nothing to quell Kilian's distrust of him. Turning towards his siblings, Kilian knelt before them so that their faces were approximately at the same level.

"Why don't you go outside and play until supper is ready, eh?"

May's lips quivered as her eyes flicked towards Bluebeard, "B-but, I wanted…"

"No buts, May. Not today," Kilian interrupted her. "Why don't you go catch starbugs? It's been such a long time since we've created the constellations with them."

Her eyes roamed the space between Kilian and Bluebeard, but eventually, she tugged on Willis's arm and began leading him out of the cottage. Her small voice could be heard in the doorframe as they exited the room, "C'mon Will, let's go catch the stars."

Once his siblings had left the room, Kilian sat down in the wooden rocking chair opposite Bluebeard. Bluebeard's eyes followed Kilian as he sank into the chair. Kilian's muscles were taut and sore from the day's work and the hard wood of the chair pressed into his tired body, but Kilian was thankful to be sitting. He looked at Bluebeard without speaking.

The older man blew smoke rings in Kilian's direction. They changed shape the closer they got to Kilian's face, and he realized that the smoke had taken the form of a lizard with giant wings. *A dragon,* Kilian realized. *What is it with this man and dragons?* Finally, Bluebeard snuffed out his pipe and placed it into a velvet bag with a drawstring closure.

"Never can be too careful with our most valued possessions, can we?" Bluebeard said as he patted the breast pocket where he'd placed the pipe. "We wouldn't want to lose what we value most."

Kilian's heart pounded in his chest so loudly that he was sure the older man would be able to hear it. He could feel the vein throbbing in his neck and hoped that Bluebeard wouldn't notice. With a clenched jaw, Kilian only stared at the man without speaking. *What is he talking about?* Kilian found himself thinking, *surely he's not threatening May, Willis, and Ma.* His heart beat even faster.

When it became apparent that Kilian was not going to respond, Bluebeard continued, "Tell me why, again, you can't be my apprentice."

"Tell me why you're so insistent that I go with you," Kilian responded.

Bluebeard chuckled. "You're a fiery one if I ever met one." He tapped his finger on his chin as he spoke, "You remind me of your father."

Kilian gripped the hard wood of the rocking chair's armrest. *How did this man know his father?*

Bluebeard continued, "You even look like him. In the eyes, anyway. Such sincere blue eyes."

A lucky guess, Kilian thought.

"Did your father ever tell you about the time he met the grizzled old bear-man in the woods?"

Kilian's mind filed through all the things his father had ever said to him. They were getting more and more difficult to remember each day. Kilian feared that one day he would forget his father altogether.

"I'll take that as a no, then," Bluebeard's voice cut into Kilian's thoughts, "Well then, let me tell you a little story."

There once was a young man, not much older than yourself, Kilian Clearwater, who wanted nothing more than to explore the world. One day, as he was walking through the woods, he came across a giant bear rubbing his back on a tall tree. Now, the bear, he was a beast by all accounts, and the young man was terrified that he would be eaten alive. So, he quietly began backing away from the giant bear.
But not quickly or quietly enough.
The man snapped a branch as he was backing away and the giant bear swung his head to face the young man. It hunched its shoulders—

"Like this," Bluebeard said, as he lifted his shoulders so high they rose above his ears. "And he snarled like this," Bluebeard made a loud, throaty growl. Kilian's mother turned to face the men and listen to the story.

Well, the giant bear lumbered towards the young man at such a great speed that the man barely had time to lift his arms above his head and drop to the ground. He crouched, not making a sound and

*waited for the bear to maul him. The
great bear stepped onto the man's back
and sniffed at the man's hair. The man
could feel his ribs cracking under the
immense weight of the bear, but he
forced himself to not make a peep. Not
even a whimper.
The bear began nuzzling the man's
hands and licking his head. Still, the
man said and did nothing. The bear
stood on his hind quarters on the man's
back, putting all his weight on the man.
Still, the man said and did nothing. Of
course, the young man knew that he was
about to die. There was no way out of it.
But then, suddenly, the bear was gone.*

"I'm assuming there's a point to this, Bluebeard,"
Kilian said. Bluebeard only winked at him in response.

*The man lay crouched on the ground
with his arms covering his head and
neck until he felt a weathered old hand
scrape across the top of his skull.
'I think it's gone,' came a raspy voice.
The man slowly peeked out from beneath
his hands to see a skinny old man staring
at him. He held a gnarled, wooden staff
in his hands with feathers tied to the top.
He wore deerskin breeches and a
fringed top.
The man's chest and sides ached as he
moved, but still, he didn't whimper. It*

wouldn't do to survive a bear attack only to reveal how hurt you truly are.

'Thank you,' the young man said, 'my name is Nathanial. What's yours?'

'Bear Whisperer,' the man responded.

The two men had talked for several moments before Bear Whisperer said, 'Would you like to join me on my journey?'

Of course, the young man, Nathanial, responded with an adamant 'Yes!'

'Before we begin, I think it best to share with you a small piece of advice. It takes a strong man to survive the attack of the great bear. But, it takes an even stronger one to admit that he's hurt.'

'How did you...'

'I know many things, Nathanial Clearwater.'

With that, the old, grizzled man waved his hands over Nathanial's chest. Instantly, the young man felt his bones mending, and the bruises disappear. He had been made whole again.

Without questioning the Bear Whisperer's abilities, the young Nathanial Clearwater finally set off on his adventure.

Kilian stared at Bluebeard in disbelief. He waited for the man to continue, but when he didn't, Kilian exclaimed, "That's it! Honestly, Bluebeard, you had me believing that this story would be one, factual, and two, have a point. As far as I can tell it was neither," he breathed heavily as he spoke. "In fact, I wouldn't even be surprised if you never even met my father."

They sat in silence as Kilian's words hung in the air. Bluebeard stroked his beard. Kilian rocked back and forth waiting for the older man to respond. He sensed, rather than saw, his mother pull the wooden tray with the baked bread on it from the oven. The scent made his mouth water.

Unexpectedly, Bluebeard began to guffaw in booming peals of laughter. Stomping his feet and slapping his hands on his knees, Bluebeard managed to say, "You're so much like your father, Kilian, and you don't even know it yet."

Kilian glared at the man. Turning towards his mother, he asked, "Ma, did you ever hear Father talk about a scummy pirate named Bluebeard."

Kilian's tone only made the older man laugh harder. His mother peered at him over the baked bread. "No. But…"

"Ha!" Kilian exclaimed, "See, Bluebeard, that confirms it. You never knew my father. How could you have? He was just a blacksmith for our village."

"But," his mother's voice cut in, "he didn't tell me everything from his past."

"What do you mean?" Kilian asked as he whipped around to face his mother again, "I thought Father was born and raised here. Same as you. Same as me and May and Willis." His voice became pleading as he continued, "Isn't that right, Ma?"

He could tell from her face, even before she responded, what her answer would be.

"No, Kilian. It's not. Your father came here after…well…I don't know when. He had a haggard look about him, but he was a skilled blacksmith and quickly became a prominent fixture in our village," she paused as if considering her next words. "He rarely spoke about the things he'd done or the people he'd met. The only thing he would tell me was that he had been a great explorer until he was done with the chaos."

"But," Kilian started but then stopped. *How well did I actually know my father?*

His mother came around the kitchen table and sank to her knees in front of Kilian's chair. She clutched at his hands and tears streamed from her eyes. "I'm so sorry Kilian. We intended to tell you..." she hesitated and Kilian could tell she was holding back. She finally continued, "We always intended for you to leave the farm when the time was right. Your father knew how much you wanted to explore and experience the world. He just wanted you to have a childhood first. But then..." her voice trailed off, and she squeezed his hands tightly within her own, "But then he died."

Kilian barely heard the last of his mother's words they were so quietly whispered. He looked up at Bluebeard and saw the confirmation in the man's eyes. Kilian didn't know why the fact that his father had been more than a simple blacksmith shook him to his core, but it did. He thought he had known his father. He thought he had understood the world around him. Now, he wasn't so sure.

"It's alright, Ma," he said soothingly as he looked back into his mother's eyes. "It's alright."

The revelation didn't change anything. Without him, his ma and his siblings would be destitute. No matter how much he wanted to go on an adventure, he couldn't leave his family behind to rot.

"Ella," Bluebeard said, using Kilian's mother's given name, "would it be alright if I spoke to Kilian alone for a moment?"

She nodded and rose from the floor. She squeezed Kilian's hands one last time before walking out of the cottage. He could hear her calling for May and Willis as she walked. How he longed to follow her out the door.

Instead, he turned to face Bluebeard once more. "I have a proposition for you, me boy. One that I sincerely hope that you accept."

"Alright," Kilian said, "since you have sufficiently disrupted my family's evening I suppose you had best get on with it."

Bluebeard smirked and raised his bushy eyebrows. His eyes shifted from gray to green to blue in rapid succession, and Kilian felt like he was staring into the ocean's depths. He'd only seen the ocean once, as a child. His father had taken him to Port Verenis on the coast of the Paralosa Ocean. He could still smell the hot, salty sea air and feel the cool breeze of the ocean's tide.

"I will supply your family with everything they need to survive—food, clothing, and education—if you will join me as my apprentice."

"I don't understand," Kilian said. And he didn't. Even if this man had known his father, it didn't make sense why he wanted Kilian to join him.

"Let's just say that I need a new apprentice and I once made a promise to your father that I would look out for ya." Kilian didn't know why, but he felt as if Bluebeard wasn't entirely honest with him about his reasons. He still wasn't sure that the older man had even known his father, much less made promises to him.

"Why?" Kilian asked. "Why would my father ask anything of you?"

"Well, my boy, that might be because I owed him a great debt."

"Which was?" Kilian pressed.

"He did something for me that I could never repay," Bluebeard responded evasively.

Kilian snorted.

Bluebeard glared at him, but then said, "Listen, Kilian, I know that this may all seem like too much of a coincidence.

But the truth of the matter is that it is. I just happened to be looking for a new apprentice when I stumbled across you. You just happened to remind me of your father."

Kilian tuned out the rest of Bluebeard's speech. Although he did not trust Bluebeard, Kilian knew that the money and protection Bluebeard offered would keep the rest of his family safe, even if it meant putting himself in danger. When his father died, Kilian had taken over as the head of his family. He needed to do something to ensure that his family would be cared for. *No matter what the cost,* he thought as he ground his teeth. Kilian made his decision.

"Make a blood oath, and I'll go with you," Kilian said abruptly.

Bluebeard stared at him as he once again stroked his beard, "A blood oath?"

"Yes," Kilian said, "a blood oath. If you're not comfortable declaring, with your own blood, to the Light that you will ensure that my ma and siblings are cared for until my return, then I can't go with you."

"I see," Bluebeard responded. His voice sounded almost calculating. "And is there anything else that this oath of mine should include?"

Kilian pondered this question for a moment. "Promise that my family shall not be harmed."

"Well now, my boy, I'm not sure that I can guarantee their safety."

"I think you can."

Bluebeard sat back into the cushioned chair. Kilian could hear his siblings' voices as they neared the cottage.

"Better make your decision quick, Bluebeard. My acceptance disappears once my family returns to the cabin."

Bluebeard drummed his fingers on the armrests of the chair and looked around the cottage. Kilian followed his gaze. His home wasn't much. A small kitchen set into the side of the large room with a few chairs and bench circling a large fireplace. There were two smaller rooms at the back of the cottage where his family slept. He had shared a room with May and Willis for as long as they had been alive.

"There may be something I can do…" Bluebeard muttered.

"Terrific," Kilian stated before spitting into his hand and holding it out to the older man. "Shake on it now, and you can make the blood oath tonight."

Bluebeard raised his eyebrows at Kilian's gesture but followed suit. Spitting into his own palm, he shook Kilian's hand.

"It's settled then," Kilian said decidedly. He still didn't trust Bluebeard, and he had the strangest sense that Bluebeard's intentions weren't as honorable as he made them seem to be, but Kilian had decided that it was better to provide for his family than it was to live in fear. His father had always taught him that doing the right thing, even if it was difficult, was always the best.

May burst into the room with a sack full of starbugs. Kilian could see their sparkling light through the cotton bag and smiled.

"Who's ready to eat?" she asked as she marched right up to the bread and tore a chunk of it off and shoved it into her mouth, "I know I am!" she said through a full mouth.

Kilian just laughed.

Chapter Two

Kilian and Bluebeard walked through the Arcadi Forest towards the old shrine dedicated to the Creators. Kilian carried a small bag stuffed with all that he owned. It wasn't much. Just a change of clothes, his father's favorite book, a drawing May had given him of their cottage, and a smooth stone Willis had found near their village's creek. Still, the bag felt heavy.

In addition to the bag, Kilian had his ax strapped to his back, and a small hunting knife belted to his waist. The knife was dull, and his ax was chipped, but they were the only weapons Kilian had. Bluebeard had stared at him with sad eyes as he'd packed but hadn't commented on the poor state of his belongings. Before leaving the cottage, Bluebeard had handed his mother a large pouch of golden coins and jewels. She'd wept then. And clung to Kilian as she'd hugged him goodbye. But she had not asked Kilian to stay. He knew his mother recognized the blessing that had been offered to them in the form of Reginald Bluebeard.

"We're almost there," Kilian said as they rounded a bend in the worn path to the shrine. His torch light flickered as he swung it around the forest, looking for the telltale glimmer of stone.

"This is good," Bluebeard huffed.

For an adventuring pirate, Kilian thought, *he certainly struggles to journey through a hilly forest.*

Out of the corner of his eye, Kilian caught the glint of a sparkling stone. Turning towards it, Kilian knew they were in the right spot. A short, stone well stood in the middle of a small clearing. Its stones shimmered in the light of Kilian's torch. Quickly, Kilian snuffed the torchlight out. For several moments, he stared into the clearing in near blindness. Then, as his eyes adjusted to the darkness, the well began to glow in the light of the sister moons and starlight. Peering up into the sky, Kilian realized that there was no tree cover above the clearing.

Bluebeard stood behind him. Kilian could feel the man's hot, wet breath on the back of his neck and smell the scent of his pipe smoke on him. The smell made Kilian want to retch, but he forced himself not to.

"This is it," he whispered.

The man stumbled towards the shimmering well. His large, dark outline seemed all the darker compared to the brilliance of the well's stones. Kilian stood just within the trees' ring. It was too perfect to be natural, but Kilian had never seen anyone clearing the trees or the brush around the well.

Bluebeard drew a pail of water from the well and drank deeply from what Kilian knew was the coldest water there was in Mitier. Or so he had been told. He'd only drank from the well once when he was thirteen. It had been a celebration of his entrance into what his village called 'the awakening.' According to the traditions of his people, every man and woman between the ages of thirteen and seventeen were expected to discover their calling. Drinking from the well was supposed to ensure that one would be successful in this journey. It had been two years since he'd drank from the well and Kilian didn't feel any closer to achieving this goal. Perhaps his adventures with Bluebeard would change all of that.

Bluebeard drew a long, thin blade from within the folds of his coat. It glimmered slightly in the darkness, a bright white light. To Kilian, it almost seemed like the glow of a falling star it was so brilliant. The blade's glow faded quickly into the darkness of the night. Squinting his eyes, Kilian watched as Bluebeard deftly sliced the palm of his hand. Without being able to see the gash on the other man's hand, Kilian knew that the cut would run from Bluebeard's wrist to the place where his middle finger joined with his palm. Reflexively, Kilian flexed his own hand at the pain he knew Bluebeard must have felt as the blade sliced his skin and muscle.

In the light cast by the well's stones, Kilian watched Bluebeard's shadowy figure wipe his bloody hand across the entire perimeter of the well. The man's blood did nothing to disrupt the steady glow of the stones. If anything, the blood oath seemed to make the stones shine even brighter. Where Bluebeard had been in constant shadow, his form was now illuminated by the light. Kilian gasped as he watched the other man become enveloped by the well's light.

Through the darkness Kilian heard Bluebeard recite the blood oath's words:

"Let the Light, and all the Creators know,
I, Sir Reginald Bluebeard, of the long
sword and Watery control, do so pledge
me to the protection
Of the Clearwater family. Let it be hence
that until my last breath,
My last ounce of strength, my last drop
of blood, that the Clearwater family
shall be shielded from all despair.
To this, I pledge with my blood. Let it be
known.
Let the Light demand."

The light emanating from the well swelled until it encompassed everything and everyone within the forest clearing. Kilian was momentarily blinded as the light seemed to explode all around him. He felt an immense pressure flow over him, nearly knocking him off his feet from its force. The pressure rushed, like a heavy wind pushing its way through a tunnel. Kilian felt as if he were secured in place by the pressure. It filled his mind, his body, every sense of the world he held.

A shrill shout filled the air, and Kilian wondered if Bluebeard had been injured in some way by the magic of the shrine. He shuddered at the thought.

Then, as suddenly as it had come, the pressure relinquished its hold on Kilian's body, and he slumped to the ground in a giant heap. He remained there for several moments as his breathing normalized and he felt his senses return to him. Glancing up, he saw that the well's stones still glowed faintly in the distance. A section of the well was clouded by a large, dark form.

Bluebeard, Kilian thought, as he leaped to his feet and rushed into the clearing. The trees swayed and moaned as he entered the shrine's grounds. He gulped as he heard the wind whisper, *"Run. Run. Run."*

He ignored the warning.

By the time he reached Bluebeard's shadowy form, the older man was just beginning to rise from the ground. Even in the dim light of the well, Kilian could tell that the older man had been sucked dry of all his energy. His eyes drooped, and his cheeks sagged in a way they hadn't before. Giant splotches covered Bluebeard's face, and his hair had changed from seaweed green to gray. Kilian gasped.

"What are you so surprised by, boy?" Bluebeard snapped. He held out his arm, and Kilian helped the man rise to his feet. "If you can't handle what I look like without my magic, then you don't deserve to be my companion."

Kilian looked closer at the older man. His back was stooped, and a medium-sized hump protruded from the space between the man's shoulder blades. His hands were as wrinkled as his face was with the same strange spots covering them. The cut on Bluebeard's hand oozed a greenish liquid that Kilian wasn't quite sure was blood.

"What are you?" he asked.

Bluebeard laughed, and Kilian felt the force of the man's magic sweep over him until he felt the urge to laugh as well. He forced himself not to.

When Bluebeard's laughter finally died away, the older man bellowed, "I am who I am, Kilian Clearwater, same as you. And there is much for us both to discover about the other."

Well, that's not an answer, Kilian thought, but said nothing. If Bluebeard wanted to keep secrets from him, that was all right. He would just be sure to keep a few secrets of his own. If he had any. Bluebeard seemed to know more about Kilian's past than he did.

"Now, listen here, Kilian. That blood oath I made, included you in it. You can trust me now."

It had been Kilian's experience that people who said that they could be trusted were typically the ones who couldn't be trusted at all. *What if Bluebeard's magic somehow negates the blood oath?* Kilian thought with a sinking feeling in his gut. Then again, if this really was Bluebeard's true form, it seemed strange that he would have allowed Kilian to see it. Sighing, Kilian decided that the best thing for him to do was to believe in the man before him.

"I understand," Kilian whispered into the darkness.

"That's good," Bluebeard responded, his voice rough, "that's quite good."

The older man clapped a thick, hot hand on Kilian's shoulder. Kilian forced himself to not shudder at the man's touch. They stood like that for several moments, and Kilian sensed rather than saw that Bluebeard was examining his face from the dim light of the well. Once again he heard the trees whisper in the wind, *"Run, Kilian. Run."*

A cold sweat formed on Kilian's brow the longer he stood in silence with Bluebeard's hand on his shoulder. He heaved a great sigh as he waited for the older man to lead the way from the Light's Shrine; however, Bluebeard appeared content to stare at Kilian in silence as the well's light continue to glow a dim green.

"You don't trust me yet, and I can understand why." Bluebeard said abruptly and squeezed Kilian's shoulder. "But what you need to understand—what you will know with time— is that I am the only living creature who knows who you truly are and what your existence means for our world."

The heat from Bluebeard's hand intensified on Kilian's shoulder until he felt as if the man's hand was burning him without flame. He gulped in pain, but let not a whimper pass his lips. He could feel blisters bubbling and spreading across his skin. He could smell the singed hair that covered his broad chest and his shoulders. He could hear Bluebeard's heavy breathing—as thick as his own.

What can my existence possibly mean for the world? Kilian thought. His thoughts tumbled through his mind in rapid succession. His father had been something more than he'd appeared. Kilian found himself wondering if he had a destiny greater than the ones he'd imagined for himself. He doubted it. He hadn't been anything more than a poor blacksmith's son. Despite his dreams of adventure and triumph, he didn't actually believe that he could be anything more.

"Stop!" Kilian shouted into the night, "Just stop, Bluebeard." His whole body trembled as the heat emanating from Bluebeard's hand disappeared and was replaced by the bone-chilling grasp of a dead man's clutch. Kilian gasped in surprise.

"Kilian, you have nothing to fear from me," Bluebeard said as if he were able to read Kilian's mind.

Kilian wrenched free from Bluebeard's grasp and took a step backward. He glared at the older man through the darkness.

"What was that?" he asked. He could still feel the fire and ice imprint of Bluebeard's hand. He felt weak. Old, even.

His whole body seemed to quake under the gentle breeze wafting through the clearing.

"I needed to replenish my strength," Bluebeard declared, his voice stronger than Kilian remembered it.

"What do you mean?" Kilian asked, his voice shaking. He reached towards Bluebeard as if to shove him further away. His arms trembled from the weight of lifting them.

It was then that he noticed the same strange splotches covering his own hands that he'd seen on Bluebeard's face only moments before.

"What have you done to me!" Kilian asked as he stared at his hands. Despite his feeling of weariness, he didn't feel any different than he had before. But, Kilian knew that if he were to see his reflection, he would find his face covered in the splotches.

He stepped towards Bluebeard angrily. "What. Did. You. Do. To. Me?" he enunciated each word with venom.

"As I said, I needed to replenish my strength." Bluebeard picked at his nails nonchalantly as he spoke and Kilian had the sudden urge to throttle the man standing before him. "It's nothing that won't pass in a couple of days," Bluebeard finished.

Kilian felt his jaw drop but could do nothing to stop it. "What do you mean it could take a couple of days to pass?" His voice rose with a pitch of anxiety. "Bluebeard, I'm warning you, if you've done something to me, I will never forgive you."

"It is truly nothing, Kilian. Besides, we wouldn't have been able to continue our journey without this little 'procedure,' as I'll call it. You'll barely feel the effects after you get a good night's sleep."

A knot formed in the center of Kilian's stomach. Bluebeard was apparently avoiding telling Kilian those things which were the most important for him to know. Kilian wasn't even sure if the blood oath Bluebeard had made was valid, considering he'd just been injured by the man.

Bluebeard strode past Kilian with a lightness of step that he hadn't had before the blood oath. Kilian's bones ached as he turned to follow the man. His heart beat faintly in his chest, so faintly in fact, that Kilian thought for a moment that his heart had stopped. He breathed in deeply and held his breath for several seconds, trying to suppress the rage that was creeping over him.

"Bluebeard!" he yelled through gritted teeth, "I have had quite enough of your vagueness and cowardice."

At Kilian's words, Bluebeard spun around. In the dim glow of the Light's well, Bluebeard's face twisted into a disfigured scowl. His eyes seemed to glow a bright green with red pupils. His brows were knit together, and his teeth overhung his lips in perfectly sharp points. Gills ran the length of Bluebeard's exposed neck. Kilian nearly screamed, but then the vision of Bluebeard's face disappeared as quickly as it had come.

"You dare to call me a coward, Kilian Clearwater?" Bluebeard's voice came in a low hiss. Something about the way Bluebeard spoke gave Kilian courage.

Despite his quivering body, Kilian planted his hands on his hips and said in a very clear voice, "I do, and you are."

Smoke billowed from Bluebeard's mouth as he opened it to speak. Kilian couldn't see clearly in the darkness, but he somehow knew that the smoke would be blue.

"You insolent little fool," Bluebeard snapped.

"Tell me what you did to me," Kilian commanded.

He heard the older man sigh. "You are a stubborn one, aren't ya?" All of the malice and anger had left Bluebeard's voice. All that was left was amusement. "You are your father's son," he whispered so quietly that Kilian wasn't sure he'd heard the man correctly.

Bluebeard shook his head and looked straight into Kilian's eyes through the darkness. "I siphoned some of your strength."

"Ok," Kilian began, but then Bluebeard continued.

"I can temporarily use the strength and energy of the people around me to replenish my magical supplies following a draining experience. Since you were the only one around after the oathing, I decided it would behoove me to just use yours. As I said before, you'll recover after a few days."

Kilian regarded the pirate with loathing. "You turned me into an old, aching man!"

"One of the side effects," the older man replied. "You'll get used to it, now that you're my assistant."

Kilian looked at the splotches on his hands. His heart still beat rapidly in his chest. He wasn't sure that he wanted his youth to be taken from him at regular intervals.

"And what if I decline your...er...irregular way of staying young?"

"Then I will have to kill you," Bluebeard stated matter-of-factly.

"But you just pledged..." Kilian began.

"I just vowed that I would stop despair from taking hold of you. Not that I wouldn't kill you if it suited my purposes."

Kilian replayed the oath in his mind.

"Let it be hence that until my last breath,
My last ounce of strength, my last drop
of blood,
that the Clearwater family shall be
shielded from all despair.
To this, I pledge with my blood. Let it be
known.
Let the Light demand."

Bluebeard was right. The oath did not include anything about keeping him or his family out of harm's way. It just stated that they would be shielded from despair. *What a fool I have been*, he thought to himself as he glared at Bluebeard.

"Now," Bluebeard said, seemingly done with the current conversation, "shall we continue onward in our new journey together?"

The first response that came to Kilian was to resolutely declare 'no.' However, he doubted that Bluebeard would accept this answer and rather than battle with the older man about their journey, Kilian whispered, "yes," from chapped lips.

Gathering the remnants of the travel supplies Bluebeard had left outside of the tree's circle, Kilian followed the pirate into the dense trees of the Arcadi Forest. Despite his reservations about his traveling companion and his anxiety about how the man would use him in the future, Kilian felt excited to be venturing from his home village for the second time in his life.

Father, let me discover who you really were, Kilian thought to himself as he pushed past several small tree limbs that overhung the path. *Keep me safe. Help me find who I am.*

Kilian wasn't exactly sure why he was speaking to the dead. He had never believed that those who entered the afterlife had any understanding of the living world. Instead, they idly watched as their once loved-ones deteriorated and died, thus joining them in their useless existence. It was comforting, in a way. After death, there would be no more pain or suffering. *"Keep going. Keep going. Keep going,"* the trees seemed to whisper.

Chapter Three

Kilian and Bluebeard traveled in silence for three days following the blood oath. Kilian attempted to speak to the pirate on several occasions, but the older man only grunted in response. Eventually, Kilian stopped trying to talk to him at all and followed behind him in irritated silence. Bluebeard had been correct about one thing: the spots covering Kilian and his aching bones subsided the further they traveled from the Light's Shrine. Still, the change in his body did nothing to alleviate his discomfort at the pirate stealing his youth to begin with.

As they journeyed, Kilian replayed the oathing ceremony in his mind. It had happened so quickly that he hadn't had time to process what he'd witnessed or what he'd heard at that moment. Now, as they continued to travel through the Arcadi Forest towards Port Verenis, he had all the time in the world to replay Bluebeard's words in his mind. The old pirate had mentioned that Kilian was destined to be something greater than he had ever imagined. He'd said that Kilian would become used to living as an old man for days at a time. He'd revealed that his family was not actually protected from harm.

Kilian knew one thing for sure. He hated Sir Reginald Bluebeard.

And not with the hate a young child feels towards their parents when they aren't given everything they desire. This was a deep-seated, virulent hate that Kilian knew would be difficult to remove now that it had been embedded within him. It had only been strengthened by Bluebeard's refusal to speak with him. Now, each step they took further and further from his home, Kilian's hatred grew. He no longer desired to go on an adventure—to have the journey of a lifetime. He simply wanted to destroy the man who had stolen him from his family.

Kilian's anger propelled him forward. On the morning of the fourth day, Bluebeard finally broke the silence.

"I know yer angry with me, boy. I can feel the putrid energy pouring out of ya," the pirate had inclined his head towards Kilian then and looked at him through a single, slit eye as he continued, "but there's no reason for us to avoid having our conversation now."

Kilian regarded the older man with shock. "You can't possibly know what I'm feeling. We haven't talked this whole time," he said petulantly.

"Wrong," Bluebeard responded.

Kilian just shook his head at the older man and pushed his heels into his mare's belly. She instantly moved forward, rushing past Bluebeard and his horse. They'd picked the horses up during the second day of their journey, from a small stable on the outskirts of Brilla. The city was nestled in the heart of the woods with several paths leading into it. Kilian had tried to convince Bluebeard to enter the town for supplies, but Bluebeard had refused. He'd mentioned something about the city having too many elves present. Kilian had tried to press him on the issue, but in the end they'd added an extra day of travel by foot to avoid entering the small city.

Bluebeard had chosen the horses without consulting with Kilian. He'd chosen a sweet-faced mare by the name of 'Bitey' for Kilian and a larger, sturdier brute named 'Hunter' for himself. Kilian had never before met a horse with a predator's name. Still, Bluebeard seemed to cherish the wild beast. From the moment Bluebeard had straddled Hunter, the great horse had bucked, twisted his head this way and that, and disobeyed the pirate's commands. At one point, the horse had bucked so unexpectedly that Bluebeard had risen out of his seat and it seemed to Kilian the pirate should have fallen to the ground in a giant heap. Unfortunately, this was not the case. Somehow, Bluebeard had been able to stay in the saddle.

That had happened near the evening meal the day before. Ever since then, Hunter had allowed Bluebeard to ride him without incident.

"Halt!" Bluebeard shouted after Kilian.

Bitey, despite Kilian's commands, stilled and stood quivering on the rutted path. Kilian didn't blame his mare. She was scared, and Bluebeard had a very commanding presence. He stroked her mane carefully and whispered softly in her ear. Still, Bitey continued to shudder.

"What was all tha'about?" Bluebeard shouted as he reined in beside Kilian. The pirate's eyes darted between Kilian and the mare. "Why would ya run like that, boy, when there's clearly no place for you to go."

"We'll see about that," Kilian said as he tugged at Bitey's reins. She did nothing but lower her head and nibble at a small patch of grass beneath her hooves.

Sighing loudly, Kilian turned to face the old pirate. "I suppose this was your plan all along, wasn't it?"

"What was?" Bluebeard asked, his voice void of any emotion.

Slapping his hands on his thighs, Kilian yelled in frustration, "You know exactly what I'm talking about, Bluebeard! Yet, you continue to provide only the vaguest of answers. You stole my youth. You took me from my family. You…you…"

"Oh, don't act all high-and-mighty with me, boy," Bluebeard spat as he spoke and a giant glob of greenish mucus splattered onto the dirt path. Kilian had to swallow the bile that rose up in the back of his throat. "You wanted to do this. You wanted to escape your pathetic life in that small village. You wanted to explore the world. And so, you shall."

"I want to go home," Kilian said, refusing to look at the older man. He knew Bluebeard was correct, but he would never admit it.

"You want to go home?" Bluebeard repeated, amusement in his voice. "You, who so desperately wanted to have at least one big adventure before you died, want to go home?" he chuckled as he looked down at Kilian. "You and I both know that this isn't true, Kilian. You don't want to go home. You just want the fantasy that has been in your mind these past fifteen years of a glorious adventure to be a reality. Well, let me tell you, life never plays out the way you anticipate it to."

Kilian chanced a glance upwards, towards the older man. Bluebeard stared at him with his cold, tumultuous eyes. They held none of the amusement his voice did. Kilian quickly looked down again.

"Yes, sir. If you don't mind. I'd like to just go home." His voice shook as he spoke and his plea sounded weak, even to his own ears.

"Well ya can't," Bluebeard stated without any hint of negotiation in his voice.

"But…" Kilian began.

"But nothing," Bluebeard finished for Kilian. "You and your ma made a bargain with me. I will continue to provide for your family in exchange for your services as my apprentice. You don't want to go back on your word now do ya, boy?" Bluebeard leaned in close and Kilian could smell the stench of mureechi and ale on the pirate's breath. "Not when yer family could suffer from your choices."

An image of May and Willis's swollen bellies flashed through Kilian's mind. His mother's eyes, lost and weary, followed.

"No," Kilian whispered. He flexed his hand as he spoke. A sense of powerlessness washed over him.

"Now tha' that's settled," Bluebeard began, "I think it's time you and I continued our little discussion."

Sighing heavily, Kilian nodded and dismounted Bitey. "Tha's better." He heard Bluebeard say as the pirate followed suit.

The older man led Kilian and the horses off the path towards a small clearing. They were less than a day's ride from Port Verenis, but for some reason, Bluebeard seemed to be stalling. Although Kilian couldn't remember how long it'd taken to travel to the port, he'd talked to enough traveling merchants to estimate the distance. Even calculating in the extra day they'd spent traveling around Brilla and purchasing the horses, they should've been at the port by now.

They weren't.

Kilian fingered his dull, chipped knife as he followed Bluebeard through the forest brush.

"I wouldn't if I were you." Bluebeard's voice came out in a low growl. "It's not worth the risk."

Kilian released his hold on his blade. *How does Bluebeard always seem to know what I'm thinking and planning?* Kilian thought.

"I really do need to teach you how to protect yourself from my powers, Kilian," Bluebeard said, almost as if to respond to Kilian's question.

Wind swept through the trees and Kilian sensed them urging him onward. He hadn't heard the trees talk to him since the Blood Oath ceremony, but he felt their presence. He couldn't explain the sensation; he just knew that the trees, the Light, his father—something—was telling him to keep going now that the Blood Oath ceremony had taken place. It was too late to turn back, too late to run. Now, it seemed as if he were being told to learn everything he could from Bluebeard about his past.

"What kind of powers?" he finally ended up asking. His voice sounded weak, even to him; it came out in such a small chirp.

"All kinds of powers, my boy. All kinds."

"Specifically?" Kilian pushed.

Bluebeard spat again. This time, the mucus was less globby and thinner, but still, it was grotesque. Kilian choked down his desire to grimace at Bluebeard but felt unable to look the older man in the face. Then, out of seemingly nowhere, Kilian felt the intense urge to begin singing.

He started bellowing one of the old tavern songs his father had sung to him as a child. It told of a fair sea lass who sailed the ocean blue. She brought fortune to all who allowed her passage on their ships, except for one. She had fallen in love with him, yet her magic failed to supply him with good fortune, and he fell into ruin. She'd died in childbirth soon thereafter.

It was not a happy tavern song, and Kilian had never been sure why his father had sung it to him. He'd never sung the tune—at least that Kilian could recollect—to May or Willis. Despite this, Kilian remembered every note and every word. When he had finished that tune, he opened his mouth to sing again. Only this time, Kilian momentarily paused before beginning the song.

Why am I singing? he asked himself. He hated singing in front of other people. His voice sounded like one of those chirping frogs that lived in the Arcadi Forest. It was not something people generally enjoyed listening to. He tried to stop singing, but couldn't. It was as if there was a puppeteer inside his mind, pulling the strings to the rest of his body. And then he felt it, Bluebeard's presence invading his mind.

"Get out!" he screeched. "Now!"

Still, he felt Bluebeard's presence.

Anxiety coursed through him. He didn't know how or why Bluebeard had entered his mind, but he certainly did not like the idea of the older man being able to control his every move. Focusing on the sense of Bluebeard in his mind, a shadowy figure of the other man appeared to him. Kilian began building a stone wall between himself and the Bluebeard phantom. When that didn't work, he reached out with one hand and pushed on the presence with so much force, he knew he would've knocked Bluebeard down had it been his physical form. Instead, Bluebeard disappeared into a cloud of smoke only to reappear a few feet away.

Kilian growled in frustration and lunged at Bluebeard's wispy form. He fell right through the man's body. *It's only a dream*, Kilian told himself. *It's only a dream.*

Bluebeard appeared right in front of him with a long, steel cutlass. Kilian screamed although he wasn't sure whether the scream happened in his mind or in real life. A shield appeared in Kilian's hand and he held it up in defense of Bluebeard's attack. The shield disappeared after blocking Bluebeard's first attack. However, the pirate didn't stop waving his cutlass at Kilian—not even when the blade sliced through his arm. *It's only a dream*, Kilian whispered. *Please tell me that this is only a dream.*

"It's only a dream, Kilian," Bluebeard said.

Kilian opened his eyes, and the image of Bluebeard with the cutlass disappeared. Instead, the older man stood before him with his arms crossed and an apple in his hand. He bit into the apple and juice sprayed Kilian in the face.

"Wha-what was that?" Kilian asked as he wiped the sticky juice from his brow.

"Your first lesson," Bluebeard responded.

Kilian stared at Bluebeard with a blank expression. "You're joking, right?"

Bluebeard laughed and small chunks of apple flew from his mouth. One landed on Kilian's cheek, and it took all of Kilian's willpower to not run away from Bluebeard, screaming.

"'Course not, my boy. If you're going to be my assistant, you'll need to know how to block your mind from persuasion.

45

That little game we just played was your first introduction. Good job on creating the shield. Most times the host is paralyzed within the first blow and can't defend itself against the assault. You, though, put up a solid defense."

Kilian's stomach clenched as he listened to the man talk. He wasn't sure what Bluebeard had meant by being paralyzed, but he was sure he didn't want to find out.

"You're sure you haven't done this before?" Bluebeard asked as he dropped the apple to the ground and placed his meaty hand on Kilian's shoulder.

The moment Kilian felt Bluebeard's hand touch his shoulder, the world around him faded away into a blurry haze. He blinked his eyes frantically, afraid that Bluebeard was trying to invade his mind again. Instead, he was transported back to his youth.

May's cry rang through the trees, and Kilian's heart tightened. It was the cry of a babe, not of a little girl. Instead of trees, Kilian was surrounded by flat farmland. A small cottage—his cottage—stood in the background with a wisp of smoke billowing from its solitary chimney. Kilian's father stood before him. Kilian stopped breathing as he saw his father's face. His dark brow knit into folds as he bent down to talk to a little boy. *That's me*, Kilian realized as he continued to watch his father.

Nathanial Clearwater had always been a strong man, but Kilian had almost forgotten how powerful his father had been. His muscled arms wrapped around the boy Kilian as he whispered into his ear. Nathanial had a broad, tan chest covered in a mat of curly hair. His eyes were a brilliant blue shade that was uncommon in their village. He kept his hair shaggy and let his natural curls fall in ringlets around his ears. Seeing him now took Kilian's breath away.

"Whenever you feel like someone is entering your mind, Kilian, all you have to do is close your eyes and imagine yourself as a great warrior. You will be. That's the power of our minds, my son. We can do and become anyone we wish to be."

His father's voice was warm and soft and kind. It held none of the edge it did when he was talking to the traders. The sound of his father's voice brought tears to Kilian's eyes. He let them pour down his cheeks without embarrassment.

"But Father, how can I tell if someone's trying to enter my mind?" the boy Kilian asked.

Kilian waited for his father to respond. The scene seemed foreign to him and yet so familiar at the same time. It was as if he were watching actors put on a show from a book he'd read but partially forgotten. Or maybe a dream that was fading quickly into forgotten memory.

His father looked down into the boy Kilian's face and smiled a warm, sad smile. "You'll know because it won't feel like you."

"But that doesn't make any sense!" Kilian shouted. Or, at least, he thought he shouted. He mouthed the words, but no sound passed his lips. He looked around the scene, bewildered.

"But…what if it does feel like me?"

The sound of his own voice drew his attention back to the scene. His father bent down and gently caressed the boy Kilian's cheek with his rough hand. At the same time, Kilian felt a warmth pass through him. He smiled as he smelled his father's familiar pine and oil scent. It was faint as if a memory of his father had been unlocked by Bluebeard's magic.

"It will feel like this," his father whispered.

At first, Kilian didn't feel anything. He thought the way he had always thought and sensed everything as normal. He watched his younger self close his eyes and drift off to sleep. His father cradled his younger self's head in the palm of his hands and gently nestled the little boy into the tall grass at their feet. He stood looking at the sleeping child for several moments before looking up and staring Kilian straight in the eyes.

Does he see me? Does he know I'm here? Kilian thought. He held his breath and waited. He so desperately wanted to speak to his father again. To have him cup his cheek and cradle his head. For the first time in several months, Kilian felt the gnawing need to have his father back in his life.

"Father," he whispered, "I've missed you so much." Still, no sound emanated from his lips.

As the soundless words escaped him, his father's eyes widened, but still he said nothing. He just continued to stare into Kilian's eyes. Kilian realized that he had an intense urge to go swimming in the creek. It started out as just an inkling but grew into a ravenous, uncontrollable desire. He began stripping his clothes from his body and walking towards the small creek that ran behind his family's farm.

"This is what it feels like to have someone enter your mind, Kilian."

Kilian stopped walking. He still felt the urge to go swimming, but a thought crept into the recesses of his mind. *I don't actually want to swim.* It repeated over and over again, as faint as a buzzing fly. And just as annoying. He took a few more steps towards the creek and then stopped again when he realized he'd forgotten why he wanted to head that way.

The idea of swimming slammed into him, much more insistent and bodily than it had before. Kilian let a silent scream erupt from deep inside him. And he suddenly found himself confronted by an armored knight. The knight sat atop a giant stallion with flowing silver hair. The knight's armor was polished to a brilliant sheen. Kilian took a small step away from the knight, but as he stepped back, he realized there was another knight behind him. Everywhere he turned there was another knight.

Fear coursed through Kilian's veins, making him twirl in a frenzy. Hard metal scraped across his skin and for a long moment, Kilian believed that he was about to die.

"Calm your mind, Kilian. I am right here with you. There is nothing to fear."

Even in death, his father's voice was the most calming entity on the planet for Kilian. Breathing in deeply, Kilian allowed his mind to still and the image of the knights to become separate from himself. Then, with as much strength as he could muster, he shoved out with the palm of his hand. Three of the knights went flying into the air and disappeared into nothingness.

Turning to the next three knights, Kilian shouted, "Get out of my head!"

The knights transformed into tiny shards of their former selves and dissolved into the night sky. Dusting his hands off, Kilian turned to face his father and younger self once more.

"Well done, my boy. Well done," his father was saying to the child Kilian. "One day, you will learn about your abilities and save the world. Hopefully, the small amount of training I am permitted to provide you will protect you until then." The boy Kilian looked up at his father with such a look of admiration that Kilian felt his stomach drop.

Kilian's heart pounded in his chest. For just a moment he'd thought that his father had been speaking to him. But it was only a dream—a memory. And, with that singular thought, Kilian felt a pulling sensation at his naval as the world began to meld together. He closed his eyes to stop the movement from making him sick. He only opened them again when the pulling sensation had stopped.

"Apparently, you have been trained before," Bluebeard's rough voice said as Kilian's eyes adjusted to the world around him.

He was once again surrounded by trees. But he could still smell the smoke and grass and oil of his family's farm.

"Apparently," Kilian said weakly as his stomach stopped churning.

"Why didn't you tell me you knew the basics?"

"I didn't know," was all Kilian could say.

Bluebeard just shrugged before saying, "Didn't seem to stick much. All you could muster was that small shield, and it didn't last but one onslaught. You'll have to do much better than that in the future, Kilian."

Kilian picked at his nails and refused to meet Bluebeard's eyes. He wasn't sure that he wanted to learn how to block magic. Not if it meant that he wouldn't be able to see his father anymore. If he concentrated, he could still hear his father's voice. It was faint and fading, but it was there. It had been real. He'd actually seen him.

"I know what yer thinking, Kilian, and yer wrong."

"Wh-what do you mean?" Kilian asked.

"I can see it in your eyes. You think that you were actually there. That what you saw was more than just a dream. And you'd be right. It was. Only, it was a recessed memory that caused all of those emotions within you."

"Does that mean I can see him again?"

Bluebeard spat some more mucus onto the ground before answering. "You can, but I doubt that you'd want to, considering what happened to the last person who tried to interact with their deceased loved ones through their memories."

"What's that?" Kilian asked anxiously.

"They died."

Kilian and Bluebeard stared at one another for several long moments as Kilian contemplated Bluebeard's words. Kilian did not want to die.

"But, it appears that yer father taught you how to do all of this when you were a child. This is good. It means that all we have to do is unlock yer memories enough for the training to come back." Bluebeard rubbed his chin absentmindedly as he continued to stare at Kilian. "You've retained some of the muscle memory, or else you wouldn't have been able to conjure that shield the way ya did."

Kilian nodded once but said nothing. His father had trained him, but he had no recollection of this. If May had been a baby at that time he'd witnessed today, Kilian knew he couldn't have been more than eight years old. At that age, he should've been able to remember his father doing that. He should've been able to block Bluebeard's attacks on his mind.

But he didn't and he couldn't. He didn't say anything to Bluebeard about it, but Kilian vowed to himself that he would unlock his forgotten memories. He vowed that he would discover what happened to make him forget them.

Chapter Four

By the time Kilian and Bluebeard made it to Port Verenis one and a half days later, they were both hot, hungry, and a tad bit angry. Kilian, in particular, was in a foul mood. The previous two nights had been thwart with bittersweet dreams of his family, especially his father. He'd tossed and turned the whole night. At various points, he'd thought about waking Bluebeard to see if he held a remedy for such ailments, but Kilian had ultimately decided not to tempt his luck. Instead, he had suffered in silence. To make matters worse, Bluebeard had resumed his stoic silence for the remainder of their travels. This had meant that Kilian was no closer to learning the mysteries of his past or how to block Bluebeard from entering his mind since they had not practiced any techniques during this time.

Now, as they rounded the last bend in the road, Kilian was less than excited to have finally reached their destination. In other words, he was too tired to care. However, when Bluebeard reined in Hunter and swept his arm out across the expanse before them, Kilian's breath caught in his chest. The city before him was unlike anything he had ever seen before.

Houses crested the low-hanging clouds. They all had wood and metal roofs, unlike the fiber-woven roofs of his village. The buildings were so tightly fitted together that there was quite literally no space between them. Each structure was painted a different color. Some were a brilliant blue or a faded yellow. Others had been painted the color of flowers like pink, purple, and dark red. Cobblestone paths wove their way through the close-knit town. Even from the top of the hill, Kilian could smell the scent of the city wafting on the heavy sea breeze. The smells were so jumbled that Kilian had difficulty differentiating them, but there were hints of fish, fresh bread, and excrement. Men and women of all varieties and species walked about the city. Kilian caught hints of their movements in the burning torches shining in the darkening sky. Their voices carried on the wind along with the clamor of their activities.

The city was not as impressive to Kilian as the harbor was. Giant ships rocked in the waves; they were so massive that they looked like the sea serpents his father had told him about in his youth. Kilian shivered slightly at the memory. The ships' sails were tied tightly to their masts, but Kilian could imagine what the great beasts looked like when their sails were spread wide across the sky. Some of the masts reached so high that Kilian was sure that they touched the heavens. Long oars Kilian knew would be too heavy to heave by a single man hung from small round holes carved into the side of several ships. Twinkling lights flickered through portholes, casting reflecting light upon dark water.

Kilian was still examining the city before him when Bluebeard clutched tightly at Bitey's reins. Kilian's mare tucked her head deep into her chest in submission. Kilian didn't fight against Bluebeard's command. Instead, he glanced at the older man and noticed the deep ridges that had formed around Bluebeard's pursed lips.

He's worried, Kilian realized as he continued to regard the pirate.

Bluebeard made a tsking noise that sounded like a squirrel packing away a grouping of nuts and being interrupted by another animal. Kilian stifled a laugh at the sound and Bluebeard glared at him.

"Come on, boy. It's getting late, and there is much that we need to do," Bluebeard jerked the reins as he spoke and Bitey immediately began moving forward. The hill was steep, and there was a broad ridge on one side of the hill that sloped into a rocky sea embankment. Kilian gulped and sent up a silent prayer to the Light that his mare continued to be sure of foot. It had taken them so long to reach Port Verenis that Kilian had almost started believing that Bluebeard had different plans about their travels altogether. Now that they were here, Kilian didn't know what to expect next.

"Er, Bluebeard, how long do you think we'll stay in the city?"

Bluebeard sent him a sideways glance and grimaced. "For as long as it takes to gather a crew. My first mate, Narcon, should be attending to that matter. He's been expecting us."

Kilian wondered why, if this Narcon had been waiting for them to arrive, they had taken so long to complete their journey to the port town.

"I've had a bit of trouble with the royal navy, you see," Bluebeard grumbled beneath his breath. Kilian glanced at the old pirate.

"What kind of trouble, Bluebeard?" Kilian asked.

Instead of answering, Bluebeard reached into one of his saddlebags and pulled out a long, green cloak from within it. It seemed to shimmer in the fading sunlight, shifting colors to match the world around it. Kilian stared in awe. He had heard of such cloaks, but he had never actually seen one. They went by many names: invisibility cloaks, hidden cloaks, elven cloaks. Kilian had always heard them called cloaks of indistinctness. They were quite valuable as only a few remained in the whole of Mitier.

"Whe-where did you get that, Bluebeard?" Kilian said in a stammering voice.

"Stole it of course," Bluebeard responded automatically.

"What! From who? Where?"

More questions were on the tip of Kilian's tongue, but Bluebeard interrupted, "From one of the Macaian princesses. Had to fight her for it, but I won. Barely, of course. Those princesses are quite skilled in swordplay... among other things." Bluebeard winked at Kilian after his response and Kilian had the distinct feeling that he did not want to know in what ways Bluebeard had 'bested' the Macaian princess.

"Are the rumors about the cloak true?" Kilian began.

"Listen, boy, once we enter the city limits, I'll need you to pretend to lead Hunter for me. No one will be able to see me with this here cloak, and I'd prefer to keep it that way until we're in my safe house."

"There's a safe house?!" Kilian asked before he could stop himself.

"Yes," Bluebeard muttered in an exasperated tone. "Listen, don't screw this up, boy. I'll whisper directions to you, but you'll have to pretend like you do not hear anything," Bluebeard paused and then said, "don't say anything back to me. I wouldn't want the townspeople to think you muddle-minded."

Kilian nodded but didn't respond. He watched in awe as Bluebeard wrapped the cloak around his shoulders. At first, all Kilian saw was Bluebeard's seemingly decapitated, floating head. However, that, too, soon disappeared as Bluebeard brought up the hood of the cloak. Kilian held the reins to both of their horses with sweaty, shaking palms. He still wasn't sure why Bluebeard was so wary of the naval officers residing within the port's boundaries, but he doubted that he wanted to find out. Taking a large gulp of air and counting to three, he led their horses towards the security gate. The officers within barely glanced at him as they passed into the port's limits. Kilian exhaled loudly once they were safely within Port Verenis.

Smokey torches were the first thing Kilian noticed about the city. Their fumes clouded around him as he breathed in and barely masked the dirty scent of too many people living in too small a space. Kilian nearly gagged at the overwhelming stench. The second thing he noticed was how cramped the streets were. There was barely enough room between the walls for two horses to pass in a horizontal line. With the various merchants and people milling about, even in the evening hour, there wasn't enough room for both Kilian's and Bluebeard's horses to travel together. Kilian had to lengthen the reins on Hunter and ride ahead of him.

They passed by one intersection within the town where the streets formed a little ring around what was apparently a well. Several tables were set up around the perimeter of the circle where merchants were cooking various foods. Their aromas were spicy with hints of sweetness tucked in. Kilian's mouth watered. It had been almost a week since he'd had anything other than hard bread and scraps of cheese. One table had a whole goat strung between two poles over a raging fire. Kilian's stomach grumbled, but Bluebeard didn't stop, so neither did Kilian.

They passed through the square and continued on down the main road for another quarter mile, or so Kilian estimated. Here, another well was situated. It was much more ornate than the previous one, and it appeared that people were not partaking of its water. No buckets were tied to the stone rod that hung between two pillars above the well. All around it, tiny mosaics formed images of the Creators.

There were eight Creators in total, all of whom were said to still live in their secret places within Mitier. They were said to be the first gifted by the Light. They had been given the task of seeking out those who were worthy of the gift and bestowing upon them the Light. Countless numbers of Mitierians had bowed before the Creators only to be rejected. Or worse. Still, the people had continued to seek the Creators out. They built shrines to the Light and whispered desperate prayers to the chosen ones. Some had been chosen. Some of their children had been gifted, and then their children after that. Entire species had passed down the Light's magic for generations until there were none who remembered a time without the blessing. Centuries passed and the Creators vanished into lore and myth.

The shrines had remained. Those who were faithful continued to adhere to the ways of old. Others only used the shrines to conduct rituals, like the coming-of-age ceremony Kilian had taken part in when he'd turned thirteen. Clearly, the people of Port Verenis had not practiced the traditions of old for quite some time. Kilian sighed in dismay.

"Turn left at the first side street once we've left the intersection," Bluebeard whispered in a gruff voice, breaking Kilian out of his thoughts.

Kilian glanced at Hunter and hoped that he looked Bluebeard in the face. He doubted that he had. Without a word passing his lips, Kilian urged both horses forward at a slightly quicker pace.

They were almost through the intersection when a horn blasted, and a cold, boney hand clamped down on Kilian's shoulder.

"What's yer name, boy," the man attached to the hand asked. He was a slender man with a curled mustache that stretched far beyond the lines of his face to either side. He had a mop of carefully trimmed salt and pepper hair atop his head and wore a justice-keeper's uniform. The blue and green leather stretched across a well-toned body. Kilian gulped at the image of the man before him.

"Good evening, Officer," he began, his voice trembling a bit. He clenched his hand tightly around the reins of both horses. "I don't believe you have any reason to have stopped me. As you can see, I am just bringing my horse home after he escaped from my family's barn," he said as he avoided answering the justice-keeper's question.

Stupid, Kilian thought, *why couldn't I come up with a better lie than that?* Thoughts tumbled through his mind as he tried to think of a way to make his story sound more believable.

The slender man eyed him with bright, beady eyes. Kilian forced himself not to flinch when the man's eyes narrowed.

"Where's your house then?" the justice-keeper asked in a high-pitched tenor.

"Just up the street there," Kilian pointed dismissively down one of the streets leading away from the courtyard.

"Just up there," the justice-keeper repeated. He turned in his saddle to glance at the street Kilian had pointed at. His expression was hard and unreadable. Kilian gulped.

"Yes," he said in a trembling voice.

"I see."

They stared at each other for several seconds. Kilian resisted the temptation to wipe away a stream of sweat that slid down the side of his forehead. It fell into his eye with a momentary burning sensation, but still, Kilian maintained eye contact with the man before him.

Finally, the justice-keeper blinked and Kilian stole a glance in Bluebeard's direction.

"Well then, if there's nothing else you need," Kilian began.

"I've never seen you here before," the man finished.

"Excuse me?"

"As I said, I've never seen you here before. I've been working as a justice-keeper for the past six years and I ain't never seen the likes of you before."

Kilian's back stiffened reflexively, and he felt a swath of tension wrap around his shoulders and neck.

"My ma just moved us here." It was the only thing he could think to say, yet even as he said it, he knew how weak of an argument it was.

"Which street did you say you lived on again, son?" The way the justice-keeper said son made Kilian's stomach tighten as if it were a rope being tugged on.

"I haven't quite remembered the name, yet. You'll have to forgive me." Kilian's voice trailed off as he caught the look in the man's eye.

The justice-keeper reached into the folds of his uniform and pulled out a thin wooden rod. He pointed it at Kilian's chest and whispered, "You best be tellin' me the truth, now, boy."

Kilian was just scrambling to come up with a substantial response to the man when a petite woman with graying hair and a plump body waddled up to where the horses stood and tugged on the justice-keeper's boot.

"'Cuse me, sir, I don't mean to be trouble, but I need to steal this young man away from ya."

The justice-keeper peered down at the woman with narrowed eyes.

"Do you know this boy?" he asked. His voice was full of shock and Kilian couldn't help himself but smirk.

"Of course, you minnow-minded man. This is my son!" she jabbed her finger into the man's abdomen for emphasis.

The man looked between Kilian and the woman. She didn't particularly look like Kilian. Her face was too long, and her eyes were the wrong shade, but the justice-keeper apparently decided that the relationship between the two people wasn't worth disputing.

"So sorry for the inconvenience, ma'am," he bowed his head as he spoke. Kilian's smirk grew into a broad, toothy smile.

"I told you I just lived down the way," he couldn't help himself from saying.

The justice-keeper turned his horse away without a response. He looked like the sort of pompous child one sees at the market during the toy season when he's finally been told 'no.' Kilian's smirk deepened.

"You shouldn't have done that." Bluebeard's voice barely registered in Kilian's mind. He glanced askance at where he thought the older man was situated on Hunter but said nothing. "That justice-keeper will be on the lookout for you in the future now," Bluebeard continued.

Kilian's smile faded a little, but he managed to keep a mangled half-smile plastered to his face. He had already decided that he wouldn't let Bluebeard see the fear he'd felt during his conversation with the justice-keeper.

Just then the little old woman tapped her hand on Kilian's thigh. He looked down at her wrinkled face and smiled brightly.

"Thank you so much, Grandmother."

"Grandmother?" the woman scoffed. "Who do you think I am, boy? Some wizened old woman who makes everything better?" Her brilliant topaz eyes gleamed in the starlight. "I'm just a shade older than you!" she raised her hands up to the sky in the dome of one who is about to pray to the Creators and the Light. "Careless boy," she muttered under her breath as she clutched the reins from both Bluebeard and Kilian.

Her brow furrowed as they made their way onto a narrow side-street to the left of the courtyard. Kilian dismounted from Bitey and followed closely behind the old woman.

"Yer not from around these parts," she stated matter-of-factly. "And you shouldn't have been usin' my gang's turf to fight yer battles with th'justice keepers. It won't do, I tell ya. It won't do."

Her voice was so steady and firm that Kilian had to take a second look at the woman. She had graying hair that fell in curly wisps around her wrinkle-lined face. Yet, her cheeks were rosy, and there was a fire in her eyes that made Kilian believe that she probably wasn't quite as old as she first appeared. In fact, her eyes were her most distinctive feature. They were a brilliant topaz that shimmered in the starlight. Kilian had rarely seen such beautiful eyes. However, when she grinned at him with a toothless mouth, Kilian balked at her. He tried not to, but he had always been taught that the hygiene of the mouth was akin to the cleanliness of the soul. He leaned away from her.

"What's yer problem?" she asked, her voice hard as a rock.

Kilian waited for Bluebeard to interject, to save him from his embarrassment, but the older man said nothing. Sighing heavily, Kilian responded, "It's just that... I've never seen someone without a single tooth in their mouth before," he paused, considering and then asked, "how do you eat?"

She erupted in a trill of chirpy laughter. Her narrow shoulders shook, and her plump body jiggled slightly as she let the sound of her mirth roll over her. Abruptly, she leaned in close enough for her nose to touch Kilian's and whispered, "I gum the food is all. An' I eat mostly the soft bits."

Her breath smelled like the bottom of a piss pot after it had been sitting in the hot sun for several days. Kilian wrinkled his nose in disgust but said nothing. She stayed like that, nose-to-nose and staring into Kilian's eyes for several seconds before determining something. Kilian wasn't sure what, exactly, it had been, but he was sure he would find out.

Turning her back towards Kilian, she once again began leading the horses down the narrow side street. Sighing heavily, Kilian followed her.

But not for long.

Within moments they were standing in front of an old tavern. The sign hanging above the door in peeling paint read 'The Flying Eagle.' The old woman tied Hunter and Bitey to a knotted post outside of the tavern before entering the establishment without looking back at Kilian to ensure that he had followed.

He did, of course. There was nothing else left for him to do. He hoped that wherever Bluebeard was that he was happy he had gotten them into this predicament. He wasn't even sure the older man was still with them. He didn't put it past a pirate to jump ship the moment he sensed danger, even if it did mean leaving a man behind.

The moment Kilian entered the small room at the front, he gagged. The air was so clouded by smoke that Kilian felt his lungs heave and shake with every breath he took. Someone was playing a piano at the back of the tavern. To Kilian's left, there was a long wooden bar where a dirty man with a large gut and a stained shirt stood behind the counter. He spat into a pot the moment his eyes fell on Kilian.

"Ah, Mave, whatcha got there?" A voice that was young and whiney said from somewhere in the smoky room. Kilian instantly didn't like the sound of the voice or the tone that it carried. He looked about the chamber, trying to identify where the voice had come from but didn't see anyone else there.

"Just a new recruit," the woman—Mave—responded. She was now sitting at one of the many tables that filled the space. She leaned back into a cushioned chair and motioned for Kilian to take the seat across from her. He hesitated, but only for a moment, before crossing the room and sitting down.

Mave tapped her finger on her cheek absently as she regarded Kilian with a frank expression on her face. Kilian wasn't sure why, but he felt as if he could trust this woman. She had saved him, after all. Didn't he owe it to her? He was sure he did. Though he wasn't quite sure what it was, he owed her. The man from behind the counter brought her a tall glass of what Kilian could only assume was ale from its frothy golden color. She took a long swig from the bottle, the brown liquid ran down her chin and dripped onto her already soiled clothing. She wiped her arm across her face and belched loudly when she was done.

"So, boy, tell me yer story," she said before taking a smaller, shorter sip from her mug. She propped her feet up on a twisted, wooden table. Her shoes were worn and patched, and Kilian could smell the putrid smell of her feet, even from the distance between them. He started to wrinkle his nose but stopped himself when he caught Mave looking at him from beneath one cracked eyelid.

"There ain't much to tell, honestly. I'm just tryin' to get passage on a ship is all."

"A ship to where?" she asked as she took yet another sip of her ale.

"Not sure yet. Just wanted to get away." The lie sounded false, even to his own ears, but Mave didn't seem to notice. She just nodded and took another sip.

The young, whiny voice piped in, "You can't stay here if that's what you're thinking, we barely have enough…"

"That's enough, Jordel!" Mave yelled as she sat bolt upright up in the cushioned chair. She glared at the teenage boy who wandered out into the center of the room from the shadows by the piano. The music abruptly stopped. The boy's face looked stricken as if he weren't used to being yelled at by the older woman.

"What have I told ya about interrupting me when I'm speaking to guests," Mave spat. The boy glowered but stood his ground. Mave continued, "Get out of here. Get." She waved her hands at him dismissively.

The boy shot Kilian a reproachful glance before casually making his way towards the front entrance of The Flying Eagle.

Mave watched him go, her eyes bolted to his backside. She didn't seem to be breathing, and Kilian wondered if he should offer her some other type of refreshment other than her ale. But, when Kilian heard the loud 'thud' of the door being slammed shut behind Jordel, Mave turned to look at him with a broad smile.

Kilian thought he heard her whisper, "stupid child," beneath her breath before loudly saying, "You can unveil yerself now, trickster."

Kilian's eyebrows rose, and his jaw dropped. "What are you..."

"That's quite enough of that, Kilian," she said as she slammed her drink onto the table between them. "It'll do you no good to lie to me. I know he's here. I could sense him the minute I laid eyes on ya." She licked her lips as she spoke. The ease Kilian had felt only moments before vanished, leaving him with a cold sense of dread. *Why does this keep happening to me?* he thought. Kilian had always prided himself on being a good judge of character. Since meeting Bluebeard, he wasn't so sure that he was.

Floorboards creaked, and balls of dust floated into the air as the figure of Bluebeard emerged from beneath the folds of his cloak. The older man strode right up to Mave, his face dark with anger, and planted his hands on his hips before her.

"Well, if it ain't the blue devil 'imself," Mave said. There was something in her voice, Kilian wasn't quite sure what it was, but it sounded almost like flirtation to him.

Kilian looked between the two people before him. He couldn't see Mave's expression past Bluebeard, but he could imagine the anger she must be expressing at having Bluebeard standing before her. She apparently knew the old captain and Kilian found himself wanting to learn more about how they knew each other. He certainly hoped she would be an ally and not a foe. Despite the sense of cold dread Kilian now felt, he willed himself to believe that she would be a friend. After all, she had saved them from the justice-keeper.

Bluebeard leaned down and picked Mave up in one smooth swoop. He cradled her in his arms in such an affectionate way that it made Kilian blush with embarrassment. Mave's face lit up, and it almost looked like Bluebeard was clutching a much younger woman in his arms. He kissed her passionately on the lips, their entire bodies melding together. Kilian felt embarrassed as he watched Bluebeard kiss Mave. He quickly looked away, fire burning in his cheeks. This had not been what he had been expecting.

"Er, excuse me," he began. His voice was barely above a whisper, and even with only two words escaping his mouth he stuttered.

Bluebeard waved him off. It wasn't the kind of friendly 'hello' wave Kilian was accustomed to. No, this was the wave that universally told people to bugger off and leave him to his own devices. Sighing heavily, Kilian got up from his seat and went to find himself something to drink other than ale and spirits.

The noises of the two of them made his skin crawl. They sounded like two wild animals mauling each other in the night. Kilian shuddered. He hoped he never sounded like that, even if he was in love. To distract himself from the awkwardness of the situation, Kilian entertained himself by looking around the main room of the tavern. He noticed things he hadn't upon his initial entrance into the building. To one side of the main room stood a large bookcase laden with all sorts of jars and bottles. A stack of tattered books was piled onto one shelf, their spines so cracked that Kilian couldn't read them. He crept closer.

The jars and bottles were all labeled: Lemon Seed, Sugar Water, Snakebite, Tallow, Straw, Cat's Nails, Rice Grains. The list continued, but Kilian couldn't make any sense out of the labels. All of them seemed to be common enough things, yet to bottle and store them seemed ludicrous to him. *She must be a witch*, he found himself thinking. He had no proof for that, of course, but it would explain so many things, including how she had 'smelled' Bluebeard from the start.

Kilian was just about to pull the top book from the shelf when a large, sweaty hand clamped down on his shoulder.

"You best be leaving that to my Mave, ya hear?" Bluebeard's voice was husky and wet in Kilian's ear. Turning to face Bluebeard, Kilian realized that he found it difficult to look the older man in the eyes. Looking down didn't make it any easier. Bluebeard's pants were untied, and Kilian could see the hairy mess beneath his clothes. Already he could feel his face blushing. Bluebeard followed his gaze and immediately stuffed his undershirt into his trousers before tying them off again.

"I suppose we best be tellin' ya the story of how I know Mave," Bluebeard continued, his cheeks flushed a rosy red. He beamed at the old woman who was panting in one of the side chairs.

"Oh, okay," Kilian muttered as he followed Bluebeard back to the front of the tavern.

Bluebeard twiddled his thumbs and peered at the older woman through his eyelashes. Mave actively dug at the dirt collected beneath her nails. Her already wrinkled face seemed to furrow even more as she concentrated on the thin line of black in her otherwise pale pink nails. Kilian looked between the two of them and waited. His leg itched just above the ankle, but he resisted reaching down to scratch it. Instead, he sat ramrod straight in his chair with his hands resting lightly on his knees. Tapping his finger gently, Kilian fought the urge to relieve himself from the itch.

Bluebeard cleared his throat with a loud choking sound before turning his whole body to face Kilian.

"You're probably wondering who this beautiful woman is," he began, "and I can answer all of those fine questions I'm sure you have wandering around in your mind."

"Uh... sure," Kilian said. The itch seemed to be traveling up his leg. Gritting his teeth, he kept himself from rubbing his leg on the back of the chair.

Mave dropped her hands into her lap and stared at Bluebeard with an expression that Kilian couldn't quite place, but it was somewhere between shock and dismay.

"I thought you told me to never discuss your gift in front of th'others," she said in a shrill voice that hurt Kilian's ears.

"He already knows, Mave."

"Oh," she whispered under her breath before turning to stare at Kilian with a bewildered look on her face. Louder, she asked, "What makes him so special? Weren't my boys better than this one?"

She looked Kilian up and down then. Her countenance remained unimpressed. Kilian gulped down the pool of spit that had accumulated in his mouth as he forced himself to appear as passive as possible. He nearly gagged as the itching crept up to his groin.

"Not now, Mave," Bluebeard exclaimed in an exasperated tone before turning back to Kilian, "You see boy, Mave here used to be my first mate. And not just on our ship. In everything." His eyes brimmed with tears as he spoke and Kilian had the sickening feeling once more that he was intruding on something private. "But then time continued to pass, and she grew older, less able to handle the passage of the seas. I had to leave her behind, but I never forgot her."

Bluebeard turned to look at Mave as he said the last line. Her eyes flashed with anger as she pursed her lips and sank back into the chair. Kilian squirmed slightly as the itch reached his naval.

Yelping, he stood up from the chair and began shaking his whole body.

"I know, it's a terrible thing that I done, leaving Mave here on her own, but I couldn't help it," Bluebeard was saying as Kilian struggled to untie his pants to scratch. His skin burned as his nails raked across the irritated areas.

"Wha-what are ya doing, son?" Bluebeard gasped as he stood up from his chair.

"It itches!" yelled Kilian. He hopped from one foot to the next as he tried to relieve himself of the itch. All he succeeded in doing was to cause an intense burning sensation across his entire body. And, it still itched.

Mave made a tsking sound as she rose from her chair with surprising speed.

"Where does it itch, Kilian?"

"Everywhere!"

She hobbled over to the bookcase Kilian had been inspecting when Bluebeard had interrupted him. She muttered under her breath as she pulled vials and jars from the shelves. She kept some of them, but mostly, she tossed the jars into a woven basket beside the shelf. Meanwhile, Kilian continued to shake and scratch. He couldn't tell where the itch was going, but he could already feel the inklings on his chest.

"Ah ha!" Mave yelled as she clutched a small, wooden box in her hand. "I knew this were the cause."

She ambled over to where Kilian still stood scratching and shaking. She seemed to move so slowly that Kilian almost believed she would never make it to him. Then, without looking at him, Mave knelt down and waved her hands over Kilian's body. He felt the itching move across his shoulder blades and down his spine. He twitched as the sensation swept across him. Beads of sweat rolled down the side of his face as he attempted to keep himself from reaching around his body and scratching at the itch.

Suddenly, a thin, black insect about the size of a silver coin leaped from Kilian's body and landed in the wooden box Mave held out before her. Instantly, the itching across Kilian's entire body receded until it was nothing more than an odd tingling on his skin. That, too, seemed to fade the longer Kilian stared at the figure of Mave kneeling before him with the box clutched shut between her palms.

"Wha-what was that?" Kilian asked in a hoarse voice.

"That, me boy, was a Narwag. And his name is Arte," Mave stated matter-of-factly.

"You named that *thing?!*" Kilian exclaimed before he could stop the words from tumbling out his mouth.

"Well, of course, you silly little boy," she caressed the top of the box lovingly as she spoke as if it were a precious child for which she had longed.

"You can't be serious," Kilian responded more firmly. He clenched and unclenched his hand reflexively as he spoke.

Mave stared at him, her mouth slightly ajar. Her eyes glittered a bright topaz as she turned to face Bluebeard.

"This kid you've chosen is a bit of a dunce, ain't he?" she asked through the side of her mouth. She spoke quietly as if Kilian wouldn't be able to hear her even though she was less than a foot away from him.

"Well, so far he ain't been the sharpest blade in my belt, but he is what I've been looking for in an apprentice. He's malleable and quick to please."

"I see," Mave said as she glared at Kilian with those strange topaz eyes. She grimaced in what resembled a smile as she noticed that he was looking at her. Kilian did not smile back.

"I think that I have a real chance with this one," Bluebeard was saying. "Well now, what's all this about?" Bluebeard nearly shouted when neither Kilian nor Mave responded.

Startled, Kilian glanced at Bluebeard, whose face had taken on a reddish-purple hue. "What's wrong, Bluebeard?" Kilian asked, confused.

"I see you looking at my Mave," Bluebeard grumbled.

Kilian wrinkled his nose. "It's just that I don't understand why we're here. I thought we were meeting your crew."

"Well now, you have," Bluebeard said flatly.

"What? But you said…"

"I lied."

Kilian looked between Mave and Bluebeard. Mave's cold eyes observed the two men interacting, and Kilian had the unnerving sensation that he was being watched by a predator determining her next steps before the final attack. He swallowed hard before turning to face Bluebeard squarely.

"I think we should leave," he tried to keep his voice steady as he spoke.

"Nonsense," Bluebeard said with a wave of his hand. "There's no reason to be acting this way, Kilian."

Kilian felt the heat rise to his cheeks. The anger inside him seemed to burst.

"All you've done since I've met you is lie to me!" Kilian snarled, "No more, Bluebeard! I'm done." Kilian crossed his arms over his chest and peered straight into Bluebeard's eyes. The older man didn't blink or flinch or do any of the other things Kilian had imagined when he'd been speaking. Instead, there was so much mirth contained in the older man's eyes that Kilian felt his anger deflate to nearly empty. He clenched his jaw as he tried to determine his next steps.

"You know the bargain we made, Kilian Clearwater," Bluebeard said with a half-smile.

Kilian was just about to respond when he noticed Mave turn towards him. Her eyes narrowed and her lips pursed. Small creases formed on her chin where the skin had been pulled up from her sagging jaw line. Her eyes changed from their once brilliant topaz into a blazing red as she peered at Kilian.

"You didn't tell me he was the Clearwater boy, Bluebeard," she licked her lips as she spoke.

Kilian's heart stopped beating for what felt like the entire length of a minute. *What does my name have to do with anything? How does she know who I am?* He thought as he took a subtle step away from the pair. His heart started beating again.

It felt like a sledgehammer being pounded into his breastbone as he took another step backward.

Bluebeard shrugged nonchalantly and said, "Didn't think it was important."

Mave took a menacing step towards Bluebeard and jabbed her finger into his chest with such force that her entire body shook when she struck the bigger man. "You mean to tell me that this... this boy," she gestured at Kilian with a quick swipe of her hand, "is the son of Nathanial Clearwater and you didn't think it was important?" her eyes bulged as she spoke.

Kilian took another furtive step backward. He shifted his eyes towards the door, but he stopped when he heard Mave mention his father. His hands quivered as he contemplated making a run for it and waiting to find out what else Mave might reveal about Bluebeard's intentions. The old pirate stood with his hands on his hips and kept his eyes firmly locked on Mave's. Kilian hesitated a moment longer.

"You are full of surprises today, Reginald Bluebeard," Mave said, her voice still tinged with anger. There was something else in her voice that made Kilian's stomach drop. Not for the first time he wondered what Bluebeard's true motives were for finding him and taking him. He once again took a step backward before turning his back on the others and racing towards the door.

He didn't make it far. Bluebeard reached out a massive hand that clamped firmly onto the space between Kilian's shoulder blades. The old pirate pressed firmly into Kilian's flesh with his thumb, and a tingling sensation passed through Kilian's arm. Kilian tried ripping away from the other man, but Bluebeard's hold on his neck forced him to remain locked in the other man's grasp. Kilian groaned in what might have been considered a whimper and let Bluebeard lead him back to where Mave stood. Her eyes still blazed, and once again Kilian felt his heart skip a beat.

Mave ran one long, bony finger down the length of Kilian's jaw line before looking back up at Bluebeard.

"Now that I know what ta look for, I see his father in him."

She clutched Kilian's chin between her fingers as she spoke. Her fingers dug into the soft spots on Kilian's face, and he felt bruises begin to form beneath her touch. Kilian could smell her stench even from where her hand cupped his face. It made him want to gag it smelled so strongly of decay and herbs. Forcing himself to not jerk away from her, Kilian stared straight into her eyes.

"He even acts like his father used ta," Mave said with a laugh.

"Let go of me you bitch," Kilian said. Mave dropped her hand from his face but brought her other one up in one swift, seamless motion. She backhanded him before he could ready himself for the blow. Colorful stars danced in front of what was otherwise a black universe before Kilian's head lolled forward and his eyes opened again. A small trickle of blood seeped from his lower lip.

"Now Mave, there ain't no reason ta do that to 'im."
Bluebeard's voice was loud—too loud—in Kilian's ear. It made a wave of nausea pass through him.

"This boy is my ward, and I'm set to take of him until he fulfills our bargain," Bluebeard continued his voice firm. Bluebeard clutched both of Mave's hands in one of his own and squeezed. She cried out in pain and Kilian heard the snap of a bone.

"You'll not be hurting him, Mave," Bluebeard spoke softly yet it seemed to boom in the quiet of the tavern. Tendrils of his beard slithered around his face like a snake during a charming session. It began to glow a fiery blue. Kilian's vision swam as he tried to determine what he was seeing. *Can his beard really be on fire?* Kilian thought through the haze.

Mave held Bluebeard's gaze, her face impassive. She seemed younger, somehow, in the light of Bluebeard's beard. Until she finally looked away. Bluebeard released his hold on Mave, and his beard instantly ceased its glow. Mave fell away from him, shuddering as if he had struck her. Bluebeard hadn't. At least, Kilian hadn't seen him physically hit her, but he couldn't be certain what effect the fiery blaze had had on the older woman.

"We're leaving," Bluebeard said curtly as he began walking towards the entrance of the Flying Eagle. Kilian swayed slightly as he took a step to follow Bluebeard. His head felt like a thousand tiny blades were being stabbed into his skull. He used one of the chairs to steady himself as he took a deep breath and released it slowly.

"Com'on boy," Bluebeard said without looking back.

Kilian flicked his eyes at Mave. She still remained huddled on the floor, rocking back and forth. He heard her mutter to herself as she clutched the box that contained Arte tightly to her chest. Her hands trembled as she slowly turned her gaze towards Kilian. He watched her movements in slow motion as if he were in a dream sequence that he didn't honestly believe was happening. She lunged across the space between them. Her eyes were closed, but she landed with surprising accuracy right in front of Kilian.

Her bony hand raked at his arm until it found a hold on his wrist. Her skin was icy cold. Kilian had a momentary vision of Mave's flesh disintegrating into tiny flecks of gray skin and her eyes opening to reveal blazing red eyes before she became the old woman again. Her nails dug into his skin, and Kilian felt the trail of hot blood roll down his wrist and onto his hand. She brought her other hand up as if to strike him again. Kilian recoiled from her. He saw her hand move towards him, crashing into him. Closing his eyes, he waited for its impact.

Her attack never came.

Kilian opened his eyes to see Bluebeard standing over him, his beard such a brilliant, blazing blue that it temporarily blinded him. The older man was holding Mave around the neck with a single hand. She was scratching and thrashing at him, struggling to break Bluebeard's hold on her, but to no avail. Kilian watched as Bluebeard squeezed his hand even tighter around her neck. He heard the faint pop of her neck snapping and saw her body slump lifelessly to the ground when Bluebeard dropped her. She lay in a crumpled, unmoving heap.

Bluebeard's face filled Kilian's vision as the older man leaned down. "Kilian, it's time we were leaving," he said, his voice impassive.

Kilian stood motionlessly. His muddled mind tried to piece together everything he had just witnessed, but he struggled to make sense of it all.

"Kilian," Bluebeard's voice came more forcefully now, "we need to go."

Kilian knew Bluebeard's tone meant that this was a command, not a request, yet he couldn't seem to make himself move. He looked down at Mave's body. He knew the older woman had hurt him and would have, most likely, killed him had Bluebeard not intervened, but he couldn't shake the memories of his father's body lying in the snow. Crimson blood had poured from the black holes that covered his body. His body smoldered slight as Kilian called out his name. He had been the one to find his father's body.

An accident. That's what the townspeople had said it had been. His father had been testing a new composition of powders. He'd believed that he'd be able to create an explosion if he could just find the right combination of materials. He hadn't kept any notes about his attempts nor had he revealed to Kilian which powders he was using at the time of the accident. He'd simply gone out to the empty fields closest to the Arcadi

Forest and blown himself up. Kilian shivered. Closing his eyes, he forced the image from his mind.

"Kilian," Bluebeard bellowed loudly into Kilian's ear, "we need to leave." The larger man scooped Kilian into his arms and began to carry him across the space between Mave's dead body and the entrance to the Flying Eagle.

"Put me down," Kilian said weakly. He thrashed against Bluebeard. His fist caught Bluebeard's nose, and he felt something crack. Bluebeard grunted but didn't put Kilian down.

"I said, PUT ME DOWN!" Kilian shouted as he tried to roll out of Bluebeard's grasp.

Bluebeard laid a large palm across Kilian's forehead. Kilian felt a wave of heat pass through his body, starting at the place where Bluebeard's hand met his skin. The pirate's beard once again began to glow a brilliant blue. And then there was only darkness.

Chapter Five

The sour smell of burning cypress mixed with something else was the first thing Kilian noticed when he woke from his dream. He stretched his arms high above his head and yawned. His muscles ached. *I'll have to ask Ma for some salve,* he thought and then continued, *I wonder where she got the cypress wood from?* She always said that burning cypress was sure to bring good luck to all who were present. It had been a tradition in his family to burn cypress wood on the last night of their village's festival of lights: Lumosan. Kilian smiled as he remembered how his father would journey to the wetlands bordering the Seppiet River. He would always bring back treats for Kilian and his siblings. They hadn't been able to afford the time or money to get cypress wood for the festival for the past two years, not since his father had died.

Kilian's smile slipped away at the remembrance of his father's death. Clenching his teeth to distract himself from the memories, Kilian opened his eyes. He wasn't in his family's cabin. *Where am I?* he thought. Instead of the room he shared with his siblings with its three small cots neatly made on its three open walls, Kilian was in a room with a single bed. However, the room was larger than the one back home, and it had a large, glass window that let in a trail of pale morning light. Kilian could feel the cool draft of the night that still lingered in the room, despite the fire he knew was burning. He lifted his head from the lumpy pillow and a searing pain passed from his temple to the middle of his forehead. Sweat slid from his temple down the side of his face. Closing his eyes again, Kilian took a deep breath and readied himself to sit up.

"I wouldn't do that if I was you."

The voice was soft, close, and vaguely familiar. Kilian tried to remember where he knew that voice from, but he couldn't quite grasp the threads attached to that particular memory.

"I ain't sure what Mave did to ya, exactly, but I figure she must've used her magic to really pack a wallop on you."

Kilian cracked one eye open. A tall, muscular man with a narrow waist sat on a plush chair beside him. His hair and beard were braided with metallic beads woven into the strands. The man puffed out mureechi smoke from a long, thin pipe. A fire crackled in the hearth behind him. Smooth, white branches hung over the stones in front of the fireplace. *Well, that's where the cypress smell is coming from*, Kilian thought.

The man leaned down and placed a hand atop of Kilian's. He wasn't sure why, but he had the strong urge to tug his hand away.

"You've been outta it for three days now, boy," the man paused as he eyeballed Kilian. Even through his muddled mind, Kilian didn't like the way the man was staring at him. "I finally decided the best thing ta do was light some cypress and wait," he said as he puffed some more on his pipe.

A tingling sensation crept up Kilian's hand the longer the man kept his hand on top of his. It didn't hurt, exactly, but it almost felt the way his legs did right after they'd fallen asleep: slightly numb with a hint of sensation.

"What are you doing to me?" Kilian mumbled. Then, in a groggy tone, Kilian continued, "Who are you?"

The man said nothing as he continued to stare at Kilian and maintain physical contact with him. Kilian tried to move his hand away but found that he lacked the strength to do so. Feeling trapped, he began to ramble about how he needed to be going, that his ma would be waiting for him, that he needed to chop more wood for the winter. Meanwhile, the tingling sensation continued to creep up his arm and flood into his body. It felt warm, almost like a caressing hug, except for the occasional twinge of something prickling his skin uncomfortably.

"It will all be better soon, Kilian," the man said as he patted Kilian's hand. It was at this moment that Kilian realized his entire body felt warm and prickly. He tried to speak but found that he couldn't open his mouth anymore. Fear crept up within him but was quickly squashed by the warmth that had flooded his body. His headache receded and, for a brief moment, Kilian felt a complete sense of peace.

The feeling did not last long. A wave of intense nausea struck Kilian. He tried to lean over the bed, but he still couldn't move. His body shook uncontrollably, and his head felt like a knife was being shoved straight through the middle of it. He tried to scream, but couldn't. Helpless, Kilian let the pain consume him.

Just as suddenly as it had begun, the pain ceased, and Kilian realized that he remembered everything that had happened to him since meeting the man—Bluebeard—in the forest. Kilian groaned audibly as he looked over to see that Bluebeard was still standing over him.

"What did you do to me this time, Bluebeard? Steal more of my life from me?"

The older man shifted his gaze over Kilian's face. Kilian couldn't read Bluebeard's expression, but he assumed that the older man was just trying to figure out how much of a lie he could get away with.

"I see you remember me now," Bluebeard said gruffly.

Kilian's lips turned down into a small frown as he regarded the older man. Bluebeard was wearing a different set of clothes. *Clean clothes*, Kilian realized. His beard had recently been trimmed, and, despite its length and assortment of metallic beads, it now resembled something more civilized than it had before.

"Where are we?" Kilian asked. The last thing he remembered was Mave attacking him. And her dead body slumped on the ground after Bluebeard had snapped her neck.

"In the safe house, we were set to arrive at before you got us into that bit o'a mess." Bluebeard did not sound accusatory. In fact, there was a bit of humor in his voice.

Kilian sat up and rubbed his jaw and cheek where Mave had struck him. He expected the spot to be tender to the touch, but it wasn't. *Why doesn't Bluebeard sound more upset about Mave's death?* Kilian wondered. *They had been lovers after all.* Once again, a knot formed in the pit of Kilian's stomach as he thought about the older man's lack of compassion for others.

"I believe that it's time," Kilian said as he stood up from the bed, "that you told me exactly what happened. No lies, Bluebeard, just straight facts."

He looked around the room before finding a fresh set of clean clothes in his approximate size on top of an intricately carved wooden trunk by the window. They were finer than anything he had ever owned before. Even when his father had been alive, they had never been able to afford clothing as rich as these. The dark red linen shirt flowed between Kilian's fingers like water. The breeches had so many pockets and secret hideaways sewn into them that Kilian was afraid he would put something in his pocket and never find it again. A leather belt with loops attached to the sturdy yet pliable material was tucked beneath the pants.

Kilian knew Bluebeard was watching him as he slid the clothing on, but he didn't care. He was determined not to say anything until the older man told him the truth. As Kilian pulled on the shirt, he realized it smelled like a fresh breeze rising off the hills from his village. He smiled a small, sad smile to himself. *If only I hadn't left*, he thought as he turned to face Bluebeard.

"You'll be needing your ax to go with that belt," Bluebeard said as he motioned towards a rack at the back of the room. Kilian's ax had been old, chipped and familiar. The one nested into the rack was double-edged. Both blades were narrow and sharp. The curved edges of the blades were engraved with dragons breathing fire into the symbols of life and death. Kilian lifted the ax from its place in the rack. It was much lighter than he had expected. The hardwood of the haft was reinforced with metal bands that were also engraved with the symbols of life and death.

Kilian gripped the ax tightly in his hand. It felt comfortable, almost as if the haft had been designed specifically for him. He swung the ax a few times to see how it felt when in use. The motion felt natural. He smiled as he tucked it into his belt.

"You'll not be using that for wood cutting, let me be the first to tell you that," Bluebeard said. Kilian heard the man grunt as he stood from his chair. "This here is the Labrys Ax and can be traced all the way back to the creation of Mitier. The Creators themselves gave it t'me."

Kilian frowned at this and turned to face Bluebeard. "If that's the case, then why give it to me? It must be one of the most precious things you own."

Bluebeard scratched his beard profusely. Kilian didn't believe the older man had an itch—he just wanted to stall. Kilian wasn't sure if the ax had been forged by the Creators or if Bluebeard was just trying to fool Kilian once again.

Finally, the older man said, "It weren't never really meant for me." He looked down at his hands as he spoke and began picking at the bits of mureechi still left in his pipe. "I tried to give it to yer father once. He wouldn't take it."

Kilian paled at this. *If my father didn't take it then neither should I*, he thought. The thought pained him. He had never felt so comfortable with an object before.

"Why didn't he take it?" Kilian demanded.

"It weren't really meant for him neither," Bluebeard said.

"Then why give it to him?"

Bluebeard looked up into Kilian's face at this. "It was always meant for you," he whispered.

"What do you mean it was always meant for me?" Kilian's voice trembled as he spoke. He watched as Bluebeard rubbed his chin. He wondered what the older man was thinking, but stood with his arms crossed over his chest, waiting. Bluebeard tapped one thick finger on his cheek and then gestured towards another wooden chair that faced the fire.

"I think it's time that we had a talk about the things your father never told ya," Bluebeard spoke in a deliberate, clear voice. Kilian hesitated, but only for a moment before moving over to the chair and sitting down. He scooted the chair as far away from Bluebeard as the room would allow and leaned back with his feet stretched out before him. Crossing his arms over his chest once more, Kilian sat in silence.

Bluebeard cleared his throat loudly and once again picked at the remnants of the mureechi leaves in his pipe. He looked everywhere except at Kilian's eyes. Kilian waited.

With a loud sigh, Bluebeard began, "Your father was the first apprentice I ever took on." Kilian was surprised by this information but didn't say anything. He was determined to wait out Bluebeard's uneasiness, until he had heard everything there was to hear.

"He'd been raised as a fisherman in the tiniest village I'd ever visited. I woulda never found him, except my ship had taken port at Angelico, and I had decided to roam the surrounding areas to find new crew men. There were always those who hungered for a way to escape their lot in life. Your father was no different, at least at first." Bluebeard took a sip from his flask. He wiped the back of his hand across his lips when he finished, drops of copper-colored liquid soaked into his sleeve.

"That all changed the first time your father saved me life. In the dead of night, we hit one of the largest storms I've ever been through. Waves flooded our decks and our ship were but sunk. A massive wave thrust me into the sea. Your father jumped in after me. I had never seen such bravery before. After that, I took him on as my first mate. He was the best first mate and apprentice I've ever had. I thought one day he'd take the reins from me." Bluebeard paused as he finished this bit of his story. Kilian waited impatiently for the older man to continue.

"We went on a lot of journeys together. Light's End! We even faced dragons together in the Forgotten Isles. Did he ever show you the scar he had on his thigh?"

Kilian shrugged. He couldn't remember his father ever showing him a scar before, though he'd seen some on his father's back and chest.

Bluebeard shook his head and muttered, "Damn shame that your father never took pride in the things he'd done. He made me—both of us—rich. We saw the world together. He shoulda told you 'bout it all."

Kilian didn't know how to respond to Bluebeard's outburst, so he continued to sit silently on the hard, wooden chair. So far, Bluebeard had only talked about his father, not about why the Creator's would have forged an ax especially for him or why his father had decided to leave Bluebeard's company. Until then, Kilian was determined to remain silent.

Bluebeard waited for several minutes, clearly expecting for Kilian to respond in some way. When he didn't, Bluebeard continued, "That scar was caused by the merking himself. He's a gnarled beast with the largest tail I think I've ever seen. The old merking, Posidi, jabbed his trident into your father's leg. I don't think I've ever seen someone take a stabbing like that without a single whimper before. But your father did. Tough as nails, your father."

At this, Bluebeard pulled a small wooden box from within his jacket pocket. Opening the lid, Bluebeard stuffed a large quantity of the mureechi leaves into his pipe before lighting it. The distinct odor of the drug engulfed Kilian, making him want to cough, but he forced himself to focus on a single spot on the fireplace as the wave of nausea passed over him. Bluebeard chuckled as he watched Kilian.

"But that's probably a better story for another time," Bluebeard said abruptly. "What you really want to know about is that ax and why your father left me, is that right?

Reluctantly, Kilian sighed out a low, "yes," before returning to his stony silence.

"'Right then," Bluebeard began, "ya see, your father captured the interest of several of the Creators. It might not seem like very many years now, but your father was my apprentice for seventy years before he left me."

Kilian jerked his head at this, "Wait, what?" *Surely, I misheard him. There's no way my father was Bluebeard's apprentice for seventy years!* Kilian thought as he waited for Bluebeard to finish taking a draw from his pipe.

"You heard me correctly," Bluebeard said with a slight rasp in his voice, "your father was my apprentice for seventy years. I was teaching him how to take over fer me when the time came. Sadly, his time to leave me came first."

Bluebeard made the sign of the dead by crossing his middle finger over his index one and twisting his hand in front of his face.

"I taught him my trick for preserving my youth. He used it a few times—"

Kilian stopped listening to Bluebeard for several moments as the thought of his father sucking the life out of someone else sunk in. His father—the person who had always protected him, taught him how to be a man, who had brought him treats during Lumosan and loved him and his siblings fiercely—had stolen someone else's life. Disgust and anger began to creep into Kilian's memories of his father, distorting the image he had clung to in the year since his father had passed.

"No," Kilian whispered, almost to himself. Then, louder, "NO!"

"No?" Bluebeard asked with a puzzled look on his face. "No what?"

"You've got the wrong person," Kilian said quickly. "My father would never've used that magic to keep himself young. He was too kind and proud to do that. He taught me—"

"He taught you to be a simple farmer and to accept the lot that has been given to you, Kilian. I thought your father was the bravest man I knew, but in the end, he turned out to be nothin' more than a coward."

"No!" Kilian shouted, his voice echoing around the small room. "Stop lying to me, Bluebeard!"

Kilian rose from his chair and advanced on Bluebeard so quickly that Kilian was sure he'd be able to at least get a punch in before Bluebeard incapacitated him. Instead, he struck open air as his hand passed mere inches away from Bluebeard's face. Bluebeard's eyes narrowed in on him, and he caught Kilian's fist in the palm of his hand. Kilian fought against him to release his hand but to no avail.

"Don't be foolish, Kilian," Bluebeard whispered. "You've seen what I can do. Don't believe for a second that if I'm willing to kill my Mave, that I won't do the same to you."

Kilian stopped fighting against Bluebeard. Instead, he stared straight into Bluebeard's eyes and said, "Don't ever call my father a coward again, Bluebeard."

Bluebeard held Kilian's gaze for several seconds before nodding. Kilian tugged his hand out Bluebeard's grasp and sat back down in his chair. "You still haven't told me how you came to be in possession of this ax or why it's meant for me," Kilian said flatly.

"I was getting there, boy, I was getting there," Bluebeard chuckled as he responded, clearly amused at Kilian's outburst. "You really are so much like Nathanial."

There was a long, awkward moment where they both sat in silence after this statement. Finally, Bluebeard cleared his throat again and said, "The Creators reward those who demonstrate great strength. They decided to honor your father."

"For what?" Kilian asked before he could stop himself.

"That, me boy, is a much longer story for a different time. What ya need to know is that yer faher met with the Creators. They blessed him with a great many things, including the greatest gift of all: the gift of a prophecy."

Kilian found himself sitting on the edge of his seat. No longer leaning back with his legs stretched out in front of him, Kilian leaned in towards Bluebeard. The old pirate spoke in a quiet voice with the misty smoke of his mureechi swirling around him.

"Only it weren't a prophecy 'bout him. The prophecy they gave was about you."

One of the cypress branches in the fireplace crashed to the bottom of the hearth. It sent glowing embers into the air, mixing with the mureechi's smoke. Kilian jumped at the sound. He slowly leaned back in his chair again and closed his eyes as he tried to think. *If there is a prophecy about me, why didn't my father ever tell me about it?* His mind wandered to all the secrets that had been uncovered about his father since meeting Bluebeard.

"If there is a prophecy about me, there must've been a good reason for my father to keep it from me," Kilian found himself saying out loud. His heart hammered in his chest and he realized he was holding his breath.

"You're right, son. He had his reasons, though I never agreed with him 'bout it."

"What do you mean?"

"Well, he said that whatever thing you were supposed to accomplish would make you a great warrior. He stated that because of this, the Light would use you as its hero in the days to come."

"Those don't sound like reasons to keep this from me," Kilian interjected. He was once again sitting on the edge of his chair. His hands were clasped in front of him, and Kilian could feel the pounding of his heart through the soft flesh between his thumb and index finger.

"Those weren't the reasons he never told you," Bluebeard said slowly. "He never told you 'bout the prophecy because it described yer death."

"Kilian's lips momentarily formed a small 'oh' before he pursued them. "And why should I believe you?"

"Because the Creators came to me with this ax. They told me I needed to convince your father to stay on with me, to raise you right."

"But I hadn't even been born at that point. How did they know—"

"The Creators know everything, Kilian Clearwater, and it would be best if you remembered that."

They remained silent for several moments. Kilian tried, unsuccessfully, to let this information sink in. His father had kept his destiny from him. He'd kept Kilian from the life he knew Kilian wanted to live. He'd forced Kilian to toil away on a farm. All these years, Kilian could have been out seeking his destiny. A surge of anger coursed through him. *How dare he*, Kilian thought as he pinched the soft flesh of his hand until it hurt. *How dare he keep this from me!*

But then, an image of his father's face came to his mind. He remembered all those times his father had tried to teach him survival skills, the way he had stroked his hair when he'd been sick, the way he'd looked at him with pride in his eyes. His father had loved him. Kilian knew that. But, he couldn't let go of the knowledge that his father had let him go through the Awakening Ceremony knowing that Kilian would never find his path in their village. This prophecy—this destiny—the Creators had spoken of: it was the journey he was meant to go on. Even if it would mean his death.

"Do you know what the prophecy spoke of? Do you know the specifics?" Kilian asked hopefully.

"I'm sorry, Kilian," was all the older man would say.

Chapter Six

Hours later, Bluebeard called Kilian to the lower floor of the new inn they were staying at, a bright, whimsical place called "The Scarlet Lily." Six chairs sat around a wide, round table. Bluebeard had already claimed the seat closest to the small fire that crackled in the stone hearth. Fresh flowers adorned the bookcases and side tables around the room. A large vase with an impressive arrangement of tiger lilies and orchids sat on the floor. Apparently, Bluebeard wanted to be able to see everyone who sat at the table. A barrel of ale had been hoisted onto a pouring table directly behind Bluebeard.

Kilian took a seat on the far side. He remembered the words Bluebeard had spoken to him that afternoon. The old pirate hadn't known what was contained in the prophecy, but he was willing to help Kilian fulfill the first part of Kilian's destiny. He needed to become such a great warrior that the Creators would honor him. Kilian still wasn't exactly sure what Bluebeard had in mind to achieve this task, but he had decided to believe in the man, even if he did steal away his youth periodically. He would die anyway, so what did it matter?

Creaking floorboards in the hallway outside of the room where he sat with Bluebeard drew Kilian's attention. He turned his head just in time to see a stout man with a long, grizzly beard enter the room. He had a dark, purple scar that ran the length of his chin to his forehead. Kilian winced at the pain that must have caused and stared in amazement at the fact that the little man still had both of his eyes. The shorter man nodded in Bluebeard's direction before taking a seat next to the pirate.

"Welcome Narcon," Bluebeard said as he poured a pint of ale from the barrel behind him. The man drank deeply from the cup and then held it up in Kilian's direction as if to toast him. Kilian smirked at the man. It was slightly ridiculous to him that the man didn't even know who he was and he was already toasting him.

Laughter wafted into the room followed by a pair of sisters. Or, at least, Kilian thought they were sisters. They had long, luscious hair that fell in braids down their backs. Flowers had been woven into the tresses, creating a fragrant odor around the pair of them. Their faces were delicate, and thick eyebrows framed violet eyes. Yet, they wore loose fitting clothing that created a boxy shape around their bodies. They both had deep, throaty voices that were hard to identify between feminine and masculine.

"Ah, Adrienne and Alex, it's about time you got here," Bluebeard smiled as he greeted the pair. "It's been too long, my friends."

They bowed in response to Bluebeard's greeting and took their places at the table. Bluebeard did not offer them cups of ale. Instead, Kilian watched as the pair drew a tall glass bottle filled with a liquid Kilian had never seen before from deep within one of their satchels. They poured the thick liquid into silver cups, also produced from their satchels.

"To you, Narcon," they said in unison as they raised their glasses towards the stout man. Narcon drank deep from his glass in reply.

The five people at the table sat in silence. Adrienne, Alex, and Narcon continued to drink noisily from their glasses. Kilian watched as Bluebeard rapped his fingers on the wooden table. He kept glancing at the door as if he were expecting someone else to arrive. Somewhere, a clock's chime indicated the evening hour.

Sighing loudly, Bluebeard stood up and went to close the heavy double-doors leading into the room. Just as he was about to seal the doors shut, a lithe woman with a deep-cut bodice and breeches stormed into the room. Her dark, chestnut hair fell in curls with coppery streaks gleaming in the firelight.

A long sword hung at her hip and swung when she moved. She glanced around the room and nodded in greeting to the others. When her gaze fell on Kilian, he found it difficult to breathe.

She had the most beautiful blue eyes he had ever seen. They were like a mixture of ice and sky mixed into one with violet starbursts exploding from the pupils. They seemed to look straight through him into his soul. Her caramel breasts pressed against the confines of her tight blouse, nearly popping out from beneath its lacings. Kilian exhaled deeply as she passed by him to take the only remaining seat at the table: the one right next to his. She smelled of chocolate and pine needles and salty air. Kilian breathed in deeply, filling his senses with her.

That is until he noticed that everyone at the table was staring at him. Startled, Kilian sat up a little straighter and said, "I'm sure most of you are wondering who I am—"

The woman beside him snickered lightly. "We know who you are, Kilian Clearwater," she said with a distinctly Borgandian accent.

"You do?" Kilian stuttered in surprise.

"Oh, lay off him, Tavia," Bluebeard said sternly as he slid a tall mug of ale down the table to her. Her eyes gleamed merrily as she winked at Kilian before sipping daintily from the mug. She burped loudly after taking the sip and smiled broadly at the rest of the table.

"Good one," one of the twins, Kilian wasn't sure which said as they attempted to produce their own belch. It came out as a tiny little thing. The rest of the room erupted in laughter and pounded their own drinks on the table.

"It is good to be together again," Narcon roared as he waved his mug back and forth. Ale sloshed over the sides of the cup, splattering against the wooden table. The others murmured their agreement. This continued for several moments until

Bluebeard finally raised his hands high above his head. This instantly quieted the four other people at the table.

"You all know why we're here," he began. Kilian looked about the room in confusion. *I certainly don't know why we're here*, he thought in dismay.

"We're gathered here today to start what may be our last adventure together."

"Here, here!" Tavia chanted. Bluebeard raised an eyebrow at her, and she quieted down again.

"There will be much peril as we begin and, hopefully, finish the task that's been laid out before us. But, my friends, should we be successful in our endeavors, we will accomplish what so few have before us. We will meet the Creators firsthand, in person, with our glory at our feet."

The crew drank to this. Kilian felt a growing sense of uneasiness as he waited to be clued into what this meeting was actually about and what it had to do with him.

"Kilian here, son of our fallen brother, Nathanial Clearwater, has a destiny to fulfill. Will we let him fail in this task, my friends?"

"No!" They all responded.

"Good, then let us begin our planning."

"Excuse me," Kilian said in a small voice. When no one even glanced at him, Kilian stood up and said "Excuse me!" again in the loudest, most commanding voice he could muster.

All ten eyes turned in his direction. Bluebeard glowered slightly at the interruption, but Kilian didn't care. "I don't believe I was briefed like the rest of you. Can you please explain to me what's going on?"

The four newcomers turned their whole bodies towards Bluebeard as they waited for him to respond. The older man began laughing loudly. Narcon joined him, although a bit more anxiously. The others sipped at their drinks.

"Kilian, me boy, I thought you understood what was to happen after today's conversation. We're going to help you achieve your prophecy."

Kilian blushed. Bluebeard had promised to help him discover the contents of the prophecy and fulfill his destiny; he just hadn't thought that anyone else would be invited on the journey. Slowly, he nodded and once again took his seat at the table. Kilian sank deep into his chair, embarrassed that he had interrupted Bluebeard for what now seemed so obvious. Tavia reached over and patted his arm lightly. Kilian looked up at her, and she winked before turning her full attention back to Bluebeard.

"To become a great warrior, this lad here will need to accomplish some of the greatest challenges the whole of Mitier knows," Bluebeard was saying when Kilian finally stopped thinking about what it would be like to kiss Tavia and instead began listening to the old pirate. "Our lives will be in great peril as we escort him to these places. Though, we won't be able t' help him should he fail in any of the tasks."

Kilian's heart skipped a beat at this last phrase. He knew how to chop wood and scavenge for food, but he wasn't confident in his abilities to defeat the armies or monsters it would take to be considered a great warrior.

"The first of these tasks will be the easiest, o' course. You know the lore: the key to the Beyond rests in the hands of the forgotten."

Kilian, of course, did not know the lore, nor did he have any inclination about what Bluebeard was speaking of. However, instead of interrupting again—the way he wanted to—Kilian waited for Bluebeard to continue. The twins penned notes on a long piece of parchment. The blue ink from the bottles they produced from within the folds of their clothes flowed across the page without blotting.

"The Labrys Sword itself is plunged deep into the heart of the sea serpent, Malmadi. To reach the sword, we will need to make a visit to the new merking."

At this, Narcon slammed his cup on the table and stood upon his seat. "Captain, we will follow you to the ends of the world, if need be, but let us not follow folly. Surely you remember that we barely made it out alive the last time we met with the merking. Ol' Nathanial was the only one who assured us of our escape, and that was only because he let the merking stab 'im with his trident."

Bluebeard had told him that his father had been stabbed by the merking, but he hadn't mentioned that this had allowed the entire crew to escape from the clutches of the king. He leaned in a little, waiting to hear what other details Narcon and the rest of the crew would reveal about his father.

"That was the old merking, Narcon, and under much different circumstances. 'Sides, we'll have another Clearwater with us this time."

Narcon stared at Bluebeard for a heartbeat before lowering his gaze in submission. "As you say, Captain."

Bluebeard nodded and then continued, "Once we have the sword, we will then have to face the most dangerous quest of 'em all," he paused.

Kilian found himself leaning forward, almost falling off his seat.

"We will journey beyond the borderlands of the Forgotten Isles."

Tavia shivered as Bluebeard spoke, distracting Kilian. She hugged herself as the older man continued, "We will battle against the growing darkness of the Shadow Knights."

"No," Tavia whispered as she continued to cradle herself. The twins dropped their pens upon the table, splattering ink across the wood. Narcon drank deeply from his cup and did not look at Bluebeard. The room seemed to grow colder, even though the fire continued to blaze in the hearth. Kilian had never heard of the Shadow Knights before, but they didn't sound as scary to him as the merking or the sea serpent. Still, the reactions of the others made him nervous.

A hesitant knock on the door interrupted the silence. Without hesitation, Bluebeard lumbered over to the door and unlocked the bolt. A scraggly girl with a mop of straw blonde hair and plaid dress stood in the doorframe. Her apron was stained with grease and Kilian could smell the distinct odor of horse manure, even from where he sat at the table. The girl bobbed her head and looked down at the ground as she spoke.

"I'm sorry to interrupt, m'lord."

Bluebeard burst into laughter. "I ain't no Lord, child. Call me Captain or Bluebeard, but never m'lord."

The girl blushed a deep scarlet before murmuring, "Sorry m'lor—I mean Captain." Her face turned an even deeper shade of red. Kilian thought the girl would faint from embarrassment, but she continued, "There's a man here said he needed t'speak with you. Was quite insistent that you come t'meet with him."

Bluebeard glanced back at the rest of his crew. "I wasn't expecting anyone else," he said. "Do you have a name for this guest?"

"N-no, Captain." Her voice trembled as she spoke. "I'm sorry m'l-Captain. But Ms. Burcham said I needed to come get you." Her voice shook as she spoke and Kilian had the distinct impression that she was about to cry.

"It's alright, girl." Bluebeard reached out and patted her on her shoulder. "Go on now, lead me to our visitor."

The girl bobbed her head again and quickly spun around. Bluebeard followed her from the room. The rest of the crew stood from the table and followed him without being asked. Tavia grabbed Kilian's arm and pulled him along behind her. A wave of warmth spread up Kilian's arm at Tavia's touch but was immediately replaced by the clutches of anxiety as he made up the rear of their group.

"Don't be nervous," Tavia whispered just before they continued to follow the girl to where their unexpected visitor waited for them.

"I'm not nervous," Kilian lied. He wondered how she had known what he'd been feeling. *Can she read my mind the way Bluebeard seems to?* Kilian pondered before a bead of sweat streamed into his eye. *No*, he thought, *I'm just a mess. Anyone who is paying attention would have been able to identify that I'm nervous.* The thought warmed him, if only by a little. She had been paying attention to him. He smiled in spite of himself.

They filed into the airy entrance of the Scarlet Lily. Like the room they had just left, this room was filled with vases of fresh flowers. The room smelled exactly like Kilian imagined a whimsical place like this inn would: floral, clean, and with a hint of freshly brewed tea. As if on cue a kettle could be heard whistling from a room to his right side. The young maid bobbed her head once and then scurried away, presumably to fix the tea, but there was no way to be certain since she said nothing as she left.

A teal clock ticked on the wall farthest away from them; it was weathered, but Kilian found its smooth edges and carved depictions of mermaids beautiful. A warm breeze bristled Kilian's hair as they stood in the entryway. A figure with a fluttering black cloak stood next to the open doorway. The newcomer's face was shrouded by his—or her—oversized hood. Bluebeard's party formed a semicircle around the figure. Kilian gulped as he noticed the gleam of a blade flash from a stray sunbeam streaming in through the door.

"Bluebeard," a loud, nervous voice said from somewhere behind the counter. Kilian leaned forward to see a fat man with a long mustache that curled around his plump cheeks wipe his hands across a pristine white apron. This was not the person Kilian had been expecting. He'd thought the inn would have been run by either a young, willowy woman or by an old, free spirit. This man was something entirely different.

"Ah, Mr. Burcham, thank you for entertaining our, eh, guest while we concluded our business," Bluebeard smiled widely. The man nodded before turning and walking to a small room behind the counter. The room seemed to grow colder without him in it.

Kilian turned his attention back to the newcomer. He instantly wished he had decided to wear the ax to the meeting. As it was, he had no weapon to defend himself should the cloaked figure choose to attack Bluebeard's party.

"I see you have started without me," the voice was icy, hard, and distinctly feminine.

Bluebeard, seemingly unperturbed by the tone of the woman took a step forward and replied, "You aren't welcome here."

The figure drew a long, wooden staff that Kilian hadn't noticed before from her back and slammed it into the wooden floor of the entryway. The hood fell back from her face with her movements. Her sharp blue skin seemed to glow in the sun's light. Her raven hair fell in curls around her face. Her golden eyes flashed like lightning as a brilliant blue light encircled her.

"I have a right to be here," she said. Her voice maintained its icy, hard tone. Her gaze held Bluebeard's with such ferocity that Kilian felt sure she was about to attack the man. "It is you who have broken the trust bond, Reginald Bluebeard."

Trust bond? Kilian had never heard of such a thing. Kilian's eyes flicked towards Bluebeard to see how he would react. The older man simply stared at the cloaked woman with a tight-lipped expression. He said nothing.

The woman shrieked slightly; her voice clogged Kilian's ears with a ringing sound he couldn't seem to shake. Disoriented, Kilian stumbled a bit and fell into one of the twins—he couldn't tell which.

"You have the boy. I can sense him," she looked about the room as she spoke until her eyes latched onto Kilian. Kilian gulped loudly as she took a step towards him. "You do not look like the child of Nathanial Clearwater," she began, "You're too—scrawny."

She said this last word as if it were the worst smear she could think of to describe him. Kilian had never heard himself described as scrawny before. He was slender, to be sure, but he was muscular. The woman took another step towards him. The air around Kilian seemed to become dense and icy. He swore he could see his breath misting in the air with each breath he took.

The woman reached out a hand towards Kilian. An intricate web of purple silver veins coursed beneath what appeared to be paper-thin skin. Kilian almost believed that he could see her heartbeat within those veins; they pulsed rapidly as she stretched her fingers out to him. Kilian had the sudden urge to go to her. At first, it was like the buzzing of a bee, a faint hum telling him to come closer to her. The longer he resisted the urge, the stronger and more insistent it became. His entire being seemed to burn with an icy fire for its failure to be close to her.

"Enough."

Bluebeard's voice cut through Kilian like a dagger does a block of cheese: grating, yet somehow smooth. It was enough to melt some of the tension growing inside of Kilian.

The woman, instead of stopping, thrust her hand out even further and waggled her fingers at Kilian. She took a small, yet noticeable step towards him. To Kilian, it felt as if a heavy chain had been placed about his neck, pulling him all the closer to the cloaked woman. His mind raced with questions, fear, excitement—everything he had always imagined love to be. *Am I in love?* Kilian shook his head. *Where did that idea even come from?* His body shook as he inched his way towards her. It seemed as if the whole world faded away into nothingness. All that remained were him and the woman. Her golden eyes widened as he took a large step forward.

Something unbearably hot latched itself to Kilian's arm. A cry of pain escaped his lips as he tugged against the shackles that seemed to hold him in place. Whatever held him grew tighter upon his arm, pulling him away from the cold—away from the cloaked woman.

"I said enough," Bluebeard shouted. This time, the older man's voice along with the burning sensation on his arm won. Kilian's consciousness seemed to fall through the air and land firmly back into his body. He hadn't even realized that he was having an out-of-body experience until the weight of his clothes pressed in upon him. The room seemed to blaze with a blinding light. He knew it was nothing more than the dull sunlight streaming in through the open door and a few candles lit in the entryway, but even that small amount of light seemed too much.

Tavia's hand held firm to Kilian's arm. *The burning sensation must have been her*, Kilian thought bewilderedly. He looked into Tavia's face to see her regarding the cloaked woman with a wide array of emotions. Kilian could identify contempt, concentration, envy, and a smidgen of desire before her face became blank. Kilian blinked, wondering if he had imagined the expression on Tavia's face or if it had really looked the way he had seen.

The cloaked woman spun around, her cape fluttering in the breeze. She faced Bluebeard head on.

"You should not have kept him from me, Bluebeard," her voice was as cold as Kilian had felt only moments before. "I have the right—"

"You have the right to nothing, Kaldeena. You gave that up when you abandoned him."

The woman scoffed. "I never relinquished my right to him."

"He don't know you as you would have him, Kaldeena," Bluebeard began.

"Nathanial stole him from me. You know this!" her voice became shrill as she continued, "I carried him, I gave birth to him, I have a claim to him!" She took another step closer to Kilian. She was now no more than two steps away from him. If Kilian had wanted, he could have reached out to touch her. Strangely, and despite the urge he had felt only moments before, he did not feel the desire to go any closer to her than he already was.

Bluebeard sighed loudly. "Kaldeena, you can't do this. He don't know," he sputtered over his words as if he were struggling to find just the right way of saying whatever it was that he intended to say. Kilian watched with rapt attention. A sinking sensation had sprouted in his stomach that didn't seem to be going anywhere anytime soon. Kilian had the distinct impression that he knew what Kaldeena was talking about, but couldn't quite admit it to himself. And so, he waited.

"He needs to know the truth, Bluebeard!" the woman, Kaldeena, cried out. Her voice echoed in Kilian's mind. He did need to know the truth. He needed to figure out every bit of truth there was in the world. He needed to understand why Mitier—and beyond—functioned the way it did. He needed to know who his father was. Mostly, he needed to know about the prophecy.

Then, as if as an afterthought, she snarled, "You're the one who took him from me. It is only right that you be the one to give him back."

Bluebeard and Kaldeena stared at each other for several moments. The rest of Bluebeard's crew stood motionless within the room. Kilian wasn't even sure that they were breathing, their bodies were so still. It was only the light squeezes upon his arm from Tavia's grasp that let him know that she was still alive. Kilian was comforted by the small reminder that she was still there with him.

"It's not for you to decide, Kaldeena." Bluebeard's voice came out in such a soft whisper that Kilian was not entirely sure he had even heard the man speak. "Nathanial was the boy's father. You have no claim."

"No claim?" she repeated, her voice just as soft as Bluebeard's had been. "We will see about that, Reginald Bluebeard."

The blue glow around Kaldeena burned even brighter. Kilian shielded his eyes from the brightness. The inn's door slammed shut with a resounding bang as the air within the room seemed to be sucked towards the blue globe. Its force ripped at Kilian, pulling him along with it. Tavia held fast to his arm. He could feel her nails digging into his skin as he was pulled towards the ball of light. Kaldeena was a dark shadow in its center. Somehow, Kilian could hear Bluebeard muttering an incantation in a language he had never before heard. There was a loud popping sound and the light dissolved into darkness.

The room became deathly silent with the absence of Kaldeena and Bluebeard's argument. The room was in total darkness. The fire and candles had been extinguished by the pull of the air. Kilian shivered slightly as his muddled mind tried to piece together everything he had just witnessed. *Why is it that every time I feel like I'm starting to figure things out, something happens to shatter that notion?* Kilian thought as he tried to see what was going on in the room. His eyes were slowly adjusting to the darkness, but still, he could only make out vague shapes. No one spoke. No one moved. Tavia's hand still rested on Kilian's arm, but it no longer squeezed him reassuringly. Kilian felt the way he had on the day he'd buried his father: utterly, and undeniably alone.

A small burst of light formed as if from nothing in the center of the room. The small brilliance illuminated the crew's faces, including Bluebeard's. Kilian was aghast to see that the older man had lost much of his youth during his confrontation with Kaldeena. His face sagged, and the strange, brown splotches had reappeared on his skin. When he finally spoke, his voice came in ragged, hard-fought puffs.

"I didn't anticipate," he began.

"We know," Tavia interrupted.

"We understand," the twins agreed.

"Just one more obstacle to overcome," Narcon bellowed.

"I'm sorry," Bluebeard finished. He wheezed softly in the still mostly dark room. The older man lifted his eyes to Kilian's and searched his face. Kilian wasn't sure what Bluebeard was looking for, but he assumed the older man found it because he dropped his gaze from Kilian before continuing.

"There are many dangers that we will have to face— much more than we ever have before," he coughed quietly into the palm of his hand. The cough sounded wet. Kilian winced at its sound. He knew Bluebeard would want to steal part of his youth before the day was over.

"I cannot guarantee how many of us will make it back to this inn. Nor can I guarantee that we will be successful in the end." His entire body shuddered as he spoke. "I just know that we cannot let this boy," he stuck one long, bony finger out in Kilian's direction, "live his life without ever knowing who he is. We have to try."

The others nodded in agreement. Despite everything that had happened, Kilian still wasn't sure he was worthy of all of the attention Bluebeard, and the rest paid him. In his mind, he was still nothing more than a blacksmith's son. But still his heart beat faster, and images of a life filled with adventure, courage, and accomplishment filled his mind's eye. These were the things he had dreamed about as a child. These were the things that he'd heard tales about, only those stories had been of other men in other times. Never had Kilian believed that he could be one of those myths.

"Well then," Bluebeard continued, "if we are all in agreement, I think it best that we begin."

As soon as the words were spoken, Kilian felt Tavia's hand rip away from his arm. Its absence left a void Kilian hadn't known could exist. He hungered for her touch again, for the warmth of her skin upon his. In that same instant, Kilian felt a pain sweep through the side of his head. He tried to reach up, to ward off whatever had struck him, but the blow came again. This time, Kilian dropped to the floor in a heap. He tried to keep his eyes open, to see what had attacked him, but the world around him had become hazy. Strange shapes moved above him. Whispers filled his mind, but he couldn't latch onto the words—couldn't understand.

And, with that, Kilian sunk once again into unconsciousness.

Chapter Seven

The world violently pitched to and fro. Kilian cracked one eye to see that he was in a dimly lit room. Well, if you consider a hole that was just large enough to hold a small, swinging hammock, a peg for a lantern, and a crate for personal effects a room. The place smelled like excrement mixed with brine. Kilian gagged and nearly vomited on himself as he continued to swing in the soft lull of the hammock. No one else was in the room, but then again there wasn't space for another person. There was barely enough room for Kilian.

Standing up, Kilian's head brushed the rough wood of the ceiling. Cursing under his breath, Kilian looked about the room to see if anything else was there to remind him of where he was and what had happened. He stumbled slightly in the space of the two steps it took him to reach the crate. Looking down, Kilian realized that it contained a second set clothes along with a simple, but heavy and well-made cloak. The ax Bluebeard had given him rested on top of the clothing. Kilian sighed in relief. He really needed to get out of the habit of being knocked out and waking up in strange places. At this point, it was becoming a habit. And one that Kilian did not want to keep.

A creaking noise outside of the room made Kilian jump. His head cracked into the ceiling, causing him to yelp in pain. Within seconds, the door to his room was open, and a shadowy figure stood in the dim light of Kilian's single candle.

"I see you're finally awake then," one of the twins—Kilian wasn't sure which one—said as they entered the room. Kilian squinted up at the person standing before him and sighed in frustration. Even with a scrutinizing look over, Kilian still couldn't tell which twin it was.

"Barely," Kilian grumbled as he pushed himself as far up against the back wall to make room for the newcomer. "I'm sorry," he said in an agitated tone, "but I don't quite remember," he trailed off as he was speaking.

"I'm Adrienne," the twin responded.

Kilian waited, hoping that Adrienne would reveal what pronoun to properly use. He didn't want to give offense, after all. When the waiting turned into an awkward silence, Kilian finally asked, "Can you at least tell me where we are? The last thing I remember is the strange woman in the Scarlet Lily."

Adrienne blushed a dark purple at Kilian's question, though Kilian wasn't exactly sure why. The awkward silence continued. Kilian shifted his body so that he could see Adrienne's face more clearly in the dim candlelight. He cleared his throat to say something else when Adrienne finally said, "You're aboard the Dragon's Breath."

"Ok," was all that Kilian could think to say. They stood for a moment longer in silence.

"Come on then," Adrienne said as they tugged on Kilian's sleeve and pulled him out of the room. The ceiling was higher here, but not by much. Adrienne led him down a short hallway that had doors on either side of it. The hallway was dark and had a musty, salty smell to it. The world still seemed to swim before him, and Kilian found himself bouncing into the walls on either side of him. Kilian counted the number of doors as they passed. There were eight total, but he wasn't sure where they led.

At the end of the hall, a steep ladder climbed the short distance to the ceiling. Adrienne climbed up first and released an iron latch. The moment the door opened a torrent of wind and rain slammed into Kilian, nearly pushing him over. Gritting his teeth, Kilian forced himself to climb up the now slippery ladder. Pulling himself up into the room above, Kilian sank to the ground as he looked around him. Two large masts towered above him, their soggy sails tied to a long pole that stretched across the sky like a cross. Cold water sloshed onto what Kilian now knew was the deck. He shivered as the waves crashed over him, soaking him to the core.

Lightning flashed across the sky, and the ship pitched violently. Adrienne didn't seem to notice the ship's turmoil. Instead, they walked nimbly up to the back of the ship. A giant, wooden wheel with spokes sticking out on all sides loomed ahead of them. Bluebeard's distinct form stood behind the wheel. His beard glowed faintly blue. Another crack of thunder and the sky became lit with the purple and white strike of lighting. The faint glow in Bluebeard's beard disappeared.

Shadowy figures moved about Bluebeard, following commands Kilian didn't understand. Adrienne left Kilian to join the others. None of them paid Kilian any attention. With the rocking of the ship and the continuous crash of cold water onto him, Kilian felt his stomach roll and cramp. It tightened so much that Kilian was afraid he would throw up right there, in front of everyone, but he was able to maintain his composure.

"Come here, boy," Bluebeard's voice rang out above the crash of the thunder and the waves, and Kilian complied. Bluebeard looked Kilian up and down as if to assess how he had recovered, but didn't say much as he continued to deftly maneuver the Dragon's Breath through the sea.

"Tie yerself to the mast, boy, or go back below. We can't risk you being thrown overboard. Adrienne shoulda left ya down there anyway," Bluebeard's voice was gruff and hard, but Kilian caught an underlying note of relief.

"Where are we, Bluebeard? I have a right to know," Kilian said as he stood his ground firmly.

"Yer in the Paralosa Ocean on me ship," Bluebeard responded. Kilian assumed the older man sighed after responding, but his voice was swept away by the rapidly increasing gusts of wind.

"You have a lot of explaining to do, Bluebeard," Kilian yelled, as he tried to keep his voice louder than the raging wind.

Bluebeard made a dismissive sound but kept his hands firmly planted on the wheel of the ship. A blast of cold sea water sent Kilian stumbling backward and for a moment Kilian believed that he would fall overboard on the narrow deck. He flailed his arms wildly as he attempted to regain his balance. He steadied himself before another wave crashed into the ship's side. The force of the water shoved Kilian against the low wall of the deck. His back bowed over the wood. Salty spray soaked into his already wet clothes. Kilian screamed, but his voice was lost in the wind. He felt his body slip and, for a second, Kilian was sent floating into the space between the sea and the sky.

A firm hand grasped Kilian's arm and hoisted him back onto the deck. Kilian coughed as tears welled in his eyes as he realized that he was still alive. Blinking up into the rain, Kilian tried to see who his savior was. In the darkness, he couldn't discern his rescuer's face. A flash of lightning stretched across the sky, illuminating her face. Tavia stood before him, panting heavily. Her blue eyes held a fierceness that Kilian had never seen anyone hold before. She met his gaze before nodding once and returning to her post. Kilian's eyes trailed after her as she went as he huddled in the middle of the deck. He inhaled deeply several times, trying to control his breathing.

He felt the pulse of the ship as she continued to absorb the brutal thrusts of the sea. He felt the ship's torment as she continued to push through the tumultuous water. Kilian stared listlessly into the sky. It was so dark that Kilian couldn't see either of the sister moons or any of the stars that typically created a patchwork of twinkling lights. Kilian had always found the night sky comforting. Now, in the darkness, all Kilian felt was empty. It was only the occasional flashes of light and deafening cracks of thunder that kept him from falling into despair.

Somewhere, from the recesses of Kilian's mind, he remembered what Bluebeard had told him to do: tie himself to the mast or go back below deck. Despite the terror of the storm, Kilian found its torrent beautiful. He knew that the only option he had was to tie himself to the mast. Sighing heavily, Kilian forced himself to crawl to the mast amidst the blasts of wind and water. Debris from the deck swirled around him, occasionally scraping across his body. Still, he continued to crawl until his hands met the dripping, solid wood of the mast.

His fingers slipped over the rough rope as he tried to tie himself to the mast the way Bluebeard had instructed. Each time he got close to achieving his goal, the ship rocked and send a spray of cold water dousing upon him. His hands trembled as he finally pulled the knot tight against his waist. Closing his eyes, Kilian breathed in deeply and rested his head against the smooth, hardwood of the mast. Through the storm, he could see the faint blue glow of what he knew was Bluebeard's beard. He made a mental note to ask Bluebeard about his glowing beard after the storm had passed—if it ever passed.

***

The smell of cooking bacon woke Kilian several hours later. He was still tied to the mast, his clothes were stiff from the salty ocean water, and he smelled like a barrel of fish that had been sitting in the sun for too long, but at least he was alive. His muscles ached from sitting upright for so long. He tried stretching, but that only made his body tense and hurt even more. He slouched back against the mast. *Why did I ever agree to go with Bluebeard?* Kilian thought as he tried to work up enough strength to untie the rope and go searching for that bacon. He had just cracked open his eyes again to begin this task when a pair of muddy, stinky boots thumped before him.

Kilian drug his gaze from the boots up the person's body to their face. He was shocked to discover that it was not Bluebeard standing before him like he had expected, but rather one of the twins. *I really do need to learn who is who*, he thought as sunlight streamed into his eyes, making him grimace.

"My brother really should have never brought you on deck," Alex-or was it Adrienne-said. "He has such a hard time distinguishing right from wrong sometimes."

Kilian opened his mouth to speak but found that his throat was much too dry and his lips much too chapped to speak.

"I told him, I says, 'Adrienne, you done did a disservice to the captain.' He didn't know what to say then."

Well, at least that clears up which twin I'm talking to and what gender they are, Kilian thought as he willed his body to stand up. His bones creaked as he pushed them out of the position they had been in for the last several hours.

"I told him, "Adrienne, you're gonna have to apologize to the captain and to that lad there. I did."

Kilian nodded out of habit. His mother often told long, rambling stories with little to no meaning. Still, he always listened to her with rapt attention. Or, at least, she thought he had. Most of the time Kilian had let his mind wander, just like it was now.

Stretching out a hand, Kilian let Alex pull him up from the deck. His lower back screamed at him in dismay as he pulled his arms high above his head and stretched for several seconds. Alex laughed when Kilian's stomach growled noisily.

"I almost forgot!" he exclaimed as he motioned for Kilian to follow him. "Narcon made us a real Borgandian breakfast, he did. Learned the techniques from his travels. Pork bacon and fried eggs. Best enjoy it now, though, 'cause we won't be eating this way for the rest of the journey."

Alex continued to ramble about the food, his brother, and the previous night's storm until they arrived at a small room in the hull of the ship. A glittering fire smoldered in a small pit in the center of the room. Smoke billowed from the fire, causing Kilian to cough loudly, but that didn't stop him from plopping into a narrow wooden chair close to the fire. As he leaned in close to the fire, Kilian noticed that there was no wood beneath the flames, only a small, smooth rock the color of the sun.

"It's a Sun Rune," Adrienne said as he placed a plate of assorted meats and pastries in front of Kilian. Steam rolled off of the food in waves, and Kilian's stomach grumbled once again.

"A what?" Kilian asked as he shoved a forkful of egg into his mouth.

"A Sun Rune," Adrienne said matter-of-factly. "You know, those things that sailors use to make fire without the fear of burning up the boat."

Kilian shook his head as he slowly chewed another mouthful of food.

Adrienne burst into laughter, "You're joking, right?" He slapped his hand on his leg as he spoke and jeered at his brother, "Can you believe that this boy has never heard of a sun rune?"

Kilian blushed as the twins bantered back and forth about how sheltered Kilian must have been to never have heard of a sun rune before.

"Enough," a feminine voice said from the doorway. Kilian looked up just in time to see Tavia stride into the room. She wore a tight-fitting shirt and vest with a deep V in the front. Her breasts pressed against the constraining fabric of her top, seeming as if they could burst from her clothing at any moment. Kilian blushed an even deeper shade of maroon and looked down at his food as Tavia came to sit next to him.

Adrienne handed her a plate as well and proceeded to begin cleaning up the meal. Even in the kitchen, his movements were graceful, almost as if he were dancing. Kilian watched in awe as the brothers sashayed across the room, carrying plates and bowls to their respective storage places. They seemed comfortable on this ship, much more comfortable than Kilian could ever imagine himself feeling here.

"Today we begin your training, Kilian," Tavia said, her voice calm with a hint of music to it. Kilian watched the way her lips moved when she spoke. She had beautiful, plump red lips. He wondered what it would feel like to touch them.

She laid a hand on his arm, "Narcon is to be your first lesson. May the Light bless you."

Kilian was still watching her lips when Tavia stood and began walking to the door. "I'm sure you'll do fine," she said, "Just watch out for his fists, Kilian. You've never known pain until you're hit in the eye by one of Narcon's fists."

"Wait, what?" Kilian called after her, but Tavia did not return.

Suddenly, Kilian wasn't as hungry as he thought he had been. Leaping up from his seat, Kilian ran after her.

"What do you mean, 'watch out for his fists?' Do you mean to say that I'm actually going to be fighting him?" Tavia's heels clicked on the hardwood floor of the ship. "Of course," she responded without stopping. They reached the end of the ship, and she began climbing up the ladder. "How else are you supposed to learn?"

"I just thought," Kilian paused as he considered what he was about to say. He wasn't exactly sure what he thought his training would entail. "I just thought that maybe I wouldn't have to get hurt on my very first day of training," he finally said as he reached the top of the ladder.

"If you're going to be ready for the Shadow Knights, then we're going to have to accelerate your training." Tavia pulled a rope to release the second sail as she spoke. Kilian watched her work the ropes and sails with interest. He had always imagined life on a great ship, exploring the ocean. Now he was on one, and he wasn't sure he wanted to be here at all.

"I see," he said quietly as he continued to watch her movements. He wanted to ask more about the woman from the inn, about the Shadow Knights, about everything he was learning about his father, but Kilian didn't know how to formulate his thoughts into words or his words into questions.

"'Bout time you got here," a loud voice from behind him said. "I've been up for hours waiting for ya to git ur lazy ass on deck."

Kilian spun around to see the short, stalky Narcon standing behind him with two broad axes in his hand. He grinned at Kilian's shocked expression.

"We ain't got all day, boy. Let's get to it then."
Narcon led Kilian to the front of the ship. Kilian estimated that the deck was thrice the length of his arms span, but it felt cramped as Narcon dropped the axes to the ground and planted his feet about shoulder length apart, knees slightly bent. He stared at Kilian for a long moment, clearly expecting him to do something, but Kilian wasn't sure what he needed to do.

Finally, Narcon said, "Well don't just stand there, boy. Follow my lead."

Embarrassed, Kilian mimicked Narcon's stance as best he could. It felt uncomfortable. His body still ached from sleeping upright and tied to the mast.

"Good, good," Narcon was saying as he transitioned into another stance. This time one foot was forward, and his arms were up in a protective brace. Kilian followed Narcon's lead.

"Each morning we will go through this routine," Narcon said after they had passed through a series of twelve different stances. "This will teach you to be strong and quick." He picked up the axes as he spoke. "That way, I won't kill you."

Kilian barely had time to register this last remark before Narcon had tossed him one of the axes and began charging at him with the other. The ax slipped in Kilian's hand as he hastily tried to bring it up to block the blow. It clattered to the deck, leaving him without defense or weapon. Narcon stopped the swing of his ax just before the blade would have nicked Kilian's right forearm.

"Pick it up," the shorter man said. His eyes darted down to the fallen ax and then back up to Kilian's face. Kilian paled.

"I'm not…"

"Don't say that you're not ready, my boy. We don't have time for your worries. You either learn now or you die during the first—and easiest—of the challenges. Your choice," Narcon bellowed as he stepped away from Kilian and assumed one of the stances he taught Kilian only moments before. This time, his body was turned sideways with the ax lifted to shoulder height. He snarled at Kilian.

Kilian quickly retrieved his ax from the deck. His hands were so sweaty that he feared he would drop it again, but he managed to maintain his grip. He got into the first stance that Narcon had taught him and tried to remember the small tidbits Bluebeard had taught him on their journey to Port Verenis. It wasn't much.

Narcon thrust his ax at Kilian's legs this time. Kilian stumbled backward, narrowly missing the bite of Narcon's ax. Kilian fumbled as he tried to remember another one of the stances. He swung the ax out wildly. Narcon sidestepped each of Kilian's attempts to strike him. Cursing under his breath, Kilian lunged at Narcon, throwing his entire body weight into the attack. Narcon easily avoided the assault and Kilian plummeted to the ground, propelled by the force of his attack.

Narcon laughed as he waited for Kilian to get up from the deck. Kilian was breathing heavily now, sweat dripping from his brow. He resumed the first stance Narcon had taught him, firmly planting his feet on the deck. Kilian heard movement behind him and turned to see that Tavia and Bluebeard had joined them on deck. They watched the bout, an expression of amusement on their faces. Anger bubbled inside of Kilian. He didn't want Tavia to see him flounder. He wanted her to see him succeed.

Turning back to face Narcon, Kilian lifted his ax once more, this time with two hands. He charged at the other man, his ax raised high above his head. It was a short distance between them, but Kilian felt like he was witnessing his attack in slow motion. He sensed when Narcon shifted his stance and began to swing his ax out at knee level. He felt his own muscles tighten as he leaped from the deck and landed on the other side of Narcon's ax. A wave of heat passed through him as he brought his own ax down, aimed directly at Narcon's skull. He could see how the attack would go, how the ax would embed itself in Narcon's body. Too late, he realized that he wouldn't be able to stop his blow. The momentum of his swing was too strong to break.

Just as the ax was about to cleave Narcon's skull in half, the blade twisted in the air and swiped down the right side of Narcon's body, missing the man's flesh by mere inches. Kilian once again fell to the deck on the other side of his opponent.

What?! Kilian thought as he spun around to face Narcon again. The half-sized man was smiling.

"Did ya feel that, boy?" Narcon's voice was gravelly and hard, but it held a hint of awe in it.

"Feel what?" Kilian asked as he assumed one of the crouching positions Narcon had shown him that morning.

"You be Light Blessed, me boy."

Kilian certainly didn't feel blessed, but he didn't say this to the other man.

Laughing, Narcon began an aggressive assault on Kilian. Kilian attempted to block it, to scramble away, but he was too slow. Narcon feigned a swing at Kilian's neck before raising a fist and slamming it into Kilian's cheek. Blood sprayed from Kilian's mouth, and he felt as if all of his teeth had been knocked loose. He crumpled to the ground, holding one hand to his face.

"Get up," Narcon commanded.

Kilian glanced at where Tavia and Bluebeard were standing. They looked on with interest but said nothing. Sighing, Kilian rose to his feet once more.

Again, Narcon came at him, this time using a combination of maneuvers so quickly that Kilian couldn't keep track of what he saw much less anticipate how to defend himself. Narcon slammed the handle of the ax squarely into the middle of Kilian's chest. The force of the hit knocked the breath out of Kilian's lungs, and he staggered. Coughing, Kilian got into another stance.

"That's enough for today, I think," Narcon said, as he looked Kilian up and down. "You did well, boy."

Kilian wanted to laugh at this but didn't have the strength or the air to do so. His entire body ached and not just because of sleeping tied to a mast this time. He could feel the bruises already forming on his skin from where Narcon had struck him. He didn't think he had any broken bones, but it was hard to tell. During that entire exercise, Kilian had only been able to almost hit Narcon once. *At least that's something*, he told himself as he handed the ax back to Narcon. *I could have failed even to do that.*

"Be sure to be up by sunrise tomorrow, boy. That's when we will start every morning." With that, Narcon spun on his heel and walked towards where Tavia and Bluebeard still stood. He whistled as he went and Kilian had the distinct impression that the other man had enjoyed beating him.

Sighing heavily, Kilian sank to the deck panting. His entire body shook as he let the exhaustion overtake him. He had thought, when he'd awoken that morning, that his body couldn't feel any sorer. He had been wrong. He wasn't even sure if he could move again, much less do anything other than sleep. He closed his eyes and breathed in deeply. The gentle rocking slowly lulled him.

"Kilian," a soft voice said close to his ear. He stirred, jumping to his feet. The movement pulled at his already tense muscles, causing them to spasm. He jerked in pain as the muscle spasm ran up his body. Finally, after the last spasm had ceased, he looked at the person who had disturbed him.

It was one of the twins. Kilian thought it was Adrienne, but he still wasn't sure.

"I'm sorry to disrupt your nap, Kilian, but it's time." Kilian blinked at him, still dazed from his bout with Narcon. "What?" he mumbled.

"Well, it's already midday, Kilian. It's time for Adrienne and me to teach you about disguises, and cunning, and all those other things you'll need to survive."

It's Alex, Kilian realized. *I'll have to get better at this.* Then, in a faint voice, he asked, "Disguises? Cunning?" Kilian knew he sounded like a dunce as he spoke, but his muddled mind couldn't piece together everything that Alex was saying.

"Kilian, if you are to be the greatest hero known to Mitier, it is time that you begin to think like a great hero."

Kilian blinked. Alex stared at him, his grin broadening into an almost painful looking smile as he waited for Kilian to respond.

"Ah, there you are!" Adrienne said as he walked up to stand by his brother. When Kilian looked at him, he had to do a double-take. Adrienne was wearing a light blue vest jacket with a delicately embroidered pattern of flowers and butterflies covering the entire length of cloth over a bright white blouse. Instead of trousers, he wore what looked to be a mix of a skirt and pants all rolled into one. Didn't Alex call his brother, well a brother? Kilian was no longer sure and, he realized, he wasn't certain he cared. Shrugging, Kilian let the twins lead him to a wooden table on deck that Kilian hadn't noticed before. It had a series of hinges down its middle and, Kilian realized, could be folded in half. Kilian bent down for a closer inspection of the legs and realized that they, too, had hinges built into them.

"It's a technique only the best and most notorious travelers know about, Kilian."

Kilian looked up to see who was speaking. It was Alex. He, too, was bent down and inspecting the table with an odd expression on his face.

"Did you know that I helped design this?" Alex did not wait for Kilian to respond. Instead, he clapped him on the shoulder and continued, "Well, of course, you didn't. You didn't even know these contraptions existed." He fiddled with the hinges on the leg closest to him for a moment. Kilian remained silent, hoping that Alex would continue talking about how he came up with this design.

Alex continued, "There are several of us out there, seeking to develop the next invention that will make life just a little bit easier than it was before. Your father was one of them, before he exploded himself, that is."

Kilian looked at Alex with a shocked expression on his face. Of course, he knew that Bluebeard had known that his father had passed, but he hadn't anticipated the others knowing the exact specifications of the way it had happened. He narrowed his eyes at the other man.

"Ah, come now, Kilian, don't look at me like that. It's widely known within my community of thinkers that the work we do can sometimes be dangerous. I think your father was trying to find a weapon that would keep you safer for longer. It just killed him was all."

Kilian had known that his father liked to tinker with scraps of metal and that he had always been working on a new project. He remembered when his father had created a way to pump water from the well into the house.

It was on a sunny day out with just enough wind that the heat hadn't become sweltering. Nathanial had spent the entire morning digging a ditch between their small cottage and the well out back. The freshly turned dirt smelled old to Kilian as if it had been sitting there for hundreds of years without ever being disturbed. Kilian liked the smell of the freshly turned dirt. It reminded him of how he thought the Creators would smell like if he ever got the chance to meet one of them. Kilian played with the fat, pink worms that moved about as their home was destroyed by his father's digging. The worms felt like a mixture of wet slime and smooth ripples as they wiggled on his open hand. Kilian laughed as one of the worms tickled his palm. They wriggled right off his palm and into the old-smelling dirt beneath him.

Sad to see them go, Kilian, reached down and plucked the first thing his fingers made contact with. To Kilian's dismay, he had picked up a giant, hairy black spider instead of a worm. It had one long orange stripe streaking up its back. Kilian hated spiders more than anything else in the whole of Mitier, with their eight long legs and their many eyes. Kilian always felt like the spiders were up to no good. And there Kilian was, holding the largest spider he'd ever seen in the palm of his hand. His entire body trembled as the spider stretched its front legs out and began exploring Kilian's palm. He screamed.

His father instantly dropped his shovel and rushed to Kilian's side. He scooped the spider into his larger, rougher palm and tossed it into the tall grass behind them. Kilian still held his palm out, staring at it as if his flesh had betrayed him.

"I hate spiders" he complained in the whiniest voice he could muster. "They're scary," he said. Shame filled him as he spoke. His father wasn't afraid of anything, and he wanted so much to be fearless and brave. He wanted to make his father proud of him.

"Can I tell you a secret?" His father's voice was soft and carried on the wind like a gentle caress. Kilian looked up at him, his eyes full of unshed tears. His father smiled at him. It was the type of smile that makes your body tingle with warmth from your toes to your head, and Kilian instantly felt safe. He nodded his head earnestly.

Kilian's father squatted in the field until his eyes were level with Kilian's. He rested one massive, warm hand on Kilian's shoulder and peered into his eyes. Kilian never felt as safe as he did when he was with his father.

"I get scared all the time," his father said.

"Wha-what?" Kilian stammered. His puffy red cheeks paled at the thought of his father being afraid of anything.

"It's true," his father continued, "sometimes, I get so scared that I can barely move."

Kilian looked down at his feet, considering his father's words. Twilight began to creep in around them as the twin moons rose in the western sky and the sunset in the same location. Eventually, they would meet in the heavens. Kilian always loved when the moons and the sun met. He imagined that they were father and daughters of the world, meeting each other time after time. He looked back up at his father and sighed.

"What do you get scared of?" he asked in a small voice.

"Oh, lots of things," his father responded with a chuckle. "Mostly, though, I get scared that my past will come back to haunt me."

"We won't be getting into the building of things before we reach the Forgotten Isles," Alex said, pulling Kilian from his memory of his father. Kilian hadn't thought about that conversation for years, and yet it had felt like it had just happened. At least now he would learn a little bit more about the past that his father had been so afraid of.

Kilian shook his head. He couldn't think about those things now. Uttering a faint "why" beneath his breath, Kilian pulled a sheet of the design closer to him and examined the minuscule drawings of parts that fit together and what looked like wheels interlocking with another similarly shaped wheel. None of it made sense to Kilian, and he wasn't sure why anyone would draw such a thing.

"For starters, we don't have time to cover the basics of ingenuity with you. We barely have time to train you on strategy and tactics before we reach the Forgotten Isles," Alex said in response to Kilian.

It was then that Kilian noticed that while he and Alex had been discussing the hinges and the art of building, Adrienne had placed some items on the table including a selection of maps and diagrams depicting battle formations, the muscles in the body, and various descriptions of strategies for hand-to-hand combat. Kilian had always dreamed of being a great warrior, but he had never imagined that there would be so much training involved with becoming one. A lump formed in his throat as he thought about what he was missing at home. His brother Willis and his sister May were probably just coming in from doing their chores. His mother would be baking fresh bread since they had the money to do so now.

They have the money to do so now, Kilian repeated this to himself in his mind. *Because of me, they can eat.* His jaw clenched at this thought as his resolve solidified.

Alex tapped one finger on an image of a man holding an ax. "This is what we will be teaching you."

"But I thought that's what Narcon was…" Kilian had begun before Alex interrupted him.

"Narcon will teach you how to put our lessons into action. Any buffoon can swing a sword or an ax wildly and without discipline. It is only the true masters that understand strategy."

Adrienne handed Alex a tattered, yellow slip of paper. Kilian leaned forward, trying to decipher the images drawn onto the paper. They all seemed like gibberish to him. There were lines drawn in different colored inks that spread across the paper the way water trails through sand, leaving seemingly unusual patterns in its wake. Each color seemed to be a code for something, though Kilian wasn't sure what.

"What is this?" Kilian asked in a breathy tone. He snatched the paper from Alex's hand. The paper felt thin in his grasp as if it could crumble into dust with just the wrong movement. Kilian traced his finger down one of the lines. Something about this drawing called to him. He knew he must be going insane. There was no way a piece of paper could speak to anyone. And yet it did. The lines seemed familiar somehow. He wasn't sure how. The way they flowed over the page. The way they made sense, even in their disorder. All of it seemed to mean something. He looked up at Alex and Adrienne. The twins were staring at him with rapt attention. He blushed at their intense gazes but held up the piece of paper.

"What is this?" he asked again.

The twins shared a look that made Kilian's stomach drop. "Tell me what it means!" he nearly shouted when they didn't answer. They continued to stare at each other in silence. Kilian had the sense that the twins were communicating without words as they continued to stare into each other eyes. Angrily, Kilian slammed his fist down on the table, "I'm not a child! Please, just tell me what this is."

He placed the piece of paper in front of the twins. "These lines, they seem so familiar," he said as he again traced one of them. "It's almost as if..." he trailed off as the twins turned to face him again.

"This is a map through the Forgotten Isles, Kilian."

That didn't make sense to him. He had never traveled anywhere beyond his little town before. He had heard tales of the Forgotten Isles, of course, but they had been nothing more than myths to him, a relic of the past. He had even seen maps of Mitier, including the island nations of Borganda and Macai. Never had he seen the shapes and sizes of the lands beyond the Forgotten Isles depicted on a map before. Kilian had always assumed this was because those lands remained uncharted. Apparently, he had been mistaken.

"Kilian, do you know why your father took you to live in that village Bluebeard scraped you out of?"

"What do you mean took me to live? I was born there," Kilian said quickly. *I was born there, wasn't I?* All of a sudden, Kilian wasn't certain he could trust the things his parents had told him all the years that he'd gone from a child to a man. His mother had given birth to him shortly after she'd met his father. They'd had a whirlwind romance that had turned into a lifetime together. Well, at least all of Kilian's lifetime.

Alex and Adrienne shared that knowing glance once more. The action infuriated Kilian.

"I'm not a child!" he hissed. "If there's something you feel like I should know, then you should just tell me!" Kilian shoved away from the table with an angry, loud scraping noise. "If you don't want to tell me anything, that's fine. But you can't expect me to play along with your little training."

"Sit down, Kilian," Alex said in a cold, calm voice. "We will tell you everything we know, but you must first calm down."
Kilian sputtered for a moment. He glanced around the deck, stared up at the blazing yellow sun, looked everywhere but at the twins standing before him.

"Forgive me, Kilian," Adrienne whispered, "but if it is you who wishes to learn our secrets, then you must learn your very first lesson."

"And what would that be?"

"Patience."

Kilian scoffed.

"It's true," Alex said. "What my brother says will make you a great leader."

Kilian crossed his arms over his body and waited for the twins to continue.

"This map…" Adrienne began.

"I don't care about the map right now!" Kilian shouted. "I want to know why you said that my father brought me to my village."

There was a long moment of silence. The only sound to be heard was the lapping of the waves against the ship as they crashed down upon the planks over and over and over again. Kilian's heart thumped rapidly in his chest. The yellowish-red sun beat down on Kilian's back, causing a line of sweat to form between his shoulder blades. Kilian desperately wanted to wipe away the beads of sweat that slowly spread across his exposed brow but didn't dare move.

"It is not our place to tell you these things, Kilian."

"Not your place?" Kilian repeated. "What do you mean it's not your place?!"

"We mean that any discussion you want to have about your heritage must be brought on by your mother."

"Who's all the way back home in Lunameed," Kilian mumbled as he slumped back into his seat.

Adrienne reached across the table and laid his hand upon Kilian's. He smiled sheepishly at him, and Kilian felt as if he were a child being cajoled by an aging uncle. He laughed quietly to himself. None of this made any sense. All he had done since coming on this quest with Bluebeard was end up with more questions about who he was.

"We would tell you the story, Kilian if we felt it were our place. But it just ain't," Adrienne said as he continued to hold Kilian's hand. Kilian only sighed in response.

"You know who should tell you these things, Kilian?" Alex said.

Kilian looked up at the other twin, a wry expression on his face. "Who?" he asked sullenly.

"I can almost guarantee that if you ask Bluebeard at the proper time that he will tell you your story."

Kilian laughed nervously beneath his breath. "You're joking, right?" he tapped his fingers on the table as he spoke. "Do you honestly believe what you're saying, or do you just not know any better?"

"Is there a difference?" Alex asked. Kilian rethought what he had just said. Was there a difference between truly believing what you say and simply not knowing the difference? He wasn't sure, not anymore at least.

"Kilian," Adrienne said before Kilian had a chance to respond to Alex's question, "I want to tell you a story about patience so that maybe you will start to understand. We can cover strategic planning at a later time." He paused and regarded Kilian with a hard expression, "If you can't learn how to be patient without losing hope then you will never be a true hero."

"What do you mean?" Kilian asked before he could stop himself.

"What do I mean?" Alex responded with a hint of laughter in his voice, "My dear boy, I mean that there have been other candidates—like you—who have started out strong—like you—but who have ultimately failed at their quests because they weren't willing to be patient."

"That can't be true," Kilian said, "there's too many…"

"Myths? Legends? Stories about heroes who completed insurmountable tasks only to falter in the end? Why yes, yes there are too many of those. They all end in failure." Alex leaned back in his chair and stared at Kilian. "You can be so much more than those legends of old, Kilian," he finally said.

A chill ran down Kilian's back as if he had just read the last words of a dying man. Even his heart seemed to turn to ice as he regarded the twins. He struggled to breathe in and a cold sweat formed on his brow as he tried yet again to breathe. He couldn't. Air seeped into his lungs the way the last drops of water ran from a bucket, slow and tedious.

"I can't be one of those legends," Kilian began.

"But you must be," Alex finished.

They sat in silence for several moments. The sun and the moons met in the sky, signaling the evening hour. Kilian's stomach rumbled, and he realized just how hungry he was. He started to rise.

"Kilian," Adrienne asked in a sweet, melodic voice. "Don't let us forget to tell you the stories of those who came before you."

"I know them," Kilian retorted, his voice incredulous.

"Not the way we tell them," Adrienne said firmly, "but you will."

Chapter Eight

Kilian's body ached. It ached more than it had when his father had made him carry two sacks of stones from the quarry to their house to replace the hearth. It ached more than it did when he'd spent his days chopping wood just to have a meager amount of food for his family during the winter months. They had been on the ship for five weeks without making port. Each day, Kilian had gone through a series of training sessions with the twins and Narcon. In the mornings, he practiced fighting followed by at least two hours of studying battle tactics with the twins. After the evening meal was the second rotation of either training or studying. To Kilian, it seemed like a never-ending sequence of being pushed beyond his limits. He was exhausted. And, his body ached.

Now he lay, with his arms stretched up as far as they would go above his head, upon the deck. The gentle rocking of the ship tempted him to sleep, but he knew that if he let himself succumb to the temptation of rest that he wouldn't be able to pull himself out of the reprieve. A faint line of golden and pink light faded into the darkness of the beyond. The beyond was not something Kilian had ever considered before, but now it was the only way he could describe the seemingly endless leagues that stretched out in front of him. He could barely remember what the sun looked like setting behind the hills of his village. He missed his life there and yet he didn't at the same time.

"Kilian," a melodic, feminine voice said. Kilian turned his head slightly to see Tavia standing before him. She wore soft leather trousers and a clean, blue linen shirt beneath a longer, heavier leather jacket. The jacket was fastened beneath her bosom with a single silver clasp. Her breasts, in their usual fashion, pressed against the confines of the leather jacket. Her dark, chestnut hair glimmered a coppery red in the setting sun.

Her perfectly red lips were pouted slightly as if she were trying to think of something but couldn't quite remember what it was. Kilian's heart beat faster and a thin line of sweat beaded on his brow. Despite being confined to the close quarters of the ship, Tavia had spent such little time speaking with him, that he almost believed he had done something to upset her.

"Y-yes?" he finally stammered, once he controlled his breathing enough to respond to her.

She raised one eyebrow at him but squatted down to speak with him. The distinct smell of chocolate and pine needles mixed with the salty scent of the air. Kilian sat up and leaned in close to her. She scrunched up her nose and leaned away from him instantly, and his heart fell.

"You need a bath!" she exclaimed as she pulled out a small cloth from her jacket pocket and held it up to her nose. "Have you washed at all this entire time?"

Kilian tried to remember the last time he'd bathed himself. He couldn't. With a sigh, he shook his head.

"You know, we may live on the road—well, in this case, a ship—but the least you could, AND ALL OF YOU," she said loud enough for the others to hear, "could do is wash yourselves every morning and night. Light's Sake! We're surrounded by water."

"Saltwater," Kilian grumbled beneath his breath. His shame was not enough to break him of his exhaustion.

"What was that?" Tavia asked, her wild eyes flashing like lightning.

"Nothing," Kilian hurriedly replied. "It's just that, how can you expect me to care about being clean when, and I'm going, to be honest here, all I do every day is train?"

"I expect," she said, enunciating each syllable as she spoke, "you to have enough self-respect that you will never let yourself become the pauper."

Kilian stared at her blankly. She stared back at him with her tumultuous eyes. A shiver ran down Kilian's back, causing him to break their eye contact. When he looked back at her, she held a smirk on her face.

She sniffed, loudly, before saying, "You do realize that you smell like a wheelbarrow of dung," she paused briefly and then finished, "that's been sitting out in the hot sun for a week." Kilian bent his head down and twisted it until his nose was pressed into his armpit. He sniffed.

"I don't smell anything."

"Of course not!" she responded, "you've become acclimated to the stench." She pinched her nose and stood up. "You have ten minutes, Kilian. Go clean yourself and then we shall begin."

Kilian tried standing up, but the muscles in his legs refused to respond. They burned, and a spasm shook his lower calf. Kilian groaned in pain.

Tavia bent down, a look of concern briefly passing over her face. It was quickly replaced with a look of appall. "Haven't you been stretching the way Narcon is teaching you?" she demanded. Her voice was like ice in his veins. Kilian flinched at its tone.

"Of course," he began. He hadn't really been following the stretches the way Narcon had taught him. In fact, most days Kilian was so exhausted that he had foregone that bit of training altogether.

Kilian gulped at her penetrating gaze and felt the heat rise in his cheeks from his lie.

"I know you're not telling me the truth, Kilian," she stomped her foot loudly as she spoke, "You must promise me that you will always tell the truth."

Tendrils of her hair fluttered in the sea breeze. They swept across her face in a graceful, tantalizing motion. *Everything about her is tantalizing*, Kilian thought as he let his eyes drift once again from her face to her bosom. Heat coursed through him, giving him new energy. He jumped up from the deck.

"I promise," he whispered as he brushed his fingers across her face, pushing the curls of hair away to reveal her face. Faint sparks like lightning flowed from her skin to his. *Light! But her eyes are so beautiful*, he found himself thinking as he leaned in closer.

She swatted his hand away with a quick flick of her wrist. His skin stung where she'd slapped him. He stepped away, his shoulders hunched, and his face hidden.

"What are you doing, Kilian?" she demanded. Her voice no longer held the light, musical quality it normally did. Instead, this voice was harsh and cold. Kilian flinched with every word she spoke.

"I'm sorry," he whispered over and over again until she, with one hand on her hip finally cupped her hand under his chin and forced him to look at her. Her eyes rolled like an ocean in a storm. The violet starbursts seemed to grow as she stared into the depths of his eyes. Kilian's heart hammered in his chest, and he breathed heavily in her grasp.

"You will never try to kiss me again," her words were clipped and monotone. Kilian didn't understand how she could be so calm when he felt so alive. Her eyes roamed over him, and Kilian felt a hunger like he never had before.

She slapped him. He blinked. The slap hadn't hurt, exactly, but it had forced him to break eye contact with her for a moment. The heat left his body and all he was left with was the dull ache of his body and now his heart.

"Kilian, listen to me," she whispered so quietly, Kilian wasn't even sure she was speaking. He thought, for a moment, that maybe he was hallucinating her voice. But then, she continued, "This can never be. I am sorry."

Kilian raised his head to glance at her. Despite the coolness of her voice, her eyes continued to storm. He wasn't sure—couldn't be sure—but he felt certain that she felt the same as he did. *Maybe one day I'll be able to sway her*, he thought as he nodded. *One day, I vow that I will.*

She raised her eyebrow at him once again, as if she had been able to read his thoughts, but didn't broach the subject further. Instead, she pulled out a small stone, no larger than a pebble really, from her jacket pocket and rubbed it between her thumb and pointer fingers.

"Do you know what this is?" she asked. The pebble glittered in the low sun. It cast rays of pink and red across her skin, highlighting her caramel features.

Intrigued, Kilian reached out and snatched the stone from her hand. It felt warm in his palm. An errant beam of sunlight struck the pebble. Tiny facets had been carved into the stone. They reflected the light and seemed to make the stone shine with all the radiance of the sun. Kilian gasped.

"It is impressive, is it not?" Tavia whispered.

Kilian nodded as he continued to stare at the beauty encompassed by that one small stone. It would have taken a master carver days to have chiseled away all those facets, he realized as he tried to count their number. He found that he couldn't.

"You still have not answered my first question, Kilian," she clutched the pebble from Kilian's hand and pocketed it within the folds of her jacket. "Do you know what that was?"

Kilian felt as if Tavia had taken something precious from him. His fingers itched to take back what had been taken from him. *Wait*, he thought, *that can't be correct. I—it's another piece of magic*, he realized.

He slumped his shoulders, but stared straight into her eyes as he spoke, "I don't know what that was, but I know that it was part of the Light's magic." He dropped his hand to his side. His fingers flexed as he forced himself to refrain from tackling Tavia and searching her until he found that pebble again.

"It is," Tavia began, "one of the nine stones of creation."

"The what?" Kilian asked.

Tavia rolled her eyes exaggeratedly. "Are you telling me that your father, the great Nathanial Clearwater, never taught you about the stones of creation?"

"N-no," Kilian stammered.

Clasping her hands in front of her, Tavia exclaimed in a sing-song voice, "then I shall just have to teach you the history of magic as well as the basics of control."

"You want to teach me magic?" he asked, his mind not quite catching up with the conversation.

"Well, of course, Kilian," she batted her eyes at him and smiled a full-on smile. Her lips glistened in the setting sun like a thousand tiny stars in the night sky. Kilian had no idea what she used to make her lips shine the way they did, but he found himself thinking about how tantalizing those lips were. He leaned in closer to her. Their lips almost touched. He could feel the heat pouring out of her. He could smell her chocolatey, fresh scent. She slapped him, not gently enough to be teasing, but definitely hard enough to sting.

"Kilian!" Tavia exclaimed, "What are you doing?" She took a step away from him and shook her head. Kilian was breathing heavily, and he clutched one hand to his cheek where her hand had met his skin. He believed he could still feel her touch. "Snap out of it, Kilian," she nearly shouted, "We have a lot to cover, but I know you'll be able to rise to the occasion." She smiled sweetly at him and put her hands on her hips. "We don't have time for your boyish fantasies." Her words stung. *They aren't childish fantasies*, he thought. *They're real.*

"I'm sorry, Tavia," Kilian began, "but I think I need a moment."

Tavia let out an exasperated breath before storming off. Kilian watched her go in silence. He breathed in heavily and tried to still his heart from beating as quickly as it was. *She's too old for me*, he told himself. *She would never want someone like me.* These thoughts did nothing to quell his desire for her. Clenching his hands into fists, Kilian jabbed at the empty air in front of him as a way to relieve some of the tension that had built up inside of him. It didn't work. Sighing heavily, Kilian made his way slowly to where Tavia stood.

She leaned against the waist-high railing of the ship with her arms stretched out wide. Spray fell upon them as Kilian joined her. A smirk spread across her face as Kilian drew near.

"Shall we begin your first lesson?" Tavia asked, her voice deep and breathy. Kilian felt a twinge of desire but forced himself to focus.

"Yes," he replied. "I think so, anyway."

"Good," she said simply. "Then let us begin."

What followed was either the worst or the best training session of Kilian's life. Unfortunately, he couldn't decide which it was. She pressed her body against his and taught him how to properly hold his body. She taught him how to protect himself against magical forces. She lectured him on the uses of different herbs and spices. Kilian's head continued to ache from his earlier exertion, but he forced himself to keep listening to her. Even when his eyes began to droop, he forced himself to remain alert to her words.

Before he knew what had happened, the sun had set, and Kilian was once again lying flat on the deck, barely able to think much less move.

"You did well this evening, Kilian. You have much to be proud of," Tavia said as she packed away the things she had brought with her to demonstrate how magic was supposed to work. Kilian hadn't been able to do any of the things she showed him except to block her from entering his mind. He sent a silent prayer of thanks up to Bluebeard for teaching him protective magic early on in their journey. She did not wait for him to respond. Instead, she wandered off to the bowels of the ship.

Starlight filled Kilian's vision as he stared straight into the sky. It was more beautiful than he had ever imagined, this world without light save the sun, moon, and stars. Sure, they had torches and candles and stones that glowed with heat, but so few of these items were used that Kilian had learned how to find his way around the hull of the ship without proper guidance. A milky strand of what looked like dust flowed through a cluster of stars at the top of his vision. It seemed to Kilian, as he stared up at those stars, that his troubles and woes all seemed so insignificant in the majesty of the world. He doubted that the Creators or the Light had spared him any thought at all. He was but a spec in the vastness of the world around him. *How could I have ever thought that my little village was so big*, he questioned. *Why had my parents never taken me from our home? Why had they never showed me the world?* These thoughts followed Kilian into a fitful sleep.

***

Loud shouts stirred Kilian from his slumber. Groggily, he opened his eyes and peered around the deck. His clothes were soaked with ocean spray and dew. Light from the twin moons cast long shadows all around him. Somewhere Kilian smelled the putrid scent of something burning. *That can't be right*, he thought as he pushed his body into a sitting position. Loud footsteps thudded behind him, and Kilian heard the scrape of metal on metal. He spun around, and all he saw was chaos. Narcon, Alex, and Tavia stood shoulder-to-shoulder fighting against a group of ten men, all dressed in identical black robes. They seemed to be holding their ground, but another group of black-robed men was approaching them from the side. Bluebeard stood at the wheel. His beard glowed with a brilliance Kilian hadn't seen since they'd boarded the ship. Kilian saw the captain's lips move before he hurled a blazing ball of flames at the men approaching the rest of the crew from behind. Bluebeard's skin grayed at the effort, but he immediately began summoning another ball of flames. Still trying to pull his thoughts together, Kilian pushed himself up into a standing position.

Rough hands immediately pulled him back down. Kilian cried out in surprise before one of the hands covered his mouth and pulled him closer to the railing. Large crates and a barrel of ale provided shelter for them as Kilian's captor forced him into a crouching position. Kilian's mind raced in a thousand different directions as whoever it was continued to hold his mouth shut.

A pair of guards stalked past their position. They wore navy uniforms with a silver crest embroidered on their chest. One of them, the one closest to Kilian's position, carried a massive sword in both hands. They wore battered plate armor on their shoulders and knees. *What are they doing on the ship?* Kilian thought as he watched them walk by. The one with the sword peered around the deck as if searching for something. For one long, awful moment, he glanced in the direction where Kilian and his captor hid in the darkness. He squinted his eyes in their direction but did not stop his companion to further investigate the shadows between the crates and the barrel.

Kilian heard his captor sigh heavily behind him before releasing their hold on Kilian's body. Spinning around, Kilian came nose-to-nose with Adrienne. His hair was disheveled, and he appeared as if he hadn't slept all night, but there was a look of defiance in his eyes that left a fire in Kilian's stomach. He burned to join the fray.

Adrienne shoved Kilian's ax into his hands. Kilian weighed it in his grip. Somehow, it felt lighter than it had when Bluebeard had first given it to him.

"Follow my lead," Adrienne whispered as he inched towards the boxes. Kilian held his breath and waited. It seemed to him that if they were going to survive this assault, then they needed reinforcements. A hurling ball of flames skidded on the deck before them. The nauseating scent of burnt hair filled Kilian's nostrils and, when Adrienne pulled his face back, his eyebrows had been singed off. Despite this, Adrienne motioned for Kilian to follow him beyond the crates. Kilian could still hear the sounds of men crying out in pain and the shriek of metal on metal, but he forced himself to swallow his fear. Though is hands shook as they grasped the ax, he nodded at Adrienne.

No sooner had Adrienne stood up as he crawled out from behind the crates than his entire body went rigid. Kilian barely had time to pause and sink back into the shadows before Adrienne's body twisted at odd angles. He heard the sharp snap of bones breaking as one of Adrienne's arms was bent upwards at a ninety-degree angle. Adrienne's face remained in the same expression it had when he'd been—Kilian wasn't sure what. But his eyes, they darkened from the pain.

"No," he whispered under his breath as one of Adrienne's knees audibly popped out of position.

Adrienne's body remained suspended in air, so close to Kilian, yet Kilian knew, somehow, that if he tried to help his friend that he would suffer the same fate.

"Kaldeena," Bluebeard's voice echoed over the ship. The sounds of fighting died away at the sound of his voice. "If you wanted to talk, you should have just asked." Bluebeard's voice was cold and slid like ice over Kilian's heart.

She strode into the middle of the deck, her long cloak fluttering behind her. Her skin emanated a soft blue glow as she planted her hands on her hips and scanned the ship's deck. She scowled when she didn't find what she was looking for.

She snapped her fingers and Adrienne's body drifted towards her. His head bobbed in the air as he moved. His expression still had not changed, but Kilian saw a single tear rolling down his friend's face.

She laughed softly and inspected her long nails before raking them across Adrienne's once beautiful face. A trail of blood blossomed on his pale skin. Kilian shuddered.

"You expect me to believe that you would have let me onto your ship without these acts of violence, Bluebeard?"

Seamlessly, Kaldeena pulled a small dagger from a belt at her side. Sapphire and ruby jewels gleamed in the soft glow of her skin. The silver blade seemed to hum slightly as she flourished it around before her as if it were a fan and not a knife.

"Kaldeena," Bluebeard said, his voice a threat.

"Yes, Bluebeard," she responded innocently as she waved it in front of Adrienne's face. Kilian couldn't be sure, but he thought he saw Adrienne's eyes grow larger at the sight of the blade.

"Put the dagger down, Kaldeena." It was a command. There was no other way to interpret Bluebeard's words.

Kaldeena laughed hysterically.

"Kaldeena," Bluebeard said again, more forcibly.

Kaldeena continued laughing.

Bluebeard summoned a small ball of flames in his hand. It glowed brightly in the dark night. Kilian stared, transfixed as Bluebeard raised his hand and aimed the ball of flames right at Kaldeena's head. She didn't seem to notice as she began moving gracefully around Adrienne's still floating body. Bluebeard, as if in slow motion, released the ball of flames. It soared through the air so quickly that Kilian barely saw it move. To him, it seemed as if the flames were a comet in the sky.

His entire head moved with the flames. They burst into a spray of cinders as they struck their target.

"No!" Kilian shouted.

Adrienne's body still floated in the air, but where his chest, so solid had been, there was now only a mass of smoldering, melted skin. Kilian sank to his knees, tears welling in his eyes. "No," he whispered over and over again.

Kaldeena still danced around Adrienne's body. She continued to brandish the blade she'd plucked from her belt. It seemed to disappear from the speed of her gestures.

Bluebeard marched towards Kaldeena, his own blade now in his hands. His face looked so impassive to Kilian. *Does he feel anything?* Kilian found himself thinking. *Doesn't he know how much Adrienne meant to me? And Alex. Poor Alex.*

Kaldeena stopped moving around Adrienne's body and held her blade up to the soft spot between his chin and his neck. Even from the distance that separated them, Kilian could see Adrienne's vein still throbbing in his neck. *He's still alive.* The thought passed so quickly that Kilian wasn't sure he'd even thought it at all. *He's hurt, badly, but he's still alive.*

Bluebeard abruptly stopped moving. He was still too far away from Kaldeena to make his sword useful in a fight against her. A smile spread across her face.

"Where's the boy, Bluebeard?" her voice was like ice in Kilian's veins. She had done all of this because of him.

"Out of your reach, Kaldeena."

She smirked at Bluebeard's response and pressed the blade more firmly against Adrienne's skin. Bluebeard noticeably tightened his grip on the hilt of his sword.

"You have no claim to him," Bluebeard said, his voice calm, but firm.

"Oh, and I suppose that you do?" Kaldeena replied in the same calm, loud voice. Her golden eyes seemed to glow in the night from within her pale, icy blue skin. They stood like that for several moments, both staring into each other's eyes. Kilian held his breath as he looked between them. A trickle of sweat ran between his shoulder blades as the tension continued to rise. The scent of Adrienne's still smoldering chest lingered in the air. Kilian's grip on his ax tightened. *I could*, he began to think, *but no. She wants me.* The air became a thick wall of smoke and pressure. Kilian's eyes looked beyond Bluebeard and Kaldeena.

And he saw Alex. His friend clung to Narcon, who was holding him tightly. His entire body seemed to sag. At that moment Kilian knew what was to come. She would kill Adrienne. There was no bargain, nothing that they could do to save him.

Unless, he thought.

"More than you," Bluebeard whispered, his voice carried on the wind like the gentle caress of a mother's kiss. It drew Kilian's attention back to the scene before him.

Bluebeard swiftly charged towards Kaldeena with his sword held before him. He moved so quickly Kilian could barely see the blur that made up his massive frame.

Adrienne slumped to the ground as Kaldeena brought up her dagger to defend herself. Her blade was shorter than Bluebeard's, but she was even quicker than he was.

She swung her blade out at him, the jewels gleaming in the faint light of her skin. Bluebeard zipped around her swing as if he had been anticipating the move. Despite his large size, he moved gracefully, as if he were in a tranquil dance. Kilian watched in amazement as he shifted between stances fluidly. He seemed to adapt to her attack and defense as easily as he steered his ship. To Kilian, it seemed as if Bluebeard had all the control in the world.

They tested each other, each advancing on the other in quick succession. Kaldeena's body appeared to hum in the night air, and a rippling bubble of air expanded around her body before tightening to her form. It glowed faintly as she continued to spar with Bluebeard. Then, as if from nowhere, a small shield materialized on her arm. It was the same shiny metal as her dagger with a jewel inset into the middle of its width.

Bluebeard snarled and lunged at Kaldeena. His sword flew through the air as he tackled her. Kilian watched with bated breath as Bluebeard straddled Kaldeena and pressed her hands firmly into the deck. She squirmed beneath his weight. Without hesitating, Bluebeard plunged his sword straight into Kaldeena's chest.

And his sword shattered.

Kilian didn't see the sword shatter. Rather, he heard the bits of metal scraping against the wooden deck as he was blinded by a brilliant blue light that seemed to emanate directly from Kaldeena's body. The light exploded, shoving Kilian back into the crate behind him. His head cracked against the solid planks of wood, and a wave of nausea passed over him. Sucking in a deep breath, Kilian counted to twelve, and the feeling stopped.

Leaning forward, Kilian saw Bluebeard kneeling several feet away from Kaldeena, his hands raised to his chest. He looked old, frail even. His skin had turned a sour pale and his hair had turned gray. *He needs another infusion*, Kilian thought as he stared at the old captain. Small, dark spots covered one side of the captain's face, and many of his teeth were missing. *I wonder if this is what he truly looks like*, Kilian considered.

Kaldeena laughed mirthlessly as she twirled the dagger between her fingers. "Fool," she said loud enough for everyone on deck to hear. She dropped the knife and it dug into the hard, smooth wood of the deck. She began to stride towards Bluebeard, her face a mixture of lust and hatred. *She's going to kill him*, Kilian realized. Anger flared within him.

Without considering what he was doing, Kilian stepped out from behind the crates and charged straight at Kaldeena. He screamed loudly as he rushed towards her, his ax raised before him. She turned, slowly, as if she had not a care in the world—except for her eyes. Her eyes swarmed with a mixture of emotions, the greatest of which was desire.

As Kilian ran, his ax began to spread warmth up his arm. He felt strong—stronger than he had ever felt before. His mind cleared, and he could clearly see the actions he needed to take. Breathing in deeply, Kilian shoved his shoulder into Kaldeena's chest, knocking her to ground.

As if from muscle memory, only quicker and more powerful, Kilian brought his ax down in a crushing blow. His ax scraped against the metal of Kaldeena's shield. Kilian's blood pumped through his veins at a swift pace. He felt exhilarated by the fight. He swung his ax again and again. He was swinging his ax so rapidly that if Kaldeena had been a normal opponent, she would have already been cleaved by his blade. All Kilian could think about was swinging his ax, breaking through her shield, taking revenge.

One of her guards lunged at Kilian from the side, knocking him off balance. Kilian's vision went red as he quickly adjusted to the imbalance. Gripping his ax tightly in his hand, Kilian swung his ax and cleaved the man in half. The soldier's face barely registered his pain before his top half slid off of his bottom. Looking around, Kilian saw the other soldiers—the ones who had been attacking his crew, his friends—standing all around him. Some held weapons, others looked on with looks of horror on their faces.

Releasing a primal roar, Kilian charged at the guards. His vision red, his heart pumping rapidly, Kilian brutally attacked all of them. He moved so quickly—and thoughtlessly—he didn't know who or what he was cutting down. Blood splattered his face and slid into his mouth. The coppery taste riled his emotions even more. He twisted and swung, cutting down another of the guards in a powerful blow to the neck. Spinning around, Kilian's ax sliced through the legs of one of the guards, sending him toppling over the rail of the ship.

Kilian lost count of how many people he cut down. All he knew was the desire to destroy, the rage of battle.

Panting, Kilian spun around, looking for any remaining guards. Blood covered the deck and ran in streams over the sides. Mangled bodies lay all around him. Some groaned pathetically. Kilian deftly slammed his ax into each of their heads as he moved about the deck, searching for something. From the corner of his eye, Kilian saw a dark shadow moving towards him. Without pausing, he gripped the ax with both hands and swung as forcefully as he could towards the direction of his assailant.

He swiped through air.

Grunting, Kilian spun around, his ax forming an arc around him. Still, he swung through thin air. Fury rose within him. Kilian bellowed out a loud roar and began twisting around, searching for his elusive assailant.

"Kilian."

The voice was soft, feminine, and pleading. Kilian hesitated for but a moment, trying to place where he knew that voice from. It sounded like a delicate set of chimes ringing in the wind.

A pair of thick, muscular arms wrapped around Kilian and pulled him to the ground. Kilian thrashed against him, trying to break his hold—to no avail. Suddenly, a second set of hands appeared from the darkness and wrenched his ax free from his hand. The moment the handle fell from Kilian's fingers, it was as if all of his emotions were pulled away from him as well.

Kilian felt numb, cold even. He shivered violently in the wake of his loss. Images flashed through his mind. Countless eyes faded into the unseeing. Desperate cries crowded out all other sound. It was as if Kilian were watching himself from the outside. He saw the things he had done. He smelled the scent of their blood and excrement as the light faded from their eyes.

I did this.

Kilian stopped struggling against whoever it was that had been holding him. He continued to shake uncontrollably as his captor slowly released him from his grip. Kilian covered his face as a single tear slid from his eye. He somehow knew that it was leaving a clean streak on his otherwise blood smeared face.

I did this.

He heard muffled murmurs from somewhere close by. The scent of burning wood and flesh filled the air. Slowly, Kilian stood up and turned in the direction of the murmurs. Tavia, Narcon, and the frail-bodied Bluebeard stood in a semi-circle around Alex, who was cradling Adrienne in his arms. Even through the darkness Kilian could see that Alex rocked back and forth. His lips moved in the recitation of the old words—the ones reserved for the deepest mourning.

"No," Kilian whispered beneath his breath. He took a step towards them. His entire body rebelled against him. Even before the fighting Kilian had been exhausted. Now he felt as if his body were not his own. He felt weak and exhilarated all at the same time. His breathing came in ragged gasps as he continued inching his way towards where Alex held what Kilian knew would be his dead brother.

Adrienne, Kilian thought. He couldn't quite believe that the person who had been so patient with him was really gone.

The sound of Alex's laments cast an eerie tenor to the night. What few fires remained cast shadows over the faces of

Kilian's companions. For the first time since he had begun this journey with them, he felt like a complete outsider. They had known Adrienne and loved him. Kilian had only barely met any of these people. Although he had felt connected to them in a way he never had with the people in his village, here, at this moment, he was the intruder.

Kilian was close enough to them now that he was able to see Adrienne's face. A small cut had been sliced across his neck, barely deep enough to have caused his death. *There's not enough blood,* Kilian found himself thinking. But, when he got closer, he realized that the wound had spread an intricate pattern of dark lines throughout Adrienne's body. His lips were cold purple and his eyes were open, revealing empty black sockets.

"What happened to his eyes," Kilian asked, though he wasn't sure if he spoke these words out loud or not. None of the others looked at him. They continued to stand silently with the brothers.

Kilian's body ached, and he had the overwhelming desire to sink to the floor and sleep. It was covered in blood and grime, but somehow Kilian didn't find these things as repulsive as he once had. Vague thoughts of his ax passed through his mind as he sank to the deck.

"No you don't," a loud voice in his ear said.
Kilian blinked rapidly, trying to piece together his thoughts. His back and legs cried out at him as he slowly stood back up.

"Come on now," the voice said as a pair of hands turned Kilian away from where Alex continued to hold Adrienne. "Come on," the voice said commandingly.

Kilian followed who he soon realized was Narcon down the ladder to the hold of the ship. The older man barely spoke as he led him to Kilian's room.

"Wh-what happened?" Kilian mumbled groggily. Images of the battle swept through his mind. *Did I really kill all those people?* He wanted to ask, but couldn't force the words out of his mouth. Instead, he asked, "Where's Kaldeena? I didn't see her body above?" He hesitated a moment and then asked, "And where's my ax."

"Calm yourself, boy," Narcon said in the most monotone voice Kilian had ever heard the man use. Narcon hesitantly placed a hand on Kilian's shoulder before continuing, "She's gone, son. She escaped in the chaos of your rampage."

"NO!" Kilian shouted. "She can't—" Kilian stopped speaking. *What have I done?* He had killed all those people. No, he hadn't just killed them, he'd slaughtered them. He'd refused them mercy, even when they'd begged for it. Even after the danger had passed and the soldiers had been incapacitated, Kilian had continued to kill them.

And Kaldeena had gotten away.

"Adrienne," he said, "what did she do to him? I saw the cut. There wasn't enough blood. He shouldn't be dead. He can't be—" his voice trailed off as Narcon held his finger to his lips.

"She used one of the creator's blades, Kilian."
Kilian stared at the older man blankly. He had never heard of a "creator's blade" before. Narcon must have realized that Kilian didn't understand what that meant because, after a short pause, he continued.

"Creator's blades are weapons that only one of the eight originals can bestow upon those they deem worthy. They don't work like normal weapons. The smallest cut spreads the darkness right through the person, killing the soul. It's a fate worse than death, Kilian." His voice quivered as he spoke.

They stood in silence for several moments. Kilian shivered. He couldn't imagine what a fate worse than death felt like, but he could imagine the agony that Alex must be feeling. He remembered what he had felt when he'd found his father's charred body in the clearing. A lump swelled in his throat.

Blinking away the unbidden tears, Kilian whispered, "And my ax." His voice hung in the air the way the last note of a flute did at the end of a sad story. Kilian shivered again.

"Tavia has it," Narcon responded flatly. He turned to leave then, but Kilian quickly laid a hand upon Narcon's arm, stilling the older man.

Narcon lifted an eyebrow at him and silently waited for Kilian to remove his hand from his arm. Taking the hint, Kilian let his arm fall beside him. He clenched his fist tightly as he considered what he wanted to ask.

In slow, deliberate words Kilian finally said, "Why does Kaldeena want me so much? Why would she kill Adrienne... especially with one of those blades? It doesn't make any sense to me, Narcon."

Narcon sighed heavily, and his shoulders visibly slumped. The older man smelled of sweat and blood, but when he leaned in and held Kilian tightly to his chest, Kilian didn't resist the man's embrace. In an odd way, the putrid smell was comforting. He had grown to know this older man during his time on the ship. Wrapping his own arms tightly around Narcon, Kilian squeezed the older man.

Without warning, Narcon pulled away from Kilian and stated in a flat tone, "There are many prophecies in this world Kilian. Some of them contradict each other. Still, others describe how someone important will die. The rarest tell of what will come to pass that will have a significant effect on the world. It is Kaldeena who first received the prophecy about you," he paused.

Kilian let out the breath he hadn't realized he'd been holding. That woman—that murderer—knew the prophecy. She knew what he would do.

Narcon continued to eye Kilian with a thoughtful expression on his face. Kilian, wanting to reassure his mentor, took a step forward and placed his hands on Narcon's upper arms. He smiled. Narcon did not smile back.

"Bah," he exclaimed. "I always speak outta turn." He once again pulled away from Kilian. "I'm sorry, m'boy. You will have to figure this one out on yer own. It's not my place to tell you of the past—or the future."

With that, Narcon fled from the room.

Kilian stood in silence for several moments. He tried to hold onto as much of the night's events as he could, but eventually, the exhaustion he had been stymieing for so long overtook him. He didn't even undress before he fell into bed and began to snore.

Chapter Nine

In the beginning, there were eight who were chosen and gifted with the power to claim and gift others. They were the Light's chosen ones. They were our gods.

For centuries, they sought out the greatest warriors and heroes of the time and granted them unheard of powers. Some were given the gift of flight. Others were given control over the winds and the seas. Still, others were given the power to create, much in the way they could. To the worthiest, they granted entire species gifts from the Light that could be passed down for generations. Still, in every generation and in every race, there were those who were special. Those were chosen.

I'm not quite sure when that began to change.

Perhaps it was when the Creators began to tell stories of the things they had seen. Perhaps it was when the Creators granted others the gift of Foresight. Regardless, there were those who began to believe that they alone had deciphered the cryptic nature of the prophecies and that they alone could discover the ones meant to fulfill them. The arrogance of these sects has never ceased to amaze me.

-From the personal journal of Navalara the Bard,
Oracle of the Second Order

***

Twin mountains loomed before Kilian. The air was cold and smelled of rotten eggs. Cries filled the air. Kilian scanned his surroundings, frantically looking for the owners of the voices. Everywhere he looked all he saw was desolation. Dwellings were burned to the ground, their charred skeletons laid bare in the twilight. Some still smoldered, sending tendrils of smoke into the hazy sky above them. The ground beneath his feet squished with the unmistakable sound of sticky mud. Kilian grimaced as one of his feet clung to the ground. As he wrenched it free, he realized that there was a trail of footsteps leading forward. Still, Kilian followed the footsteps. His calf muscles burned as he climbed the first slope of the mountain to his left.

His ax hummed softly to him as he climbed. He wasn't sure how he knew it was his ax; he just knew. It carried the notes of sorrow and hatred upon its rhythm, making Kilian shiver slightly. It had gotten so cold; he wasn't sure when. His teeth chattered as powerful gusts of wind plummeted against his body.

"So, you have come," a voice echoed through the hills.

The world around Kilian seemed to warp and fade away. He fell through space as if he weighed little more than a feather in the breeze. His stomach twisted and flopped as he was pulled through the sky. Or, at least, he thought it was the sky. Stars seemed to twinkle in the darkness of night, their glowing radiance called to him.

He began to fall more quickly now. Ribbons of distorted light waved around him the faster he fell. Kilian knew he would hit the world soon. That he would perish. He braced himself for the impact, tucking his head between his knees and whispering a silent prayer to the Light for protection.

It didn't help.

He landed in a tangled, bloody mess upon one of the ridges surrounding his home back in Lunameed. He could hear his sister May and brother Willis playing in the distance. Their voices traveled on the wind and gently caressed him. A deep yearning filled him. How he longed to see them again, to play with them the way he had before their father had died. Memories of his father filled his vision; he blinked in an attempt to block out the tears that had swelled there.

The ground shook beneath his feet, and Kilian stumbled and fell. He scraped his hands against the rough rocks. Crimson blood poured from his hands, splattering on the ground beneath him.

It wasn't his blood.

His sister lay at his feet, her neck sliced open. Her cold, dead eyes remained open, staring at him with an accusing expression in them. Willis lay next to her, his limbs turned in odd directions. Kilian could hear his whimpers over the hum of his own heartbeat. Shadows etched in darker shadows fluttered through the hills around him. Startled, Kilian turned and ran into the forest behind him.

As he ran, fires caught hold of the trees all around him. Sweat dripped down his back, though he wasn't sure if it was from the heat of the flames or the panic rising within him. His sister's voice echoed in his mind carrying the melodic sound of death. The further Kilian ran, the closer her voice seemed to be.

His skin turned to ice. Shivering, Kilian breathed out a cloud of condensation. The forest surrounding his home had disappeared as had his sister's voice. A dark void filled his vision. Everywhere he looked, all he saw was emptiness.

"So, you have come at last," a deep, booming voice said from somewhere within the void. Kilian squinted, trying to see if any shapes were moving behind the cloud of darkness before his eyes. He thought he could see something. It slithered over the ground like a snake, yet stood tall like a man. The glint of metal reflected from the small torch Kilian clung to in the darkness. He couldn't remember when he'd started holding the torch, but he was happy to have it.

"It has been too long, old friend," the voice said.

"Old friend?" Kilian asked.

"Do you not remember me then?" the voice chuckled lightly.

A withered hand with skin stretched so tightly over its bones that it looked more like a skeleton than anything else reached out from the darkness. In its palm, it held a shimmering orb of blue light. Shapes and images zipped through the orb.

"They contain my memories," the voice said. "And it is time that you remember."

The orb shot through the air aimed right at Kilian's head. He stood, motionless, unable to decide. As the sphere of blue light slammed into Kilian's face, it burst into tiny shards of brilliance.

***

Kilian woke to darkness.

His brow was drenched in sweat as was his arms, back, and the thin sheet that separated him from the hammock. The gentle rocking of the ship seemed at odds with the dream he'd escaped from. *Was it a dream?* Kilian wasn't sure anymore. Everything had seemed so vivid, so real.

Something moved in the darkness. Kilian couldn't be sure, but he thought he saw the outline of a person's shape leaned against the wall. Yes, there. He had seen the person flick something into the air and catch it. *This must have been what first drew my attention to him*, Kilian thought. The person flicked the something into the air again. As Kilian continued to lay motionless in his hammock, staring into the darkness at the shape, he began to reimagine the things he'd dreamed about.

Did one of those shadows—the man with the withered hand—follow me from my dream? He knew it was an impossibility. He knew that he should close his eyes and go back to sleep. He knew that the most likely scenario was that whoever was standing in his room was just a figment of his imagination. None of the things he used to calm himself made his fear any less. *I watched Adrienne die tonight*, he told himself. *I saw his eyes. They were the same—*

The person, whoever it was, opened the door to Kilian's cabin and slipped out into the hallway beyond. Kilian's stomach churned, and he felt as if he were going to vomit. His body still ached from the training and the battle. He still couldn't seem to remember everything that he had done. He remembered feeling powerful and undefeatable. He remembered fighting against his enemies. With a shiver, he remembered the smell and taste of the soldiers' blood as it splattered onto his face. The thrill of seeing and tasting that blood had pushed him to continue. He had enjoyed—no, he had *loved*—the thrill of battle. Some part of him yearned to battle more, to kill more.

I am a monster, he thought, *a total and complete monster.*

Shaking his head, Kilian pulled his blanket up closer to his chin and turned his back on the door. He wouldn't allow himself to be afraid anymore. He couldn't. There was too much at stake that Kilian wasn't willing to risk losing. *Besides*, he told himself, *I fought an entire army today and won. What is one person, even if that one person was creepily watching me sleep, going to do to me?*

Still, his heart continued to hammer in his chest. He felt like the boy he used to be who would curl up on his mother's lap and let her sing him to sleep. How he wished he could curl up on her lap now. He couldn't, and he knew that. He had bargained away his ability to receive her comfort or even to see her the day Bluebeard had wandered into his life.

A loud click coming from his cabin door disrupted his thoughts. *He's back*, Kilian thought as he tried to remain as still as possible. He struggled to keep his breathing as normal as possible, but the louder the footsteps got to his bed, the more alarmed he became.

"Kilian," a raspy, old voice said as a hand shook him gently. "Kilian," he repeated.

Kilian recognized that voice, even in the layers of fatigue and age he knew had been molded onto him. He rolled over and glared at Bluebeard. Soft light filtered in through the now open door. Kilian, who had opened his mouth to tell Bluebeard to go away, closed his mouth abruptly.

The older man still wore the clothes he had been wearing during the battle. They were stained a dark brownish-red and, as Bluebeard kneeled before him, Kilian could smell the distinct scent of old sweat and piss. Bluebeard trembled as he sank to his knees and his hands, outstretched before him, shook violently as he slowly clasped Kilian's hands. They were as cold as ice and as wrinkled as a sheet that had been freshly laundered. Bluebeard's once clear eyes had become clouded and white. He bowed his head, shielding his face from Kilian's gaze as if he knew Kilian were looking at him with pity.

He was, of course looking at Bluebeard with pity. How could he not? The older man reeked of failure and despair.

"Kilian," Bluebeard muttered under his breath. "You did," he paused, "You saved me ship."

Images of Kilian cutting down all those soldiers flashed through Kilian's mind. He momentarily felt the excitement, the need to battle, before it quickly faded.

"I also got Adrienne killed," he said as he yanked his hands away from Bluebeard. Then, in the most accusatory tone he could muster, he said, "Actually, maybe it wasn't me. Maybe it was YOU who got him killed."

Bluebeard's shoulders sagged at the mention of Adrienne's name. Kilian instantly felt guilty for blaming the sad, frail man before him. It was hard to remain angry with Bluebeard when he had lost his youth and strength.

"You're right," the older man whispered softly. He rocked back and forth as he spoke and Kilian felt a strong twinge of guilt and remorse. "You're right," Bluebeard said again. "It's my fault. It's all my fault." He wrangled his hands before him. "I should never have…" he paused.

Kilian waited for but a second before eagerly asking, "You should never have what, Bluebeard? What, exactly, is that you shouldn't have done?"

"I should never have fetched you," he said in a monotone voice that seemed to come automatically from him. "I should never have let your father take you from me, to begin with."

Bluebeard looked up at Kilian as he spoke and, despite his blind eyes, peered straight into Kilian's.

"What do you mean you should have never let my father take me from you?" Kilian asked in a slightly trembling voice. He had tried so hard to keep it at a steady level, but his body and mind were both exhausted.

"I knew when you were born that you would be the one," Bluebeard continued in his same monotone voice. "Even at birth, you shone with the brilliance of a thousand stars. We knew—all of us—that you had been blessed by the Creators. When I held you in my arms, I could feel your strength, even then. I knew that the ax was meant for you. I knew that you would one day help me find the Creators to receive my own blessing."

Something nagged at the back of Kilian's mind as Bluebeard spoke. *How could Bluebeard know what I looked like when I was born if I had been born to my ma and father back in Lunameed?*

"I wasn't born in Lunameed, was I, Bluebeard?" Kilian's voice came out in an eager chirp as he spoke. From the recesses of Kilian's mind, he heard a voice whispering, "I carried him, I gave birth to him, I have a claim to him." As if from a fog, Kilian remembered.

Even as Bluebeard hesitantly muttered "no" in softest of tones, Kilian knew.

"Kaldeena is my mother," he did not ask it as a question.

"Yes," Bluebeard responded, still wringing his hands.

Kilian stood from his hammock and began pacing around Bluebeard in the small cabin. It couldn't actually be considered pacing; the room was too small. It was more like hopping from one foot to the other as Kilian considered.

Finally, he said, "I will give you part of my youth, since I know that's the true reason why you came here this morning, Bluebeard." His voice was cold as he spoke, but he also heard hints of control. Somehow, Kilian didn't feel like the little boy he had been when Bluebeard had first taken him from his home. "I will give you my strength, and you will give me back my ax."

Bluebeard opened his mouth to speak, but Kilian shushed him. "I'm talking now, Bluebeard. You will have your turn." *When did I become so demanding?* Kilian thought as he continued, "Then, you will tell me everything you know."

For a single, short moment, Kilian believed that Bluebeard would say no, that he would deny Kilian's request. But, as if Bluebeard had been compelled to follow Kilian's demands, he nodded.

"I need to hear you say the words, Bluebeard."

"I swear it," Bluebeard mumbled.

"Say it louder," Kilian commanded.

"I swear that if you give me your youth that I will tell you everything I know about ya," Bluebeard said in a loud, clear voice that didn't match his appearance.

"Done," Kilian said as he stretched out his hand and allowed Bluebeard to take it.

The moment their hands clasped Kilian felt the pull of Bluebeard's magic on him. It seemed to be sucking out his energy in a slow, steady stream. Kilian's muscles flattened, and he felt as if all of his strength were being removed. His mind became muddled as he continued to remember the dream and the battle.

It's time.

Startled, Kilian opened his eyes and stared at Bluebeard. The older man had his eyes closed. His entire body glowed a brilliant blue. He looked calm as the wrinkles and spots on his body faded away into smooth, muscled skin. Bluebeard's face filled out as weight was added to his frame. The longer he remained in contact with the Kilian, the more he looked like his familiar self.

Kilian! The voice rang in Kilian's mind. He knew that voice.

Father? He asked. Deftly, Kilian constructed a barrier between Bluebeard's invasion of his body and mind so that the older man wouldn't be able to tell what he was thinking. After weeks of training, Kilian had managed to block Bluebeard's attempts to enter and control his mind. Furthermore, Kilian had been able to keep a weak barrier up during in the infusions.

An image of his father's face filled his mind. He looked as he had when Kilian had been a child. Nathanial Clearwater had been a proud, sturdy man. He had worked hard every day to supply for the Clearwater family. He had loved his mother and his siblings, of this Kilian, was sure.

Father. He whispered again in his mind. He felt the barrier flicker as he peered around the recesses of his mind, searching for a way to fully shield his father's image from Bluebeard.

You're not safe here, me boy. I always knew— his father's voice cracked with emotion and, although Kilian couldn't see his father's eyes, he knew that he would have seen tears in them.

Why aren't I safe? Kilian thought. *What do you know?* His father's image disappeared, leaving Kilian standing in a dark abyss. *Father,* he cried out. The sound of his own voice reverberated in his mind the way his voice had in the caves by the river. *Father!* he shouted again. *Can you hear me? Please, I need your help.*

Although Kilian was only speaking in his mind and, although Kilian was confident that his discussions with his father whenever Bluebeard took an infusion were figments of his imagination, Kilian couldn't quite let go his desire to hear his father's voice.

The image of his father stood before him. His silhouette oscillated as he stood before Kilian. He grasped something in his hand, but Kilian wasn't quite sure what it was.

Kilian, his father whispered, *you're not safe here*. It was the same line he had said before.

Why aren't I safe, Father? I don't understand.

I couldn't save you. I'm sorry. His father's shoulders sagged as he spoke and the brilliance of his image's edges seemed to fade slightly.

Don't go! Kilian pleaded. *Please, Father, don't leave me again.*

"That enough Kilian," Bluebeard said as he pulled his hand from Kilian's grasp.

Kilian blinked. He had fallen into his hammock during the infusion process. His arms felt weak, and he knew that if tried to stand that he would fall. Bluebeard, on the other hand, stood tall and muscular before him. He looked even younger than he had when Kilian had first met him.

"How much did you take?" Kilian asked accusingly. "Enough to repair the damage caused by Kaldeena."

Kilian pulled his blanket up above his shoulders to hold off the cold. It didn't work nearly as well as he would have liked and he shivered as a gust of wind filtered in through his open cabin door.

"What, exactly did she do to you?" he asked after a moment.

Bluebeard coughed quietly before saying in a baffled tone, "I'm not exactly sure what she did. I've never seen anything like it, Kilian. It was as if all the magic I had summoned to destroy her reflected back on me."

They remained silent for several moments, each considering the meaning of Bluebeard's words. Finally, after much consideration, Kilian asked, "What did she do to Adrienne?" Kilian leaned forward, not caring that his blanket dropped slightly, letting in more of the cold. "I only know what Narcon told me."

"She used one of the blades forged by the Creators. They were not meant to take life through greed and vengeance."

"What were they intended for then?" Kilian cut in. Bluebeard coughed again. "They were created as a way to protect the Light's will. The Creators forged them out of their own magic and dipped them in the Light's pool to temper them. They are the rarest and most treasured of all the artifacts formed by the Creators."

Kilian thought through Bluebeard's words. If he were to believe what the older man was saying, then this Kaldeena woman had, at some point, been blessed by the Light. She was one of their chosen.

Remembering his dream and the words Kaldeena had spoken during their first encounter, Kilian steeled himself to ask the most difficult question he had been considering.

"Is she really my mother?" his voice shook as he spoke. Bluebeard raised an eyebrow but gave no other indication that Kilian's question was out of line.

"Bah, Kilian, you don't really want to know the answer to this question, do you?"

Bluebeard's answer was enough. A sinking feeling pressed down on Kilian's stomach, and he felt like he did when he jumped from highest cliff above their family's farm.

"She is, isn't she? That's why she's come after me. It isn't because she wants to harm me or the mission, it's because she wants to have a relationship with me." his voice grew more and more excited as he spoke. "She probably wants to help me."

A sense of exhilaration filled him. His mother had been blessed by the Creators. He wasn't just a nobody from a nowhere town. He was something—someone.

"Kilian," Bluebeard spoke slowly, deliberately, "You don't know what you're saying. It's not like that. Your father… he took you away from her."

"And he was wrong to do so. Think about it, Bluebeard. What if she's only doing these things because she wants to know me."

Bluebeard breathed out heavily. "Ach, boy, can't you see that what you're saying doesn't make any sense. She murdered Adrienne right in front of you."

"That could have been an accident."

Bluebeard glared at Kilian, his expression hardening. "You know nothing, Kilian Clearwater." Raising his hands in frustration, Bluebeard stomped around the cabin. It was only a few stomps—the cabin was rather small—but it was enough to make Kilian pause.

"Your father was the same way the first time he met Kaldeena. By the Light! He loved her. He did everything she asked. He even betrayed me," Bluebeard stopped speaking as he uttered the last of his words. A look of surprise crossed his face. "I hadn't been intending on telling you that one."

"How did he betray you? 'Sides, I thought Kaldeena had been part of your crew as well," Kilian pointed at Bluebeard with one long, knobby finger, "The things you say don't add up, Bluebeard. I want you to tell me the truth."

"I am!" Bluebeard shouted unexpectedly. "It's not me fault if you can't see the truth when it's right in front of ya, Kilian. Your father betrayed me to help Kaldeena. She was blessed by the Creators. With the dagger and—" he stopped speaking.

"And with what," Kilian prompted.

"You," Bluebeard finally whispered. "The Creators gave her you."

Kilian felt cold as ice as Bluebeard's words pressed down on him. Everything he thought he'd known had been a lie: his parents, his siblings, his entire life. *You're not safe here, Kilian.* His father's voice hung in his mind. Was it a warning against Bluebeard or something else entirely? Kilian wasn't sure.

"Then… Nathanial wasn't really my father?" he finally asked.

"No, Kilian, that's not what I'm saying at all. Your father loved Kaldeena with a passion that only the Creators could understand. But, she was barren. For good reason, if you ask me," Bluebeard stopped speaking when he saw the look on Kilian's face, "Right," he said uncomfortably. "That isn't really what I meant, son. It's just that, Kaldeena doesn't have a mothering bone in her body. She'd kill you in an instant if she thought it would benefit her."

Kilian stared into the distance. This wasn't what he had signed up for. He wanted an adventure. He had wanted to do something great with his life—to be a hero. *Maybe not all those who venture out are meant to be heroes*, he thought morosely. *Maybe I'm not supposed to save the world*. The thought made Kilian feel empty. He looked about the cabin that he had been calling home for over a month. The sharp image of his sister lying on her back with her cold, dead eyes staring up at him flashed through his mind.

He let out a small gasp. Shaking his head, Kilian lay back into the hammock, letting the natural sway of the ship lull him gently.

"Son, you have to believe me when I say that your father thought he was doing the right thing."

"Yeah," Kilian muttered.

"Believe it or not, but your father got out from under Kaldeena's spell. He was the first. We didn't believe it when he left, or when he took you with him. But, as we got to know your mother better, the more we realized that she was like rot spreading through our lives. She spoiled everything. And now she is trying to do the same to you."

Kilian slammed his hands against the wall. "Why should I believe you?" he shouted. "You've been lying to me this whole time, Bluebeard. And now—" he trailed off. "And now I've murdered all those people. And Adrienne's dead. And now you're telling me that it's all my fault—or rather my father's fault."

His voice shook in spite of himself. He wished he hadn't been so gracious with his strength. Bluebeard had taken so much of it, and now Kilian felt as if he wouldn't even be able to get up from the hammock. It was nice, after all.

"Your father was the best man I knew," Bluebeard said. He ground his fist into the palm of his other hand. "Kilian, I'm try'n to do what's best for you. Your father would have wanted this for you."

"Bah," Kilian sniffed. "If he really wanted this life for me then he wouldn't have hidden me away all these years, now would he have?"

The silence that followed clung to the air like a spider clings to its prey. Kilian's head ached from the visions that plagued him and the nearly unbearable fatigue. He cradled his head gently in his hands as he let the silence fill the space between him and Bluebeard. Rolling over, he turned his back on the older man.

"Just go away, Bluebeard. I don't want to talk anymore." Bluebeard did not say anything as he left the room. The only reason Kilian knew he had gone was the nearly inaudible click of the lock fastening into place as his cabin door closed.

I don't know when. I don't know how. But I know that I will get out of here when the time is right, he vowed to himself. *This is not what my father wanted for me. And I am no hero.*

***

The ship's deck was the same dark wood it had been before the battle. Not a speck of blood could be seen anywhere. The places where Bluebeard's fireballs had struck the deck had been rebuilt as if nothing had happened at all. Kilian strode across the deck, his face lifted to the sky. They had arrived.

It had been one week since Kaldeena's attack, but to Kilian, it still felt like it was yesterday. The soldiers' bodies— the ones Kilian had murdered—had been shoved overboard during the night. Not a single one had remained on deck by the time Kilian came up. For that, he had been grateful. His dreams of the slaughter were enough for him. He didn't need to see the evidence as well. The same morning—after Bluebeard had taken an infusion from Kilian—they had wrapped Adrienne in a sheet of finely woven cloth and pushed his body out to sea. In many ways, Kilian still felt numb. He wasn't sure how he was supposed to feel or how he was expected to express those feeling when he finally did let himself feel anything at all.

In the distance, mist swam around tall pillars of stone. Kilian remembered what Adrienne and Alex had taught him about the pillars. They were carved to depict the original eight. Squinting his eyes, Kilian tried to make out their shapes, but the ship was still too far away and the mist still too thick to see. In any case, they had reached the Forgotten Isles, and it was time for Kilian to face his first test of valor. Still, Kilian did not feel anything: not fear, not anxiety, not excitement. He simply felt numb.

"You look so pensive today, Kilian," Tavia said as she walked up to stand beside him. Light, but she was beautiful. In the days following the attack, Tavia had been the only one who had continued to train Kilian. Alex, understandably, had been avoiding him—and everyone else it seemed. Narcon had simply said that he needed time to rest his old bones, but Kilian believed he knew better. Something had happened to him the night of the attack. He'd been like a wild animal out for the kill. And none had survived. He had seen the fear in Narcon's eyes when he'd looked at him. And Kilian had known.

I am the monster in the night.

Tavia laid a tentative hand on Kilian's shoulder, drawing his attention away from his thoughts. Her chocolate hair shown in the sunlight filtering through the clouds above in an array of gold and copper. Still, her eyes drew him in with their storms. He leaned in closer.

She turned her head to stare out across the sea.

"Do you feel ready to face this first challenge, Kilian?" her voice was soft.

"I'm ready for anything," he responded, thought his heart hammered in his chest and he felt the tendrils of doubt swirling in his mind.

She drew her lips into a half-smile and raised one eyebrow at him. "If you say so, Kilian."

He leaned in a little closer. He could feel the heat emanating from her skin and smell her spicy scent.

"This first challenge is more a battle of will than of mind, Kilian."

He nodded at her words in an attempt to play at confidence.

"I have seen how Adrienne's death has affected you," she paused before turning to face him, "how the battle itself has thrown you."

The storm raging in her eyes calmed as she peered up at him. Although Kilian had wanted to ask for his ax back, he had refrained from doing so, and Tavia had avoided discussing his ax—and what it had done to him—until now, it seemed.

"Do you know where the ax came from, Kilian?"

He shook his head. Bluebeard had told him that the ax had been a gift from the Creators. It dawned on him that this ax could have the power that Kaldeena's dagger had. *Does that mean that when I killed those men that I separated them from their souls?* He almost let the question spill from his lips but found that he couldn't find it within himself to utter the words.

"It's the Labrys Ax," Kilian said simply. "That's all Bluebeard told me about it."

Tavia tsked loudly as she dug her nails into the railing of the ship. "He should not have given this weapon to you so soon."

Kilian was surprised at the anger in her voice. He glanced at her and saw that the storm had once again fired up within her eyes.

"You are not ready," she barked roughly. "And your father is to blame." She stuck out her bottom lip as she spoke in the cutest, most innocent way that Kilian had ever seen. Her lips seemed to glisten in the sunlight. Before Kilian could stop himself or before Tavia could turn away, Kilian bent down and quickly kissed Tavia right on the lips.

They're so soft, he thought as he wrapped his arms around her body, pulling her tightly against him. He moaned softly.

She slapped him.

A searing pain shot through Kilian's cheek. *Not again,* he thought as he rubbed his fingers across his already swelling skin.

She shook her head at him as she took a step away from him.

"This cannot be, Kilian Clearwater," her voice quaked as she spoke, "There is too much at stake for you to be distracted by… by…" she trailed off as he took a step and closed the gap between them.

"If I am to face these challenges, and put myself in danger in the process, I want to have experienced everything that life has to offer."

Before she could move away from him, he bent down and kissed her again. He trailed his fingers down her back until they rested at the hollow where her spine met her hips. It was like lightning was passing between them. Kilian felt exhilarated in a way he hadn't felt since his father had died. He pulled her closer to his body and wrapped her hair around his fingers.

"Stop," she whispered faintly when he pulled way for air. "Please stop, Kilian."

He pulled back, a stricken look on his face. *Did I read her wrong?* He thought. *Does she not want me the way I want her?* Kilian couldn't believe that it was true. She had clung to him during that kiss. He knew it.

"Why?" he finally spat. His tone was harsher than he intended.

Tavia scoffed at him before disappearing below deck. Kilian watched her go. *Are all women like this?* He had only ever known his mother and sister well enough to form an opinion about them. He certainly hoped this wasn't common. Unsettled, Kilian stared out across the sea, towards the now closer stone pillars. He could just make out the larger shapes carved into their sides. His first challenge had come.

As the sun began to set, Kilian went below deck. Alex passed him in the narrow corridor that led to Kilian's cabin. Knowing that they wouldn't be able to talk much once they reached the isles, Kilian grasped Alex's arm in the spur of the moment decision.

"Alex," he began.

"Let me go, Kilian." Alex's voice was deep, harsh, and entirely different from the one that Kilian had become so used to.

Startled, Kilian released his grip on Alex's arm. Alex immediately began walking away from Kilian.

"I'm sorry," Kilian called after him in a small voice.

It must have been loud enough for Alex to hear because Kilian saw the other man's shoulders tense and his whole posture became more upright. He turned around and faced Kilian with the hardest expression on his face that Kilian had ever seen from anyone. All the mirth, curiosity, and easiness had fled from Alex since Adrienne's death. It's my fault, Kilian reminded himself. It's all my fault.

"You're sorry?" Alex spat. "Let me explain something to you, Kilian. Your being sorry doesn't bring Adrienne back. Your being sorry doesn't change the fact that Adrienne's soul was cut away from him. It doesn't change the fact that I am honor bound to Bluebeard to complete this mission even though I'm not convinced that you're the great hero we thought you would be. Who knows, maybe the prophecies were wrong. Or maybe we interpreted them wrong. It doesn't matter, and I don't care."

Even from the distance between them, Kilian could hear how heavily Alex was breathing. Shadows danced on Alex's face from the flickering candle he held in his hand. To Kilian, it seemed as the if the shadows and the light were dueling, trying to determine who would win the heart of Alex.

"I'm sorry," Kilian said again more firmly. "I didn't know any of this would happen."

At this, Alex barked out a loud laugh. It too was harsh and carried notes of anger within it.

"When you fail in this challenge tomorrow, Kilian, I will be the first to help Bluebeard dispose of you. That's what he does to those he no longer needs."

A chill passed through Kilian. *You're not safe here.* The words reverberated through his mind. He opened his mouth to speak, to say something back to Alex, but the man had already climbed the ladder. He was gone.

Kilian stood in the corridor for several moments. He felt paralyzed. He didn't know how long he stood like that. None of the others passed through the passageway the entire time Kilian stood there. He thought about everything he'd been through, everything he'd seen. *And this is only the beginning*, he told himself.

Kilian sucked in a deep breath and released it slowly. He knew what he wanted to achieve. He knew that he wanted to become one of the heroes that would be talked about for ages. If he was to believe Bluebeard, his family line already had a history of pleasing the Creators. There was no reason that he should fail.

I'm ready for this.

Steeling himself, Kilian finished walking down the corridor and into his room. There, in his hammock, lay the Labrys Ax. *I really do need to come up with a name for it*, he thought. The silver metal of its blade gleamed in the light pouring in from the corridor. He smiled broadly as he walked toward it and gripped its hilt. As he lifted the ax, he knew that this weapon had always been meant for him. He had been planned for since the beginning. The Creators had planned for him. And, he vowed to himself, he would not fail them.

Chapter Ten

The channels between the pillars became too narrow for their ship to safely pass through. Instead, Bluebeard had ushered them into the smallest rowboat Kilian had ever seen. It was little more than a raft. The edges curled up on the sides to create a shallow barrier between the water and the base of the vessel. Narcon and Alex pulled large oars through the water. Water splashed into the ship as they rowed. They occasionally grunted as the sun beat down upon them and the swift current of the channel pushed them in errant directions. Giant fish swam beneath the murky surface of the water. Kilian could just make out their massive, black shapes. He hoped they were the friendly kind and not the ones he'd read about that had a thirst for blood and meat.

Mist floated around the small boat, making it difficult to see more than a hand's length in front of them. Through the mists, Kilian could see shadows rising up from the water, their forms not moving at all. Although Kilian knew that they were the giant stone pillars, he found it difficult not to let his mind wander to the stories he'd read as a child about the giants who lived in seclusion. His father had approved of these stories and had always pushed Kilian to imagine what it would be like to be hated by everyone. These giants had built the mountains and dug the lake. They had forged metal from their farts.

Yes, Kilian remembered, *their farts*. He had always laughed at that part of the story. Now, he was too scared to smile, even with as pleasant a memory as the stories he'd read with his father. He tried to remember what his father had said about the giants that lived beyond the Forgotten Isles. Well, not exactly beyond. No one truly knew what lay beyond the isles. Even the maps Adrienne and Alex had made him memorize only depicted the vaguest drawings of what explorers believed were beyond the isles. Even the few who returned to Mitier following their travels beyond the isles could little describe what they had seen. Most returned mad.

Kilian shivered, despite the warmth of the air. Although mist covered the lands and the sky was gray and full of shadow, the air was warm and smelled like a lush forest. It seemed odd to Kilian. But then, they couldn't see onto the isles. Perhaps the amount of water that flowed through them allowed for lusher, fuller plants to grow.

The sound of rocks splashing into the water startled Kilian, and he jumped slightly in the boat. It swayed dangerously. Bluebeard glared at him from the front of the boat, his blue eyes a torrent.

"Remain calm, Kilian," the older man whispered.

The sound of more rocks splashing into the water followed. Kilian frantically looked around them, but he could see nothing. Everything was clouded by the mists. More pillars lined the channel they were rowing on ahead of them. Although these appeared to be thicker, shorter stones, they still towered over the boat. Kilian knew they would have towered over him, even if he had been standing next to one of them. He gulped as he saw the leg of one of the pillars move.

Bluebeard must have seen it too, Kilian realized, as he motioned for Narcon and Alex to stop rowing. He motioned ahead of them, his lips pressed into a thin line. He didn't speak, so neither did Kilian, although it was killing him to not ask the series of questions that burned within him.

Kilian held his breath as he heard splashing right in front of the boat. Water sprayed upon the crew. Kilian opened his mouth to yell, but Tavia wrapped her hand around his mouth. The pressure of her fingers on his skin was so firm that Kilian knew he would have bruises in the shape of her hand. He didn't care. The current that passed between them—he knew she had to feel it too. The boat rocked a few more times violently. It felt as if something heavy were swimming beneath it, kicking it as it went along. Kilian quivered despite himself and clutched his ax tighter in his hand.

Unlike the night of Kaldeena's attack, it felt cold in his grasp. The knotted wood of the handle fit snuggly within his hand. It almost felt as if it had been shaped specifically for him, the grip felt so natural. It reverberated gently in his hand each time he imagined the foes he would have to face, but the blinding red vision and the overwhelming sense of power did not overtake him. In some ways, he was sorry for this. Whatever had passed between him and this ax had made him powerful, indestructible. He would need that again if he were to accomplish this first task.

I don't even know for certain what I'm supposed to do, Kilian thought as Narcon and Alex began rowing again. They moved slowly, carefully through the channel. Kilian had to strain himself to hear the sound of their paddles striking the water's surface. Peering behind him, Kilian saw that they were cradling their paddles in their hands the way a lover does their other half. Still, their arms wove the paddles in and out of the water. It dawned on him that not once during all of his training sessions of the twins, Narcon, Bluebeard, or even Tavia had any of them told him what he was supposed to do during this first mission. All he knew was that the key to the Labrys Sword rested in the hands of the forgotten.

Does that mean that I'll have to find the key somewhere among these carved pillars? Kilian looked up at one as they passed by it. This one depicted a woman with long, curly hair. Her face was serene, and she held a stack of scrolls to her chest. The carvings on her legs would provide many footholds if Kilian were expected to climb up one of the pillars. That wouldn't be so bad, he decided.

"We'll get out here," Bluebeard whispered to Kilian as he held up his fist and the others stopped rowing. The ground sloshed beneath his feet as Kilian stepped out of the boat. Mud seeped up the sides of his boots, covering them.

"We have to keep moving," Bluebeard said. He held up a tiny metal disc with strange silver markings covering it. The writing glowed faintly in the dim sky. He pointed the disc in different directions before eventually motioning for the others to follow him.

Kilian jumped as a rock splashed into the water right behind him. He spun around, hoping to see if there were more to follow, but all he saw was the boat and one of the pillars. He couldn't even see the other side of the channel; the mist was too dense. Sweat beaded on his brow as he followed Bluebeard past a bend in the canal. Here, the small rivers abruptly stopped flowing. Before them stood eight pillars. They were taller than the ones they'd passed coming in. Their massive heads rose into the sky, above the line of mist so that they were mere blurred lines of what Kilian knew they depicted. It was eerie, staring up at those pillars that looked like decapitated giants to Kilian.

The pillars were different shapes and sizes. Kilian had never thought of the Creators as being human before, but none of the pillars seemed to suggest otherwise. They were, all eight of them, clothed in richly detailed robes. Each Creator held a different item in their hands: a long bow, a set of scrolls, a sword, a pitcher of what Kilian assumed to be the Light's Water, a massive ax similar to the one Kilian wore tucked into his belt, a flute, a hammer, and a key.

A key! Kilian did a double take of the massive, stone key the last statue held. It had a simple bow and a long, narrow blade with a few protruding grooves. Ignoring Bluebeard's signal to remain where he was, Kilian walked up to the pillar holding the key. He was surprised that it depicted one of the female Creators. Through the mists, he could see her long, curly hair spilling down her back. The ends of it brushed the small of her back. Her robes were carved with intricate patterns of stars and moons. A giant sun had been etched onto the center of her chest. He still couldn't see her face through the mists, but he could imagine that, whoever the sculptors had been, they had given her beauty.

The sound of crunching rocks beneath feet drew Kilian's attention to something moving behind the massive stone. It moved through the mists with a strange gate. It was almost as if the person were slumped to one side and dragging one foot behind them. Despite himself, Kilian took a step back from the pillar. The thing in the mists kept coming.

"Bluebeard?" Kilian asked as he took another step backward. His voice shook enough that he was sure it would alarm the older man.

"What is it now, Kilian?" Bluebeard said in an exasperated voice. Kilian stole a quick glance at the older man and realized that he too was facing the pillars and squinting his eyes into the mist. In vague detail, Kilian saw other shapes moving along behind the pillars. He gasped as the first of the shapes moved beyond the set of pillars.

Strands of skin hung from its face in gray blobs. Pus seeped from blisters and tiny holes covering their skin. Even from the distance, Kilian could smell the pungent odor of rot. Their clothing was tattered and dirty. His heart hammering in his chest, Kilian tried to think of what he should do. He didn't want to get close enough to these—he didn't even know what to call them—things to chop them down with his ax.

"Steady now," Bluebeard said as he drew his massive sword from its scabbard. His skin began to glow a brilliant blue in the mists. The fog pulled away from Bluebeard with a hissing sound, allowing Kilian to see the creatures moving towards them more clearly. Blood sputtered from their mouth in thick, black goo and each of them had at least one wound somewhere on their bodies. From these, Kilian could see the same black goo seeping from what appeared to be bite marks.

"Bluebeard?" Kilian asked again as he took several quick steps back. He was now standing in line with the others. They formed a circle, their backs to each other. "I thought you said this was going to be easy," Kilian whispered.

"It is," Bluebeard murmured. Kilian felt the older man move beside him and realized that Bluebeard had rushed at the creature closest to him.

His blade swiped through the creature's arm, spraying the thick pus all over the ground. A shield of translucent light clung to Bluebeard's body, repelling the black pus. Bluebeard swung through another one of the creatures that was standing right beside him; his sword lopped off its right arm. Despite the massive wound, the creature kept walking. It raised its nose into the air and sniffed loudly before moving forward. Bluebeard came from behind and slammed his sword into the creature's chest. Once again black pus seeped from the creature's wound. Kilian grimaced as he caught a whiff of its scent. He had never before smelled something so grotesque. It smelled the way Kilian imagined a heap of dung and old meat would smell after it had been allowed to sit in the hot sun for several days.

Bluebeard cursed as he withdrew his sword and the black pus ran down the hilt of his sword. The shield of light he had created for himself seemed to falter as the pus molded itself to his hand. He glowed brighter as he used his magic to swipe it away. Unfortunately, this left a hole in his magical shield. Part of his hand was completely uncovered and, as Kilian watched, he failed to rebuild the magical shield at all. The creature let out a throaty, gurgling laugh. Or, at least Kilian thought it was a laugh before it continued forward.

"Don't let the pus touch you," Bluebeard croaked.

Fear swept through Kilian like a raging storm. Thoughts zipped through his mind in rapid succession. He barely registered one before a new one came to mind. In each of them, he saw his friends destroyed by these creatures. His ax hummed at his side. Kilian still hadn't drawn it from his belt. Maybe we can just escape, he thought as he turned to see what the others were doing. At least twelve of the pus-ridden creatures were advancing on them from behind. Kilian groaned as he realized that they were surrounded. Remembering the battle tactics that Alex and Adrienne had taught him, Kilian strained to see beyond the initial set of creatures advancing on them. To his dismay, he saw that a whole hoard of them huddled in the mists. They weren't moving, but Kilian knew what they were.

Blue light sprang from Bluebeard's fingertips, leaving a shield of light clinging to Kilian's body. Glancing around, Kilian realized that Bluebeard had done the same for the others. Kilian looked at Bluebeard and realized the strain the use of that much magic had put on him. The older man's shoulders sagged, and he moved sluggishly against the creatures. He'd hacked off arms, cut through legs, and stabbed them straight through. Nothing seemed to stop the creatures from their advance. Where their black pus struck Bluebeard's magical shield, holes sprang up, leaving him defenseless. Kilian didn't know what the pus would do to him if it touched his skin, but he didn't like the odds that it was something good.

Bluebeard continued trying new ways of attacking the creatures. Still, they advanced. They were so close now that Kilian could see the details of their faces. They had hollowed out eyes and skin that looked as if it had been shredded in places. The skin held a greenish-yellow tinge to it that reminded Kilian of a dead deer he had once found half-rotted in the forest. His stomach squirmed as he realized he needed to draw his ax and begin to fight.

His ax hummed even louder in his hand as Kilian gripped its hilt and breathed in deeply. His vision did not turn red the way he had expected, but he did feel more powerful with his weapon in his hand. He took a step towards the closest of the creatures.

Tavia screamed behind him, pulling his attention away from the creature as it leaned in towards him, pus dripping from its mouth. A glob of pus had eaten through her magical shield and attached itself to her skin. Where it touched her, a black rot spread. Tiny holes appeared on her skin. He looked into her eyes, and all he saw was terror.

No, he whispered to himself. *No!*

Somewhere, deep inside of him, rage burst free from its cage. Kilian charged straight at the creature that was still attacking Tavia, despite her now lethargic movements. He raised his ax high above his head and slammed it down into the creature's skull with a loud thump. The creature gurgled on its blood and pus before slipping from the ax's blade and sinking to the ground. Its mouth moved open and shut several times before finally stopping. It did not get up or grab at Kilian.

Kilian immediately turned to face Tavia. Her face was streaked with tears, and he saw a scared vulnerability in her eyes that disturbed him. He bent down to examine her wound, careful not to touch the black pus that resided there. It had completely eaten through her skin, revealing bone. Clenching his teeth, Kilian used what little magic he could summon from his training with Bluebeard and tried to wipe the pus away from her skin. She whimpered, but the pus didn't budge.

Kilian looked up to see that Bluebeard was now engaged with three of the creatures at once. His shield of light had so many holes eaten into it that Kilian was certain it was no longer providing any type of protection. Still, Bluebeard did not appear to have been harmed by the pus yet. Kilian glanced around him, searching for the others. Narcon had deftly cut one of the creature's arms and legs off. It fell to the ground in a puddle of its own pus. Still, it struggled to move towards Narcon. He was careful not to step in the thick liquid, but Kilian could tell that he was running out space to walk as he cut off the legs of more creatures.

Alex, on the other hand, had apparently observed Kilian incapacitate one of the creatures and was now focusing his attacks on the creatures' heads. He used a bow and arrows to pierce their eye sockets. Several of the creatures dropped to the ground in a gurgle of blood and pus. For the ones that Alex couldn't knock down this way, he used a long pole to wallop them in the heads. With a sickening crunch, Kilian watched as three more creatures were felled by Alex's staff.

Tavia's eyes glittered with tears as she sank to the ground. Kilian could see that the black pus was slowly seeping into her veins. They now ran with a dark tinge to them. She whimpered and clung to his hand. It pained Kilian to see her in this way. She reminded Kilian of his sister, May, every time she became sick. Sweat made Tavia's hair slick, and Kilian could already start to smell the twinges of rot emanating from her skin.

He pulled himself out of her grasp and whispered, "Wait here," as he dashed off towards Bluebeard. For as many holes in his shield as he had, Bluebeard had not been struck by the black pus. Kilian waved his ax above his head and cut through two of the creatures at once. There were more coming from all sides. *How many are there?* He thought, panicking slightly. They were coming in droves now. Muscle memory pulled him into the power stance Narcon had made him practice every morning. Kilian felt the heat rising from his ax, propelling him forward.

Not yet, he told himself. *Not until I let Bluebeard know.* He forced the power seeping from his ax back into his weapon. He didn't know how he was able to control it; he just knew that he needed to try to save her. Kilian drove his ax home into the skull of one of the creatures closest to Bluebeard. The thing exploded into a puddle of black pus and bones. The creature's matter slid down Kilian's magical shield, leaving holes in its wake. Cursing, Kilian barreled through the rest of the creatures so that he was directly in front of Bluebeard.

"You need to help her!" he shouted as he stopped one of the creatures from touching Bluebeard in a break on his face. Bluebeard's eyes had taken on a glowing hardness that Kilian had never seen before. He blinked at Kilian as if he didn't recognize him and swung his sword clean through the stomach of one of the creatures as it clawed at Kilian. At the same time, Kilian cracked his ax into the neck of a creature that was moving faster than the others. He cut its head off in the mighty swipe of his ax.

Grunting Kilian swung his ax up once more. His ax hummed with power as he pulled upwards. The ax met the underside of one of the creatures, cleaving him in half from groin to neck; the metal slid through the creature's left shoulder as Kilian pulled himself back into the basic stance Narcon had taught him.

"Bluebeard!" Kilian yelped as one of the creatures coughed and a glob of pus flew out of its mouth, straight at Kilian's head. He ducked, and the glob struck another of the creature's in the face. "Tavia needs you!"

He pressed his back to Bluebeard, guarding the man's back as more creatures filled the clearing they had made.

"You can't let her die!" his voice cracked as he spoke. He felt Bluebeard's back sag behind him.

"Where is she?" Bluebeard asked in a voice devoid of emotion.

"Over by Narcon and Alex," Kilian responded. He snuck a glance at the other two men. They seemed to be faring well, although the multiple holes in the protective layer of magic Bluebeard had placed upon them.

Kilian heard Bluebeard grunt loudly and felt the man's weight against his back disappear. He swung out with his ax as he turned around to ensure that Bluebeard was helping Tavia.

As he did so, he drove his ax through the legs of one of the creatures that had been approaching him from his left. The ax bit into the creature at the knees, sending it sprawling to the ground. Without pausing, Kilian heaved his ax up and then back down, straight through the creature's skull.

He glanced once more at where Bluebeard now knelt by Tavia. Kilian could see his lips moving and the spark of his magical blue light being applied to Tavia's arms and hands. Her skin had taken on a milky pallor that made her look like one of the undead creatures from the stories Kilian used to read about in his father's books.

One of the creatures grabbed Kilian by the arm and leaned in to bite him. Its teeth chattered loudly as it pulled Kilian close enough to it that he could see the bristle of a half-grown beard on the creature's face. Black pus oozed onto Kilian's arm where the creature grasped him. Another creature grabbed him from behind, pulling his shoulders back and revealing an opening to his neck. Kilian's hands became sweaty on his ax as he tried to squirm free from the creatures' grasps. Their sharp claws dug into his skin. Thankfully, the protective magic prevented them from breaking his skin, but Kilian could already see that the black pus was eating through his magic.

His ax hummed with its power. Despite his fear and reticence to use its magic once more, Kilian let the ax take control. He felt its warmth spread through his body. His skin glowed a golden color as he jerked himself free from the two creatures. Breathing heavily, Kilian cleaved one of the creature's skulls in two. Bone shards and dark pus splattered the ground as Kilian wrenched his ax free. His vision turned red as one of the creatures tugged at his leg. Kilian cut through the creature's neck in a single swing. Pus covered his arms and face as he continued chopping through body parts.

He didn't notice how many holes had spread across his protective shield as he pummeled several of the creatures in the head with the haft of his ax. Each one made a crunch as the skull shattered. His body felt strong, stronger even than when he had battled against the soldiers on Bluebeard's ship. Nothing could stop him if he just kept moving.

Somewhere in the recesses of Kilian's mind, he remembered Tavia. He remembered how her eyes swam like the Paralosa Ocean. He remembered how her lips stretched into that smile. He pulled back until he was only feet away from where Tavia lay on the ground. Bluebeard cradled her in his arms like a small child.

Narcon and Alex joined Kilian, forming a protective circle around Bluebeard and Tavia. Their shields had nearly disintegrated, but still, they fought on. Kilian nodded to them in appreciation but did not wait to see if they acknowledged him in return. The hordes of creatures rushing in from the mists had dwindled. Countless bodies, covered in their own gore lay in mounds around them. Everywhere they stepped, black pus puddled on the ground.

A loud horn sounded in the distance. Kilian stilled as the creatures looked about in surprise and stopped attacking. Kilian's blood continued to boil, and his vision remained red. All around him, the creatures backed away, their pus-ridden bodies disappearing into the mists. Confused, Kilian looked over to where Narcon and Alex stood. They slumped to the ground, their bodies completely worn out by the attack. Kilian's heart beat too quickly in his chest for him to do the same.

The loud horn sounded again. It carried the notes of mourning Kilian was used to at funerals. Nervous, Kilian stepped closer to Bluebeard.

"What's happening?" he asked the older man from the side of his mouth. He spoke as quietly as he could. The mists were so thick that he couldn't see much beyond the pillars. He knew something was out there, something that could control the beasts that had attacked them.

Bluebeard continued to minister to Tavia. His skin turned an ashy gray as he used the remnants of strength Kilian had provided him early that week. Wrinkles formed on his skin and dark spots crept along his brow.

When he finally spoke, it came out as a croak, "Kilian, I need your help."

"Now?" Kilian asked. His ax still vibrated in his hand, and his heart pounded loudly. "We're kind of in a bad spot here, Bluebeard."

"Clearly," Bluebeard responded, to Kilian's dismay. *Why is it that this man always seems to give the worst kind of answers when we're in an actual bind?* Kilian thought as he squinted into the distance. He thought he had seen something moving through the shadows.

Bluebeard grasped Kilian's hand, and Kilian immediately felt the man enter his mind. He barely had time to throw up a defensive wall around his thoughts and memories before Bluebeard began to suck away some of Kilian's energy.

"Not too much," Kilian gasped as he felt a sudden decrease in his strength. "I have to be able to fight," he whispered weakly. "Bluebeard?" he asked.

The older man did not respond as he continued to pull from Kilian's youth.

"Stop!" Kilian shouted. "You need to stop now!"

A burst of energy coursed through him and exploded outward. Kilian saw a flash of golden light burst from his body and expand out through the surrounding area. Bluebeard's grip on his hand was pushed away with the explosion. When the light dissipated, Kilian was left standing with his ax raised above his head as if ready to swing. Bluebeard huddled away from Kilian. His wrinkled and splotching skin had disappeared from the infusion, but his eyes spoke of fear.

The horn trumpeted again. This time it sounded like it was just beyond the perimeter of the eight pillars of the Creators.

Kilian winced as he saw Bluebeard immediately begin performing healing magic on Tavia. *I should have given him more*, Kilian thought. *He needs it to heal Tavia.* Kilian reached out as if to touch Bluebeard to begin the infusion again, but the sound of hooves on the stony ground drew Kilian's attention towards the pillars once more.

A man clothed entirely in white appeared from beyond the pillars. He rode upon a giant steed whose muscular body gracefully navigated the pus-covered ground. Even with the distance, Kilian could see that the man's robes were embroidered with silver thread. The material gleamed with the brilliance of the sister moons. His white hair flowed over his shoulders. Tiny gemstones had been woven into his hair. They glowed through the darkening sky. *How late is it?* Kilian thought as he tried to control his breathing. Despite the power pouring into him from his ax, Kilian felt weak. Whatever he had done to push Bluebeard away had also used up a portion of Kilian's strength in the process.

"Kilian Clearwater," the man said in a clear, firm voice that did not match his old figure. "So you have come at last."

Chapter Eleven

Kilian stared at the man in white. His hands felt clammy and he knew his face must be registering some of the shock he felt. *Does everyone know who I am?* Thoughts tumbled through his mind as the power that had so freely flowed from his ax began to wane. His knees felt weak, and he noticed for the first time just how many holes had formed on his protective shield. It glowed only faintly now. Kilian could only assume that the golden light that had emanated from his ax—his body—had somehow also protected him from the black pus.

He shot a sideways glance at where Bluebeard still cradled Tavia in his arms. Her breathing came out in ragged, shallow breaths. Kilian looked back at where the man in white continued to sit on horseback. He sat so nonchalantly that Kilian could almost believe that he had been there all along, that he was merely a stone statue. He was not, however, and Kilian knew that the longer he stood in silence, the more difficult it would be to figure out exactly what was happening.

He opened his mouth to speak, but, as he did so, Kilian noticed a row of men and women also on horseback create a line behind the man in white. They all wore pale green robes covered in silver embroidery in intricate patterns. Kilian gulped. His body ached, and he had a roaring headache. He wasn't as tired as he had been the first time his ax had stopped feeding him power, but he still felt exhausted.

The line of people on horseback stood resolutely before them. Breathing in deeply, Kilian forced himself to take a step forward.

"I am Kilian Clearwater," he stated as clearly as he could.

"We know who you are," the man in white responded. "The question is, who will you become?" he smiled broadly as he spoke. He had a broad, toothy smile that Kilian thought looked ridiculous on his slender face. His long, white hair curled at the ends, giving him a distinctly relaxed look despite his auspicious robes.

Remembering why he had traveled so far to make it to the Forgotten Isles, Kilian took another step towards the man in white. "I am here seeking my destiny."

"Ah," the man said with a knowing tone in his voice. "So we were correct." He looked down each row of people behind him. They all nodded to some unspoken question. He turned back to Kilian and continued, "We have been waiting for your arrival for far too long, young one. Far too long indeed."

Kilian wasn't sure how to respond to that. He was only fifteen, after all. Well, almost sixteen, but he didn't think that mattered too much now that he was away from his family. They had been the only ones to celebrate his birthday with him. The thought sent a dozen happy, now remorseful memories spiraling through him like a knife cutting into a piece of meat. *I can't think of that now,* Kilian thought. *I need to figure out who this person is and how I can leverage this encounter to find the key and get out of this place.*

Tavia moaned behind, making Kilian cringe. He looked back at her. Bluebeard had laid his hands upon her chest and was muttering an incantation. Although his hands glowed blue from his power, nothing seemed to change her condition. She moaned again, this time louder. Resolve settled upon Kilian the longer he looked at her face. He couldn't leave her like this. He didn't know exactly what the black pus did, but he somehow knew that he didn't want to find out.

With a grace Kilian had never seen before, the man withdrew from his saddle and began to walk towards Kilian. He was taller than Kilian had expected with long legs and arms. Wherever he stepped, the black pus disappeared and was left with green foliage in its place. The bodies disintegrated into nothing more than cinders that blew away in the mists. He carried nothing on his body save for a small flute tied around his waist by a long silver chain.

The man in white walked straight past Kilian and bent down to meet Tavia's gaze. Her brow was covered with sweat, and her eyes had taken on a glassy haze. Kilian stepped from foot to foot as he tried to calm his nerves.

"She was attacked by" Kilian paused as he tried to decide what to call the creatures that had attacked them. Finally landing on 'those things,' he continued, "those *things*, whatever they were."

The man raised one eyebrow as he stared at Tavia. He gave her a half-smile before turning to face Kilian.

"What would you give me if I could save her?" his voice came in a melodic tenor as he spoke. Kilian found himself compelled to give this man whatever he asked for.

"I would do anything to save her," he said with candor. The man in white smiled more broadly. "Would you really, Kilian Clearwater?"

The way he asked this last question gave Kilian pause. It made his skin crawl and his resolve waiver. He stole another glance at Tavia. Her once perfectly red lips had turned gray, and tiny cracks covered them. She writhed in pain as the pus continued to spread its poison throughout her body. Bluebeard continued to pour his strength into her, but Kilian could see that it wouldn't be enough. He couldn't let her die. He couldn't.

"I would," he finally said.

The man in white clapped his hands together and laughed robustly. "Excellent!" he exclaimed. "This is truly wonderful."

The man in white gently rolled up the sleeves of his robes and placed the palm of his right hand on the initial wound Tavia had sustained from the pus. Kilian watched as the man closed his eyes and began to chant beneath his breath. A bright white light flowed through his veins, making his skin glow. The wind picked up all around them as the man continued to chant. Kilian moved closer to where the man knelt by Tavia. *Please let this work*, he said to himself. *Please*. Kilian did not often pray to the Light, but at this moment he wanted nothing more than for her to be saved.

The glowing light passed from the man in white to Tavia. Her veins, once clouded by black and purple pus turned a brilliant white. They stayed like that for several moments as the man continued to chant over her body. He spoke so softly that Kilian couldn't hear what the man was saying. His lips moved rapidly, and Kilian could hear the echoes on the wind as it swept past him. The mists thickened the longer they stood, and Kilian found himself becoming uneasy. What if those creatures came back? He could tell by just looking at Narcon and Alex that they were too exhausted to fight. His own body sagged beneath his weight and he felt the undeniable urge to simply lay down and go to sleep. He couldn't, of course. He had come here for a purpose and that purpose, he vowed to himself, he would keep.

Abruptly the howling winds ceased, and the mists lightened as if releasing a heavy load. Overhead, Kilian could faintly make out the brightest stars through the mist above. He looked back to Tavia and the man in white. The gray pallor of her skin had all but disappeared, and the wound on her arm had healed. She blinked up at Kilian with clear, calm eyes and smiled.

"Thank you," she mouthed towards Kilian. He nodded, a smile fluttering on his lips. *Is it just me or is this the part when she's supposed to be eternally grateful. Could it be?* He bent down and took her hand. It was clammy and felt like he was holding a dead fish, but she didn't pull away from him the way she would have before. Kilian, feeling emboldened by this, leaned in and tucked a small strand of hair that had fallen out of place behind her ear. His fingers grazed her cheek as he did so and she leaned into his touch. He lingered there, with her head resting on his hand before he realized that everyone—literally everyone—in the area was staring at them.

Coughing, Kilian drew his hand back quickly and turned to face the man in white. He didn't know why, but he had the sudden urge to bow to the man. The man chuckled lightly as Kilian bent his knees and dipped his head forward. He had never been taught, not even by the twins, how to properly bow. The motion felt awkward to him, and he quickly lifted his body again.

"Thank you for saving her," Kilian said. "How did you know what to do?" Kilian remembered the strange trumpet of a horn before the man in white appeared, and the pus-ridden creatures disappeared. *There has to be some connection*, his mind kept telling him in a nagging way. The thought left him with the uncomfortable realization that the man in white could have just played out an elaborate trick to gain favor from him.

"You are most welcome, Kilian, son of Nathanial Clearwater. It has been many moons that I have waited to meet you."

Kilian peered into the man's eyes as he spoke. They were a bright tan that seemed to glow in the dim light. In them, Kilian could see an intelligence that almost came off as cunning. Kilian decided that he did not like what he found in them. He shuddered involuntarily and saw the man's eyes narrow as he continued to stare at Kilian.

Abruptly, the man said, "My name is Kha-ael-ido, of the Khael people. You will not remember them."

Kilian nodded. Then, feeling as if he were expected to do more, he bowed again. The man in white burst into a fit of laughter as Kilian stood once more.

"For the hero spoken of for ages, you certainly do not know the etiquette of meeting one of the Creators," the man said jovially.

Kilian's mouth gaped as he realized what Kha-ael-ido just proclaimed. *It couldn't be, could it?* his mind thought frantically. He glanced at the giant statues forming a line before him and then back at the man. For all Kilian knew this man was a con artist who waited for people like him to show up here. *But then, how had he known who I was? How had he banished the creatures? How had he saved Tavia?* Kilian blinked, trying to stall for time as his mind continued to work through this revelation.

"I can see that you have many questions, Kilian of Lunameed. Come," he said as he clapped his hands and his attendants—still on horseback—turned and began to ride beyond the pillars, "let me provide you refreshment and rest from your journey. We can discuss the boon you must grant me in the comfort of my home."

Kilian looked to Bluebeard for the proper response, but the elder only stared into the distance. Kilian couldn't tell if he were battle-shocked after the near death they had faced at the hands of the pus-ridden creatures or if there was something else happening. In reality, it didn't matter to Kilian. He needed Bluebeard to snap out of whatever was bothering him and be the captain.

Kha-ael-ido stared at him with those eerily tan eyes, a thin smile curled on his lips. "There is no need for you to be wary of me, Kilian Clearwater. As long as you are a guest, there is no need for fear."

"And if we do something to displease you?" Kilian asked before he could stop the words from spilling from his mouth. *Or if I overstay my welcome?* Kilian thought with more than a little twinge of fear.

The man in white's eyes flashed with a bright, almost frightening light, as he said, "Then we shall see."

Without waiting for Kilian to respond, Kha-ael-ido walked, with graceful, quick steps to his horse. To Kilian's dismay, Narcon, Alex, and Bluebeard all rose to follow the man. They shrugged as they passed him as if to say 'this is best we can do for now.' Only Tavia lingered behind. She grasped Kilian's hand as the others turned away from them and began to follow Kha-ael-ido's entourage beyond the pillars.

"Do you think we can trust him?" Kilian asked, weariness threatening to break down his resolve.

"He saved me," Tavia said simply. "Besides, if he is telling the truth, he may be the only person on these isles that can help you find the key."

She squeezed his hand as she spoke and Kilian felt her warmth spread up his arm and through his body. *She is glorious*, he found himself thinking as he looked down at her face. She smiled up at him, her perfectly luscious lips within inches of being kissed. He began to lean down.

Tavia turned to face in the direction in which Kha-ael-ido had led the rest of their crew. "Come," she said, tugging at his arm. "We have nothing to lose from following him, Kilian, and everything to gain."

Sighing, Kilian allowed himself to be led towards the rest of their group. Any lingering doubts he had about who Kha-ael-ido was and whether he could trust him were shoved to the side as Tavia continued to hold his hand. All Kilian could do was think of her and how grateful he was that she was finally showing him affection.

***

Several hours later, after Kilian had taken the first real bath he'd had since boarding Bluebeard's ship, Kilian sat in the window seat in his room. The view looked out over the lush gardens. Kilian had been surprised by the beauty of Kha-ael-ido's home after their journey through the mire and grime of the isles. One moment, Kilian had been sloshing through the mud.

The next, he had walked out into the most enchanted place he had ever been. The house shone like a beacon in the darkness. Kilian had no idea how Kha-ael-ido had made his home to be luminescent, but it was a marvel the likes of which Kilian had never seen before. The stone was carved with depictions of the greatest heroes of Mitierian lore. Kilian had trailed his fingers over the carvings as they walked past the outer buildings of the estate. Every visible wall had massive windows that opened out onto the grounds.

The grounds, much like the house, were marvelous. Unlike the rocky terrain of the isles, the estate was covered in colorful, lush plants that sent an array of smells wafting through the air. Kilian had heard bees buzzing as they deposited pollen from one flower to the next. Although Kilian knew many of the plants from growing up surrounded by farmland, there were many he had never seen or smelled before. He felt like he stumbled upon a living dream, one that reminded him of the best things from home.

Now, as Kilian sat in the window with a cup of hot cider clutched between his hands and looked out over the grounds, Kilian couldn't believe his good luck at having been saved by Kha-ael-ido. He was the kindest man he had ever met; he was sure. No sooner had they arrived at his estate than he had offered them all a warm bath and a chance to rest after their battle. Kilian tried to remember his exhaustion after having faced the pus-ridden creatures, but found it difficult to grasp. It didn't matter anyway. He was safe now.

The smell of roasted hog wafted through his chambers accompanied by the scent of baked apples and cinnamon. Kilian loved baked apples and cinnamon. They had been a rare treat at home. His mouth watered at the mere thought of enjoying the dessert. Kha-ael-ido had invited them to join him for dinner that evening so that he might explain his presence in the Forgotten Isles, and so that he could request his boon from Kilian.

Now that Kilian had seen how Kha-ael-ido ran his household, Kilian no longer feared the repercussions of his promise. The man had been nothing but kind to him, and Kilian had no doubt that he would use his boon as a betterment for the people who lived on his estate with him. Kilian snuggled deeper into the luscious robe he had found waiting for him once he got out of his bath. It was white, like everything else in Kha-ael-ido's estate, and it smelled faintly of jasmine. He breathed in deeply. *I could get used to this*, he thought as he leaned against the window frame and dangled one foot from the ledge.

A loud rapping on his bedroom door made Kilian jump. He rushed to the door, wrapping the robe tighter against his naked body. Feeling like a fool for not dressing after his bath, Kilian pulled his door open to reveal Tavia. She was more beautiful than he remembered, in the soft white glow of the house, dressed in a flowing white dress with purple flowers sewn onto its hem. No trace of her injury remained on her face. Kilian's heart began beating rapidly in his chest as the scent of her perfume caught him. She smelled like warm vanilla and strawberries on a hot summer day.

Realizing that he was staring awkwardly at her through the doorway, Kilian motioned for her to enter his room. She brushed his arm as she passed through the doorway. Kilian remained motionless for a heartbeat. Breathing in a shuddering breath, he finally forced himself to follow her into the room.

"Thank you, Kilian," she spoke in a smooth, melodic voice that melted Kilian's heart.

"For what," he squawked. He immediately blushed as he spoke and was thankful when Tavia either didn't notice his abrupt change in octave or chose not to comment.

"For saving me, of course, silly," she batted at him playfully.

"Oh, I didn't do anything," he said, waving her off, "it was mainly Bluebeard and Kha-ael-ido who saved you. You should thank them instead of me." He looked down at his hands as he spoke. He could feel the color rising in his cheeks; he just hoped she hadn't noticed.

She grasped his arm with her hand in a gentle yet firm embrace. "If you hadn't ensured that Bluebeard broke away from the fighting and if YOU hadn't made that promise to Kha-ael-ido, I don't think I would have survived the attack," her bottom lip trembled as she spoke.

All Kilian could think about was leaning down and kissing those too perfect lips. He closed his eyes and counted to three. When he opened them again, she was still there, holding his hand. In one sudden, graceful movement, Tavia stood on her tiptoes and kissed Kilian lightly on the cheek. Her lips were soft, and her scent reminded Kilian of warm night snuggled up with his siblings before the fire. He smiled at her as she withdrew. The touch of her lips lingered on his cheek.

"You must learn to be more..." she paused as she tapped her finger on her chin and looked up the ceiling. Her eyes were still the color of the ocean, yet they no longer swam in tumultuous waves as they did the first time Kilian had met her. Her brow crinkled as she continued to think. "Bah!" she finally exclaimed, "I cannot think of the word that best describes what you need to do and be, Kilian."

"Oh," Kilian let slip. He hung his head slightly, trying to decide which was better; believing that she could love him or knowing that she was beyond his grasp.

She cupped his cheek with her hand and stared into his eyes. Her expression was warm and inviting. "Oh Kilian, there are so many things yet for you to learn." She stroked his cheek with her thumb gently as she spoke. Her fingers were so smooth and gentle; it was as if the wind itself were caressing him. He leaned into her caress, closed his eyes, and released a silent sigh.

She immediately pulled her hand away. The coldness that followed was jolting. Kilian opened his eyes to see that her face was mere inches away from his. If he leaned forward, even a little, he knew that their noses would touch. He blinked, considering. Her eyes had taken on the storm again. They raged like so many of the storms they had passed through on their journey to the Forgotten Isles. He blinked again.

Her lips were on his before he opened his eyes again. The surprise of feeling her on him caused him to panic slightly. He didn't know where to put his hands or where to hold her. His leg shook uncontrollably, like a dog wagging its tail. Embarrassment filled him as he realized that she would probably be able to feel his leg shaking so much. He fidgeted. She pulled away.

Kilian stood breathlessly before her. He raked his hand through his hair as he tried to think of something to say. The longer they stood there in silence, the more difficult it was for him to form his thoughts into words. He opened his mouth, then shut it again. Tavia looked down at her feet, avoiding his eyes. Kilian felt crestfallen as thoughts coursed through his mind in rapid succession. *Did I do it wrong? Was it not good? I thought it was good.* Kilian couldn't stop the doubt from crowding out everything else.

Finally, Tavia said, "You should get dressed, Kilian. The dinner will be served soon." With that, she twirled in the most feminine way Kilian had ever seen her take on before.

He watched her leave his room. She did not look back at him. As she left, Kilian began to doubt whether she had kissed him at all. This uncertainty continued to plague him as he quickly dressed in the white linen trousers and shirt that had been left out for him. They felt just as luxurious as the towel had. The linen was so smooth and silky that Kilian almost didn't believe that it had been created from natural fibers. He glanced at himself in the tall mirror as he was leaving his room. His arm muscles bulged beneath the shirt. Kilian could see the clear definition of his stomach through the thin, tight shirt. His face had lost its extra fluff since he'd been training with Bluebeard and the others. The eyes that stared back at him were hard and calculating. They carried the grief of those who had fallen, but they also glimmered with hope.

"I can do this," Kilian said out loud, even though no one else was there. He blushed at the realization that he hadn't just thought the statement, but he believed it was true. He believed he could become the hero spoken of in the prophecies. And, apparently Kha-ael-ido believed in him as well. Nodding to himself, Kilian made his way down the large marble hallway to the banquet room. The attendants from earlier lined the sides of the corridor. They did not speak to Kilian as he passed. Kilian had the eerie sensation that they had been placed there specifically to ensure he would make it to the feast.

Even in the hallway, Kilian could smell the succulent scents of roasted meats. His mouth began to water the closer he got to the banquet hall until, finally, he entered the room and was confronted by the vast array of foods available. The first things he noticed were tables laden with desserts of every kind. Even before his father had passed, his family had never been able to afford the various delicacies available at this feast. A whole roasted hog was speared through its length and hanging above an open fire pit to one side of the room. This seemed out of place to Kilian, but it was only a fleeting thought as he noticed the different vegetables and fresh fruits lining the table. Greens, reds, purples, and yellows covered the table. It was as much a feast for his eyes and his nose as it was about to be for his mouth.

Narcon and Bluebeard were already seated at the table. Kha-ael-ido strode from the back of the room towards Kilian. He had changed robes. Although still white, they were embroidered with an emerald green that clearly showed the designs stitched into the cloth. As Kha-ael-ido got closer to where Kilian stood, Kilian could see that the robes now depicted the great heroes of old. The man seemed to glow a soft, white brilliance that, although not painful to look at, made Kilian uneasy. He dismissed the thought as Kha-ael-ido embraced him in a massive hug that did not match the decorum his graceful, tall frame suggested.

"Kilian, it is so wonderful that you have made it here at last!" he exclaimed as he clapped Kilian on the back. "We have been waiting for someone like you for so terribly long."

"You have?" Kilian asked, confused.

"Why, yes!" Kha-ael-ido pulled Kilian over to where a small table laden with food stood. Several chairs were crowded around the table to provide a semi-private enclave in which people could talk. As they sat, Kha-ael-ido looked about the room with a conspiratorial expression upon his face. Finally, as if deciding that they were not in danger of being overheard, he leaned into Kilian and said, "You must know the prophecies about you and how exciting they are for the eight of us."

Kilian, who had been about to pop a ruby grape into his mouth, dropped the grape onto the floor at the same time his jaw dropped.

"I, uh, well—" he closed his mouth.

Kha-ael-ido burst into a fit of laughter at his stumbling. In between ear-splitting guffaws, he was able to say, "My dear, dear, sweet, innocent boy."

Kilian felt a wave of unease wash over him. *What have I gotten myself into?* he thought as Kha-ael-ido slapped his hands on the table and continued bellowing with mirth. The older man motioned for one of his attendants to come over to the table at which he and Kilian sat. The one who responded was a girl of maybe no more than ten years of age. She still wore her hair in braids down her back. Her face bore no expression upon it as she turned to face Kha-ael-ido and Kilian.

Bobbing slightly, she said, "M'lord."

"Ah, Natalie," Kha-ael-ido said with a sigh. "I see that you are still insisting on wearing your hair in those braids. Have you made a decision yet about when you'll be taking them out?"

Kilian looked between the master of the house and his servant. They eyed each other with a type of hard stubbornness that Kilian had not expected to see from any of the servants. His uneasiness dissipated as he saw the older man break out into a broad smile.

The girl laughed softly before saying, "As I've said before, m'Lord, I won't be taking these braids out until at least the age of thirty-two."

Thirty-two! Kilian thought in outright disbelief. He had never heard of any woman who waited until the age of thirty-two to court and have children.

"Bah!" the older man muttered in a jovial way. "Thirty-two is too young. You should at least wait until you're in your fifties." He winked at her.

Kilian stared at the pair of them, dumbfounded. This had not been what he had been expecting. Kilian sunk slightly into his seat, feeling as if he were the intruder now.

As if reading Kilian's mind, Kha-ael-ido turned to face him. "Natalie is one of my finest pupils," he said as he motioned for Natalie to take a seat. She did so without a word. Kilian looked at the girl a little more carefully. She had strawberry blonde hair with a smearing of freckles around her cheeks and nose. Her pale skin hinted at being sun-kissed, but didn't quite make it. She had bright green eyes that reflected an intelligence in them that Kilian found intriguing. She smiled up at him.

"It's a pleasure to meet you, Natalie," Kilian said, remembering the manners his ma had taught him. She bobbed her head low and then looked back up at him.

"Natalie, dear, can you please recite the second prophecy starting at the third stanza?" Kha-ael-ido asked in a mildly amused tone.

"The third stanza?" she asked, quickly looking up at the older man. "But what about—"

"The third verse, my dear. That's where we should begin," he said, cutting her off.

Kilian felt the prick of unease settle on his stomach again but waved it off as Natalie began to recite.

"A hero will come, who will accomplish great deeds. Born of the magic, pure as the Light. To unknown battles, he plunges. The hero will vanquish. The hero will save. The hero will one day proclaim. The Light has strengthened and purged the world. The Light has taken back what was once its own. Fearless in battle and in love. The hero will save us, below and above."

"That will be all, Natalie," Kha-ael-ido said suddenly. Natalie blinked at him. Kilian thought he saw her lips twitch as if she wanted to argue with him, but she just nodded her head and quickly scurried away.

"You are the hero, Kilian Clearwater, born of magic. Your mother and your father both were blessed by us, the Creators," a small smile crossed his face as he looked absentmindedly across the room. His eyes seemed to glaze over. "All this time, we have been waiting for you."

Another spike of anxiety passed through Kilian. "I'm sorry Kha-ael-ido, but I have to be honest with you. All that Natalie said seemed like nonsense to me. Besides, how do you know that I'm the one spoken of? There wasn't anything in what she said that would make me believe that I'm the one you've been waiting for."

His heart hammered in his chest as he spoke. He didn't want to offend Kha-ael-ido, especially after all the wonderful things he had done for Kilian and the rest of Bluebeard's crew. He just didn't like having the expectations of the whole world placed upon him when he didn't even know what he was supposed to be doing.

"As it is with all of the great ones," Kha-ael-ido began, "so must you follow the path to greatness that has been laid before you. Have no fear, Kilian. We will guide you to your rightful place."

"That still doesn't explain why you think I'm the one spoken of!" Kilian fumed. His head ached from the sudden anger he felt. It was as if his body were fighting against the negative emotions coursing through him.

"Kilian, Kilian," Kha-ael-ido said, as he placed a hand on Kilian's shoulder. A warmth passed through Kilian, and the older man seemed to glow more brightly for a moment. All the tension Kilian had been holding in his body melted away at Kha-ael-ido's touch. "There is no reason for you to be feeling this way," he continued. "I am only here to set you on the right path."

"The right path," Kilian repeated. His mind felt dull, sluggish even. "I am on the right path," he said.

"Yes!" Kha-ael-ido proclaimed loudly. "Yes, you most certainly are on the correct path, Kilian Clearwater." He left his hand on Kilian's shoulder.

Kha-ael-ido's hand was warm and firm, like an embrace from a close friend. Kilian still felt the tendrils of doubt sweeping through him, but they were small and hidden in the recesses of his mind. Kha-ael-ido leaned in close to Kilian. Kilian could smell the man's cologne. It smelled like sandalwood and musk. It was not an unpleasant smell as much as it was unexpected. Kilian started to lean away from the older man, but Kha-ael-ido slid the hand holding Kilian's shoulder around Kilian's neck and pulled him closer.

Their noses touched, and Kilian felt the jolt of lightning pass between them. Kha-ael-ido's voice turned cold and hard. "You owe me a boon, Kilian Clearwater, and I would have it done."

The man's breath was like ice on Kilian's face as he breathed out in a long sigh. Kilian looked into the man's eyes and saw that they had turned ruby red with black veins coursing through them. Just as quickly as Kilian had noticed their red color, they changed back to blue-almost-white. Kilian jolted away from the older man.

"Who are you?" he asked, his voice quivering. "Who are you really?"

"Why, my dear boy, I am exactly who I said I was. I am Kha-ael-ido, the seventh of the Creators."

"You can't be," Kilian nearly shouted. "The Creators are supposed to be good, full of the Light. They are meant to bring peace to the world. Not—" he paused, unable to come up with the words to describe what he wanted to say. *Not what? Destruction? Despair? Anger?* Kilian wanted to say so much more than this. "You just can't be," he finally finished.

"Oh, and you think you know what the Light has intended, Kilian Clearwater? Do you honestly believe that you understand anything about what our God means to accomplish?" There were notes of humor in Kha-ael-ido's voice that made Kilian cringe. The older man looked him up and down. "Of course not, my boy. You may be the hero spoken of in our prophecies, but you know nothing of the greater good your journey will bring to our world."

Kilian fumbled for his belt, reaching for his ax. It wasn't there. *Of course not!* Kilian remembered. *I left it in the bed chamber.*

"Tsk, tsk, Kilian. I am so disappointed in you," Kha-ael-ido said as Kilian looked about the room in search of another weapon. "Do you honestly believe that you can harm me?"

Kilian looked over to where Tavia, Bluebeard, Narcon, and Alex were sitting at a table. They did not look at him as he approached. Their eyes were fixated on the food before them.

Juice from one of the plump peaches on the table drizzled down Alex's chin from where he had just taken a bite. He did not wipe it away. It was as if his crew members were in a different time, unable to see or hear Kilian. He waved his hand in front of Tavia's face, just to be sure. She didn't even blink.

"What did you do to them?" Kilian asked, his voice rising with each word.

"Nothing that will harm them," Kha-ael-ido replied. "Believe it or not Kilian, but I am simply doing this to prove a point to you." He picked up a grape from a nearby table and plopped it into his mouth. "You must first believe that I am one of the Creators before you will be able to make good on my boon."

Kilian glanced back at his friends. They did not appear to be in any immediate danger. He looked back towards Kha-ael-ido. He held a toothpick between two fingers and was digging at a bit of dirt underneath his fingernails. Kilian coughed to cover up his disgust at the older man. Kha-ael-ido did not appear to notice.

"Do you promise that you will release my friends if I hear you out?"

"Of course," Kha-ael-ido replied calmly. "I have no use for them in my collection."

Kilian wondered what Kha-ael-ido meant by his collection, but was too afraid to ask. Instead, he said, "It's a deal then. Tell me what you want, release my friends, and we will try to achieve whatever it is that you want."

A smile curled across Kha-ael-ido's lips. "Yes," he whispered. He rocked back and forth on his heels as he regarded Kilian with a look that sent a shiver down Kilian's back. He felt like a horse at the market, being evaluated for sale.

"Once you have achieved greatness, all I ask is that you return to the Forgotten Isles and join me here."

Cold dread spread throughout Kilian's body. "What, exactly, do you mean by 'join me here,' Kha-ael-ido?"

"I mean that you will stay with me. Here," Kha-ael-ido clarified. "You see, these isles can become quite lonely and boring," his eyes flashed to the ruby red color they had been earlier, and his body glowed a brighter white. "You see, Kilian, I was chosen to protect these isles, and really all of our world, from what lies beyond our borders."

"The Shadow Knights," Kilian whispered beneath his breath.

"Yes," Kha-ael-ido said, "the Shadow Knights."

The words hung in the air between them like a dead weight just waiting to pull them into the void. Kilian shivered again, though he still wasn't sure exactly what the Shadow Knights were.

"But," Kilian began, "surely you can leave this place? If you're one of the Creators, surely the others invite you—"

"Bah!" Kha-ael-ido cut in. "The others have chosen to exile me. They tell me they don't agree with my methods of training the holders of the Light. Imbeciles," Kha-ael-ido spat the last word as if simply talking about the other Creators left a rotten taste in his mouth. "They should know better," he continued, "They were there when the whole world began. We all were," he continued muttering.

Kilian stared at the older man. Kha-ael-ido was now pacing about the room, his long cloak fluttering behind him. He talked to himself as he walked. Kilian thought about interrupting him but didn't want to intrude on the older man's thoughts.

"The Light charged us with gifting its magic onto its other creations. It gave us the power we needed. It's not my fault the power is so difficult to contain." His eyes gleamed as he spoke and his mouth seemed to froth.

"Uh, Kha-ael-ido," Kilian broke in, "I don't mean to be rude, but I still don't understand what you need me for." He stumbled over his words as he spoke and his cheeks flushed. The rest of the crew still sat in a frozen state. Kilian gulped as he waited for the older man to reply.

"Why I need you to return to me once you've achieved your goal?" he paused briefly to cough into a handkerchief before continuing, "I know that if you were to choose me above all others that the others would finally allow me to leave these isles."

He smiled broadly at Kilian, like a snake ready to attack its prey. Kilian unconsciously leaned away from him. Muddled thoughts swept through his mind as he tried to figure out what to do. He wanted to talk through it with Bluebeard or Tavia, or even Alex. He couldn't. Like a fly caught in a web, Kha-ael-ido had spun his web beautifully.

"Done," Kilian said simply. He flicked his eyes over to Tavia. *Will she follow me?* he thought for the briefest of moments before looking Kha-ael-ido straight in the eyes. "I promise to return to the isles once I've completed the tasks."

Kha-ael-ido clapped his hands and the world around them began to bustle with noise again as they roused from their frozen state. Kilian nodded at the man before rushing over to the members of the crew. He ate the decadent food, flirted with Tavia, and had the nagging sensation that there was something he was missing.

It wasn't until Kilian climbed in the plush feather bed Kha-ael-ido had prepared for him that he realized what he had missed earlier. The older man had spoken as if Kilian were some prize to be won by the Creators. Bluebeard had led him to believe that the Creators didn't know who he was and that he had to complete these tasks to gain their favor. If he were to believe Kha-ael-ido, the Creators had already blessed him and were now waiting to see what he would do with their gifts. They were waiting for him to choose one of their order to praise. These thoughts plagued him as he drifted off into a fitful sleep.

Chapter Twelve

Who knows what games our gods play on us. They are all-powerful. They are in and of everything. We cannot begin to fathom their powers or what inspires them to bless us. We are but children in their eyes and never will be more. In all my journeys, I have still yet to discover what makes them tick. Perhaps I will one day.

-From the personal journal of Balbin the Adventurer

Sunlight poured into Kilian's eyes, waking him to the hot, damp morning. His clothes clung to his body in wet splotches. Rolling over, Kilian heard the crack of rocks as his body fell onto them. *Where am I?* he thought, groggily. The last thing he remembered was being in Kha-ael-ido's mansion and falling asleep in the softest feather bed he had ever encountered. Mud seeped between his fingers as he felt around himself. Lifting his head, Kilian realized that he and the rest of Bluebeard's crew were back at the pillars of the Creators. Long shadows covered the rest of the crew, but Kilian lay closest to the water and directly in the sun. No mist covered the ground, and the heat from the sun closed in around him.

Looking up, Kilian realized that he could now see the faces of the Creators clearly etched into the stone pillars. He looked for one to be similar to Kha-ael-ido but found nothing in the eight faces that even came close to resembling the older man. Where is he, anyway, Kilian thought as he stood up and slowly walked towards the others. Narcon snored loudly, and his rumbling voice shook the stones around him. Kilian smirked as he woke the war master first.

As Kilian bent down to wake Tavia, he noticed that a note had been pinned to her blouse by a silver pin in the shape of a lute.

"My dearest boy, by now I am sure that you have surmised that you have been dismissed from my household. My creatures will not harm you this day, though I am certain that you have already figured out that I am the one who sent them to attack you. You can understand that I had to be sure that you were among the party disturbing my isles. The key that you seek is already within your grasp. Good luck, Kilian Clearwater.

-K

P.S. Do not forget our bargain. I'll be seeing you soon."

Kilian dropped the note to the ground. As it fluttered in the air, it turned into the black pus the creatures had emitted during their battle the day before. Kilian's stomach churned as the pus dropped to the ground and sizzled as it ate through the rock on which it had landed. Anger surged through him like a gust of wind but died quickly as Kilian remembered the last line. "The key that you seek is already within your grasp." He still held the silver pin. Clutching it in his palm, Kilian walked over to where Bluebeard slept. Without pausing, Kilian kicked Bluebeard in the abdomen, causing the man to sputter as he awoke.

"The devil with ya!" Bluebeard shouted as he scrambled to his feet. "What's wrong with ya, Kilian?" he asked as he rubbed his belly. He glowed a faint blue as he did so and Kilian knew that he was healing any bruises Kilian's kick had caused.

Kilian thrust the hand containing the silver lute pin in front of Bluebeard's face. "Do you know what this is?" Kilian asked, his voice cold.

Bluebeard blinked at the pin. His eyes were glazed from sleep dust and confusion, but Kilian didn't care. He repeated himself, "Do you know what this is?"

"It's a pin," Bluebeard muttered. "But I fail ta see why a simple pin warrants the kick you just laid upon me, Kilian." The captain glared, but Kilian maintained his ground.

"I learned a lot of things last night, Bluebeard," Kilian paused, hoping Bluebeard would jump in and explain himself. Kilian knew who he was, after all.

"Ah, is that right?" Bluebeard asked with a chuckle, "And what is it, exactly that you think you've learned, Kilian Clearwater?"

"That you're using me," Kilian huffed. "And that you're one of them," he said as he pointed up at the pillars. "Don't try to deny it!"

Bluebeard looked from Kilian's face to the pillars and back to Kilian's face. He narrowed his eyes at Kilian before bursting out in a fit of boisterous laughter. "You have got to be daft, son. To think that you actually—I mean actually—believed that I was one of the Creators." Bluebeard slapped his hands on his legs and continued laughing. Narcon, Alex, and Tavia walked over to see what Kilian and Bluebeard were discussing.

"Can you believe it, men—and Tavia—this here twerp believes that I am one of the Creators!" Bluebeard's voice was loud and full of laughter, yet his eyes remained cold and hard. Kilian gulped as he waited for what was coming next. It didn't take long. Bluebeard stopped laughing and stared Kilian straight in the eyes.

"Listen to me, boy, I am no Creator. Never have been, and never will be. The only reason I picked your sorry self to join us was because of your father," Bluebeard paused and then said, "and the prophecy, o'course."

Kilian opened his mouth to speak, but Bluebeard shot him the stormiest look Kilian had ever seen cross the older man's face. He promptly closed his mouth and gestured for Bluebeard to continue.

Bluebeard looked around the clearing where the pillars stood. "Now, it's no surprise that Kha-ael-ido tricked you into believing otherwise." Bluebeard rubbed his chin, thoughtfully. "He was my mentor, all those years ago."

"But… it seemed like you had never met him before!" Kilian exclaimed loudly.

"Ah, hush now, Kilian. I didn't know it was him t'start with. But now that we find ourselves here, I realize what I should have realized before. It's him," Bluebeard finished simply.

"Uh, Bluebeard, I don't think that really explains how you know," Kilian prodded.

"Bah!" Bluebeard grumbled. "It was my mentor's classic stunt. He would coax people into a trap, cajole them with gifts, and then rob 'em blind," Bluebeard smiled as if remembering something pleasant. "He was the best at what he did, always playing games with his guests. It was all illusion though. Every bit of it."

Kilian stared at Bluebeard, dumbfounded. "You find this funny!" he finally asked aghast.

"Course I do m'boy. It seems I can still be outsmarted by the best o'them."

Kilian clenched his jaw and stared at the older man, a fire brewing in his belly. "So he's not one of the Creator's then?"

"Of course not! Did you actually believe that, Kilian? How daft do you have to be? No, he is the same as me. Fact o'matter is, he's the one who taught me how to stay young. Seems like he's got quite a retinue to keep him young enough, though it was a surprise that he adopted the guise of a wise old man," Bluebeard chuckled to himself. "During my time with him, he went by the name of Paprike and had golden hair and a fat belly. The eyes are the same though."

Kilian's palms had turned sweaty, and his grip on the silver pin grew slick. He looked from the pin to Bluebeard and back again.

"But then," he trailed off as he desperately tried to figure out a way to make sense of everything. Tavia laid her hand on his shoulder, triggering a thought. "But then how come Tavia got so sick when the black pus touched her arm? How was it Kha-ael-ido or Paprike or whoever he was, was able to heal the wound?" His voice sounded more confident that Kilian felt.

"Oh, that wound was real," Bluebeard said. "I'm not quite sure how he managed it, but those creatures have been lurking around these parts for as long as the isles have existed. It's a wonder that he has been able to not only survive on the isles but to become the creatures' king."

The answer did not fully satisfy Kilian, but he let it go. For now, he thought as he placed the pin into the deepest recesses of his pocket.

"You brought us into the isles without warning us of the dangers," Kilian said. It was not a question. "Why should I trust you to tell me the truth about any of this. You've lied so many times before."

"Choose to believe what you will, Kilian. But I am on a mission to gain favor with the Creators. You're the one mentioned in a prophecy. Together we can both achieve our goals," Bluebeard roamed around the clearing, clearly searching for something, though Kilian wasn't sure what.

"Fine," Kilian muttered. "But I want to find that key and get out of here."

Bluebeard bent down and picked up something from the ground. He shielded whatever it was in his hands before quickly slipping it into his coat pocket.

"That's easy, now that the spooks are gone." Bluebeard turned around and pointed up to the top of one of the pillars. "The female Creator is wearing the key around her neck."

Kilian groaned. This is precisely what he thought would happen. He would have to figure out a way to climb to the top of that pillar, without falling or damaging the stone. Even in the morning dew, the sun beat down on him, making him sweat. *Well*, he thought to himself. *This should be fun.*

Indeed, it was not fun. Kilian spent the better part of the morning making it about a quarter of the way up the pillar just to have his fingers slip on the wet stone and go crashing back to the bottom. Bluebeard, Narcon, and Alex had gone off into the distance to explore the isles. Only Tavia remained, which made it even worse for Kilian as he couldn't stop thinking about the kiss they had shared or the humiliation he felt every time he fell from the pillar.

"It's too high," he finally said to her after about his thirtieth attempt.

She smiled crookedly at him and said, "The Creators must really want to test your mettle."

He let out an exasperated cry and kicked the pillar. Pain shot up his foot and through his shin. *Great*, he thought, *now I'll have a bum leg as I try to climb this light forsaken monstrosity*. He thought about kicking the pillar again for good measure but decided against it when he realized that Tavia was watching him from the corner of her eye. He walked around to the other side of the pillar and gently kicked at the stone base.

"I was just trying to decide how sturdy this thing is," he said meekly.

She cocked an eyebrow at him but didn't respond. Kilian knew she probably had seen the whole ordeal and had seen right through him. He heaved a massive sigh and stared up at the face of the Creator depicted within the stone. From what he could tell, the Creator was young and beautiful. It was surprising in a way. He had always imagined the Creators as old and wise. His eyes trailed down her body, and Kilian began to notice the crevices etched into the stone where her robes formed creases and folds. He noticed how her knees were bent slightly.

The curves form a pattern, he realized as he continued to stare at the pillar. Yes, he could see it now. Wiping the sweat from his brow, Kilian dried his hands on his pants. He let out a deep breath and began to climb. Jagged shards of rock bit into his hands as he slid them into the narrow handholds. The many creases that had been carved into the pillar did not provide deep hand and foot holds. In fact, many of them were difficult for Kilian to fit even his tiptoes onto. Sweat bubbled on his forehead and began to run into his eyes causing them to sting.

Kilian momentarily thought about wiping the sweat away, but quickly dismissed the notion. He couldn't risk losing his position on the pillar. This was the furthest he had ever gotten in the climb. He allowed his body to fall back. His arm muscles strained as his fingers clung to the grooves carved into the stone. The sun blared in his eyes, but through the brightness, he could see that he was more than half way up the pillar. Smiling, Kilian carefully pulled himself flush with the stone.

Maneuvering over the arms will be the most difficult part, he thought as he began his ascent again. The Creator held one of her arms to her chest, causing an enormous bulge that Kilian would have to climb over. He glanced down to see if Tavia was still watching him.

It was a mistake. The ground seemed to shoot up at him and then fall away. His head felt lightheaded and his body, already covered in sweat, began to sweat even more. He released a small cry as he pulled himself closer to the pillar. His fingers began to cramp from the exertion. *I can't stop now; I can't stop now; I can't stop now.* He repeated this over and over in his mind. He was too close to reaching the top to let a little fear of falling stop him. Yet, as he pulled his left hand off of his hold, he had the instant sensation of falling.

He wasn't, of course, but that didn't stop his mind from telling the rest of his body that he was going to fall to his death. Closing his eyes, he reached blindly up and used his fingers to find a hold. The muscles of his arm and side began to tremble as he strained to pull himself up one-handed. Thankfully, after all the hours he had spent training with Bluebeard's crew, he had enough strength to dangle one-handed until he could find a second hold with his right hand. He hung from the side of the arm, gently swaying back and forth.

Using the momentum of his body in motion, Kilian swung his legs up and wrapped them around the bulging arm. For one long moment, he thought his legs would simply slide off from the slick stone, but he squeezed his legs tighter and found that he could straddle the stone and keep his place. His arms didn't stretch completely around the statue, but he wrapped them as far around as they could go. He breathed a sigh of relief. He was now hanging upside down from the arm. Only a few feet were separating him from the key. *I'm going to make it!* he thought excitedly as he rested for a moment. The air was cooler this high off the ground. The sun was still blinding and hot, but there were also cool breezes that gently caressed Kilian's hair as they swept by. None of the winds were forceful enough to fling him from his position. For that, Kilian thanked the Light.

Slowly, Kilian began to shimmy up the forearm until his legs met the hand. At this point, his butt was higher than his head, giving him the strange sensation of hanging from a tree the way he used to as a kid. He laughed lightly at the thought. His father would loop his legs around a tree branch and let himself fall until his knees caught him. His father had turned the activity into a game. He would coax Kilian into hanging upside down from the tree and then compete to see who could hang the longest. His father always won. Somehow, it never seemed to stop Kilian from wanting to play along. Even in those moments of panic, which Kilian thought that he would fall from the tree and crack his head open, he always knew that his father would be there to catch him. He had been safe.

Now, as he hung upside down from the arm, higher than he had ever hung before, Kilian repeated the words his father had always said to him, "Son, there's no reason to fear. I am right here with you."

Kilian released the breath he had been holding. Resolutely, almost defiantly, Kilian crunched his abdominal muscles and swung himself up to the top of the arm. From this high up, Kilian could see Bluebeard's ship bobbing in the distant waves. A cool breeze whipped at his hair. It wasn't robust enough to knock him off of his perch, but it startled him all the same. Birds chattered, causing white noise all around him. *So this is what it feels like to be on top of the world*. He smiled to himself.

The stone hand curled into a fist around an enormous key. Steadying himself, Kilian began to walk across the giant hand towards the key. A glimmer of gold caught his eye as he walked forward. It seemed so out of place to Kilian, considering the pillars were white and gray stone. Falling to his hands and knees, Kilian inched his way towards the golden glimmer. As Kilian crawled, he noticed that the hand was cracked and charred beneath his fingers. The further up he climbed, the deeper the cracks became.

Cursing under his breath, Kilian flung himself at the glimmer of gold. As the force of his weight pushed down on the arm, it began to crumble beneath him. The arm slowly began to fall away from the rest of the pillar. Loud thumping sounds followed as enormous chunks of rock plummeted to the ground.

Kilian had the momentary sensation of being suspended in the air; it was almost as if he were not falling at all. He stretched out his hand, trying to grasp the tiny gold key that came loose from the stonework. He swiped his hand at it, desperate not to lose it in the chaos of the fall. Cracks spread across the rest of the pillar and mountains of dust wafted through the air as the stone began to disintegrate before Kilian's eyes. A primal yell escaped his lips as he realized there was nothing for him to grasp to stop or slow his fall. What felt like hours lasted only a few seconds as he fell through the sky and came crashing down in the rubble beneath him.

***

Kilian's head throbbed and he could barely breathe when he finally woke up hours later. Coughing, a cloud of gooey, dark dust spilled from his mouth in pools of drool. *Well, that's attractive*, Kilian grimaced. Like before, his entire body ached. Gently, he sat up and realized that he was back in his cabin on the ship. *How did I get here?* he wondered. Then, as his memories reformed, *where is the key!*

Kilian lunged from the hammock in a violent, jerky motion. His muscles tensed as he stood and he heard the unmistakable crack of his ribs as they buckled under the weight of holding him erect. Gingerly, Kilian pressed one hand firmly down on his side as he tried to gauge the amount of damage he'd done. A searing pain shot through his entire body at the touch. He moaned loudly, his entire body shaking as the full weight of the pain settled upon him. Closing his eyes and gritting his teeth, Kilian attempted to climb back into the hammock. His head spun when he moved, and pain washed over him once more. Breathing in deeply, Kilian prepared himself for the pain before slowly sinking down. His abdominal muscles shuddered uncontrollably as he sank back into the hammock. By the time he had finally settled, Kilian had a fine sheen of sweat coating his forehead. His skin felt cold, and he shivered, even beneath his covers. Kilian coughed again as he gasped from the pain. Gritty drool trailed down his chin. Using the back of his hand, Kilian wiped it from his face before realizing that it was more of the same black dust he had coughed up earlier.

Fear prickled within him. *Is this how the pus-ridden creatures began to transform? Had they started out like normal people?* These thoughts and more clouded Kilian's mind as he tried to remember the last thing he could. He kept coming back to the sensation of falling. The glimmer of a golden key spinning in the air. The pain of crashing into sharp, hard rock. The darkness.

Kilian shuddered involuntarily.

He remembered the darkness. It had swarmed around him, suffocating him. Like a deep, dense pool, Kilian had tried to swim through the muck. He had tried to find the glimmer of the gold and the light of the sun. He had tried. And, he had drowned in the ever sinking pull of the darkness. It was as if icy manacles had been shackled to his wrists, dragging him further and further into the depths of the darkness. Terrible, disturbing images had flooded his mind. They were too dull and fuzzy for him to remember them now. But the absolute terror they had infused within him had remained. Kilian remembered cowering in the darkness, dark tears streaming from his eyes. His breath came out in misty ice. He had been completely alone.

No, not alone, he remembered. Adrienne had been there. *It had been Adrienne, hadn't it?* Kilian tried to force the memory, tried to seize control of it. The image was fuzzy. The lone figure walked towards Kilian and rested one soft hand upon his brow. Kilian leaned into the touch, more dark tears spilling from his eyes. It was then that light had begun filling Kilian's senses once more and the image of Adrienne had started to fade. Kilian had stretched out his arms towards

Adrienne, pleading for him to stay. In the brightness of the light, Kilian had seen Adrienne say something. *What did he say?* Kilian thought, trying to remember.

Pain seared through Kilian's abdomen, pulling him away from the memory. It was then that he realized that he had stood up once more from the hammock while he had been in his dreamlike trance. Frustration coursed through Kilian's veins as he tried to dull the pain. *I was so close*, he thought wearily. If only he had had a few more moments in the vision, Kilian knew he would know what Adrienne had been trying to tell him.

Sighing, Kilian lifted his shirt to inspect the damage done to his ribs. Clean bandages had been pulled tight around his waist. They tugged on his skin as he moved. Dried blood clung to his skin in scabby dark patches. They bled slowly whenever Kilian move his body too quickly. Kilian didn't know much about medicine or the art of tending wounds, but he knew he had injured himself more when he'd stood up. The loud cracking noise was evidence enough, even without the breathtaking pain that still throbbed within him. Kilian leaned against one of the cabin's walls for support as he tried to stop the room from spinning. Sliding his fingers over his head, Kilian felt the rough cloth of yet another bandage. His left cheek and the soft tissue around his eye were swollen and tender to the touch. Even without looking in the mirror, Kilian knew that he would see a man completely bedraggled.

He didn't care.

All he cared about was whether or not he had accomplished his mission or not.

A soft rap on the door drew his attention. Kilian hobbled over to the door and found Alex waiting outside. Although Alex preferred to keep his face clean-shaven, he sported a full-grown, grizzly beard that made Kilian uncomfortable. Alex's clothes were unkempt and wrinkled. His eyes had turned a dark, almost unnatural color. All the vibrancy that had been alight within Alex seemed to have disappeared.

Alex snarled a mean smile at Kilian and motioned for Kilian to follow him out of the cabin door. He did not speak to Kilian as they slowly moved down the ship's hallway. Kilian stumbled with each roll of the ship over the ocean waves. And, each time he slammed into the wooden planks of the hull, he had to bite back a whimper. *I killed his brother*, he reminded himself as he tried to think of something—anything—to get Alex to talk to him. The ship lurched and Kilian, unable to hold himself steady in his battered state, fell straight into Alex's back. They both went tumbling to the ground in an unruly heap.

Alex raised a fist up into the air and, for a single moment, Kilian thought that Alex would slam that fist straight into his face. He closed his eyes, waiting. In all honesty, Kilian wasn't sure how much more pain he could take. He could feel the bruises spreading like a flowering blossom across his face. He breathed in and then out again several times, still waiting for the blow that never came. Kilian cracked one eye—his only good eye at the moment—and stared up at where Alex still had his fist raised in a menacing way. He could see how Alex's shoulders shook with every breath he took. He could see the anger—the hatred—in Alex's eyes as he continued to look at him.

"You should be dead," Alex finally whispered in the deepest voice Kilian had ever heard from him.

"You're right," Kilian immediately responded, "I should be dead." He paused, considering. Alex still had his fist raised, but his eyes didn't look quite as angry as they had before. "But I'm not," he said, staring straight into Alex's eyes as he did so.

Alex let out a ferocious cry as he swung his fist down, narrowly missing Kilian's head. Kilian felt the wind sweep across his face, Alex's hand had been so close. Still, Kilian did not close his eyes or look away from the other man. Alex's shoulders sunk and Kilian heard the thundering cry of despair rise up from within Alex. Silently, Kilian released the breath he had forgotten he was holding and leaned into Alex. The other man did not pull away from him, though he did push a little against Kilian's chest.

"I'm so sorry, Alex," Kilian whispered. "I'm so sorry." They remained like that for several moments before Kilian finally pulled away from Alex and stared up the other man's face. Tears stained Alex's cheeks, and his eyes were streaked with violent red lines.

"I'm sorry," Kilian repeated one last time.

Alex shook his head and wiped the snot and tears from his face. His features became hard again as he wordlessly stood from the floorboards. He waited for Kilian to stand up but did not help him when Kilian struggled to find the strength to pull himself up from the ground. His head pounded as he fought to maintain consciousness. With a cry of pain, Kilian forced himself to a standing position and followed Alex to the top deck.

Bluebeard stood at the wheel, the wind whipping through his hair. He looked younger even than the first time Kilian had met him. His muscles bulged beneath his tight linen shirt and his eyes gleamed in the cool twilight. Alex strode up to Bluebeard and immediately handed him a scroll bound with a leather cord. Digging into his coat pocket, Alex also pulled out a small leather pouch and tossed it at Bluebeard's feet.

"What's this?" Bluebeard asked, his voice booming. His beard began to glow with the hum of Bluebeard's magic.

"I'm done," Alex said, his voice hard and thin as ice. Kilian shuddered. He wasn't sure if it was because of the cold or because of the hardness of Alex's voice. He looked between the two men. Bluebeard's expression had changed from that of the pleasant captain to one that was calculating and intense. Alex remained stoically firm in his face and body posture.

"I'm done," Alex repeated, his voice louder and more firm this time. "The next time we make port, I'm leaving. You can't stop me, Bluebeard. As you can see from the agreement that you drew up when I first signed on for this mission with—" Alex paused, his voice cracking slightly. He sucked in a breath before pushing it out in an almost violent hiss.

"Adrienne," Bluebeard whispered for Alex, his voice gentle.

Alex nodded before continuing, "You were the one who wrote this contract, Bluebeard. So you should know what my signature on it means."

Tavia and Narcon came to stand beside Kilian as Bluebeard stared down at Alex with a wild look in his eyes. He didn't say anything, but Kilian could tell that the captain had plenty that he wished to say. He doubted that any of it would be civil.

"I've paid my debt," Alex said, kicking the bag closer to Bluebeard. It clanked as he did so and Kilian knew that it would be full of coins.

Bluebeard did not even glance at the bag of money as he strode closer to Alex. His lips quivered as he leaned down to the other man's ear and whispered something only Alex could hear. Tavia gripped Kilian's arm as the three crewmen stood beside one another and felt the tension between Bluebeard and Alex rise.

A cold, whipping wind cut through them. Kilian winced and felt the twinge of pain as he tried to remain upright as the wind buffeted him. Tavia's grasp on his arm tightened, and Kilian felt the slow tremor of magic transfer from her into him. The pain in his ribs subsided slightly, but not enough to heal the damage that had been done when Kilian had fallen. He still ached, but the pain did not overwhelm him the way it had been before.

"It is your right to decide when the contract has ended," Bluebeard bellowed. His hair fluttered in the wind, and his eyes glowed a brilliant blue. For an instant, Kilian thought he saw the older man's features flicker to those of a giant beast. His head reared back, and a giant ball of flames shot from his mouth as if a smoldering fire raged within his belly. The image dissipated as quickly as it had materialized and Bluebeard's features returned to normal. Kilian stifled a cry of fear by biting his tongue until he felt the hot, coppery taste of his own blood.

"As I said before, Bluebeard, I'm done," Alex's voice was devoid of emotion as he stood before Bluebeard without wavering. His eyes turned more lifeless and dull the longer he remained before the captain.

Bluebeard slowly pulled the scroll's cord and unrolled the thick parchment. Bluebeard painstakingly drew his dagger and drug it across his palm. Blood bubbled from the cut and trailed down Bluebeard's wrist, staining the cuffs of his white tunic. He paused, as if expecting Alex to back down, but the younger man remained resolute. Bluebeard smeared the blood across his hand until even the tips of his fingers were coated in the bright liquid.

"You're sure, son?" he asked, almost plaintively. Kilian leaned forward, trying to make out Alex's expression at the question. He had expected Alex to feel some portion of remorse at leaving the crew, at abandoning Kilian's training. All he saw was a blankness that made his skin crawl.

"Do it," Alex said in a monotone voice.

Bluebeard pressed his bloodied hand firmly onto the scroll. It burst into blue flames as Bluebeard's blood soaked into its parchment. Strangely, no smoke curled from its flames. Kilian found himself taking several steps forward, entranced by the flaming scroll. Tavia dug her nails into his arm, stilling his movements. And, after a moment, the flames subsided until all that was left was the same scroll. Through the twilight air, Kilian could see that Bluebeard's handprint had turned a charred black. The rest of the contract remained as it had been.

He slowly rolled the scroll back up and handed it to Alex, a grim expression on his face. His shoulders seemed to sag more now, after the use of magic. Bags had formed beneath his eyes, giving him a distinctly hallowed look.

"The next port, Bluebeard," Alex muttered as he turned on his heel and stormed past where Tavia, Narcon, and Kilian stood. He did not look at any of them, rather, he stared down at his feet as he passed, anger brewing in his eyes. He disappeared below deck.

Kilian released the breath he realized he had been holding. Bluebeard returned to the wheel. The blue light emanating from him dissipated into mist. It swirled around the captain's head before joining the wind. Bluebeard stared straight ahead of the ship. Even when Tavia went to stand next to him and gently placed her hand upon his shoulder, Bluebeard staunchly ignored her. Kilian watched as Bluebeard and Tavia's silhouettes faded into the setting sun.

Part Two

Chapter Thirteen

Noomi Beach was the most beautiful place Kilian had ever seen. Rose-gold sand curved in a long line in front of him and the turquoise sea expanded beyond. Tall brown rocks covered with trees and other foliage rose up on one side of the embankment, forming a giant hill. Here the water turned dark green. A narrow staircase led up the hill to where a single structure stood. It was painted such a brilliant shade of blue that Kilian almost mistook it for another section of the beach until he noticed the red roof. Colorful curtains hung in the windows and doorframes; they wafted in the cooling sea breeze. White waves crashed against the sand bars leading into the beach. The sky was bright blue with fluffy white clouds. In the distance, Kilian could see a range of dark blue mountains reaching up into the sky. *Fire demons*, he thought as he saw smoke billowing from the top of one of them.

It had been two years since Bluebeard had docked at Port Naumesi in the queendom of Siguila on the island continent of Valqueria. According to Bluebeard, only two countries existed within the boundaries of the massive island: Siguila and Niquila. The queendoms were ruled by twin sisters who denied all advances from any man in order to maintain control of their respective countries. Rumors abounded that the sisters were excessively jealous of each other. Tension between the two queendoms ebbed and receded as the sisters vied for even more power. However, in the wake of Alex's departure from their small band, Bluebeard had declared that Kilian's training would continue in Siguila's capital city: Khaeleph.

Khaeleph was known for its extravagance, and the Queen was known for her cruelty to any who exalted her sister over her. The closer to the city's center one traveled, the more opulent the buildings became. The buildings slowly became gilded in gold, making them shine in the midday sun. In direct contrast to this, the bloodied bodies of Queen Khaela's foes could be found in the center of town squares.

Kilian remembered their third day in the capital city. He heard what he thought had been a little girl crying out in pain. Her voice carried through the streets, making him shake from fear and worry. Her voice reminded him so much of May's. It had been so long that he'd thought about his little sister that he found himself rushing towards the sound. His feet pounded on the stone walkways. The girl's cries echoed through him. By the time he reached the square, he was running so fast that, instead of skidding to a stop before slamming into someone, Kilian ran headlong into an elderly man with a cane. The man promptly used his can to beat Kilian over the head as he yelled for the guards to stop the 'vagrant' trying to rob him. Kilian fled the city square, but not before he saw that the girl who had been crying out in pain was no girl at all, but rather a young woman dressed in an ornately embroidered emerald dress. Her blonde hair was matted with dry blood, and her gown was splattered with dark spots from cuts that stretched across both of her cheeks. She cried out as one of the guards brought his blade up to slice her across the chest as well. Kilian had wanted to do something—had wanted to save her from her fate. But he didn't. He'd just kept running.

It wasn't five weeks after they arrived in Khaeleph when Narcon paid Bluebeard the contract gold and left. He had not said goodbye to Kilian when he'd left. Instead, he'd left a small notebook on Kilian's bed that detailed the training schedule he wanted Kilian to keep. Kilian had asked Bluebeard why Narcon had left, but the older man had refused to answer. Bluebeard was never the same after Narcon left. Much of the time, he locked himself away in his rooms, refusing to see anyone. Kilian had made the mistake once of going into

Bluebeard's rooms and found the captain passed out at his desk, empty wine bottles scattered and broken across the floor.

The only thing—the only bright light—in Kilian's life that made the endless training and draining from Bluebeard tolerable was Tavia. She had remained with them. She had massaged Kilian's aching muscles after hours of battle practices. She had kissed away his tears when worry for his family had overtaken him. Tavia had been everything to Kilian.

But, eventually, she too had left, leaving him with the only tangible thing he had to show for his efforts: the tiny golden key he'd collected from the Forgotten Isles.

Kilian breathed in deeply as he stood at the crest of the beach. Salt and fresh air filled his lungs. The coolness of the air was refreshing in the hot sun. It felt good to be traveling again. It felt good to finally be making some progress towards achieving his goals. *Maybe then she'll return to me*, Kilian thought as he stared out at the beach and its ocean. All he wanted was to forget the dark moments of the past two years and move forward. Closing his eyes, Kilian listened to the sound of his own heartbeat and the lapping waves crashing into the rose-gold sand. They were like a gentle lullaby, calling him to rest his weary body. He stood like that, alone on the most beautiful beach he had ever seen, for several moments as he thought about his next steps.

He was to meet Bluebeard at the Dragonfly Inn. Bluebeard had told him that he would know the inn by its red roof. And so, he had. Part of his brain nagged him to continue moving forward, to rendezvous with Bluebeard at their allotted time, but something else within him made him remain. Sure, his muscles ached from the long journey to the beach, and his eyes drooped from the romantic lullaby of the ocean, but Kilian knew that he couldn't stay on the beach for longer than a few moments. Still, he lingered, breathing in the air and wishing that he could stay in this place for eternity, or at least until he could find Tavia again.

He knew he couldn't.

Sighing, Kilian tugged on the reins of his horse, Bitey, and began the long trek to the hill on the other side of the beach. During their two-year stay in Khaeleph, Bluebeard had made arrangements for both of their horses to be transported across the Paralosa Ocean to Valqueria. Tavia had told him that it was Bluebeard's way of raising Kilian's spirits after Narcon left. It hadn't worked, but Kilian was thankful to have been reunited with his steed. He led Bitey along the wet sand leaving footprints in his wake. As he strolled along the beach, Kilian began to wonder how long the remnants of his presence here would remain. *How much does anything remain?* To Kilian, it seemed as if the world was ever-changing and that, even if he did achieve the tasks Bluebeard had set for him—even if he did please the Creators—that he would just be another hero to be sung about in songs but never truly remembered for the man that he was. *What do great accomplishments mean if there's no one to share them with?* Kilian pondered as massive waves crashed against the rose-gold sand all around him. He soon had his answer. Even the deepest of his footprints disappeared into the ocean. It gave him an unsettling feeling to know that his existence could be wiped away so quickly. He shook his head, trying to clear it of the thoughts that had been plaguing him ever since Tavia had left and begun walking more quickly towards the steep staircase leading to the Dragonfly Inn on the other side of the beach.

"Come on, Bitey," he whispered, stroking the horse's neck. Bitey nuzzled Kilian's hand and licked at it, clearly looking for a sugar cube or two. Kilian shook his head at his horse's behavior but dug into his coat pocket and handed his horse an apple he'd been saving for her. His horse immediately inhaled the apple and neighed faintly. Her breath came out in a hot puff against Kilian's skin.

Soft notes from a reed instrument—Kilian wasn't sure which one—were carried on the breeze. Kilian swept his head all around but saw nothing to indicate where the music was coming from. Just like the lapping of the waves against the sand sang a gentle lullaby, the music called to him. Kilian felt an intense desire— need—to follow the notes. He slowly began to turn his horse in the opposite direction of the Dragonfly Inn, towards the ocean itself.

Water filled his boots first as he waded into the cool turquoise water. Kilian barely noticed as his boots became water-logged and heavy the further he waded into the water. The music seemed to be coming from all around him now. It filled his mind, and he released the reins to his horse. She stood by him for several moments, pawing at the sand and neighing, but Kilian barely registered that she was there. The music called to him, pulling him further into the ocean depths.

He took a step forward, and his chin sank into the water. He felt so weightless, invincible. Everything he had ever wanted to be. He let the water flow over him, through him. He tasted the brine of the sea and wished for more. Still, the song continued.

Taking yet another step deeper into the water, Kilian felt his entire leg dip as his foot did not meet the rose-gold sand beneath. He faltered, vaguely aware that he was at the beach's drop off into the deep. He hung there, suspended between land and ocean. He tried to remember why he wanted to be on land, but only hazy memories filtered through his muddled mind.

"What are ya doin', Kilian Clearwater?"

The voice rang in Kilian's mind, unfamiliar.

"Kilian, get out of the water!" the voice was more urgent this time.

It seemed faint to Kilian. It was as if the voice ringing through the wind was insubstantial compared to the song emanating from the ocean. One of his feet dug deep into the sand, caressing the edge of the sandbar separating the beach from the ocean. The other floated above the abyss.

"Remember your family, Kilian. Remember why you're doing all of this," the voice was gruff and close.

Family. An image of May's face passed through Kilian's mind followed swiftly by Willis. His father's face hung before him as Kilian closed his eyes. A wave of nostalgia overwhelmed him as he hung in the balance. The music still called to him, pulled him to take just one more step forward. His muscles ached as he tried to maintain his balance and salty waves crashed into his body. He shifted.

"Tavia wouldn't want this for you, Kilian. She—"

The ocean's song became more insistent, almost desperate the longer Kilian wavered between the beach and ocean. It drowned out the voice calling to him from behind. It drowned out the nostalgia he carried for his family. He was consumed by an unrelenting desire to join himself with whoever or whatever was making that most beautiful song he had ever heard in his life.

Kilian let his foot fall into the abyss, and his body followed.

It was pure darkness. The deeper Kilian fell, the darker the ocean became. His lungs burned from the lack of air. Fish swirled around him, almost as if they too were dancing to the ocean's song. They seemed to sparkle in the dim light filtering through the water. Kilian felt as if he were in an enchanted world that had been hidden from him until that moment. All he knew was that he was falling closer to the music. He would be with it soon. He smiled.

Kilian felt a snap of pressure and the fish swam up and away from him. The ocean around him was complete darkness now, except for the tiny bulbs of light that filtered through the water, casting eerie green light all around him. Kilian found himself staring at the strange green light. The bulbs seemed to move periodically. They extinguished and then relit in different places. Kilian's lungs twitched. He opened his mouth to take a breath, and salty water rushed in. *This isn't right.* As he thought the words, the song abruptly stopped. A cold panic filled Kilian as he realized that he couldn't breathe. He thrashed at the water around him, and the green bulbs went dark. He was in total darkness. Kilian tried to push upwards, to swim away, but he realized that he couldn't tell up from down, everything was so dark.

Twisting around in the water, Kilian sought out any sign of the moonlight filtering from the ocean's surface. *The twin moons should be bright tonight*, he found himself thinking. *They have to be.* Kilian used a tendril of magic that Tavia had taught him to keep himself from losing consciousness, but he knew that it wouldn't be enough. He didn't have enough power to keep himself from drowning. He—suddenly, a cold, webbed hand clamped around his wrist. Kilian spun in the direction he thought the creature holding him was swimming but couldn't see anything. The water was too dark. He tried tugging his arm away, but the webbed hand only squeezed tighter. It pulled on him, and Kilian was helpless to resist it.

His mind became fuzzy from lack of air, and he found it all the harder to concentrate his thoughts. He closed his eyes and tried to focus his mind. He counted backward from ten: *ten, nine, eight, seven*—smooth lips pressed against his and pushed his mouth open with its tongue. Kilian opened his eyes but couldn't see what—or who—was kissing him. Air passed through the lips and into his mouth. Kilian felt the tension on his lungs dissipate and his mind cleared slightly. He greedily sucked in the air, heedless of the fact that he had no idea what kind of creature he was locking lips with. His tongue traced over sharp, pointed teeth and Kilian pulled back in surprise. The webbed hand released his hand, and Kilian realized that he was once again in the dark, cold water. Terror. All Kilian felt now was terror. He reached around to his back, seeking his ax, but remembered that he had tied the weapon to Bitey's pack before beginning his journey to the Dragonfly Inn.

I'm such an idiot, Kilian chided himself. *I should have known that something like this would have happened.* He clenched his teeth and kicked at the water. His body didn't move. He pushed his arms out around him, trying to propel himself upwards. He didn't move. *What's happening?* he thought as panic flooded him.

All around him the eerie green bulbs of light appeared. They were closer now than they had been before. Too close, Kilian thought. Still, he couldn't see what was causing them. He leaned towards the closest one—the one right in front of him. His eyes stung from the salt water, but he forced himself to keep his eyes wide open. *What is that?* he thought as he saw—or imagined that he saw—some sort of a large fish floating behind the green bulb of light. The shadowy bulk pulled ahead of the circle of light and entered into the illuminated section of ocean in which Kilian floated. The creature—Kilian couldn't bring himself to call it a fish—was massive. It had a rotund body that took up the majority of the space around him. A slender antenna stretched out from its forehead and ended in a small glowing orb.

The creature opened its mouth. Kilian screamed. Or, at least, he would have screamed if he hadn't been hundreds of feet below the ocean's surface. The giant creature had the longest teeth he had ever seen. They jutted out of his mouth like swords that had been inserted hilt-first into the creature's maw. Kilian tried to swim away from the creature, but, just as before, the more he struggled against the ocean, the more he remained stationary. The creature moved as if to engulf Kilian in its bite.

Kilian closed his eyes and waited. *At least I had the chance to say goodbye to Tavia*, he thought, though his heart ached at the memory of her departure.

Kilian felt a sharp tug on his arm that sent him spiraling downward through the ocean at a rapid pace. But, not before Kilian felt the swipe of the creature's bite above his head and the mussing of his hair as tendrils were caught in the creature's mouth. Kilian felt his stomach rise up to his chest and the intense sensation of being sucked downward. He felt another pop as he fell through a cold, hard barrier and onto dry ground. He heaved in a massive breath, filling his lungs with precious air.

Panting, Kilian bowed on the ground. *It's not sand*, he realized as his fingers clawed at the cold surface beneath his fingers. It was smooth and white with veins of purple, gray, and pink woven into its surface. Kilian rubbed his fingers over the surface, too thankful to be alive to contemplate where he was or how he had gotten to this place. His head pounded and Kilian spent some of his magic to give himself clarity. He felt the heat of the energy course through his body and felt the weakness that followed. But his head didn't clear. Confused, Kilian used even more of his magic, trying to clear his mind. Still, he felt no relief.

"It won't work here," a delicate, feminine voice said behind him.

Kilian, cradling his head in his hands, began to turn towards the voice.

"Wait," she whispered and he instantly paused. Her voice was musical, almost like—

"You're the one who sang to me," Kilian whispered, his voice raspy. "Why?" he panted the word, still short of breath. The question hung in the space between them for several moments. Kilian thought about what he meant by that single word. He sent a silent prayer to the Creators that she would answer all of his questions.

Instead, the girl giggled. Her laugh was intoxicating. It called to every part of Kilian's body, drawing him closer towards her. He turned towards her and saw the most beautiful woman he had ever seen. Her skin was a mixture of the glistening pearl of the structure around them and the rose-gold sand from above. Her blonde hair glistened in the light seeping in around them. Her sea-green eyes roamed over his body, as if inspecting a decadent meal. Her expression made Kilian shiver, slightly, but the sense of unease quickly faded as she tossed her hair—somehow completely dry—behind her shoulder. Her neck was slender and long. Kilian wanted to kiss that neck. To him, she was like a painting, masterfully created of pure beauty. Kilian stood from where he'd been cowering on the ground and took a step towards her. She abruptly stopped laughing.

"Not yet," she whispered, gently pushing him away from her with both hands. Kilian caught one of those hands in his own. It was dry and warm and webbed. Intricate, silver script covered the webbing. Kilian traced the designs with his finger, smiling faintly to himself. There was something familiar about that script. He just couldn't place where he'd seen something like it before. While Kilian stared at the design, still absently tracing it with his finger, the girl pulled her hand out of his and placed it behind her back. She smirked at him, her lips pressed tightly together. It would have been an ugly expression if she weren't so beautiful.

"Not yet?" Kilian asked as if just realizing what she had said. Utterly confused, Kilian looked down at his hands. *I must be missing something*, he thought as he tried to force his muddled mind to piece together everything. All he could think about was how beautiful she was, how intoxicating she smelled, how musical her voice was. For the briefest of moments, Kilian thought that there was someone else he should be thinking about, but when he tried to remember who it was, his mind came back blank.

The beautiful girl before him giggled again as she took his hand in her own, webbed hand. her touch was like a jolt to his mind, forcing his jumbled thoughts to storm through him. He remembered.

"You're the one who brought me here," he whispered, his throat aching from the salt water he'd drunk and the lack of air. His throat hurt as he spoke, as if it had been scrubbed with a washboard. Clutching his throat with his hands, Kilian irrationally tried to stop the pain from the outside. It didn't work.

"Very good," the girl responded dryly. "Most of my toys don't catch onto that until much, much later." She chuckled quietly to herself as she spoke. She had such a musical laugh.

Toys? Kilian thought as she pulled him along down a narrow path. Lifting his head, Kilian forced himself to look at the scenery around him. Surrounding him was a translucent barrier, almost like a soap bubble, only much thicker and wider. Beyond it, Kilian could see dark water beating against the barrier, but unable to push through it. Luminescent fish, flashing in an array of colors swam around the bubble. Their bodies cast light through the translucent boundary and into the area around Kilian.

Kilian and the girl stood on some sort of bridge between two buildings with a large, circular courtyard in the middle. One of the plants in the courtyard had a bulbous blue stem with orange flowers on top. Kilian caught a whiff of the flower as the girl pulled him past it and it smelled distinctly like rotten fish. Kilian gagged, but the girl didn't seem to notice. Rising up before them was an enormous mansion that was, at a minimum, gilded in the same pearl stones of which the courtyard had been constructed. The pathway connected to the mansion by way of a dark, deserted archway. Despite the faint light filling the space from the luminescent fish swimming all around the dome, Kilian could not see into the darkened hole.

His shoulders tensed and his leg muscles cramped as he considered where she was taking him.

The mansion was larger than any house he'd ever seen before. It had a massive, circular room to the left of the entrance. Large windows covered many of the walls, but several of them had been covered by thick curtains from the inside. Kilian estimated how many rooms the mansion had based on the number of windows. He came up with at least thirty rooms, but knew that calculation had to be incorrect. Glancing off the side of the path, Kilian saw that a moat ran around the mansion. Kilian wasn't sure how they got the water to stay within its track, but he was so thankful that he could finally breath again that he didn't say anything about his previous struggles.

"Where are we?" Kilian asked a little too plaintively. The girl squeezed his wrist tightly, too tightly. Kilian yelped in pain.

"Don't speak unless you are given permission," she said in that same melodic voice. This time, it carried undertones of malice within it that made Kilian shiver slightly.

She led him through the archway, which turned out to be only a small porch of sorts. It ran the full length of the building, but as far as Kilian could tell, it didn't have any doors. Vines climbed the pearl walls and wound their way around the windows of the mansion. They curled in on themselves as the girl placed her webbed hand onto a small, barnacle-laden stone in the middle of the terrace. It glowed a faint lavender for the briefest of moments as mist rose from the stone in a torrent of motion. The veranda shuddered slightly as the rock and pearl formation directly in front of them scraped to the left, revealing a hidden entryway. Kilian gasped in surprise and the girl once again smirked at him.

"You'll get used to that," she said melodiously. She took his hand again and tugged his arm. Kilian followed her through the entryway without complaint, though his heart hammered in his chest and his floundering mind continued to try to make sense of what was happening.

She led him into a massive, circular room with a high ceiling that had a skylight at its top. More luminescent fish swam above them, casting colorful light into the room. Paintings lined the walls, each more splendid than the last. They depicted scenes from what must have been songs of heroes, yet Kilian couldn't place any of them. Unease pricked at him once more, but was squashed by a roaring fire in the middle of a massive stone fireplace across the room from them. It cast a warm glow throughout the room and lent warmth to the otherwise coldness that seeped into Kilian's bones. Oversized plush chairs sat around tables laden with books. On one table a small tea kettle and two cups rested beside a tray overflowing with delicious smelling pastries. Kilian's stomach growled; he couldn't remember the last time he'd eaten. He took an involuntary step towards the food, but the girl yanked him back, making a tsking sound beneath her breath.

Apprehension washed over Kilian once more. He turned to ask the girl what was happening at the same time she leaned in close to his ear and whispered, "I have been waiting such a long time to meet the son of Nathanial Clearwater." Her voice wound around him like a snake. Only, instead of feeling terror, all Kilian felt was peace. He smiled at her. She wasn't going to hurt him; Kilian was sure of it. He turned his attention back to the room, allowing his eyes to roam over the resplendent furnishings.

More than resplendent, Kilian chided himself. It was everything he ever imagined and more. Kilian had the nagging sensation that there was something he was supposed to be remembering, but the more he tried, the more his thoughts faded away before they reached him. It was as if a barrier had threaded itself through his mind, blocking all thoughts of—he paused as he tried to remember but couldn't.

Frustrated, Kilian pulled his hand out of the girl's clasp. She narrowed her eyes at him, but said nothing as he stumbled back several steps. Strands of her blonde hair fell into her eyes as she leaned forward and whispered, "You have nothing to fear, Kilian. I will cause you no harm."

It was as if an iron fist had slammed into Kilian's chest at her words, forcing him into submission. His doubts and fears melted into the recesses of his mind as he desperately tried to hold onto his discomfort. *At least then*, he thought weakly, *I'll be able to maintain some aspect of control.* Although Kilian did not physically move, he felt himself being thrown backwards, all thoughts slipping to the background and being replaced by the girl's face. Her skin glistened like the scales of a fish in the hot afternoon sun and her eyes swam over him. Kilian collapsed to the floor, breathing heavily, but completely at ease.

A scratching noise at the back of the room caught his attention. Kilian whipped his head around, searching for what had made the sound. That part of the room was cased in shadow and Kilian had difficulty seeing beyond the ring of darkness. Breathing heavily, Kilian narrowed his eyes and willed himself to see what lay in the corner. He gasped. There, shackled to the wall, in little more than an ornate loin cloth and an ornate necklace that fully covered his bare chest was the last person Kilian ever expected to see again.

Chapter Fourteen

"What are you doing here!" Kilian managed to shout before his voice gave out. His throat still ached from inhaling the sea water.

The person chained to the wall cowered slightly and pressed himself back into the shadows. He whimpered and Kilian could see that the person was cradling his chained wrists to his chest. Kilian had seen a lot of pathetic things during his time in Queen Khaela's court, but the image of a man Kilian used to know—used to admire—made his stomach squirm. Kilian frowned. *This can't be the same person,* he thought. *There's no way that this can be the same person.* He took a step towards the shackled man, his feet padding softly on the pearl floor. The girl stepped into his path. Her eyes blazed with a hungry, angry fire that made Kilian waver. She scowled at him, her lips still firmly pressed together. Kilian's eyes trailed from hers to the figure cloaked in shadow. Her frown deepened and tapped her foot impatiently on the hard floor, drawing Kilian's attention back to her.

The girl made a tsking sound with her tongue before stepping forward so that their noses were almost touching. She peered into his eyes and all Kilian could see was his reflection staring back at him. He looked haggard with the light stubble covering his chin and his still damp hair clinging to his forehead. Kilian had only ever seen his reflection in the eyes of one other person. *What is her name?* Kilian concentrated, trying to find her face, her voice, her name in his mind, but couldn't. Every time he felt like he was getting closer to discovering her again, the woman standing before caught his attention, sending him spiraling back to where he had begun. Closing his eyes, Kilian tried to remember what seemed so elusive to him. He remembered her lips upon his and the smell of chocolate and pine needles and salty air as she caressed his skin. *Tav—*

The girl slapped him. Kilian wasn't sure which he sensed first, the loud crack of her hand on his cheek or the numb pain that spread across his face like wildfire. Kilian cracked one eye and, through it, saw that the girl was breathing heavily with her hand still raised above her head as if she were about to strike him again. Her entire body shook as she stared him down. Kilian's eyes flicked to where the man still cowered in the shadows. He found that he had no anger for the man sitting there, only pity. Still, his cheek stung and Kilian felt the overwhelming sense of anger swell within him, though it was not as powerful as it was when he carried his ax with him. Clenching his fists, Kilian forced himself to count backwards from ten as he tried to slow down the anger that was continuing to rise within him.

"You'll pay for that one," he spat.

Her eyes widened and her mouth opened into a perfect little "o" shape. Kilian imagined that he saw the flash of sharp, pointed teeth before she promptly closed her mouth and began to pout. She looked so much like his sister, May, that for a moment, Kilian felt a diminutive amount of pity for her. This was quickly replaced with contempt as the girl batted her eyes at him and began to whisper.

The sound of her tinkling, melodic voice assuaged Kilian's anger and he found himself justifying her reasons for slapping him. She delicately placed her hand on his arm and looked up at him through her lashes. "You aren't angry at me, are you?"

"I, uh, I… I don't know" Kilian sputtered. She laughed playfully as she swatted at him.

"There's no reason for you to be, now is there?" Her voice was soft and lighthearted, yet Kilian sensed hints of something much more malicious in its undertones.

Despite Kilian's conflicting emotions of unease and total beguilement, Kilian allowed the girl to lead him to a love seat situated close to the fire. The figure chained to the wall disappeared behind a tall set of chairs and a table.

"There now, isn't this better?" the girls said sweetly. Her blood red lips curled into a smile that made Kilian's stomach squirm. Regardless of his tumultuous stomach, Kilian smiled at her in reply. She seemed pleased by this response and leaned towards him. Her bosom heaved over the top of her dress and pressed into his chest and she slid her hands around his neck.

When she leaned back away from him moments later, a dainty silver chain clinked against the wooden back of the loveseat.

"My, my, you are the perfect addition," she said faintly, as if to herself. She rubbed her forehead and furrowed her brow as if she were contemplating some great mystery. Kilian fingered the collar with his middle finger, thoughts swarming his mind. How do I get out of this one? He thought frantically. Kilian had been through a lot of situations over the past two years, but never had been caught without his ax or his magic to save him.

She leaned in again and said, "You'll come to love this place." Then, after a moment's pause, she continued, "All of them do."

"Who are you?" Kilian managed to croak out. The collar burned hot against his flesh and he thought he felt the prickle of blisters forming on his skin.

"Tsk, tsk, Kilian. I thought I already told you. You are only allowed to speak when commanded."

Kilian slumped back against the sofa's back. *This can't be happening*, he told himself. *Bluebeard will find out. He's waiting for me. But… no. Bluebeard won't be coming for me. He'll assume that I abandoned him, just like the others.* Kilian's heart sank. He would have to figure this one out on his own.

The girl smirked at him. "Since I knew your father, I suppose I can let your little… mistake go." She sighed as she leaned into him again. This time, Kilian willed himself not to become distracted by her scent. She smelled like chocolate. *And pine needles*, he sucked in a deep breath at the thought. That scent was as familiar to him as was his own. *Ta—*

She kissed him, deeply, and all memories of his life before vanished. There was only her and the warmth of her soft lips on his own. He twined his fingers through her hair and pulled her closer. She moaned as he pressed his hands into the small of her back, pressing her closer to him. More frantically now, Kilian kissed her over and over again. He felt hot and knew that sweat would be covering his body, but he didn't care. All he wanted was to feel her, to taste her, to smell her.

"I missed you," he whispered, desperately, before trailing kisses down her throat to her chest. She quivered as Kilian traced the outline of her back with his fingertips. With deft fingers, he began to pull her dress away from her shoulders. He had missed her so much. *Why did you leave me?* he wanted to ask, but couldn't muster the spoken words. He kissed the soft spot behind her ear and she sighed in relief. He stroked her back and she moaned. Her chocolate and pine needle scent filled his senses. This was exactly where he needed to be. Her back arched as she pulled away from him, her smile open-mouthed and wide for the first time.

Kilian nearly screamed.

But he didn't. Jagged, sharp teeth splayed from her mouth in rows three deep. Her golden blonde hair bounced as she laughed at him. Kilian locked eyes with her and said in a flat, lifeless voice, "You're not Tavia."

Her grin widened, "No, I'm not, but it is interesting to note that you forgot her so easily."

"I didn't forget her!" he shouted. He squirmed against the weight of her on his body.

"Oh, I wouldn't do that if I were," she said, frowning. "It's not polite to rebuke someone once you've gotten them so riled up."

She yanked on the chain and collar she'd latched around his neck and Kilian instantly felt a spark of pain sear his skin. He clawed at the collar, desperately trying to remove it, but couldn't find the seam or the lock. Screaming in frustration, Kilian swiped one fist at her, but she pulled harder on the chain and he instantly dropped his hand to the collar and screamed in pain.

"Do you have any idea who you're dealing with?" she hissed. Her voice was low and poisonous.

"I don't care," Kilian retorted. His head hurt as he tried to muddle through his broken thoughts. He remembered walking on the beach and listening to sound of music playing on the wind. He remembered being drawn to the ocean's call. He remembered— "It was you who brought me here," he said calmly.

She clapped her hands delicately. "Very good, Kilian. I do believe you are the only person who has ever figured this out on the very first night." Her face flushed with excitement and it once again became difficult for Kilian to concentrate on anything but the luscious red lips of her mouth.

"Yes, he's so amazing," a voice said sarcastically from across the room. The girl immediately quit clapping. She stood and the room seemed to dim as her sea green eyes turned icy and she directed her gaze towards the chained man. Kilian shivered as a cold breeze swept the room with a swooshing sound.

"You know, Saraphina, I do believe that you are the stupidest mermaid I've ever met," the man said in a mocking tone that matched the girl's voice.

The girl, Saraphina, stomped her feet on the smooth pearl floors. The entire room shook. Kilian pressed himself away from her, his eyes darting between her and the direction where he knew the man was chained to the wall.

"Oh, come on now, Saraphina. There's no reason to throw such a tantrum," the man chuckled as Kilian scooted closer to the edge of the sofa. *If only I can slip away, maybe, just maybe, I'll be able too—*

Kilian's thoughts were cut off abruptly as Saraphina pulled sharply on the silver chain connected to his collar. She dragged him to the wall where the man was chained. The scent of piss and excrement was almost stifling. Kilian wasn't sure how he hadn't noticed those strong odors before. Pinching his nose between his fingers, Kilian began breathing through his mouth. Saraphina raised one eyebrow at him, but did not force him to stop. She simply waved her hand and the smell dissipated as if on the winds.

"You!" she hissed as she brought up her hand to strike the man chained to the wall, "I should have never brought you here." She wrinkled her nose at him. "You were never worth my time."

It was clear to Kilian that Saraphina expected the man to cower before her. Instead, he laughed. He laughed for so hard and so long that it made Kilian start laughing. Saraphina looked between the two of them and stomped her feet again, "But I didn't give you permission!" She grumbled.

"Please, Saraphina, did you really think that you would be able to control the son of the great Nathanial Clearwater?" the man asked sardonically. "You do realize that this man's father outwitted the old king."

"Men are not their fathers!" she yelled. She dropped Kilian's chain as she lunged at the man.

Kilian wavered. *I should run,* he thought fleetingly. *But, I know him.* The name came to him again as if from the depths. *Alex.* Kilian caught his eye as Saraphina slapped him across the cheek. A red mark instantly swelled on his flesh. Still, he darted his eyes towards the doorway. *To freedom*, Kilian realized. *He wants me to go.*

Kilian started to move towards the door, but something gave him pause. The last time he'd seen Alex had been the day they'd docked at Port Naumesi. Alex had hated him then and with good reason. Because of Kilian, Alex's brother had been separated from his soul. It was a fate worse than death. And Kilian's own mother had completed the deed. Not a day had gone since the battle on the ship that Kilian didn't regret wavering when he should have acted. *I could have saved Adrienne*, Kilian thought, *I won't make the same mistake twice.*

Releasing a terrible cry, Kilian charged at Saraphina. Using the chain as a whip, Kilian thrashed Saraphina on the back. A long gash tore in her dress and she cried out in pain. She opened her mouth to speak, but Alex clamped his hand over her lips, muffling her voice.

"Don't listen to her speak, Kilian. She's a mermaid and she'll control your mind if you allow it!"

Saraphina bit into Alex's flesh until blood began to dribble down her chin. Kilian heard the sharp snap of bones as she chewed on Alex's hand. Alex's brow furrowed and he let out a tiny cry of pain as Kilian looked about the room in search of anything that he could use as a weapon. Unfortunately, the room that was mostly decorated with books and paintings. Alex began to whimper as Saraphina's sharp teeth tore into his flesh.

Finally, Kilian's eyes landed on the fire poker. It was long and cast of iron. Brandishing the poker like a sword, Kilian ran towards Saraphina with the poker raised high. Her eyes widened as he brought the poker down to stab her through the chest. His muscles strained as he swung with his entire might.

The poker bounced off of her chest as if it had been made of wood instead of iron. It didn't even leave a scratch. Kilian stumbled, off balance, as the momentum of his thrust carried him to the floor. He caught Alex rolling his eyes and scrambled to his feet. Using the chain connected to his collar, Kilian wrapped it around Saraphina's neck and began to pull as tightly as he could. He saw the fear in her eyes as he tugged the chain taught. Blood spilled onto the floor from Alex's hand, but still he kept it firmly attached to Saraphina's mouth.

Kilian strained against the chain, but still Saraphina gave no indication that the chain was doing anything to her. Growling, Kilian dug into his boot and pulled out a small dagger. He tossed it to Alex who, with a steady hand, slid the blade across Saraphina's cheek. Blue blood spilled from her cheek and streamed down her otherwise pale skin. It looked so surreal to Kilian, as if he were dreaming and this were only a vague memory. Her scream brought him back to reality.

She had finally managed to stop Alex from holding her mouth shut. Her scream ate through Kilian, leaving him feeling void of all emotion. He shivered as he watched her duck out of Alex's hold and snatch the fire poker from the floor. She held it out in front of her.

"You really should be more careful," she said in that same melodic voice that threatened to control Kilian. Remembering what Bluebeard had taught him about building mental walls and protecting oneself from magical attacks, Kilian threw up the strongest one he could muster on a limited supply of energy and time. His body sagged slightly from the effort. He imagined massive cotton balls in his ears, blocking out the sound. Peace teased at the back of his mind, but Kilian drove it out with such force that Saraphina let a cry of pain escape her lips instead of words. Kilian looked at her and saw that blood trailed from her nose in a thin line.

"How did you?" she asked, wiping away the blood from her face. She looked between Alex and Kilian, her sea green eyes storming. "It's not possible!" she shouted.

She began singing again. This time, it was more of a lullaby than anything else. Only, the notes sounded forlorn and beaten down. They tugged at Kilian's heartstrings, compelling him to listen to her. He watched in horror as Alex's eyes glazed over and he began to sink to the ground. He clutched his bloodied hand to his chest, staunching the flow a little. *Not enough*, Kilian thought. *There's too much blood.*

"No!" Kilian shouted as he flung his arm out and deftly hit Saraphina straight in the throat. She immediately stopped singing and sank to the ground. She clutched her throat as tears mixed with the blood still flowing from her nose.

Ripping a strip of cloth from his shirt, Kilian wrapped it around Alex's wound. "You can't die, Alex," he pleaded, though he wasn't sure to whom. He cradled Alex in his arms. "Please, don't die." Pent up tears streamed from Kilian's eyes. He didn't care that snot joined with his tears, running into his mouth in a salty, slimy way. He watched in horror as Alex closed his eyes. Shuddering, Kilian bent his head over Alex's and tried to listen for the sound of Alex's breathing over the sound of his own heartbeat pounding in his head.

From the corner of his eye, he noticed Saraphina slinking away from him, still cradling her throat in one hand. She grasped the iron poker in the other as if it were a lifeline. Kilian lurched at her and slammed his shoulder into her chest. She somehow managed to maintain her hold on the fire poker. Through instinct, Kilian swung his arm around her and slapped the back of her hand with his own. She released a painful sounding yelp before dropping the fire poker to the floor with a loud clang. The room fell silent as she and Kilian stared at each. With deliberate movements, Kilian waggled one finger at her in a 'come hither' gesture. She paused for only a moment before scooting closer to where he sat. Her lips trembled as Kilian lifted her chin so that she was staring him in the face.

"Unlock the collar," Kilian demanded, his voice stern. Tears welled in her eyes.

She opened her mouth to speak, her razor-like teeth gleaming in the firelight. Kilian didn't hesitate before backhanding her with a loud smack. Her head whipped back and, when she finally looked back at him, her eyes were dazed.

"I said, unlock the collar," Kilian repeated. Although his heart hammered in his chest and his body felt weak, he forced himself to remain upright and stern. Alex whimpered slightly as Saraphina stepped on his arm as she moved around Kilian. His face had turned so pale that Kilian could see the faint blue lines of veins pulsing on Alex's forehead. Kilian stroked Alex's brow with his thumb, vowing to himself that he wouldn't let him die here, at the hands of yet another treacherous woman. He felt the hot anger rise within him, but without his ax, it only simmered beneath the surface, ready to burst forth in all its glory at any moment. He breathed deeply in a frantic attempt to calm his nerves. It didn't work.

Kilian waited until he heard the soft click of the collar's locking mechanism releasing and the relief of the cool metal sliding away from his skin before he snatched a handful of Saraphina's skirts and yanked her to the floor. She tried scrambling away from him, but Kilian grabbed hold of her hair. She yelped in pain as he dragged her across the floor so that her face was mere inches away from Alex's wound. She looked sideways up at him, an amused smirk forming on her bruised face.

"Look what I did to my plaything," she managed to whisper before Kilian wrapped her hair more tightly around his hand. He could feel strands of her hair pulling out of her head like weeds from a garden. She grimaced with each pop of her hair follicles.

"You will never hurt him again," Kilian commanded. "Do you understand me?"

She nodded her head, sniveling softly to herself. Kilian pushed her face closer to Alex's wound, forcing her to look at it. "Promise me," Kilian said, his voice devoid of all emotion. "Promise that you will never harm him again or else I'll snap your neck like it was nothing more than a twig."

Kilian felt a shudder run up Saraphina's spine. Although she couldn't see him, he smiled at her fear. Over the past two years, Kilian had become quite adept at managing not only his own fear but the fear of others. He slid his hand down the back of her head until his massive fingers wrapped around her throat. He squeezed.

"I promise," Saraphina finally said as Kilian's thumb pressed in on the hollow of her neck. When Kilian didn't stop squeezing, she shouted, "I promise I won't hurt him!"

"Good," Kilian said slowly, releasing the pressure from her neck but still resting his hand on her skin. "Now, unlock his chains."

Saraphina scrambled to dig the key out of her dress pocket. Her hands trembled as she quickly undid the lock. As the chains clanked to the ground, a bit of color rose to Alex's pale cheeks. Sighing with relief, Kilian grasped the discarded collar that lay on the floor beside him and quickly latched it around Saraphina's neck. She clawed at the collar, trying to find the latching mechanism. Using the last bit of magic Kilian could muster, he fused the collar into a single piece of metal. Saraphina wailed and thrashed uncontrollably.

"You slimy piece of scum!" she yelled. "When my uncle hears about this—"

"Ahem," a voice said from behind them, interrupting Saraphina's tirade. Kilian swung around, snatching the fire poker from the floor as he did so. He held it up in front of him, his muscles wilting under the weight of iron in his hands. He tried to summon the remnants of his magic, but he had used it all in breaking the spell Saraphina had placed on him. His head swam and his vision blurred, but not before he saw the distinctive blue aura emanating from the person standing in the doorway.

"Bluebeard," he whispered before collapsing to the floor.

He came to seconds later as Bluebeard poured some of his reserved energy into Kilian's nearly lifeless body.

"You shouldn't use so much of yourself next time," Bluebeard chided nervously as Kilian slowly regained his strength.

"I learned from the best," Kilian whispered, his voice hoarse. "Or don't you remember all those times I brought you back from the brink?" He meant it as a joke, but Bluebeard didn't even smile. Instead, the older captain sent a surge of energy into Kilian that left a warm tingling sensation running through his entire body.

"You have to help Alex," Kilian said, as memories slowly repopulated his mind. He sat up and shoved Bluebeard's hands away from him.

Bluebeard chuckled slightly, "Alex can take care of himself, Kilian." With that the older man pushed Kilian back down until he was lying flat on his back. Kilian rolled his eyes back as Bluebeard sent yet another jolt of energy into his weary body. Bluebeard had, apparently, tied Saraphina to one of the columns located on the far side of the room. Her arm muscles visibly strained as she futilely tugged at the silver chain. Kilian smirked.

"What you smile'n at, boy?" Bluebeard asked gruffly, assuming the pirate speech he always did at random times. Kilian still hadn't been able to figure out why Bluebeard spoke like an elite Lunameedian in some instances while in others he sounded like the broadside of a pig.

"It's just... you took the time to chain her up instead of killing her," Kilian paused, still trying to figure out exactly what to say. "I'm proud of you," he finally said.

"It was nothin'. 'Sides, we need her," Bluebeard said, shrugging his shoulders. He pulled out his pipe and began stuffing the mixture of herbs into its chamber. Kilian smelled the distinct scent of mureechi.

"Oh no!" he exclaimed, "You can't be seriously considering smoking mureechi at a time like this!" Despite still feeling weak, Kilian flailed his arms as he spoke and began pacing back and forth between Saraphina and Bluebeard.

The old captain lit the pipe and began puffing away. He gave Kilian a sidelong look as he took a long drag from the pipe. Thick curls of smoke wafted from the end of his pipe. "You know what the problem with you is, Kilian? It's that you don't know how to have a good time."

Kilian quit pacing and snatched the mureechi pipe from Bluebeard's hand. "I don't know how to have a good time, huh?" he mumbled under his breath as he, too, took a long drag from the pipe. He coughed, releasing a puff of translucent purple smoke.

Bluebeard chuckled and clapped Kilian on the shoulder. "That'll do, boy, that'll do."

"Well, if you're done with this lovely display of, uh, mentorship, I do believe that I should be going."

Both Kilian and Bluebeard turned to see that Alex had stood up and walking towards the entryway. His hand had stopped bleeding.

"What?" Kilian asked, confused, "but how?"

Alex raised his hand and admired its now smooth, scar less form. "Yes, it is some of my best work," he smiled as he spoke, but the warmth of his smile did not reach his eyes. "Runs in the family, you see. Some ancestor of mine was gifted with the power to heal by the Creators." He strode across the room until he was standing directly in front of Kilian, "Adrienne had this ability too. If not for you…" he paused and heaved in a breath. "Well, if it hadn't been for you, Adrienne would still be alive." Despite Alex's anger, Kilian could see immense pain sweep through Alex at the thought of his twin.

Kilian fumbled as he searched for the correct words to say. It had been two years since Adrienne had died at Kaldeena's hand. Kilian had thought that he'd dealt with his grief and guilt at not fighting back against his mother. *Apparently, I haven't gotten over it nearly as well as I had hoped*, he thought as he stared down at his feet, too ashamed to look Alex in the eyes.

"I'm sorry, Alex," Kilian managed to murmur as he saw Alex begin to walk away. The other man stopped midway across the room and turned to look back at Kilian.

"Sorry isn't good enough," he said softly. "Sorry doesn't bring Adrienne back to me."

They stared at each other for several moments in silence. Kilian felt as if he and Alex were trapped in a world sunken into darkness. He remembered the fear he'd felt as Kaldeena had called for him to turn himself into her before she killed his friend. He remembered the blade she'd held and the fear in Adrienne's eyes. The fear that was mirrored in his own. Fires blazed all around him and all he could see was the empty look in Adrienne's eyes after Kaldeena had cut him with her blade.

Sweat ran down his cheek and dripped on the back of his hand. "I know," he finally whispered. He knew it wasn't enough. He knew that his cowardice could never be forgiven. He had provided Kaldeena with an excuse to kill one of his friends and she'd taken it. *It was as much my fault as it was Kaldeena's*, Kilian reminded himself. *I could have saved him.* "I'm a coward," he said softly. "I don't deserve to be the hero."

"Exactly my thoughts," Alex said lightly. "You aren't a hero, Kilian, and never will be. You already failed at your first task; what makes you think that you can achieve the second?" He laughed then. It made Kilian's skin crawl and his stomach drop. Kilian shivered as he took a half-step backwards, towards Bluebeard.

"Oh, he won't be able to help you achieve the tasks he's set for you, Kilian. Bluebeard is nothing more than a coward himself," Alex spat on the ground as he spoke and flashed a glare towards Bluebeard.

Bluebeard drew his sword and swung the blade through the air in a large arc before slamming the point of the blade into the pearl floor. He glowed a magnificent blue. Alex audibly gulped.

"Now, you won't be sayin' this nonsense to me boy. Do ya hear me, Alex. Do ya?' Bluebeard growled.

"Yes," Alex mumbled as Bluebeard pulled him by the scruff of his shirt's collar. He flung Alex to the ground and stood above him with his sword pointed down at Alex's chest.

"What are you doing here anyway, Alex?" Bluebeard grumbled. Kilian detected a hint of hesitation in Bluebeard's voice as he spoke.

Alex laughed profusely at Bluebeard's question. He laughed so hard that he couldn't talk. Bluebeard kicked him, hard, in the side. Still, Alex continued to laugh.

"What are you doing here, Alex." It was not a question. Kilian could hear the command in Bluebeard's tone.

Alex shivered slightly but turned his face towards Kilian when he finally responded, "My family earned the favor of the Creators once. I figured, why not do it again." He shrugged his shoulders and leaned his head back against the smooth pearl of the walkway. "I never intended to get caught by Saraphina."

Kilian quickly glanced back into the room. Saraphina was still chained to the column. She glared at Kilian when he caught her eye but then licked her top lip in such a provocative way that Kilian actually blushed. He quickly turned his attention back to the conversation Alex and Bluebeard were having.

"This isn't your quest, Alex," Bluebeard said gently. "You know what happens to those who try to steal away someone else's destiny."

"Bah! Those are just rumors," Alex retorted. "Children's stories meant to scare people into submitting to their 'fates'. I don't believe a word of it."

Bluebeard withdrew his sword from Alex's chest and bent down so that, if Alex had sat up, they would have been at eye level. "Listen to me, Alex. This is a futile mission you've put yourself on." He placed one hand on Alex's shoulder, but Alex scooted backwards and out of Bluebeard's reach.

"Why? Because I'm not the precious son of Nathanial Clearwater?" he scoffed. "Nathanial left us, Bluebeard. He abandoned us." He turned his gaze towards Kilian, "This one is no different."

Alex's voice contained so much venom in it that Kilian felt himself shutting down. He stood awkwardly next to Bluebeard, unsure of whether to return to the room or stay here and allow Alex to continue to berate him. *I did apologize, after all*, Kilian thought as he looked down at Alex. *If only he knew how much I've struggled with Adrienne's loss and my own cowardice at letting him die.*

"You ignorant little ingrate," Bluebeard bellowed furiously. He swung his sword towards Alex's chest once more. Alex didn't even flinch as the cold metal sliced the top of his shirt, leaving a trail of blood seeping from his skin. Kilian watched in amazement as the skin on Alex's chest knit back together, completely healing the wound.

"Do you really believe that you will be able to fulfill a prophecy that wasn't meant for you?" Bluebeard's voice was hollow as he spoke. Kilian stole a quick glance at the captain and noticed that the older man's shoulders sagged a bit. "This isn't your time, lad." His voice sounded sad as he spoke. "It isn't mine either," he whispered, almost as an afterthought.

"You're wrong, Bluebeard, and I'm going to prove it to you."

They remained silent for several moments in the exact same position. Kilian breathed heavily and began to count in his head. He got to two-hundred and twenty-three before Bluebeard finally began to laugh. He lowered his sword and reached out his free hand, which Alex took. Bluebeard drew the younger man into a bearlike embrace, his shoulders shaking as he whispered, "It's been too long, my friend."

Alex reluctantly wrapped his arms around Bluebeard's rotund stomach and hugged him back. "That it has," he responded, "That it has." Finally, after Kilian had gotten to thirty-six in his counting, Alex said in a loud voice, "But don't let this fool you, Kilian. I am still going to beat you in this quest. You'll see."

Kilian grinned. "Then let the best hero win."

Chapter Fifteen

"How did you get down here?" Kilian asked as he, Alex, and Bluebeard searched through Saraphina's room.

"Yes, Bluebeard, how did you get down here," Alex asked, mockingly.

Kilian shot a glance at Alex, but said nothing about the other man's tone. He waited for Bluebeard to respond as he sifted through a notebook full of papers with script on it that Kilian had never seen before. He studied the flowing, interconnected characters of the script. The way the characters formed intricate patterns across the page. They were beautiful in the depictions of the world, but completely indecipherable to Kilian. He held one of the pages up so that Bluebeard and Alex could see.

Saraphina immediately began jabbering about how 'those pages' were part of her personal collection.

"You have no right to disturb my things!" she shouted as she struggled against the chains that bound her to the column. "Get away from there!"

Alex stalked over to Saraphina. She pressed herself against the column, her entire body quivering. Alex stood over her, his shoulders square and his chin set. He raised the sword he'd found in one of her trunks above his head. Kilian watched in amazement as a smile spread across Saraphina's face.

"Alex," she whispered in a smooth, seductive voice, "my dear, sweet, Alex." Her razor-sharp teeth flashed from behind her ruby red lips. "Put the sword down." Her voice was commanding and confident. Kilian almost found himself compelled to follow her command before he realized that she wasn't speaking to him and he wasn't holding a sword.

Alex paused, his sword hanging in mid-swing. His body twitched as he seemed to be struggling to make a choice. Saraphina opened her mouth and as if to speak again. Before a single word left her mouth, Alex let out a deafening cry and dropped the hilt of the sword into her temple. Kilian heard a sickening crunch as the hilt shattered the thin bones of Saraphina's skull.

"What have you done!" Bluebeard mumbled as he stumbled towards where Saraphina lay, slumped on the ground. He glowered at Alex, "What did you do?" he spat. He cradled Saraphina in his arms, rocking her back and forth.

Alex eyed Bluebeard, a look of contempt on his face. "What do you mean, what have I done?" he said as he took a step away from Bluebeard and Saraphina. "Bluebeard, she imprisoned me for... I don't even remember how long! She made me watch as she fed on the others." At this, Alex's voice began to quiver and he abruptly stopped talking. Kilian saw a glisten in Alex's eyes as he looked down towards his sword. "Do you even know who this sword belonged to? Do you?" he dropped the sword on the ground as he spoke. "I don't. She never gave him a chance to speak his name before she killed him. I can still remember his screams."

Kilian's stomach became queasy as he listened to Alex speak. His mind, still muddled from the exertion of using the majority of his magic, tried to piece together what Alex meant by 'she made me watch as she fed on the others.' *Who were the others?* Kilian thought as his stomach rolled. Silently, he slumped to the ground as he continued to listen to the two men argue.

"You understand, now more than most, the dangers of entering the ocean unattended by a fellow merperson," Bluebeard spoke slowly and enunciated each word. "I understand that you witnessed atrocities, Alex, but this does not give you the right—"

"The right!" Alex cut in, his voice shaking. "I have every right, Bluebeard. This... bitch," he stammered as he pointed one finger at Saraphina's unmoving body, "kept me here as her personal slave. You have no idea, Bluebeard—"

"You know that I do," Bluebeard said softly.

Alex's hand—the one still pointing at Saraphina—shook violently. Clenching his hand into a fist, Alex drew it up to his chest. The shaking subsided, but did not stop entirely.

Bluebeard's body began to glow dull blue. It was nowhere near as brilliant or a deep a blue has it had been when he'd first arrived to 'save' Kilian from Saraphina. He pressed his hands onto either side of Saraphina's face and bowed his head over hers. Kilian was too far away and Bluebeard spoke too softly for Kilian to discern what Bluebeard whispered over Saraphina's body, but as he spoke the bruise on her temple slowly began to recede.

"Stop!" Alex shouted, his entire body shaking now. "You can't do this, Bluebeard."

"We need her," Bluebeard said calmly. His blue light extinguished as Saraphina's eyes opened. She glared at Bluebeard through slit eyes.

"It certainly took you long enough to aide me in my time of need, Reginald," she purred as she leaned her head into his chest and sniffed. The uneasy feeling in Kilian's stomach tightened. *This isn't right*, he thought as he slowly stood. *This can't be right.*

"It took me as long as it should've," Bluebeard responded, his voice dull. Kilian noticed that the ends of Bluebeard's hair had turned snowy white and his eyes and turned a faded gray. "Now, no more interference," he said as he patted her on the head. He swiftly, and deftly, transitioned her body off of his and let her fall to the ground as he stood up. She glared at him, but Bluebeard didn't seem to notice.

"Alex, I understand why you want to see her dead, but it is better for us that she remains alive," Bluebeard said as he grasped Alex's upper arm. Alex shrugged him off, his face darkening.

"You don't understand, *Reginald*," he emphasized the last word as he spoke, "you're one of them!"

Bluebeard sighed. "Not anymore," he said softly. Kilian could see from across the room that Bluebeard's eyes drooped as he spoke.

"Bah! I should've known when you arrived that you wouldn't be able to let her die," Alex muttered beneath his breath.

"Of course he couldn't!" Saraphina chimed in. Kilian's eyes widened as he looked over to where she sat on the ground. Her voice took on the slow drawl of seduction as she turned her gaze toward Bluebeard, "We were engaged to be married, a long, long time ago."

"You were *engaged* to this thing?" Kilian stammered as he spoke. He gestured as Saraphina, his arms shaking slightly.

Bluebeard sighed a long, rattling sigh. "Yes," he finally whispered, "I was."

Saraphina smirked, her eyes glowing. "You couldn't live without me, even now," she said, her voice a tantalizing mixture of awe and hate.

"No," Bluebeard said firmly, "You can die, just not yet." Saraphina stopped smiling. Her eyes darkened as they narrowed upon him. "You wouldn't have saved me if I didn't still mean something to you," she hissed.

Huffing, Bluebeard turned towards her, his eyes blazing.

"The only thing you mean to me, Saraphina, is the opportunity to have some leverage against your cousin."

She barked a hard, biting laugh. "How little you have remembered over the years, Reginald. My cousin has little to do with me, as he always has." She picked at her nails as she spoke. Kilian sensed that she was feigning nonchalance, but he wasn't sure how he recognized this emotion.

"Alex, let me explain why keeping Saraphina alive is the correct move in this situation," he sauntered over to where Saraphina lay on the ground and bent down. Grabbing a chunk of her hair, Bluebeard wrenched her head up so that Alex and Kilian could see her face. "Saraphina is King Trithium's cousin. With her, we have a chance at gaining an audience with the old king."

Kilian looked between Alex, Bluebeard, and Saraphina. He realized that he was missing a crucial piece to the puzzle, but he just wasn't quite sure what that piece was. He took a step forward and asked, "What makes you think that King Trithium will care whether his cousin lives or dies?"

"Oh, he probably doesn't," Bluebeard said nonchalantly as Saraphina squirmed beneath his grasp. She squeaked in pain as he pulled roughly on her hair. "But, I doubt he would miss the opportunity to confront me after all these years."

It was then that the pieces seemed to fall into place. Kilian couldn't believe how blind he had been before. "You're a mermaid," he whispered.

"Well, technically a merman, but yes, I am of those who live under the sea where the seaweed is greener and the world is a wonder."

"Well, that explains how you got down here so quickly... and how you weren't devoured by those monsters lurking just above this place. Where are we anyway?" Kilian asked in a rush.

"We are in the borderlands of Ula Una."

"What," Alex hissed. "You mean to say that I have been this close to the merfolk's court and never knew it?" He slammed his still clenched fist to the palm of his other hand. He glowered at Saraphina. "You should have taken me to court, lady. I'm sure your cousin would have recognized me from our first visit here, so many years ago."

"What makes you think that I didn't," Saraphina spat. She clawed at Bluebeard's hand, leaving trails of blood flowing from his wrist as her nails dug into his skin. Still, Bluebeard did not release his grasp on her hair.

Alex lunged at her. Kilian watched in awe as Bluebeard flung out his arm and a bolt of brilliant blue light struck Alex in the chest. His clothes sizzled and smoked as the light burned away the cloth of his shirt. Alex screamed as he was flung backwards. He slammed into the wall and slumped onto the ground. His head lulled momentarily before he snapped back to attention.

"You knew who I was the entire time—" he cut off as his voice shook so violently that he could barely utter another word.

Saraphina laughed. It carried notes of the melodic radiance that Kilian had succumbed to only hours before, but now that voice seemed harsh and malevolent to him.

"Of course I knew who you were, Alex of Kiela. You and your sibling were such a commodity the last time you visited Ula Una." She flashed her teeth at him. "I'm so glad I got to enjoy your flesh on my own." She licked her lips as she finished speaking and a drop of her blood dripped to the floor.

Growling, Alex leapt up from the floor and ran towards her once more. Bluebeard threw up his hand and a wall of translucent blue light formed a barrier between them. Alex tried to stop himself, but he slammed into the barrier. He crumpled beneath the impact. Dark bruises covered his cheeks, chest, and arms as Alex stood up. He pounded his fists against the barrier as Saraphina smiled at him mockingly. Alex snarled and let out a hideous cry as he continued to pound his fists against the barrier.

"Peace, Alex," Bluebeard whispered. "You will have your revenge when the time is right."

Saraphina looked up at Bluebeard, a look of shock on her face. Her lower lip trembled. Bluebeard did nothing but laugh when he saw her expression. Kilian moved over to where Alex continued to beat against the barrier. Hesitantly, he laid a shaking hand upon Alex shoulder. The other man stilled as soon as Kilian's hand touched him. Shuddering, Alex sank to the ground. Kilian knelt beside his onetime friend, and held him in a tight embrace. Looking beyond Alex, Kilian saw Bluebeard nod to him in appreciation. He closed his eyes and forced the frustrated tears to remain locked inside.

"We'll stay here for the night," Bluebeard finally said. "Tomorrow, we will travel to the heart of Ula Una."

***

Kilian lay on the pallet he had created for himself on the floor. As far as Kilian knew, everyone else had fallen asleep hours ago. Still, he felt restless in a way he didn't understand. His entire body tingled with anticipation for what was to come on the morrow. The longer he lay in that too silent room with only the crackle of the dying fire and the occasional soft snore from Alex to disturb the peace, Kilian found it difficult to let his mind rest. He crossed his hands behind his head and stared up at the ceiling. Brilliant colors floated across the ceiling as the dying firelight danced through the various glass bottles spread about the room. His eyes burned from the unshed tears he'd forced himself to swallow as he thought about her. The way her lips moved when she spoke. The way her eyes were a torrent of restless storms. The way her lithe body felt against his in the dead of night. The way—

Digging into his trouser pocket, Kilian searched through the debris until his fingers found the cold metal of the key. Smiling to himself, he clutched the key in his now sweaty palm. A cool breeze swept through the room, causing the fire to waver as Kilian slowly pulled the small golden key from his pocket. Its golden edges twinkled in the dim light. He traced the edges of the key with one shaking finger. His breath came in ragged heaves and tears once again stung his eyes. Still, Kilian forced himself to remember his final night with Tavia, the night she had finally given him the golden key she'd found clutched in his hand after Kilian had collapsed with the pillar.

Nubs of candles cast flickering light across the room as a singer performed in the tavern beneath them. Tavia's skin slid across Kilian's, leaving trails of warmth behind her. Her skin was as smooth as silk. Kilian breathed in her chocolatey pine scent as he nuzzled his face into her hair. She slipped her arms around him and let her fingers trail down his back. Kilian sighed contentedly as he pulled her closer to his body.

"I'm going to miss this," she'd whispered before kissing him along his jaw line.

"What do you mean you're going to miss this?" Kilian murmured as he leaned his head back into the pillows. He closed his eyes as she continued trailing kisses over his face.

"When I leave," she responded before planting her lips upon his. Her lips were soft and hot. He leaned into that kiss as his mind raced through all the scenarios that would make Tavia want to leave them. He could understand wanting to pay off her contract to leave Bluebeard. The captain had become little more than a drunken caricature of the man he had been the day he'd arrived at Kilian's home in Lunameed. But, as Tavia delicately licked his lips and pressed more firmly into his body, he found it difficult to imagine any reason for her to want to leave him.

"I love you," he whispered between kisses.

Tavia stopped kissing him at once and pulled back, her face cased in shadow.

"You don't mean that," she responded, her voice husky and worried at the same time. "You can't."

"I do," Kilian said as he leaned up to kiss her on the mouth again. She jerked away from him, her face still in shadow. Kilian longed to see her eyes, to capture her thoughts in their expression.

"You don't," she said firmly. She sat back on her haunches and peered at him in the dim candlelight. "Kilian, you don't know what you're saying." With that, she leapt from the bed and tugged on the silken robe she'd draped over the back of the room's lone chair. The material fluttered softly as she swung it around her shoulders. Kilian watched her, his heart hammering in his chest. He hadn't intended to say those words. He'd known. He'd understood that those words weren't meant to be spoken. She turned to leave.

"Don't go," he plead, his voice quivering slightly.

Tavia paused, her hand clutching the silver knob of the door. Even through the dim light, Kilian could see that her body was shaking. He wanted nothing more than to wrap her in his arms around her and make her understand that everything was going to be alright. He would succeed in the quests. They could be together.

She turned to face him. Kilian's hands began to sweat as he waited. He found himself counting his heartbeats, too fast. She was everything to him. Opening his mouth to speak, Kilian leaned into the void between them.

"I have something that belongs to you, Kilian Clearwater," she said as she fled the room.

Kilian could hear her footsteps groan on the old floorboards as she went into her room. He counted his breathes. He had just gotten to sixty when he heard the familiar creak of her door close behind her. She once again entered his room, holding her fist out before her like it held something holy. In the short time she'd been in her rooms, she'd changed out of the robe and into loose fitting trousers and blouse. Her hair was braided and bound into a loose bun. *She never wears her hair in buns*, Kilian found himself thinking as his eyes followed her across the room.

Silently, she held her fist out in front of his face until Kilian held out one trembling hand. She dropped the golden key into his palm. The metal felt like ice in his hand and Kilian shivered.

"You have to keep going, Kilian," she said, her voice urgent. "You have to promise me that you will keep going."

Kilian's stomach turned into a pool of knots as he looked up into her eyes. Though her expression was soft, her eyes were cold. They didn't rage with the force of the typhoon they normally did when Tavia was considering a difficult decision. They were calm, as calm as Kilian had ever seen them.

"You want to leave," Kilian barely whispered, his voice catching in his throat as he tried to contain his anguish. He did not say it as a question.

"Yes," Tavia responded anyway. "I want to leave."
Kilian hung his head, his eyes wandering over the golden key resting on his still open palm. "But I don't want you to," he said in a low voice.

"It is better this way," she said. Her lips curved downward into a small frown at Kilian's expression. He swiped away the tears that escaped from his eyes.

"You'd leave me alone, with him," he said, accusingly. She didn't respond to him. Instead, she leaned down and gently kissed him on the forehead before turning and walking out of the room. That was the last time he'd heard from or seen her.

Kilian heaved an enormous sigh as he hugged the key to his chest. He had vowed to himself on the day Tavia had left that he would complete the remaining two tasks. He had vowed that he'd find her once more. The colors still danced on the ceiling above Kilian's head as he finally leaned back and let his eyes close. He slipped the key back into his trouser pocket, gently tying a stray thread through one of the ornately carved loops as he did so as not to lose the only thing he had remaining of her.

"I will find you," he whispered out loud as he drifted off to sleep.

Chapter Sixteen

Bluebeard walked in stony silence as he led the small band from Saraphina's quarters and through an intricate pattern of what Kilian could only describe as tunnels. Narrow pathways encased in tubes of the translucent magic wound their way around and through pearl encrusted buildings. The barrier between air and water seemed so thin that Kilian almost believed that he was, indeed, walking through water. Schools of fish swam over and under the barrier like any other obstacle within the ocean. *Of course*, Kilian thought to himself, *to the fish it probably seemed ordinary to have these tunnels here.* He trailed his fingers across the barrier. It was smooth and pliable and Kilian had the sensation that if he pushed hard enough, he could burst the entire structure. He shuddered as he quickly withdrew his hand.

"We'll be there soon," Bluebeard called back to the rest of the group as he shoved Saraphina forward. She hissed at him through clenched teeth, causing Bluebeard to laugh. She glared at him with a look that made Kilian's skin crawl.

"What happens when we get there?" Kilian asked. He looked everywhere but at Saraphina. Despite what she had done to him and Alex, Kilian did not want her to be harmed. He wasn't sure if it was a holdover from the spell she'd put on him or if he just didn't like seeing Bluebeard be so cruel. Regardless, it irked him that Bluebeard didn't demonstrate even the smallest amount of compassion for the woman he had once been engaged to.

"We meet with King Trithium," Alex said, his voice full of frustration. "Haven't you been paying attention at all?" Kilian shot the other man a scowl before turning to face Bluebeard.

"I mean, what will happen when we arrive at Ula Una?"

Bluebeard cleared his throat and paused for a long moment. Saraphina laughed nervously ahead of her captors. Her laugh did nothing to ease the knots forming deep within Kilian's stomach.

Wringing his hands, Kilian tried to calm his breathing. *I still don't have my ax*, he thought with a sigh. This thought only made Kilian's stomach tighten even more and he began fidgeting with his hands as he waited for Bluebeard to respond.

"One of two things, son. Trithium will welcome us with open arms or he will banish me back to the sea." Bluebeard's voice came in a deep, husky rasp. "If there is one thing I never want again; it is to be banished to the sea."

"What exactly does that mean?" Kilian asked before he could stop himself. He pinched the soft spot between his thumb and forefinger to make himself think before asking questions. Bluebeard was always more willing to answer thoughtful questions than he was to answer Kilian's streaming thoughts.

Sighing, Bluebeard grumbled, "It means that I won't be able to take the form of a man, Kilian."

"Aren't you a merman?" Kilian asked incredulously.

"I am," Bluebeard said with annoyance. "But most of our people choose to switch between their tail and their legs. It's why we've built Ula Una in two parts. We're on the human side right now, but the other side of the city is encased in water. Only the city's center has both options available in the same space. It's why the merkings have always chosen it as their place of power."

Kilian poked his finger at the translucent barrier. "How are these maintained? Doesn't it take to much energy to keep the barrier in place?" The surface of the barrier rippled like a bubble about to pop. Kilian ignored the ripples undulating across the barrier. He pushed his finger further into the barrier. The smooth, bubble-like material stretched into the shape of

Kilian's pointed finger before snapping back into place once he removed his hand.

"They do, but we have a designated team of merfolk who keep the barrier in place. Collectively, they use their magic to power the entire city of Ula Una and all of its environs." Nodding his head, Kilian swiped his hand against the barrier. It reverberated, but did not break. "Has anyone ever punctured it before?"

Bluebeard stopped in his tracks and turned his face until they were eye-level with one another. He stuck his pointer finger out and tapped Kilian on the forehead before saying, "It's happened once. I don't suggest we make the same mistakes your father did."

"My father!" Kilian gasped. "Why would he—"

"I asked him to," Bluebeard interjected. "We needed to leave the city fast. Your father knew the best way to do so was to collapse the wall, so he did."

Kilian's mouth gaped as he considered Bluebeard's words. He had almost formulated his next question when Saraphina cut in by saying, "Your father was the most deliciously mischievous person I've ever met. All the mermaids wanted to keep him for their own. Of course, your father would have none of it. He only had eyes—"

"Yes," Bluebeard said, "he did." He coughed into the back of his hand and a glob of thick white spittle landed on his skin. Kilian watched as Bluebeard wiped the goo onto his pant leg.

"Pity she turned out the way she did," Saraphina pushed, "Nathanial may well still have been alive if it hadn't been for her."

Caught off guard, Kilian turned to stare at Saraphina. "My father died in an accident," he said quickly.

"Is that what they told you?" she asked in a sickly-sweet tone. "You don't actually believe that one of the greatest sorcerers of his time could die from a mere accident, do you?"

She peered over at Kilian, a penetrating look on her face. Kilian's stomach did somersaults as he thought about her words. Old doubts shoved their way to the forefront of Kilian's thoughts.

"What do you know?" Kilian demanded as he took a step towards Saraphina. His eyes burned and he found himself hungering for his ax. With it, he knew that he could face any challenge. Without it, he felt like a weak little boy still searching for his purpose. It had been four years since he'd walked with his family to the Light's Well and drank of its water. His time of awakening was quickly coming to an end and Kilian felt no closer to discovering his destiny than he did when he'd first set out with Bluebeard. He leaned in towards her, his brows knit together and a scowl spread across his face. Kilian growled softly as he peered into Saraphina's eyes.

She did not cower before him the way he had anticipated.
Instead, Saraphina winked at him. Aghast, Kilian leaned away from her. His entire body had gone numb and he found it difficult to concentrate. The sound of her tinkling, melodic laugh clawed at his senses, dragging him out of his own thoughts.

"Poor Kilian Clearwater. Such a broken boy," Saraphina leered at him as she spoke. "Your father would have been so disappointed in you." She emphasized the 'so' as she spoke, her voice lingering on its single syllable. Her chortle turned into a harsh bark as she pulled against her restraints so that her face was mere inches away from Kilian's. "Your father wanted so much for you. That's why he stole you away—"

"Enough," Bluebeard shouted as he yanked against Saraphina's chains. Her neck crunched as he pulled her away from Kilian. Tears swelled in her eyes from the pain, but she maintained the amused, hard look on her face as she continued to stare Kilian down.

"Ignore her," Bluebeard said as he turned his back on Kilian and began walking down the path once more. Kilian shared a glance with Alex, but Kilian found that he couldn't discern Alex's expression. Alex shrugged at Kilian as he, too, began walking down the path once more. Kilian stood in the middle of the tunnel for half a heartbeat. Sighing heavily, he began to trail after the others in silence.

***

The tunnel began ascending upwards in a steep slope. From what Kilian could tell, the massive building looming at the top of the incline was in the middle of the web of tunnels. Unlike the adjacent buildings which were made of pearl, this one glowed a soft golden color. Waves of light undulated across the building's smooth surface in semi-constant patterns. Great turrets soared upwards until their points nearly touched the magical barrier above. Music floated on chilled air the higher they climbed. Kilian could almost imagine that he was at the heart of the ocean.

Carvings depicting ocean-life, including merfolk, spread across a set of double doors such that Kilian couldn't tell where one image began and the next ended. The frieze seemed to move with wavering light and Kilian found himself believing that the sculptures were alive. His mouth gaped as he pushed past Bluebeard and ran up the remainder of the incline. He pressed his face against the door, trying to see if the images would stop moving if he blocked out the light. Holding his breath, Kilian peered at the sculptures with one eye. A gold-plated fish wiggled in front of him, as if it were swimming. Kilian gasped and pulled away from the sculptures. His hands, slick with sweat, clenched as he turned to look at Bluebeard and Saraphina.

Saraphina smirked at him, a knowing look in her gaze. The left side of her lips pulled up, revealing the sharp teeth hidden beneath her lips. She snarled at him before Bluebeard jerked her chain. Kilian watched as Saraphina's eyes widened and she gasped for air. She looked like a pitiful, broken girl as she stretched her arms out to him. He remembered how safe he'd felt with her when he'd arrived to her lair. The sound of her voice filled his mind as he continued to stare at her. Yet, he remained locked in place. She writhed in pain, yet Kilian couldn't find it within himself to make any move to help her. It was as if he were standing in the courtyard back in Khaeleph. He had felt helpless then just as he did now, though he was not entirely sure why he felt the way he did. Saraphina's eyes reddened the longer Bluebeard held the chain firmly against her throat. Her body began convulsing uncontrollably and her mouth gaped open. Kilian could hear a faint hiss as she attempted to suck in air through her pinched off throat. He clenched his fist to stop himself from lunging at Bluebeard.

The old captain frowned at Kilian as he released his hold on Saraphina's chains. He shoved past Kilian so that he was standing squarely on the miniature landing before the stairs. As soon as Bluebeard's feet were firmly planted on the golden platform, the set of double doors swung open with a loud creaking sound. A cold blast of air pummeled against them followed by a loud whooshing sound. The breeze carried the mixed scent of dead sea creatures and new life. The dichotomy between these two scents plunged into Kilian like a punch to the gut. He staggered slightly as the breeze buffeted against him. He turned towards Alex, who gripped a dagger firmly in his hand. Fear rolled off of Alex like the stench of a rotting corpse. It made Kilian shiver. *This can't be right*, Kilian thought as he looked from Bluebeard to Alex. Kilian watched as Alex slinked up to where Bluebeard stood.

"This is not how it was before, Bluebeard," Alex whispered. He hunched his shoulders and let his greasy hair fall into his eyes as musical notes echoed through the open doors. Kilian looked past Bluebeard and Alex into pure darkness. Not even the hall lamps had been lit to provide light for travelers entering the enormous structure. "We can't be here," Alex said, his voice full of fear as he gripped Bluebeard on the arm. "Something's wrong, Bluebeard. You must feel it."

There was a hint of panic in Alex's voice that made Kilian's stomach churn. The golden fish and merfolk carved into the doors had vanished. Kilian didn't remember seeing them swim away, but they must have. *Or they hadn't been real at all*, he thought with a sense of panic. *Is it possible that she's manipulating my thoughts like she did before?* he wondered as he came to stand next to Alex.

"Bah," Bluebeard huffed as he pulled his arm out of Alex's grasp.

"You've been down here too long, Alex. You've lost sight…"

Alex released a raging cry as he swung his dagger straight at Saraphina's chest. Bluebeard blocked him with a single flick of his wrist. Alex pounded his hand against his chest and took on a stance that Kilian had never seen before. Alex turned his body so that only half of him was visible. He clutched his dagger in a steady hand. Feigning left, Alex slipped beneath Bluebeard's outstretched arm as he ducked and rolled closer to Saraphina. He brought his blade up as if to catch her beneath the throat.

But she wasn't there anymore. Alex sliced through thin air with his blade, his eyes ablaze. He swiped his blade in Bluebeard's direction, wildly searching for Saraphina.

"Oh, my poor, dear boy," Saraphina's musical voice whispered from within the building. Torches on the walls lit the full length of corridor to where she stood. They cast a golden sheen across the hallway. Saraphina's sharp teeth gleamed in the reflected golden light. To Kilian, she looked like one of the statues that had been etched into doors. She stood with her hands on her hips and glared at the three men. The chain still circled her neck, but Bluebeard no longer held the other end.

How did she get away from Bluebeard? Kilian thought as he stared up at the woman. Something felt entirely off to him. He shot a quick glance at Bluebeard, but the captain was whispering to Alex in a rushed whisper. Kilian could not understand what the older man was saying.

"Alex," Saraphina cooed, "it was such a pleasure keeping you these past years. I so enjoyed our time together." She smiled broadly so that the three men standing just outside of the building could see the full effect of her teeth.

Alex turned to face her, his face a scowl. He took one step towards her, his dagger still raised.

She fled.

Kilian had never seen someone move as quickly as Saraphina did in that moment. She bolted down the corridor in such a fast stride that Kilian barely saw the train of her dress before she had disappeared into depths of the building. Torchlight trailed after her, leaving them a guided path to follow.

Bluebeard placed one massive hand on Alex's shoulder. "You must learn to control your anger, Alex," he said simply before releasing the man and following Saraphina into the building.

The corridor was eerily silent as the three men followed the torchlit path. Kilian suspected that Bluebeard didn't need the torchlight to know where to take them. He was one of them, after all. The thought that Bluebeard had hidden his true nature from Kilian for the past two and half years made Kilian's blood boil. He should have known that his mentor was more than what he seemed. The insecurities he had felt during his first few months with Bluebeard resurfaced and he wondered, not for the first time, if his family really were safe without him there to protect them.

They met no one on their trek through the building. At one point, Kilian could hear the sound of music wafting through a different hallway, but Bluebeard silently shook his head and led them down a different path. The air in the hallways felt dense and wet, as if it were about to rain. The scent of fish and ocean air attacked his senses. Large golden statues lined the walls; they depicted sea creatures similar to the gold-plated designs that had been etched into the double-doors at the entrance to the building. They gleamed as if recently polished. Kilian had the unsettling sensation that the statues' gazes followed them as they crept past in silence.

Kilian bit his tongue to stop himself from crying out when one of the statues fell to the ground in front of him. The loud metal clanked against the stone floor. Bluebeard cast an angry eye upon him as he bent down and inspected the statue. Its left arm had broken off from the fall, but the rest of it was still intact. Bluebeard paled when the statue unexpectedly blinked at him. Kilian watched in horror as Bluebeard drew his sword and slammed the hilt of it into the statue's face over and over again until the only thing left was golden dust.

"Let us not tarry here any longer," Bluebeard whispered. He seemed distracted to Kilian as he squinted his eyes and looked down the corridor they had just passed through. Kilian turned to do the same, but Bluebeard grasped his arm and tugged him over the broken statue.

They jogged down the hallway, Bluebeard turning corners so rapidly that Kilian found it difficult to keep up with the captain. Alex remained at the rear, his dagger still drawn. Kilian could feel his hot breath on his neck as they raced through the building. Suddenly, Bluebeard stopped running. Kilian tried to stop his momentum from carrying him forward, but the floors were too slick and he was moving too fast. He slammed into Bluebeard with enough force to drive them both to the floor. Kilian banged his head against the ground; red light flashed through his vision and a pounding headache followed.

Bluebeard glared at him as he withdrew from their spot on the floor. Kilian cringed under the older man's gaze.

"Sorry," he whispered under his breath. Bluebeard turned away from him and Kilian wasn't sure if the older man simply hadn't heard him speak or if he had chosen to ignore Kilian altogether.

Alex strode up next to them. His face was amused as he stretched out a hand and helped Kilian rise up from the ground. The gesture surprised Kilian and he smiled at Alex in gratitude. Alex did not return the smile. Rather, he walked up to a set of doors that Kilian had not noticed before.

They were a mixture of gold, pearl, and tarnished green. Torchlight cast shadows on the doors, but Kilian could see that the same figures he had seen etched into the doorways at the entrance of the building had been turned into sculptures here. They seemed to sway in the flickering light. A loud humming sound could be heard on the other side of the door. Kilian gulped as Bluebeard strode forward and gently pushed the doors open.

Sea water rushed into the corridor. It climbed to Kilian's knees before stopping. Fish flopped in the water and wriggled past him. Musical voices sang in the massive room before them. Bluebeard strode into the room with a confident walk that Kilian tried to mirror as he followed the captain. Alex trailed behind them.

Kilian's eyes widened as they entered the room. The left side of the room was covered with plush chairs. Surprisingly, the chairs were dry. Kilian wondered at this, but said nothing.

Side tables laden with food stood between every two chairs. Men and women sat or milled about the room. They were, by far, the most beautiful people Kilian had ever seen. Their lean, powerful bodies were covered in sheer cloth that glimmered slightly in the light filtering in through the ceiling. They all had long, flowing hair in a variety of shades and colors. They stared at the three newcomers with mixed expressions of curiosity and hostility. Kilian felt his insides go cold as one of them—a woman with scarlet red hair wearing a sea foam green dress— smiled at him. Her pointed teeth snapped as she turned to one of the men sitting beside her and spoke to him. Kilian could not hear what she said.

On the right side of the room was a curved magical bubble that stretched three-quarters of the way up the walls. Water sloshed over the top of the barrier as whatever it contained breached and swatted a massive tail against the surface. Kilian could see the swirl of water as several creatures swam at a rapid pace.

A large throne stood in the middle of the room. Bones gilded in gold crisscrossed their way into forming a back to the enormous chair. A skull, full of rows of sharp teeth gleamed from the top of the back. Kilian's stomach felt queasy as he saw that there were smaller skulls—some that barely looked to be the size of a child's head—covering the legs of the chair.

A merman with a long, rainbow colored tail reclined in the chair. His bronzed, muscular body was covered in an assortment of tattoos and his blue hair was plaited into three braids. His blue eyes looked familiar as Kilian stared into them. He wore a golden ring on his middle finger that glowed softly. Thousands of small, sparkling chips seemed to be embedded within the blue stone at the ring's center. Upon the man's brow rested a thin circlet of gold with yet another sparkling blue gem embedded in its center.

Kilian gulped as he noticed a stocky, golden trident leaning against the throne. This must be King Trithium, Kilian thought as he, Bluebeard, and Alex stood close to one another in the room. Kilian felt the eyes of every merperson in the room on him. The sensation made his mind race and his hands clench. Hints of red blurred his peripheral vision. Not for the first time, Kilian longed to have his ax within his grasp once more. He silently cursed himself for ever putting it on Bitey's back instead of carrying it himself.

Kilian froze as the merking locked his eyes upon him. Uncontrollably, Kilian shook as King Trithium slowly stood from the throne. His tail glowed in a swirling cloud of purples, greens, and blues. By the time the mist had faded, he stood on two legs and began to stride towards Bluebeard. The king's face broke out into a large smile as he embraced Bluebeard and patted him on the back.

"It has been too long, my friend," he said. His voice was smooth and contained a lilt to it that made Kilian sleepy.

Bluebeard stood awkwardly with his hands clenched at his sides. He didn't embrace the king. Instead, his back straightened as King Trithium continued to embrace him. Kilian found himself wondering what their relationship had been, since Bluebeard had obviously been betrothed to the king's cousin in their younger days.

Kilian found it difficult to determine exactly what age the king was. His skin was smooth without any wrinkles. Yet, when Kilian looked into the man's eyes, he saw a dark wisdom there that spoke of old age. He must use the same magic Bluebeard does to stay alive, Kilian thought, the same magic my father used. The thought irked him. For the past two years, he had attempted—without success—to forget that his father had also stolen the energy out of people in order to stay young. Clenching his jaw, Kilian ground his teeth and waited.

Finally, the king pulled away from Bluebeard and looked into the captain's face. He was still smiling, yet the smile did not meet his eyes. From the corner of Kilian's eye, he could see that Alex still clutched his dagger in his hand. He held it up in front of him, as if he were ready to attack at any moment. He scowled at Kilian when he caught him looking in his direction and dropped his hands down to his waist.

"Reginald, come. Let us share a table together and discuss why you have returned to us after all these years," King Trithium spoke in a deep tenor.

"Of course, my king," Bluebeard responded as he bowed towards the king.

"You needn't call me that, Reginald. We are friends after all, aren't we? Trithium will do just as well." His voice carried the notes of a threat in them and Kilian shuddered slightly as Bluebeard bowed once more. The king's gaze flicked towards Kilian, but he still did not acknowledge either Kilian or Alex.

"Of course, Trithium," Bluebeard responded wryly.

The king clapped his hands and his attendants quickly brought out tables and chairs. Bluebeard and his company sat at one of the tables as dishes laden with food were set before them. Kilian sniffed at the food. It smelled of seaweed and fish.

"The merfolk only eat what they can salvage from the sea," Bluebeard muttered towards Kilian. "I never did enjoy the food down here half as much as I did what can be prepared above the sea." He grimaced as he plopped a dollop of something green and squishy onto his plate. Despite Kilian's hunger, the smell and texture of the food gave him pause.

"Are you sure it's safe to eat?" he asked Bluebeard. He glanced around the table hoping that no one had heard his question.

"'Course it is, Kilian. We aren't barbarians. Us merfolk are known for our cuisine," Bluebeard scoffed. Kilian could tell from his voice that he was offended. His cheeks flamed brilliant pink.

"Sorry," he muttered, though he didn't expect Bluebeard to respond. The older man didn't and so Kilian quickly took a bite of the green goo he'd also dolloped on his plate. It tasted exactly how it looked. It was all Kilian could do to stop himself from gagging.

"Tell me, Reginald, what brings you back to Ula Una after all these years? I thought that, considering the last time you set foot in this land, you would never return again," he sipped on a glass of green liquid as he spoke. Smacking his lips with contentment, the king continued, "It appears that I have misjudged you yet again."

Bluebeard cleared his throat in what was an obvious way to delay answering the king. Kilian froze as he noticed that Bluebeard was clenching and unclenching his fist beneath the table.

"It was never my intention to return," he finally said.

"And yet here you are," King Trithium responded, his voice cold. Kilian felt the hairs on his arm stand on end as the king continued, "Tell me why, Reginald."

"I think you know the answer to that one already," Bluebeard said calmly as he took a bite of a fishy mush.

King Trithium's eyes flashed with anger as he regarded the captain. "You will tell me the truth, Reginald, or I will make action against you."

The room fell silent as all eyes turned to face Bluebeard. Kilian had the unsettling sensation that, if King Trithium gave the command, each and every one of the merfolk sharing the table with them now would attack.

"I would have thought it was obvious, Trithium," Bluebeard paused momentary as he, too, sipped at the thick green liquid in his glass. "I am here for me throne."

A collective gasp passed through the room. The sound of splashing water drew Kilian's attention. At least a dozen merfolk rose out of the tank behind them. Their tails glowed in different shades of color before turning into legs. They rushed forward and came to stand behind Bluebeard. He nodded at them as they formed a line. Each one carried a different type of weapon. Unlike the neatly groomed merfolk who had sat around King Trithium when they'd entered the throne room, the merfolk who emerged from the water wore ragged clothing and wild, tangled hair.

"It is not your throne," Trithium said through gritted teeth, "Or have you forgotten that I won that battle?" he sneered at Bluebeard as he spoke.

"That was many years ago," Bluebeard said softly, "and under different circumstances."

Trithium scoffed. He looked like a spoiled teenager who had never been told 'no' before as he glared at Bluebeard from across the table.

"It isn't your throne!" he whined.

Bluebeard laughed, but his voice turned hard as he responded, "It has always been me throne, Trithium, even if I let you keep it warm for me these past sixty years."

Trithium's face turned a putrid purple. His eyes seemed to pop from his face as he pointed a shaking finger in Bluebeard's direction. Words failed him as he opened his mouth to speak. He started, then stopped multiple times before he finally got out, "Insolent fool."

Bluebeard only laughed harder at the insult. The wall of merfolk standing behind him lifted their weapons as if to strike, though Kilian wasn't sure whom they would set their sights on.

"Settle down, Trithium, I am only reminding you of what could be," Bluebeard said as a smile crept across his face. "I didn't want the throne then and I still don't want it now."

Trithium seemed to relax at these words, but only slightly. His eyes flicked towards Kilian again. This time they held a look of contempt in them.

"Then why are you here," Trithium asked in a childish timbre.

"I need you to grant us access to Malmadi."

The merfolk gasped once more, though this time Kilian detected it was more out of fear than shock.

"You know better than anyone that none are allowed to enter his lair, Reginald. It was, after all, how your good father died."

"Yes," Bluebeard said slowly, "it was. And now I've come to claim my vengeance upon him."

Nervous chatter filled the room as the merfolk began speaking all at once.

"I see," Trithium said. He turned his gaze on Alex and Kilian. "Tell me, Reginald, who are these delectable guests you've brought with you? Surely you wouldn't want to put them at risk in this pursuit of folly." The way he spoke made Kilian's skin crawl, but Kilian forced himself to keep his face placid.

"They chose to accompany me, knowing the risks they would have to face. Their safety is none of your concern," Bluebeard said softly.

There was a moment of silence as the two men stared each other down. Bluebeard teased his beard as he looked up at the king. Kilian wasn't sure if he fully understood the relationship, but he knew one thing for certain: King Trithium was afraid of Bluebeard. The old captain rose from his chair and, picking up his wine glass as he did so, began to walk towards Trithium. The wild merfolk followed him, though he paid them no heed. He bent down until his head was mere inches away from Trithium's and began to speak.

Just at that moment, Saraphina burst into the room. She'd changed her gown and brushed her tangled hair. Kilian noticed that the silver collar was missing from her neck as she strode over to where Bluebeard and King Trithium stood. Bruises blossomed over her neck in intricate blue and purple patterns. She did not look at Kilian or Alex as she passed them. Her gaze remained firmly locked on Bluebeard.

"Cousin," she said loudly, "this traitor has forsaken your command and returned to our lands." Her voice shook as she spoke, but Kilian could tell that most of her vibrato was for show only. "He has violated me in my own home." She lifted her chin to clearly show the markings on her skin. "I demand that you punish him in the name of the Creators."

Trithium's color paled slightly as he listened to Saraphina's words. The guards standing behind Bluebeard pointed their weapons at Saraphina. She yelped slightly as one of them shoved her spear into her back.

"Enough," Trithium shouted. The merwoman continued to jab her spear into Saraphina's back. "I said enough!" Trithium boomed.

It wasn't until Bluebeard nodded that the woman holding the spear removed her blade from Saraphina's back. The merwoman nodded at Bluebeard before taking a position behind him. She scowled at Saraphina and the king.

Bluebeard seemed to grow as he glowed a brilliant blue. He leaned in close to Trithium's ear and Kilian could barely hear the whisper of Bluebeard's voice as he spoke, "You will do as I command, Trithium, or I shall have to remind you of my position and power. Let us not forget who made the decision for you to be crowned king all those years ago."

The room turned to ice as Trithium and Bluebeard glared at each other. Trithium gave the slightest of nods and Bluebeard pulled away. He turned to face the guard of merfolk standing behind him.

"Are you willing to risk your lives for me?"

To this, they knelt on one knee and saluted him by crossing one arm over their chests. Kilian felt as if he were intruding upon something personal as he continued to watch the merfolk salute his captain. *What else is there that I don't know about this man?* Kilian pondered as the merfolk rose.

"Trithium," Saraphina whined, "You can't let him do this. He...he," she stuttered over her words as Bluebeard spun around to face her. "He robbed me of my property," she finished in huff.

"I did no such thing," Bluebeard replied calmly.

Trithium flexed his jaw muscle as he obviously tried to think of a way to appease his cousin but not offend Bluebeard at the same time. Finally, he asked, "Which property did he take from you?" Saraphina pointed in Alex and Kilian's direction. "I captured both of them from the shore. By the rights granted to me, I am their owner." She pouted as she finished speaking and batted her eyes at Trithium. "Please, cousin, don't let Bluebeard take away that which is mine."

Trithium patted her on the shoulder as he looked over Alex and then Kilian from head to toe. "Cousin, they are little more than children. I will provide you with a better catch than these."

Saraphina stomped her foot loudly, clearly not caring who saw or heard her outburst. "But I want them!" she shouted. Her cheeks flushed a deep scarlet as she spoke. "You're the KING, Trithium. It's time you started acting like it. Think what your father would have thought had he seen you now."

Trithium released a long, slow breath as he looked at Saraphina with sad eyes.

"Can I just say," Bluebeard said, breaking the tension in the room, "that, as I remember our law, they no longer belong to you? I seem to remember besting you, Saraphina, and claiming them as my own."

Her jaw dropped open as she regarded him. "That's... preposterous. There's nothing—"

"Oh, but there is," Bluebeard interrupted her. He motioned for one of the merfolk standing behind him to step forward. A male with arms the size of an ale keg stepped forward and bent down to listen to Bluebeard's words. His eyes widened at whatever it was that Bluebeard had said and he immediately departed from the room.

"What game are you playing at, Reginald?" Trithium asked as he took his seat upon the throne once more. Servants—Kilian wasn't sure if they were human or mer—milled about the room. They collected plates, half-eaten food, and empty chairs as they went. Bluebeard watched them with a cautious look in his eye as he approached the throne.

"No game, Trithium. You forget that I studied our law for years in preparation for holding the position you do now with so little effort."

"So little effort?" Trithium squawked. "As you gallivant about the whole of the world on your adventures, I remain here, protecting our people," he said incredulously. "Reginald," he said Bluebeard's name as if it were a thing to be disgusted by, "you cannot seriously believe that you have more responsibility than I do."

"Of course not, just more training," Bluebeard said without humor.

The guard returned within moments carrying a tome between his hands. Its cover appeared to have been carved from shell and bound together with dried seagrass. It was the strangest book Kilian had ever seen. The spine had been reinforced with what looked like mermaid scales, though Kilian didn't want to think about how these had been harvested. The guard handed the book to Bluebeard, bowing as he did so.

Bluebeard flipped delicately through the pages until he came to the one he was searching for. Trailing one finger down a line of text Kilian couldn't read, Bluebeard began reciting, "If a merman or merwoman successfully challenges and bests another, they may claim any prize they wish from that mer's hoard."

Gleefully he looked up at Saraphina. "You see, right here, it says that I may claim what I want after challenging you. You lose, Saraphina." He clapped the book shut and smiled at the king and his cousin.

"You... No!" Saraphina shouted. Her once beautiful face turned into the ugly scowl of a person who drains all the joy out of life. "They're mine!" she screamed, "MINE!"

"Tsk, tsk, Saraphina," Bluebeard said, "I expected more decorum from someone who was ALMOST the queen of Ula Una."

She sputtered, stomped her foot twice, and then finally twirled around and ran from the room. Kilian watched her go, a smile spreading across his face.

"Was that really necessary?" Trithium asked. He raised one eyebrow as he looked at Bluebeard.

"'Course it was. She always did annoy me," Bluebeard responded with a smile.

"Yes, well, she does have that effect on people," Trithium replied. Kilian could hear the hint of laughter beneath his response. "Come," he continued, "the sooner you get what you want, the sooner you can leave. I very much want things to return to normal."

King Trithium awkwardly led Bluebeard and his crew across the room and into what could only be described as a holding cell. On the far end of the room was a thick, stone door. A crank had been set up next to it with a system of pulleys. Kilian walked over to inspect the set-up and nearly collapsed from surprise.

"My father made this," he said hoarsely as he bent down to inspect the small maker's mark etched into the wood grain.

"He did," Bluebeard said as he laid a warm hand upon Kilian's back. "It was one of the reason's the old king—my uncle, mind you—decided to let us leave when I denounced the throne."

"Why'd you do it?" Kilian asked. He traced his fingers over the small scratches in the wood. It had been such a long time since he'd seen any of his father's designs; he'd almost forgotten what his father's maker's mark had looked like. The wood was smooth beneath his touch.

"Ah, well, I never really wanted to be the next ruler of Ula Una," Bluebeard stumbled over his words as he spoke. "My uncle never had any children. But, he took me under his wing as a lad after my own father died. One could say that he groomed me to be the next ruler. But, when I was a lad about your age I decided that I wanted to venture out on my own. It was exhilarating. I never went back." He kept his voice steady as he spoke, but Kilian thought he detected a hint of regret in his words.

"But you did. Come back, that is," Kilian said as he looked up into Bluebeard's face.

"Yes, I did. When my uncle was on his deathbed, I made your father and the rest of me crew come here. They gave me the strength I needed to formally break my betrothal to Saraphina and denounce the throne. The old king made me promise never to return here."

"Yes, he did, didn't he," Trithium said as he cut into the conversation. "And yet here you are. Be thankful that I didn't have my guards kill you on the spot."

"As if they could have achieved such a feat," Bluebeard roared as he turned to face the new king. "Don't forget that it was I who gifted you that crown, Trithium. Uncle would never have agreed to let you rule if it hadn't been for me."

"Bah!" King Trithium responded, "He knew I was the better choice. That's why he let you leave when he had the chance. Do you honestly believe that he would want someone like you when he could have someone like me rule after him?"

Bluebeard only looked at Trithium with a knowing expression in response. The other man gulped. Kilian watched his Adam's apple bob as he sucked down his own spit. The sight would have been comical if they hadn't been trying to accomplish the second goal.

The group of barbaric looking guards crowded in around Bluebeard and Kilian. Kilian could smell the stench of sweat and dead fish upon their bodies. In the compact room the smell was almost overwhelming and Kilian kept having to use some tidbits of his magic to keep himself from fainting from the stench.

"All we need is entrance into Malmadi's lair, Trithium. Once we have what we've come for, we'll leave."

The king's eyes flicked towards Alex and Kilian once more. "Which one of them is the chosen one?" he asked and then, pointing one boney finger at Kilian, he said, "I bet it's this one. He reacted to Nathanial's water-locking contraption the way only a son could."

He advanced upon Kilian, his eyes full of wonder. "Did your father teach you his techniques? Do you have the same skills as he did?"

Kilian shook his head. "I'm sorry, but no. I know only a little of what my father could do."

Trithium's face crumpled into a look of disappointment. "Well then, I guess the greatest payment you can give me is your death," he said gleefully as he motioned for his guards to withdraw from the small chamber. "No one survives an encounter with Malmadi. No one."

He laughed a viscous, angry laugh as he withdrew from the room himself. Kilian heard the scream of gears and thick rope straining against pressure points the door they had entered through slowly descended from the ceiling. *Another of my father's inventions*, Kilian thought as he watched themselves become trapped in the small room.

The room rumbled slightly as the door locked into place. Bluebeard's beard glowed a gentle blue as he scanned the room. Bluebeard's guards hung back, their eyes full of fear. *If they're afraid then this sea monster must be terrible*, Kilian thought as he looked up at Bluebeard. He reached for his ax before he remembered that it was still on Bitey's back. *Bitey! I certainly hope he's alright. It's been at least two days now since I first came here.* He hoped his horse had the sense to hide or make its way to the Dragonfly Inn like they had originally planned.

Bluebeard reached into the folds of his cloak and pulled out Kilian's ax. In utter disbelief, Kilian reached over and clutched the ax in his hand. "How did you—"

"I got it from Bitey before I followed you down here," Bluebeard said simply.

"But then—"

"Forgot I had it till now," Bluebeard interjected. "Sides, you didn't really need it until just now."

Kilian fumed as he stroked the handle of his ax. The smooth wood felt comfortable beneath his fingers and he felt the warmth of his ax spread up his hand and arm and through the rest of his body. He smiled.

"Shall we begin the second task?" Bluebeard asked as he placed both hands upon the crank to open the back door.

"Let's," Kilian responded.

Bluebeard twisted the wooden handle until the large stone door slowly began to lift from the floor. Dark water flooded the room. it was cold, colder than any water Kilian had ever felt before. he shivered as he it flowed past him. When it became waist high he heard the crack and saw the light of magic. Turning around, he saw that the guards had transformed their legs back into tails. They floated in battle stances Kilian didn't recognize.

He heaved in a deep breath and felt the heat of his ax in his fingers. The familiar tingle of anger tugged at his emotions. He pushed them down. *Not yet*, he thought, *not until I need it*. Breathing in deeply, he waited for the water to cover his head. Bluebeard created a bubble of the translucent barrier and set it upon Kilian's head. Kilian sucked in a breath and realized that is was full of air. He nodded appreciatively at Bluebeard.

The door locked into place when it reached ceiling height. Dark water poured into the room, filling it. Kilian's head scraped against the room's ceiling as the water pushed him upwards. Kilian's guard continued to cling to him, the tip of his blade pricked Kilian's back as he rocked with the waves. The entire chamber reverberated with the roar of rushing water. A sudden wave shoved him backwards with its force. Kilian slammed into his guard. Thankfully, the guard had removed his blade from Kilian's back just as the wave had crashed into them.

The chamber was now completely submersed in water. Faint green lights rippled in the darkness. Carefully, Kilian swam past the entrance to the room and into the deep, dark expanse of ocean before him. His ax cast a halo of soft light around him, but it was not bright enough to see much more than an arm length away. Spinning in a circle, Kilian tried to see where Bluebeard and the rest of the merfolk had gone. He saw nothing.

A strong current whipped past him. Kilian knew from his lessons with the twins that only something colossal could have generated enough speed and mass to produce a current like the one he had just felt. He released his barriers holding the ax's magic at bay and felt its heat course through him. His body blazed a brilliant red glow as he pushed out with his legs towards the shape swimming towards the room. The glow of his magic coursed through the water, illuminating the monster before him. Kilian gasped as the creature swung its head and swam straight at him.

Chapter Seventeen

The sea serpent's yellow and red eyes loomed above Kilian. It had a maw much like that of a snake and Kilian could see its sparkling white fangs as it unhinged its lower mandible, causing its jaw to elongate. Thinking quickly, Kilian tried to swim to one side of the creature, but it whipped its tail around, blocking his path. Kilian calculated that the creature's body must have been at least fifteen feet long and four feet in diameter; however, it was difficult to tell as the creature weaved through the water.

The bubble Bluebeard had created helped him to breath, but its translucent barrier distorted everything around him. Kilian found it increasingly difficult to see as the bubble fogged from his hot breath. The tail shot past his leg, leaving a trail of air bubbles in its wake. Kilian pumped his legs as he tried to see where the creature's head was.

Kilian felt only horror when he finally found Malmadi's head. His horror quickly turned to shame as he felt the tell-tale heat of his own waste fill his trousers. He closed his eyes. If he could face the Queen of Siguila and win, then he could face this beast. He breathed in deeply and let his mind clear as he calculated his next moves.

Malmadi floated maybe six feet above Kilian. The giant serpent's jaw stretched down past the third row of designs on its body. Kilian could clearly see its sparkling fangs in the dim light of his ax. The serpent's split tongue flicked in the water with sharp, jerky movements as it regarded Kilian with a cold, unrelenting gaze. The tongue was entirely black except for a thin, luminescent stripe of red down its center. Kilian looked all around him, trying to find a place that he could hide, but all he saw was open water. *Where's Bluebeard*, he thought frantically as the magic in his ax began to wane and the red glow of its magic faded.

Shaking his head, Kilian forced himself to focus on the task at hand. The creature still floated above him. It seemed to be waiting for something, but Kilian wasn't entirely sure what the serpent wanted. Its head weaved through the water in a consistent pattern. Kilian found it increasingly difficult to concentrate on anything except for the serpent's head. His eyes began to droop the longer he stared at the beast. Yawning, Kilian released the tension he had been carrying and let his body float in the water.

He smiled as he felt slightly warm waves gently rock him. His eyes drooped until they slowly closed. His breathing slowed as he began to envision Tavia nestled against him. Her long arms cradled his head as she gently kissed him on the forehead. Kilian released a massive sigh as his shoulders sagged and he let the water continue to rock him to and fro. Tavia clutched his hand in hers. Her hand was warm and soft. It reminded Kilian of down from a newborn chick or the fur of a kitten. He rubbed his thumb over her knuckles.

No, not knuckles. The thought passed fleetingly through Kilian's mind as he continued to grasp Tavia's hand in his. Still, the nagging thought pressed in upon him. He clutched at her hand, trying to examine it. Her hand was twined with brass and leather. The nagging sensation at the back of Kilian's mind tugged at him. *This isn't right.* He pressed in on her skin. It didn't budge. Kilian cried out in frustration as his muddled mind desperately tried to sift through its thoughts.

Kilian's vision went black. A coldness spread through his body and, when he tried to move, it felt as if he were paralyzed from the head down. He screamed, but no sound came from his rapidly tightening chest. Kilian attempted to scream again. The darkness surrounded him on all sides. His heart hammered in his chest and he felt a tightness there that he never had before. His body began to convulse.

Kilian forced himself to concentrate on his breathing. *Breathe in. Breathe out. Breathe in.* His mind began to clear as his body ached from the spasms. *Breathe out. Breathe in.* He clasped his ax in one hand. Visions of Tavia swept through his mind as he forced his eyes to open. *Breathe out.* The bubble Bluebeard had given him was shrinking. Tiny cracks had formed on the translucent barrier. *Breathe in.* Struggling, Kilian moved one finger and then another. Slowly, he moved onto lifting his ax. *Breathe out.*

His ax began to burn in his hands as he held it out in front of him. It was as if the weapon had been stoked in a fire. Despite being under water, Kilian could feel the hot fire of blisters begin to spread across his palm. Kilian dropped the ax from his hands and clung to his injured hand. It ached as he traced the line of blisters still spreading across his skin. Kilian cursed loudly as one of the blisters popped, oozing a tendril of white puss. His training kicking in, Kilian ripped a length of his shirt off and quickly wrapped the wound in cloth. The bandage was waterlogged and difficult to tie one handed, but Kilian hoped that it would be enough to stave off further injury.

As the adrenaline from his pain dissipated, Kilian realized that a faint red glow was filtering through the water directly in front of his face. In the time it took Kilian to bandage his hand, he had completely forgotten about his ax. Yet, there it was, suspended in the water as if it were being held by some invisible force. It vibrated so quickly that all Kilian could see was a blur of red light shaking in the water. His mind felt muddled as he stared at the ax in disbelief. His boot-clad feet felt heavy as he kicked his body closer to the ax.

It began to shake more violently and inconsistently. Kilian thought he could hear the hum of its power vibrating through the water. He could certainly feel the pulse of magic the closer he got to the ax. He reached out his hand—his good one—and desperately tried to grasp the ax's handle. Cold water became warm the closer his fingers got to the weapon. And then, almost as if the Creators themselves were playing a bad joke on him, his hand passed through empty water and the soft red glow disappeared.

In that instant, Kilian felt like the small, scared child he had been when he'd found his father's body in the field behind their cottage. He'd been alone then, just as he was now. He needed that ax. It was all he had left to call his own. And he had dropped it. He had let that power go. Kilian's resolve crumpled along with his confidence.

Kilian kicked as he twisted around in the water, desperately searching for any sign of that soft red glow. It was nowhere to be found. His legs ached from the constant movement and the weight of his boots. He tried flexing his injured hand. The fingers still moved, but only enough to know that he should be able to retain function.

The whooshing of water and the crackle of air bubbles startled him. Two yellow eyes blinked at him in the darkness as the red-striped tongue flicked in the water mere inches from Kilian's nose. *How did it move so quickly?* Kilian thought as he propelled himself backward. His body slammed into a solid, hard mass. Reaching one hand down, Kilian felt the smooth, sharp scales of the sea serpent's body as it wound its length around him. Kilian kicked with all his might, forcing his body upwards. His heavy boots lagged, pulling him down with every kick. Kilian screamed into the bubble and his muscles burned with the force he pushed into them.

Malmadi's body twisted around him, tightening. *Where is Bluebeard!* Kilian thought as he scrambled to identify a way, any way for him to escape the monster's clutches. The snake's jaw hung long and menacing in front of Kilian's face. It moved down, closer to Kilian's head. Already Kilian could feel the fangs sinking into his body. He could sense the pain that was about to overwhelm his body. He thought about his mother and siblings. He thought about the questions still left unanswered. He thought about Tavia.

Tavia. The name rested on his mind like a soft blanket on a cold winter night. And then anger returned.

Kilian looked beyond Malmadi's open mouth and saw the tiniest glint of a purple light emanating from the creature's back. It was then that Kilian remembered what Bluebeard had said about his second challenge.

"There's a sword!" Kilian shouted just as Malmadi's maw closed in around him.

The bubble Bluebeard had given him burst as Kilian's entire body was devoured in a single gulp by the giant sea serpent. The serpent's mouth was noxious. Slime coated his body as he felt the serpent's muscles forcing him down it's long throat. The luminescent stripe of the serpent's tongue glowed in the otherwise dark enclosure of the monster's mouth. The muscles constricted and Kilian heard his bones crack as he was compressed and pushed deeper into the bowls of the beast.

Kilian's mind began pumping through different scenarios he could use to escape. His arms were pressed tightly to this sides and the pressure of the serpent's body made wiggling even in the slightest bit nearly impossible. The muscles constricted again and he felt his body slide further down. He knew he couldn't rely on Bluebeard or Alex to save him, not this time. They had disappeared along with the band of wild merfolk who remained loyal to Bluebeard. Frustration and self-pity needled their way into Kilian's thoughts as he tried to inch his hand-his bad one—closer to his boot. He'd left a dagger there and he knew that if he were just able to reach it that he would be able to gut Malmadi from the inside out.

The serpent's muscles constricted again. This time Kilian felt the sting of acid as his face was shoved into a small puddle of slime. Kilian was cold, wet, and the slime coating his face made it impossible for him to open his eyes without the substance sliding into them. The serpent's muscles constricted again as an afterthought. Kilian heard the small pop and felt the rushing pain of his shoulder being dislocated. He gasped in pain and was rewarded with a mouthful of rotten-tasting slime. He gagged, but forced himself to keep his mouth closed for fear of inhaling more of the putrid goo. Lifting his head as much as the compressed space would allow, Kilian pressed his head against the top of the serpent's belly. It was soft here with thick bands of a hard, sinewy tissue that seemed to wrap around the serpent's entire body. *Odd*, Kilian thought.

The pain in his shoulder flamed as he put every ounce of strength he had remaining into plunging his dislocated shoulder against the serpent's body. His fingers grazed the top of his boot. *My dagger.* The vague thought meandered through his mind as he breathed in deeply. He held his breath as long as he could, dreading what he would have to do next. Breathing out sharply, Kilian stretched his hand out as far as it would go. This time, his fingers trailed across the hilt of his dagger. The metal was warm to the touch and covered in the same slime that covered the rest of his body, but Kilian didn't care. He silently cried out in joy as he repeated the motion one final time. Pain engulfed him as he felt the tendons in his arm pull and his muscles ache. Gritting his teeth, Kilian forced himself to keep stretching. Breathing became more difficult as the snake's muscles constricted again. The force of the constriction pushed Kilian's arm down, shoving it even further out of socket. His fingers slid across the hilt and desperately clutched the handle.

Weak with pain and a mind fuzzy from a lack of oxygen, Kilian pressed the small blade of his dagger against the serpent's intestinal lining and waited for the muscles to constrict once more. He knew the force of the constriction could do what he would not be able to. It did not take long. Kilian's head was slammed into the pool of slime, his nostrils filling with the thick, rotting sludge. He felt the pressure of his blade pressing against the creature's flesh and the sudden give as his blade cut a small opening. The pressure compressing his body instantly lessened as he clumsily slid the blade further along the creature's body. The constrictions stopped and were replaced with frantic squirming as the serpent whipped about in pain. The lack of compression gave Kilian the space he needed to roll over.

Using his still good arm, Kilian tore at the opening, widening it enough for him to slip his head out and into the water. He still couldn't breathe, but the water cleansed his face of the slime and he could once again open his eyes. Using all his might, Kilian kicked with his legs and pressed his good arm against the serpent's flesh as he pushed himself out its stomach. The serpent hissed in pain as a cloud of dark blood formed a cloud around Kilian. Without using his arms, Kilian slowly floated away from the serpent. Holding his dagger close to his chest Kilian began planning his next move. He needed to find that glimmer of purple again. And he needed to wrench the Labrys Sword free from the serpent's heart.

Throughout all his days of training and the beatings he'd undergone during his time in Siguila, Kilian had never been as sore as he was now. Thoughts seemed to drift through his mind in circuitous manner making it difficult for him to form a logical plan of action. His lungs burned and his head felt swollen. How Kilian wished he hadn't dropped his ax. Suddenly, as if hearing his thoughts, Kilian saw a small glimmer of red below him. Hope filled him as he propelled his body downwards, towards his lost weapon.

The glimmer of red was not his ax. Instead, as Kilian realized with disbelief and horror, the glimmer was the serpent's red-striped tongue lolling in the water. Kilian cursed as the creature reared its head and he heard a gurgling noise coming from deep within its belly. A blast of freezing cold water burst from the creature's mouth in a brilliant blue haze. It froze the water around it into solid cubes of ice. Kilian had enough presence of mind to thrust himself to the side and out of the blast's path. His injured shoulder screamed at him as he twisted his body to avoid being turned to ice. Only the long tail of his shirt turned to ice as it floated into the frozen path.

Adrenaline coursed through Kilian's body, awakening his mind and helping him to concentrate. The frozen cubes of ice glowed a soft blue that was quickly fading. However, they provided enough light that Kilian could see that the serpent had pulled back its head, revealing its body in full sight. Kilian saw the glimmer of purple in the creature's chest. Without pausing to consider the consequences of brashly rushing into a fight, Kilian pushed himself towards the creature. He zigzagged through the frozen water before finally placing his too heavy boots on a large chunk of ice. Coldness seeped from the ice through his body, causing Kilian to shiver.

He ignored his discomfort. Narrowing his eyes, Kilian could see the glimmer of purple more clearly now. The sword was stuck between the fourth and fifth row of designs on the creature's scales. Sizing up the distance between them, Kilian kicked off from the ledge of ice, using the momentum of the push to thrust him downwards. Kilian slammed into the creature's body, directly above the sword.

Kilian lunged towards the sword, dropping his dagger as he did so. With both hands, Kilian tugged on the sword's hilt. It didn't budge. Frustrated, Kilian placed both feet on the struggling sea serpent and pushed upwards with his legs. His muscles strained as his feet lifted from the beast's body. The only reason Kilian didn't float away in that moment was because of his grasp on the sword. It tethered him to the serpent in a way that he hoped the monster would never be able to break.

The serpent whipped backwards and forwards, dragging Kilian's body along with it. Kilian cried out in pain when the strain of maintaining his grip on the sword became too much. Salty water rushed into his mouth, but there was no way for Kilian to get rid of the water other than to swallow it. His stomach rolled as the salt water entered his system. Still, Kilian did not loosen his grip on the sword's hilt.

Using what little magic he had left, Kilian yanked upon the sword with all his might. The sword wiggled. Hope filled Kilian as he closed his eyes and tugged again on the sword. As the serpent thrashed about, Kilian used his own weight as leverage as he pulled on the sword. His dislocated shoulder screamed in pain as Kilian wrenched the sword with a powerful jerk. The sword erupted from the serpent's chest, showering Kilian with purple sparks. The combination of Kilian's power and the sudden release of the sword sent Kilian rocketing through the water with such speed that he couldn't stop the momentum until his body collided with one of the blocks of ice. He sucked in more salt water as he opened his mouth to scream. He heard the crunching sound of broken ice as his head slammed into the block. Kilian momentarily saw stars as he clung to the hilt of the blade as it were the one and only thing that mattered to him.

The last thing he saw as his eyes gently closed was a brilliant purple light exploding in the water before him. It seemed to sparkle as it swept around the serpent's body. A great cloud of lilac mist floated through the water towards him. Some areas of the mist were so faint that Kilian almost missed seeing them.

He opened his eyes only seconds later.

Chapter Eighteen

Eyes peered into Kilian's own. Reflexively, Kilian flung a fist at the face that belonged to those eyes. He cried out in pain and realized that he could once again breath without sucking in water. He breathed in deeply, savoring the way the oxygen helped his mind to clear. Slowly, the ache in his lungs began to subside and he began breathing normally. The eyes staring down at him blinked. They were a deep violet that sparkled in the dark water. The sword Kilian still clutched in his hands glowed faintly, casting shadows across the rest of the person's face.

The person leaned in closer to Kilian, until her head passed through the translucent barrier into the air bubble. Kilian's muddled mind struggled to make sense of what he had just seen. Their noses touched and an electric current jolted him. Blinking back tears of pain, Kilian focused on the person's face and realized that the person was a 'she.' A very attractive one, judging by the way Kilian's cheeks flushed and his eyes shot down to his feet. She giggled softly at Kilian's obvious discomfort. Cupping Kilian's chin in her hand, she forced him to look up at her.

"Thank you," she whispered, her voice a mixture of the patter of a gentle rain and the cool breeze of spring. She kissed him on the lips and Kilian felt the same electrifying heat pass through him. When she finally pulled away from him, Kilian was panting. She giggled again before leaning down to kiss him again.

Rough hands yanked him backwards and away from the woman with violet eyes. Kilian's head jerked painfully as he thudded into the solid body of whoever had pulled him backwards.

"You'll not be doing that," the unmistakable voice of Bluebeard said as he pulled the sword out of Kilian's grasp.

"Wuh?" Kilian murmured, head pounding. His gaze turned to the girl. Her pale skin gave her a ghostly pallor in the faint purple light emanating from her tail.

Bluebeard pushed Kilian into the arms of one of the wild mermen. The guard wrapped his thick, muscled arms around Kilian in a tight embrace. His dislocated shoulder sent a jolt of pain through him as the guard squeezed him. Kilian groaned, but the guard did not ease his grip.

Bluebeard growled, drawing Kilian's attention away from his pain. He and the girl seemed to be locked in some sort of standoff. The girl's shoulders were tensed and her violet eyes were narrowed into slits. Bluebeard held the purple sword in front of him. Kilian couldn't see the captain's face, but he knew it would contain a scowl.

"You are not supposed to be here," he hissed through clenched teeth. "Be gone with you."

"No, away with you," the girl said. Her voice shook as she spoke and her eyes flashed. "For centuries this has been my home, my prison. You are the one invading."

"Bah," Bluebeard said dismissively. "If it had been up to the people, you would have been exiled indefinitely. Your treachery against us all led to your imprisonment, Clara."

Kilian's gaze darted towards Bluebeard. He knew this girl. *But how?* Bluebeard's knuckles had turned white as he clutched the sword tightly in his hand.

"If we hadn't needed this sword," Bluebeard began.

"Speaking of the sword," Kilian cut in, "where is Malmadi? The last thing I remember is ripping the sword from his heart."

The guard elbowed Kilian in the gut. Kilian slumped forward, paining etched on his face as he clutched at his abdomen. Kilian heard the girl hiss. His eyes fluttered open and through blurry eyes he could see that the girl was swimming towards Bluebeard. He held the sword out before him as if it would ward her off. She paused, her eyes darting between the sword and Kilian.

"Don't hurt the boy."

"The boy will be fine."

Kilian tried to focus on the voices, but he was finding it more and more difficult to concentrate. He tried looking beyond the girl to see if Malmadi were coming for them. He saw only the dark abyss. *Why isn't the sea serpent attacking us?* Kilian found himself thinking. *It... it tried to freeze me.*

"That boy," the girl paused and Kilian looked up at her, his eyes glazed. She nodded at him before continuing, "is the one spoken of in the Hero's Prophecy. You know this is true. He wouldn't have been able to pull the sword..."

"I fail to see why this is of concern for you."

The girl stared at Bluebeard for one long moment. Her eyes bore into him and Kilian could sense that the captain's resolve was wavering. Kilian tried to remember a time in the past two and a half years when he had seen Bluebeard waver. He couldn't think of a single time.

She swam past him, her tail gliding through the water like one of the dancers Kilian had seen in the theater houses. She moved with such fluid movements that Kilian almost couldn't tell the difference between her tail and the water swishing around her. Despite his aching head, Kilian mustered enough strength to keep his eyes open. They followed her movements as she positioned herself in front of the guard who was still grasping Kilian tightly by the arm.

"Release him," she said, her voice clear and commanding. Even with his mind muddled, Kilian felt the vibrations of magic in the water.

When the guard did not immediately respond to her command, the girl said again, "I said, release him."

The force of her magic was like a ram striking against a solid door. It jolted Kilian so much that he lost consciousness for a moment. When he opened his eyes again, the guard had, indeed, released him and was cowering behind a row of other mermaids nearby. He peeked at Kilian and the girl through his hands. Kilian gulped as he realized just how powerful the girl really was. She positioned herself between Kilian and Bluebeard. Her eyes softened when she looked at Kilian, but hardened again when she turned to face the captain.

"You have forsaken your duty, Reginald. I shall not forget this in the days to come."

She held out her hand and Bluebeard, his arm shaking, laid the sword hilt first into her hand. Kilian could not see the girl's face, but he felt the wave of icy cold current pass through the water. His teeth chattered slightly and goose flesh covered his skin. The girl clasped Kilian by the arm and pulled him upwards. They zipped through the water so quickly that Kilian barely felt his stomach lift before they crested the water's surface. The translucent barrier around his head instantly burst in a spray of glittering dots. Cool air filled Kilian's lungs but also made him shiver. His skin was still covered in goose flesh and the lingering fear of Malmadi hid at the back of his mind, but he was thankful that the girl had stopped Bluebeard's guards from injuring him further.

"Who are you?" he croaked, when he finally had enough composure to form a coherent sentence.

"I have had many names over the centuries."

Kilian stared at her blankly. By no means was that the answer that he had been expecting. "Ok," he mumbled beneath his breath.

She swam closer to him. Her sparkling violet eyes stared deep into his own. Kilian had the uncomfortable sensation that she could see right through him. He blushed, but the girl barely seemed to notice. He wanted to break eye contact with her, but found that he couldn't force himself to look anywhere but into her eyes. After what felt like an eternity to him, the girl finally nodded slowly and began pulling him to the set of doors separating them from the palace.

She released Kilian's hand and began using the crank to lift the doors open. Kilian marveled at her strength. Despite her slight frame and willowy arms, she had a strength to her that was entirely unexpected. A smile spread across his face as he regarded her. She didn't seem to notice.

Clearing his throat, Kilian found himself saying, "I don't remember you being part of Bluebeard's group when we first set out to destroy Malmadi."

She glared at him at the mention of the sea serpent's name. Kilian's cheeks flushed uncontrollably.

"What I meant to say was that… where did you come from? I mean… it's not everyone who would risk their lives to stop a monster like Malmadi."

The girl scowled at him through slit eyes. Kilian gulped. He remembered the force of her magic crashing into him beneath the water's surface. He did not want to experience her wrath again.

"I mean," he fumbled for the right words, "it's just that... I just realized that I don't remember you from Bluebeard's group of soldiers."

The girl rolled her eyes at him and then said in an agitated tone, "Have you not figured it out yet, Kilian of Lunameed?"

"Figured what out? I mean…" he fumbled again, "I just can't understand why someone like you would want to join a group destined for failure."

"Except you didn't fail," she said softly. Her voice was like music to Kilian's ears. "Come now, Kilian, surely you must have recognized the signs by now."

He looked down at his hands. They were trembling from the cold. He tried to remember everything as it had happened. He glanced back at her. The faintly purple sword was slung across her back. It glowed dimly. The girl… she hadn't appeared until after he'd pulled the sword from Malmadi's heart. An idea formed in Kilian's mind.

"Were you that monster's prisoner?" he asked.

"Something like that."

Kilian searched her face but could find no hint what her response meant. He sighed heavily.

"A little help, please," she said in a huff as she struggled with the lever. Kilian swam closer to her and helped her heave the lever back until it clicked into its last notch. The door stood open. Water had rushed into the chamber, quickly filling the space.

"What now?" he asked.

"Now we wait."

"Wait?" Kilian scoffed.

"Yes," she turned to face him. "You didn't think that we would abandon the others, did you?"

Kilian blushed in spite of himself. "I just thought," he stammered as he spoke, causing the blush to deepen, "I just thought that we would be on our way."

She giggled at him. Kilian couldn't believe what he was hearing. He decidedly did not enjoy being giggled at.

"My dear Kilian, we cannot accomplish what you were meant to without the help of the captain."

"You mean Bluebeard."

"Yes, him."

"Why do we need him?"

"I thought you would have guessed by now," she pursed her lips as she spoke and provided Kilian with a look of pure annoyance. "You are the Light's Hero, aren't you?"

Kilian raised an eyebrow at her. He didn't understand her sudden annoyance with him or how she had known about the prophecy. A growing feeling of angst swelled within him.

"Who are you?" he asked. He allowed the current of the water to put a small amount of distance between them.

"Think, Kilian. Who could I be?"

"I'm not sure."

She grasped the purple sword and drew it from the sheath Kilian didn't remember her having before. It glittered in the dark water.

"You were the one who drew this sword from the heart of Malmadi," she tossed the sword between her hands. Her face was forlorn yet her eyes carried a fire in them that gave her a menacing look in the light from the sword. "Tell me, Kilian, do you know why the Creators forged weapons along with instruments of knowledge? Do you know the histories?"

Kilian fumbled. He dimly remembered Adrienne and Alex discussing the Creator's various tokens, but couldn't remember the reason each Creator had a different item. It had been more than two years since he'd been tested on this knowledge. Bluebeard certainly had never required Kilian to know.

"They, uh, all had different interests?"

She smiled at him, yet the warmth did not reach her eyes. "Yes, of course we all had different interests," she paused as she ran a finger overt the sword's glowing metal. "We all created objects of great power that represented our strengths. They also demonstrated our weaknesses," she barked the last word as if it left a bitter taste in her mouth.

Kilian stared at her. Her face was contorted in an angry snarl and she looked nothing like the beautiful woman he had first envisioned below. Another thought slowly clicked into place as he registered that she had described the Creators as 'us' and 'we.' *It can't be*, he thought. *Not again*.

"My brethren used my token against me," she spoke without emotion, yet her eyes lingered on the sword as she delicately stroked its cool metal. Her hair fluttered behind her in the water. In one swift motion, she pointed the sword at Kilian's heart. "I knew you would come."

Kilian held her gaze despite the intense desire he felt to dash away. If they had been on land, he might have. But here, treading water, Kilian knew that she could outswim him.

"W-why did they imprison you?" Kilian asked. He tried to keep his voice steady as he spoke, but knew that the stutter in his speech betrayed him. He resisted his urge to glance about the water for any sign of Bluebeard for fear that she would plunge the sword inside him.

"Jealousy," she said in a single, haughty breath. She swung the sword to and fro in a desperate, gyrating fashion. Kilian's eyes trailed the stream of purple light, his stomach tensing each time the sword passed before him. It left air bubbles in its wake.

"You're free now," he said as if to console her. She stopped swinging the sword and her arm dropped to her side. Kilian exhaled a short sigh of relief that he hoped she wouldn't notice.

"Yes," she said, her voice cold. "But for how long?"

Her eyes darted to just beyond Kilian's ear. He thought about turning his head to see what she was looking at but decided against it.

"Do you trust me?" she asked, her voice a mixture of plaintive questioning and anger.

Kilian gulped. He knew he should answer that yes, he did trust her, but somehow he couldn't quite get his voice to work.

"I think I could," he finally said after a long pause.

She nodded before reaching her free hand out and flexing her fingers. Kilian stared at her in confusion. It was like she was trying to choke the water, even though it wasn't corporeal. Her upper lip twitched as she squeezed her hand shut and twisted it slightly. Her forehead furrowed as if she were in an enormous amount of pain.

"What are you doing?" Kilian asked, worried. A thin trail of blood ran from her nose and the sword glowed so brightly that Kilian had to turn away or else be blinded.

As he turned to face the dark abyss behind him, Kilian saw the faintest flicker of red light in the distance. Squinting his eyes, Kilian leaned towards the flicker of red. It seemed to be moving at an immeasurable rate. Kilian could see a streak of red following along behind the brightest point. His body began to tingle with a familiar warmth. His eyes widened as the now streak of red sailed through the water, straight towards him.

The hilt of his ax thudded into his hand with so much force that it pushed Kilian through the water a good fifteen feet from where he had originally been treading water. As the heat of his ax spread through him, so did his resolve to accomplish the second of the tasks. Defeating—or this case rescuing—the sea serpent had been the easy part. Leaving the fortress would be another.

"A peace offering," the girl said softly.

"For what?" Kilian asked.

"For attempting to kill you."

Kilian stared at her for a half-minute before bursting into a fit of laughter.

"I think that the more accurate description would be that I attempted to kill you," Kilian stated in an amused tone.

She nodded before saying, "Still, it is best for us that you maintain your grip on that weapon. I fear that you don't treasure it the way you should." Her voice carried a reprimand in it that Kilian knew his mother would employ when vexed with him. It was the type of voice that was very rarely contradicted.

Kilian stared at the glowing red ax. "Thank you," he whispered. He looked down at the ax as he spoke and trailed his fingers over the curves of the blade. Her words caused a nagging doubt in the back of his mind. She was right; Kilian didn't honor the weapon as he should. In that moment, Kilian vowed to always revere the ax for what it was: a weapon forged by the Creators and given to him for safe keeping.

When Kilian looked back up, the girl was searching his face with an astute expression in her eyes. Kilian shuddered at the thought that she had discovered too much about him. *Maybe she really is a Creator*, Kilian thought. The thought haunted him as he opened his mouth to speak.

"Follow me," she said before he could speak. She turned around and swam towards the pressure chamber so quickly that all Kilian saw was the whir of bubbles in her wake. Seconds later Bluebeard shot past him, his massive tail flapped Kilian in the face. Kilian glared after the captain. Bluebeard, above all others, should have known that the sea serpent wasn't a monster at all. *He should have warned me*, Kilian thought angrily, *I could have killed her*. Kilian wasn't convinced this was the truth. He wasn't sure that anyone had the power to destroy the Creators. These thoughts clouded his mind as he watched the rest of Bluebeard's retinue swim into the pressure chamber. Grinding his teeth, Kilian followed them at a slow pace. The ax the girl had summoned from the depths for him sang in his hand with a fiery touch. Kilian did not know what to expect when he reentered Ula Una, but he was certain he would need his ax.

***

King Trithium sat on a dais in the middle of the throne room when Kilian and the rest of the party erupted from the pressure room in a spray of salt water. Each of the merfolk's tails sprouted into a set of legs the instant their bodies were removed from water. Kilian tried to watch how the transformation occurred, but all he could see were the bright clouds of light they emitted as their tails turned to legs. He mentally reminded himself to ask Bluebeard about the transformation once they were safely out of Ula Una. He turned his gaze towards the merfolk's king.

A small purple grape dropped from Trithium's mouth as his eyes latched onto the sparkling purple sword that the girl had dropped into a belt tied to her waist. His lips pulled into a thin, courtly smile as he examined the girl's form. Kilian didn't like how the king's eyes roamed over the girl's body. He took a step towards the dais; his clothes dripped water with every step that he took. All at once, one of Kilian's boots slid on the wet floor, causing a loud squeaking screech. King Trithium turned his attention to Kilian, his eyes cold and calculating.

"I see that you were successful, Kilian Clearwater," he said Kilian's name as if it were poison in his mouth. Kilian watched in disgust as Trithium's eyes flickered back to the girl. He recognized the look in Trithium's eye as the king studied her delicate, feminine features. "And who is this?" he asked, motioning with his hand towards the girl.

Before Kilian could respond, the girl stepped forward and bowed deeply. "My name is Clara Stinger." The sword, too long for her small stature, scraped across the floor as she bowed. The sound was jarring and made Kilian jump slightly. He could feel the tension in his shoulders mounting as he set his hand on his ax's handle. He saw that Bluebeard's hand already gripped the hilt of his massive sword. Alex, always cautious, clutched twin daggers in his hands. Kilian guessed that there were more small blades tucked into his clothing. The twins had always relied on speed and cunning to win their fights.

Turning his attention back to the king and the girl, Kilian noticed that she batted her eyes at the king in a coquettish way. Confusion filled him. *If this woman really is a Creator,* Kilian thought, *then why is she pretending to be interested in that twit of a king?* Anger coursed through his veins as another, more sinister thought popped into his mind. *Unless, of course, she really is interested in him.* Kilian flexed his fingers at the thought and set his jaw into a hard line. The longer he looked at the girl's figure, the more Kilian found himself responding to her pouted lips and lively eyes. *She's so different from Tavia,* he thought. Shame filled him as he thought her name. He couldn't believe that he had been so quick to forget her.

"It is such an honor to finally meet you." The girl's voice broke through Kilian's thoughts, pulling him back to the present moment.

"Rise," Trithium said, his voice austere. Kilian wasn't fooled. He saw how the king licked his lips slightly as he watched the girl move. Kilian's stomach dropped as he realized that, while he had let his mind wander, over fifty guards had swarmed the alcoves surrounding the room. They stood at attention with weapons drawn. Kilian frowned as he comprehended just how outnumbered their small party was compared to Trithium's forces. His ax blazed in his hand and Kilian felt the swell of its magic fill him.

The girl—Clara—straightened her back and looked Trithium straight in the eyes. Her violet gaze made the young merking's cheeks fill with color. Kilian smirked at this. He watched as the merking scrambled to regain composure. With slow, deliberate motions, Trithium stepped down from the dais and strode towards Clara. Kilian could see desire in the king's eyes. The look made Kilian's stomach squirm.

He was about to step in front of Clara when Bluebeard's hand clamped down on his shoulder. The old captain squeezed Kilian tightly before releasing his hold. Kilian could feel the anxious energy pouring from Bluebeard's body and, although Bluebeard hadn't uttered a single word, Kilian knew exactly what his mentor wanted him to do. He nodded in a swift motion that he hoped none of the guards surrounding the room noticed. The tension in the throne room was so thick that Kilian half-believed that he could see it. He sensed movement behind him, but did not remove his gaze from Trithium and Clara.

"I would have you dine with me tonight," the king was saying.

Clara giggled in an infuriating way, at least to Kilian. *If she's a Creator then she shouldn't be wasting her time with that pig*, Kilian found himself thinking. He tried to still his thoughts, but they were insistent. All memory of Tavia faded into the background as he watched the way Clara flirted with Trithium. Kilian's anger swelled.

"Ahem," he coughed loudly. The moment the sound erupted from him, he knew he had made a mistake. He felt Bluebeard and the rest of the savage mermaids standing behind him take a collective breath. Silently cursing himself, Kilian shot a quick glance at Alex. He was crouched in a defensive posture, his arms held out before him, blocking his face.

Trithium turned a disdainful glare upon Kilian. The king's face was so distorted by anger that Kilian barely recognized the once jovial features beneath the glare. He gulped, but strode forward in quick, confident steps. Although Kilian's insides went cold as the king wrenched the sword free from Clara's belt in a single loping motion, his body reacted quickly. He breathed out heavily, stilling his rapid breathing, as Trithium flipped the blade up in the air and then hurled it in Kilian's direction. Kilian ducked, but not nearly quick enough. The sword grazed the top of his head, shaving his hair down the middle in a nearly straight line. He shivered as the cold metal of the sword whipped across his skin. He heard the sword clatter to the ground behind him. *He missed*, Kilian thought before releasing a sigh of relief.

He caught Clara's gaze. Her eyes widened as she raised one staggering hand and pointed in his direction. That's when Kilian felt the warm trickle of blood sliding down his forehead. It covered his eyes and filled his nose as he breathed in deeply.

Kilian coughed and wiped at his eyes with the back of his hand. All he could see was red. All he could smell was the coppery scent of his own blood. Frantically, Kilian crouched on the ground and gently explored his head with his hands. Even without a mirror, he could tell that the skin had been stripped away from his skull.

Kilian bellowed in pain.

"Fool."

Kilian recognized the voice as Trithium's, but he couldn't quite tell how far away the king was from his position. Squinting through the blood, Kilian could see that Trithium was striding past him, towards the still glowing sword. With a ferocious growl, Kilian leapt from his crouched position and slammed into Trithium. Pain rocketed through his shoulder from the impact, but Kilian ignored it. Dropping his ax to the ground, Kilian pummeled his fist into the king's face. His knuckles cracked as his fist connected with Trithium's bones. Blood splattered him on the face, but Kilian was no longer certain to whom it belonged. All he could see was red. He pulled his fist back one last time and slammed into Trithium's cheek. He felt the skin and sinew of the king's face melt like butter beneath the force of his strike. Leaning back, Kilian took in a long, deep breath.

The roar of a fight filled his ears. He could discern men shouting and the clank of metal weapons hitting each other through the pounding of his own heart. His head ached and he could still feel the ooze of his blood as it crept out of his head wound. With slow, disjointed movements, Kilian ripped a length of cloth from his under shirt and held it up to the wound.

He jumped when a cool hand gently grasped his shoulder. Through the drying, cracked blood, Kilian could see that Clara had joined him. Her violet eyes danced with something akin to amusement. Her expression turned Kilian's stomach.

"It's alright," she cooed softly as she tugged him away from the still twitching king. Kilian, by instinct, wrapped his fingers around the handle of his ax. He instantly felt the pulse of the ax's magic course through his veins. His mind seemed to clear the longer he held it. "It's alright," Clara repeated as she rubbed his back with her free hand.

If there was one thing Kilian knew for certain, it was that it was not alright. Still, he didn't fight her when she wrapped her slender arms around his neck and hugged him close to her body.

"You did well," she whispered. There was a note of awe to her voice now.

"Kilian!" Bluebeard's voice rose above the roar of the fight. "To me!" he shouted.

Through the cloud that seemed to fill his mind, Kilian managed to push himself away from Clara and stand. His knees buckled slightly under his weight, but he felt the ax reverberate with magic. The longer he clung to his weapon, the clearer his mind became. He wiped away the remaining crust of blood from his brow and plunged himself into the battle.

Bodies pressed in around him from all sides. Kilian found it difficult to differentiate between friend and foe. Already he had cut down six of Trithium's soldiers. There was a pause in the fighting and Kilian used this time to search the fray for Bluebeard. He saw a flash of bluish-white light from his left side. Charging to the left, Kilian forced an opening within the crowd of soldiers who were fighting there. A sword bit into his right shoulder. Kilian could feel the heat of pain spread through him. Gritting his teeth, Kilian did not give the merman a chance to strike him twice. Kilian wrenched his ax up and cleaved the man's face in two. Blood spurted on him, but Kilian merely wiped it on his already too dirty sleeve.

By the time he'd reached Bluebeard the older man had cut down nearly two dozen foes. Their dead bodies formed a shallow wall around the bulky man. Kilian lithely leapt over the dead bodies and landed inside the small clearing Bluebeard had made for himself. He pressed his back against his mentor and began fighting against the soldiers who had filled in behind him.

"Where do they keep coming from?" Kilian asked in a gasp. The pain in his shoulder was making it difficult for him to catch his breath.

"Trithium must have sent for more guards the moment we arrived," Bluebeard said between swings. "He evidently did not want us to survive this encounter, even if he, himself, had to pay the ultimate sacrifice." Bluebeard paused as he swung his massive sword at an opponent. The young merman wasn't quick enough to evade being nicked by the heavy weapon. He fell to the ground with a cry as Bluebeard sliced the tendons below the knee. Kilian didn't look as he felt Bluebeard finish the assault.

Of the thirty wild merfolk who had joined them in the battle against Malmadi, twenty remained. They fought with vigor against the soldiers still streaming in from the alcoves around the room. Kilian's gaze fell on Clara. She stood amidst the battle completely unmolested by either side. A slight purple haze clung to her body. She turned to face him, her violet eyes gleaming. She smiled as her eyes met his. Kilian blinked. When he opened his eyes again, Clara had disappeared.

Chapter Nineteen

The battle ended as quickly as it had begun. Kilian's wounds seeped a steady stream of blood, though it had slowed to a trickle. His entire body ached as he wrenched his ax free from the chest of the last soldier he'd killed. In all, he estimated that he had killed nearly seventy soldiers during the battle. He'd lost count after fifty. The throne room, once opulent, now carried the scent of death and excrement as he wandered over to where King Trithium's body still lay on the ground.

He was surprised to see that the king's eyes were open and wandering about the room. Kilian bent down so that his face was mere inches from the king's. Trithium's lips moved as he stared up at the man who had smashed his face in. Kilian leaned in closer.

"Kill me," Trithium whispered, "kill me."

Kilian jerked his head away from Trithium's mouth and shook his head. Without uttering a word, Kilian strode over to Bluebeard and whispered in the old captain's ear. Bluebeard glanced over to where Trithium lay on the ground, but did not immediately respond to Kilian. Instead, he, too, walked over the broken king and bent down to listen to his whispers. He listened to Trithium for some time before slowly rising back up from the ground.

Kilian watched the exchange with an uneasy feeling in his gut. He knew Bluebeard had wanted him to wait, but he hadn't been able to stop himself from interrupting Trithium's attempt to seduce Clara. Thinking of her made Kilian scan the room for any trace of her. Since she'd disappeared in the heat of battle, Kilian had not seen any sign of her. His heart sank as he once again saw nothing to indicate where she had gone.

"You did well, son," Bluebeard said. His voice startled Kilian out his thoughts.

"I beat the king to death," Kilian said. "I didn't even have a reason to, not really. I just… couldn't control myself." His voice quivered slightly as he spoke, causing Kilian even more embarrassment.

"Was it the ax again?" Bluebeard asked.

The old captain rarely spoke about the frenzy Kilian's ax normally sent him into during battle. The question caught Kilian off-guard.

"No, it wasn't the ax," Kilian responded quickly.

Bluebeard nodded in understanding. Hesitantly, he placed one of his massive hands on Kilian's shoulder and leaned in closer.

"You are becoming a fine warrior, Kilian. Your father would have been proud."

Kilian scoffed at this. Although he hadn't heard his father's voice much over the past two years, he still remembered how kind and gentle his father had been. He couldn't imagine his father beating a man's face to pulp. He said as much to Bluebeard, but the captain waved off Kilian's complaints with a flick of his hand.

"Your father was an inventor, Kilian, but he was also a great warrior. He would've wanted you to be able to make the tough decisions. Today you did."

Kilian shrugged his shoulders and forced himself to look at where Trithium still lay on the floor.

"Did he beg you to kill him as well?" he asked, his voice a mix of petulance and curiosity.

"Yes," Bluebeard responded.

They remained silent for several moments.

Bluebeard finally broke the silence when he said, "We won't be killing him. The rest of the merfolk will follow me now that I've claimed the throne."

"You what!" Kilian asked. "When? I didn't hear you say anything."

"Just now. Trithium told me that, if I am insistent on letting him live, if I let him leave unmolested from Ula Una that he will abdicate the throne."

Kilian thought about this for a moment. It seemed irresponsible of Bluebeard to let the man who had a claim to his throne continue to live.

"That's not a very strategic answer, Bluebeard," Kilian began.

"But it is my answer," Bluebeard interrupted him. "And I won't be having you argue with me over the strategy of maintaining my rule once I take it. I gave it up once; I won't be making the same mistake again."

Kilian nodded at Bluebeard's words. He wondered how much his mentor regretted renouncing the throne in his younger years. He certainly seemed eager to reclaim the throne now.

"What about the last of my missions?" Kilian asked as he realized that Bluebeard would need to remain within Ula Una to rule.

"We will still go together, only now you will be supported by the entire force of the merfolk's military."

Kilian looked at Bluebeard in awe. "You cannot be serious," he said, his voice hoarse. "There's no way that your people will join on this quest. It's not their fight."

"It is if I say it is," Bluebeard grumbled.

"And you honestly think that these people—the people you abandoned all those years ago—will follow you now into potential destruction? You said that the Shadow Knights were the most feared creatures in all of the land."

"I know what I said," Bluebeard cut in. He eyed Kilian coldly. "I know more than you could ever hope to discern, boy. You'd better believe it."

Kilian clenched his fists as he attempted to retain some semblance of composure. Ever since Bluebeard had started drinking his days away he'd turned into a sniveling lout. Kilian chided himself for thinking so ill of his mentor, but the facts were in. Bluebeard had forced Narcon and Tavia out of their group. He had been incapable of keeping Alex among their number after Adrienne was killed. It had been Bluebeard who'd forced Kilian to leave his family behind. Kilian hadn't spoken to them in over two years, despite seeing them in the nightmares that plagued him.

"You're not a good leader," Kilian uttered before he could stop himself.

Great, he thought. *The second time in a day when I say something I shouldn't.*

Bluebeard raised his hand as if to backhand Kilian. Kilian forced himself to maintain eye contact with the older man. He narrowed his eyes as he waited for the blow that never came. Slowly, Bluebeard let his arm drop to his side.

"I know I haven't been the best these past two years, Kilian, but I promise you this: stick with me and I'll make sure you earn the favor of the Creators."

Kilian rolled his eyes. "You know, Bluebeard, I don't even know what I'm working towards. Not really. Not anymore. I thought maybe going with you would provide answers about my father. So far, all I've ended up with is more questions."

Bluebeard opened his mouth to respond but, right as he was about to speak, Alex strolled up to them and said, "So glad you found me, boys. That was exhilarating."

Bluebeard laughed. Then, as if remembering where they had left things two years ago he said, "It was good to fight with you again, Alex." His voice was gruff and Kilian had the uncanny suspicion that Bluebeard was trying to hide his sentimental side.

"Aye," Alex responded, "that it was." He smiled at Bluebeard and it was as if the years of broken friendship had melted away into nothingness.

Kilian walked away from the two men. He didn't want to be there when they began reminiscing about how great their adventures together had been. He didn't want to hear stories about his father, not from them anyway. He wanted real answers, but he knew that he wouldn't get them from Bluebeard or Alex. The wound on Kilian's head still bled, but it had slowed to such a small trickle that Kilian didn't bother to try and stop the flow anymore.

Tenderly, he reached up and felt around his head once more. A flap of skin hung from his skull. Kilian nearly vomited from the sensation of feeling the flap tug at the rest of his skin when he gently tugged on it. It wasn't exactly painful. It felt more like a dull throbbing. He momentarily thought about asking Bluebeard to heal him, but he didn't want to be beholden to the older man.

Kilian saw a small sparkle of purple light radiating through a clump of dead bodies. *The sword*, Kilian thought. He walked as nonchalantly as he could towards the glimmer of light. Two bodies lay across the sword. Kilian guessed that they had killed each other during the battle since they were from opposing sides. They each had a dagger slammed into their chests. Kilian grimaced as he rolled the bodies off of the sword and grasped the hilt in his hand.

It was surprisingly light. Although Kilian had drawn it from Malmadi's breast, he hadn't had a chance to examine the sword in detail. It was long and slender. The metal was colder than Kilian would have expected, so cold, in fact, that his fingers became numb the longer he held it. The hilt was crested with small amethyst jewels that sparkled in direct light. Kilian swung the sword through the air. It whipped through the maneuvers seamlessly. Unlike the ax, Kilian didn't sense any magic emanating from the sword.

"Its name is 'Frost,'" a small, girlish voice said. "If you wield it just so," she motioned with her hands when Kilian turned to look at the person speaking, "then you can blast a cloud of ice at any opponent!"

Kilian raised an eyebrow at the girl speaking to him. Her plump cheeks blushed profusely when she realized that she had his undivided attention.

"Is that so?" Kilian asked, a hint of amusement in his voice.

The girl standing before him had silver-blue hair that fell in ringlets around her chubby cheeks. She wore a cream-colored dress with patterns of colorful fish woven into various sections of the fabric. The girl's skin was pale and Kilian could see her veins through her skin. When she smiled, she revealed rows of long, pointed teeth. Kilian had a moment of unease. Although he had only really had interactions with a few of the merfolk, Kilian had thought that when they took human form that their teeth became more human-like. His eyes must have widened at her smile because the girl instantly snapped her lips shut and stared down at her feet.

"I'm sorry, little one," Kilian said as he bent down and stared into her eyes.

She shrugged her shoulders, but continued staring down at her feet. Kilian rubbed his chin as he contemplated ways of getting her to smile again.

"How do you know the name is Frost?" he finally asked.

The girl stole a quick glance at him, her cheeks still a vivid shade of pink. "It's in all the stories," she muttered softly.

"I see," Kilian said. "And what stories are those?" he asked. "I've never heard of swords named Frost before. Will you tell me one?"

"I can't," the girl whispered. "I'm not a storyteller."

"Ah," Kilian sighed.

The girl waited, as if expecting more of a response from Kilian. When he didn't provide any feedback, she prompted him.

"But I know a truly great one!"

Kilian flashed a smile at her. She did not return the gesture but rather took his large hand in her small one and began tugging him towards the rear doors.

"Come on!" she exclaimed as she pulled him past a group of merfolk who had fought with Bluebeard. "You have to see the stories for yourself!"

She led him through several passageways. Kilian tried to keep track of the turns, but his head was still aching and he was finding it difficult to concentrate on anything other than placing one foot in front of the other.

"This way," she whispered, almost reverently, as she led him into a narrow room with a set of statues lining one wall and a series of stained glass windows lining the other. Kilian was surprised to see that, even in the depths of the ocean, enough light filtered through the glass to cast colorful shadows about the room. The room smelled of mold and stale air. The air was cool and dusty as he stepped into the room. Grime provided a thick covering on the chairs and railing separating the walkway from the statues. Kilian noticed delicate, child-size footprints covering the floor. He glanced sideways at the girl and noticed that she was staring up at one of the windows in the center of the room. She was completely engrossed by the window and Kilian suddenly felt like an intruder in her special hideaway. Without uttering a sound, the child pointed a slender finger up at the window. She looked balefully into Kilian's face and Kilian realized that they had made it to the right place.

The first pane of the window depicted the eight Creators with their various objects. It was a classic rendering of them and Kilian glanced over it without giving it much consideration. The next pane showed one of the Creators, the one holding the sword, blessing what Kilian assumed was the first of the merfolk. Brilliant purple light burst from the sword that the Creator laid upon the figure's shoulder, as if knighting her. Kilian was surprised to see that it was a woman being honored. So many of the reports given to him of the Creators implied that they preferred men. Kilian studied the expression clearly depicted on the Creator's face. It looked almost familiar. Yet, she did not look like Clara. Kilian was certain of that.

The third pane showed a group of merfolk building Ula Una. Kilian had heard that they'd spent a century constructing the main building. Beyond that, the city was a mystery. The Creator who had blessed the merfolk was depicted with her back bent and lifting heavy stone blocks. Her hair floated as if she were submerged in water and her lavender eyes glowed. Kilian dropped the little girl's hand as he leaned towards the Creator's face. *She really does look familiar*, Kilian thought. He had the nagging sensation that he should know why.

The fourth pane depicted a great battle. Kilian wasn't sure which one. Countless merfolk lay strewn on the ocean floor, their lifeless bodies cast an eerie, dark shadow. Kilian cringed as he saw that some of the merfolk had been decapitated. Once again, the Creator was shown as helping the merfolk in their fight for survival. Her sword was drawn and it shimmered with a brightness that Kilian couldn't explain. She wore a scowl upon her face that Kilian knew, had he been facing her, would have sent chills down his spine.

The fifth and final panel portrayed the Creator being betrayed. Or, at least, that's how Kilian interpreted the artwork. Her own sword had been stolen from her by one of the other Creators. There was a look of shock mixed with misery depicted on her face. Kilian found himself drawn to her eyes. They seemed dull compared to the other images of her and Kilian wondered if this had been intentional on the artist's part. The other Creator who had stolen her sword had plunged the weapon straight through the Creator's heart.

"Oh," Kilian whispered silently as the window's hues changed from light purples, green, oranges, and yellows to dark blues, purples, and even some grays. The young girl shook her head vehemently. He opened his mouth as if to respond, but she gently flicked him on the hand and shook her head once more.

Kilian nodded and returned his gaze back to the window. Ice had formed on the place where the Creator had been betrayed. Her body writhed in pain and she seemed to disappear in a haze of mist. Light rippled through the window and Kilian almost believed that he could see the mist curling around the fading image of the Creator. The image made his chest tighten and an uneasy sadness fill him. Kilian stared at the window for several moments in complete silence.

After a considerable amount of time, the girl stood on her tiptoes and kissed Kilian on the cheek. He instantly blushed, although she didn't seem to notice. She grasped his right hand and peered into his eyes. Kilian had the uncanny sensation that he had known this little girl for far longer than he really had. Breathing in deeply, Kilian smelled the faintest scent of cinnamon. Gently, she led him by the hand from the room.

"Now you have seen," she said solemnly.

Kilian's body felt completely relaxed. His muscles were warm and supple beneath his skin and he felt happier than he had in years. *Strange*, Kilian thought.

"What was that?" Kilian asked, his voice coming out in a rush.

"That was our Lady, the Creator's shrine," the little girl responded reverently.

"I see," Kilian said. He wasn't quite sure what to say. He fumbled for the right words to say.

"The sword you carry was hers," the girl said, saving him the trouble.

He looked from the sword to the girl and back to the sword.

"How can that be?"

"You must be a dunce," she said, her voice a reprimand. "Didn't you see the window? Our Lady, the Creator's own brethren betrayed her. They were jealous of her relationship with us."

Kilian tried to remember his teachings on the merfolk. Although Kilian had been told that he would need to venture to the watery city of Ula Una, Bluebeard had been remiss in his training. Now Kilian understood why. Yet, he still wished that Bluebeard had provided him with a better history of their myths and lore.

"Why would they be jealous of her? I thought that all Creators were meant to be equal."

The little girl rolled her eyes at Kilian as her lips turned down into a deep frown. "They are equal," she said, emphasizing the 'are.' "It's just that Our Lady, the Creator took a special interest in us. Unlike the rest of the Creators who blessed all creatures of the realm, Our Lady, the Creator devoted all her time to us, her chosen race."

The girl's eyes gleamed as she spoke about the Creator and Kilian instantly felt remorseful for challenging her.

"She was our greatest champion, but she has been lost to us for centuries," the little girl paused. She heaved in an audibly deep breath before continuing, "You have returned her to us. For that I am eternally grateful."

She flashed such an enormous smile that Kilian nearly missed how sharp and pointed her teeth were. His stomach did a somersault as he realized that this little girl could chomp his hand off in one bite. His stomach seized and Kilian felt as if he were going to be sick.

"So Frost it is, then," Kilian said, a small laugh in his voice covered his nervousness. He hoped she wouldn't be able to detect his worries.

She beamed at him and Kilian's hesitation subsided.

"I'm Cordelia," she said as she stuck out her hand in a very formal way.

"Kilian Clearwater," he said as he took her hand in own and shook it. "It is a pleasure to meet you, Cordelia."

"Kilian!" a voice called from down the passageway. It drew Kilian's attention away from Cordelia as he strained to hear the next line. "Bluebeard is looking for you. You best return to the throne room."

He turned back to say goodbye to Cordelia, but she had already disappeared.

Chapter Twenty

The dead had been set to sea by the time Kilian returned to the throne room, yet the scent of death lingered in the massive room. Kilian forced himself not to think of those who had fallen as he stood before Bluebeard. Guards, both from the savage army and from Trithium's army stood at attention around Bluebeard. Trithium's rule had been weaker than Kilian had initially realized if so many of his soldiers were willing to turncoat so quickly.

"An emergency general council meeting has been called to session," Bluebeard was saying. Kilian found it difficult to focus on the captain's voice. He forced himself to watch Bluebeard's lips, hopeful that he would be able to ascertain what the older man was saying. A drizzle of red ooze ran down Kilian's cheek. He had almost forgotten his head wound during his time with Cordelia. It stung when he pressed his skin more firmly into place.

"Blast it all, Kilian!" Bluebeard muttered as he laid one hand upon Kilian's brow. Blue light flashed and Kilian felt a surge of hot energy pass through his body. He knew it was impossible, but he could have sworn that he felt his skin meld back together as his wound healed. His thoughts instantly cleared as Bluebeard withdrew his hand. It had age spots on it and the skin was paper thin.

"Thank you," Kilian said quickly. He did not want the captain to regret healing him.

"Don't thank me yet, son," Bluebeard spoke in a low growl as his eyes darted around the room. "You are going to help me reclaim my throne. I need you in top condition," he said through the corner of his mouth.

Kilian sighed. He should have known that that there was an ulterior motive for Bluebeard's kindness. The older man never healed anyone else if he could help it.

"What do you need me to do?" Kilian asked, his voice resigned.

Instead of answering, Bluebeard jerked his head towards Alex and the two of them began walking towards the pressure chamber at the back of the throne room. The purple sword—Frost—buzzed in his hand. Kilian wasn't sure if it was a warning or a sign of anticipation.

Bluebeard and Alex were engaged in quiet conversation when Kilian joined them. Their heads were pressed together and Kilian, although he tried, couldn't tell what they were saying.

"What's the plan, Bluebeard?" Kilian asked, interrupting them.

Alex glanced at Kilian, a snarl on his face. He turned and walked away from them. Kilian watched him go. He felt, well he wasn't sure what he felt. It was something between the sinking sensation of loss and turmoil of realizing a prized possession was broken.

"Once I've solidified my claim to the throne we will be leave'n for the Beyond."

Kilian's head jerked as he looked back at Bluebeard. "Wah?" Kilian instinctively said.

"Aren't cha listening, boy?" Bluebeard grumbled. "I'm going make the rest of my people accept my claim to the throne and then we will take these soldiers as an army against the Shadow Knights."

Kilian nodded slowly. He was still angry with Bluebeard. At his core, he knew that Bluebeard was not a good leader and did not deserve to be the king of the merfolk. For all his faults, he had to believe that Trithium had, at least, been a good ruler. The merfolk had followed him even after he had been assumed dead. To Kilian, that was the mark of a true leader. Bluebeard, on the other hand, had pushed all his followers away.

"I'm not sure I want to go with you, Bluebeard."

Silence. Bluebeard stared blankly at his protégé for several moments. "You can't mean that," he finally said. "Yer training's not done. There's still so much for you to learn."

"I'm sure there is," Kilian said, "I'm just not convinced that you're the one to teach me."

Bluebeard's beard began to glow a vibrant, pulsating blue. His eyes turned a hard, motionless black. The air around them turned cold and Kilian shivered.

"I'm the one who found you. I'm the one who took you away from the prison yer father created for you. You owe everything ta me!" Spittle flew from Bluebeard's mouth as he spoke, spraying Kilian with the putrid scent of his mureechi odor. Kilian crinkled his nose in disgust.

"I owe you nothing," Kilian snapped. "You need me, remember? You're the one who wants to gain favor with the Creators. You're just using me to achieve your own goal!"

The two men stared at each. Kilian's heart thumped loudly in his chest and the purple sword seemed to shake violently in his hand. It glowed a faint purple, almost washing out the blue of Bluebeard's beard.

"I think we're done here," Bluebeard finally said, his voice hoarse.

"I think we are," Kilian said. He did not break eye contact with the captain.

"I'll give you tonight to reconsider. I know you will."

"I wouldn't be so sure." With that, Kilian turned and walked away. The sword continued to hum long into the night.

***

"Kilian?" a child's voice called through his closed door. His eyes leapt open and he stared into the darkness of the room. He had wandered the corridors of Ula Una until he'd found an empty room close to what must have been the kitchen. It was warm and dry. After his argument with Bluebeard, it had been the perfect place for him to think about what his next move was going to be, now that he was leaving Bluebeard's company.

"Kilian?" the child's voice said again.

With sagging shoulders, Kilian wandered towards the door. He strapped the Labrys Sword to his back and clutched his ax in his hand. He sent a small prayer to the Creators that whoever was on the other side of the door was not a threat sent by Bluebeard. Cracking the door so that it was barely ajar, Kilian peered out into the large hallway. Cordelia stood outside, her arms crossed. She smiled when she saw him.

"I thought I'd never find you!" she said softly.

Kilian raised an eyebrow at that. "Then how did you know I was here?"

"I didn't," she replied. "I've just been going door-to-door until I found you. And you see, now I have." She smiled broadly.

Kilian laughed merrily at her. "And so you have," he responded, "and so you have."

She motioned for him to follow her and he did so happily. He found himself wondering if she was going to take him to another one of the shrines dedicated to Clara. He hoped so. He wanted to learn as much as he could about the Creator who had been betrayed by her brethren.

"So, where are we going today?" he asked cheerfully.

"My uncle wishes to see you," she said.

Kilian's stomach turned to ice and the hair on his arms stood up as if they were being pulled by some invisible force. His hand began to burn slightly as his ax hummed with magic.

"Who is your uncle?" he asked. His jaw set into a hard line as he waited for her to respond.

"The king of course," she responded immediately.

Kilian sucked in a breath. *Which king?* He thought. His grip on the ax tightened and he forced himself to steal a glance at the girl walking beside him.

Clearing his throat, Kilian asked, "What does he want to see me about?"

"I don't know," she said. "He really doesn't tell me these things," she smiled sweetly up at him. "But I'm glad he told me to find you today!" she clung to his hand as she spoke. "We're going to be the bestest of friends."

Kilian's emotions struggled between joy and turmoil. Turmoil won.

"Where is the king meeting me?" he asked again.

"I think he said to bring you to his chambers," she said. Her face crumpled as she looked up at him. "Do you not want to speak with my uncle? He really is the nicest person I think I've ever met."

Must be Trithium then, Kilian thought. *Bluebeard isn't that nice.* "I see," he said out loud. "I'm sure I'll enjoy speaking with him then."

They went past the throne and through a series of corridors. Kilian tried to keep track of their path in case he needed to backtrack quickly. *Two lefts and then a right*, he repeated. *Or was it two rights and then a left?* He couldn't quite remember. He was left silently hoping that it was Trithium he would be meeting with and not Bluebeard.

Of course, things never seem to go the way he hoped. Alex stood guard outside of the rooms and Kilian, for one fleeting moment, had thought that his prayers had been answered. Instead, he was met with Bluebeard's hard glare as he walked into the room.

"Kilian, me boy, glad you could finally make it." Bluebeard's voice boomed through the cavernous room.

"Bluebeard," Kilian murmured.

There was a single, awkward moment of silence before Kilian finally walked over to where the captain—the king—sat and said as resolutely as he could, "I wish to pay out my debt."

He didn't have a debt to pay. In his mind, he had done more for Bluebeard than the other man had ever done for him. But, of course, he couldn't say this to him.

"I see," Bluebeard said, rubbing his beard as he spoke.

Kilian knew this was the warning sign of a hard battle to be fought, but then he said, "I think it's the right move at this time."

He heard a gasp from behind him and looked back to see that Cordelia was there. Her eyes filled with tears as she listened to Kilian speak and he felt the twang of raw, undiluted magic ripple through the air. A deep shadow of sadness crept over him. He tried to push it back, to force it from his mind, but her child's magic was too strong.

"I'm sorry," he whispered as a tear ran down his cheek. "I'm so sorry, Cordelia."

Her lower lip trembled. "I thought you and my uncle were friends," she said, her voice quivering. "I see now that this was a lie."

The wave of sadness transformed into the heat of anger. Kilian's ax trembled in his hand as he looked at Cordelia in awe.

"We are—were—friends, young one."

She sniffed at him. "But no longer?"

"No longer."

"But why?" Her voice was plaintive and Kilian felt the desire to comfort her. Taking a step towards her, Kilian reached out with his free hand. She stepped away from him, her eyes angry. Kilian's heart sank. He looked from Bluebeard to Cordelia. He knew. In that moment, he knew that Bluebeard had set him up. He knew that this little girl reminded him too much of his sister, May, to say 'no' to.

He knelt down and, taking her small, delicate hands in his own, said, "But we could be friends again. In fact, I think it is high time that we were."

Her little face instantly brightened and Kilian felt the warmth of her happiness pass through his body in a fleeting burst of magic. When she smiled, it made his heart sing.

"See, I knew all ya needed was a night to calm yerself down."

Bluebeard's voice was like a buzzing bee in Kilian's mind. All he wanted to do was swat at it but he knew that if he did so he would get stung.

"Yes, Bluebeard," Kilian responded as he turned to face the older man, "I 'calmed' myself down." His voice still carried notes of poison in them.

Bluebeard gave no indication that Kilian's tone bothered him as he called to Alex, "Alex, please join us. There is much to discuss."

Alex shuffled into the room, his face a dark glower. Resigning himself to what he knew would be an unfortunate conversation, Kilian took a seat in the chair that was offered to him.

"Trithium and that atrocious cousin of his, Saraphina, will be sent to Valqueria in exile," Bluebeard said once everyone was seated.

"Is that wise, Captain?" Alex asked, his voice a low growl as he looked about the room. Kilian didn't blame him. He'd watched Saraphina completely drain people of their life and then eat them. If Kilian had been imprisoned here for as long as Alex had been, he was sure he'd be as paranoid as his companion appeared.

"It's the only option we have unless yer suggest'n that we kill 'em."

There was a short pause where Kilian could hear Alex breathing rapidly. After a time, Alex mumbled, "I can't think of any reason why that's not the most logical response."

"I see," Bluebeard said. He turned his gaze towards Kilian. "And what say you, Kilian? Do you think we should kill the king or let 'im live?"

"I think you should…" Kilian fumbled for the correct words. "I think you should let nature takes its course. Let them live. See how it goes."

Bluebeard nodded his head as he twisted a piece of his beard between two fingers. Alex drummed his fingers on the table dividing them. He glowered at Kilian from across the table as they waited.

"I do not wish to kill them. Not really. Trithium only assumed the throne when I denounced it all those years ago. I can't…"

"Bah," Alex huffed, cutting Bluebeard off. "You'd listen to a boy over me?" he sneered as he glared at the older man.

"Please don't argue," Cordelia's girlish voice chimed in. "Uncle, you promised you wouldn't argue." She knelt before him, her eyes tilted up towards his. Her lower lip quivered slightly. Kilian stared at the scene in awe. *This little girl has us all wrapped around her little finger*, he thought as he realized that Bluebeard was softening to the girl's request.

He looked up and stared at Alex with a hard expression in his eyes. "Are you with me or not, Alex?"

Without hesitation, Alex responded, "I'm with you."

"Good. Then as I was say'n, we'll exile the two of them and their closest followers to the islands," he paused and then said, "My coronation is set for tomorrow. After that, no one will dare threaten my rule." He tugged on his beard as he spoke and Kilian wondered if the man was afraid of civil war among the various factions of the merfolk.

"In one week's time, we will leave Ula Una and travel beyond the Forgotten Isles. Kilian, I expect you to train with General Balbusti during this time. He will see that you understand how the merfolk fight. This will be needed when we face the Shadow Knights."

Bluebeard said many other things that Kilian did not hear. His mind wandered as he contemplated what it would mean to finally finish this Light forsaken quest. He could return home again. He could see his little sister and brother again. He could be free again.

One thought continued nagging at him the longer he sat in Bluebeard's chambers. He couldn't imagine facing the Shadow Knights without Bluebeard's original crew. He knew that he would never be able to bring Adrienne back, but he thought he just might be able to convince Narcon to meet them at the Forgotten Isles. Perhaps he would be able to persuade Tavia as well.

Even thinking her name made Kilian's head pound. He missed her. He hated her for leaving him. He loved her. Mostly, he was ashamed that he had forgotten her. All he wanted was to see her face again and to reassure himself that she had been real—that their love had been real.

"We should find Narcon and Tavia," he nearly shouted.

Bluebeard and Alex stopped chatting and stared at Kilian with a look of bewilderment on their faces.

"We need them," Kilian said. "They complete our little band. It wouldn't feel right facing this last challenge without them."

"And this has nothing to do with you wanting to see your lover before you die, does it, loverboy?" Alex sneered.

"That's enough, Alex," Bluebeard responded. He caught Kilian's eyes, "Do you honestly believe that you'll perform better with her there? I know what she means to you, Kilian," Bluebeard paused, letting his words sink in and then asked, "What will you do when it comes between saving her and defeating the King of the Shadow Knights, Rhymaldis?"

The candle light flickered as Bluebeard uttered the leader of the Shadow Knight's name. The room chilled to ice and Kilian could see his air puff out in front of him. He shivered. No one, not even Tavia, had spoken the leader's name out loud to Kilian since Bluebeard had first made it known who they would be facing in their final challenge. *In my final challenge*, Kilian thought uneasily.

"I'd finish the task," Kilian said. He knew as soon as he uttered the words that they were a lie. Bluebeard and Alex did not look convinced either.

"You say that now, but I saw how you reacted during our battle with those pus-ridden monstrosities the first time we traveled to the Forgotten Isles, Kilian. You bowed to your worry. We cannot afford to make these kinds of mistakes against the Shadow Knights."

Kilian sighed. He knew that they were right. He could feel it in his bones. But, he could also tell that he wouldn't be able to face this last challenge without her.

"She goes or I stay," Kilian said quickly. He slurred the words together in his haste and, at first, he wondered if Bluebeard and Alex had understood what he'd said.

Silence hung heavy in the room as Kilian waited for either of them to say something. Cordelia remained seated at her uncle's feet. Kilian hadn't seen her transition to kneeling over her uncle's hands to sitting at his feet, but he was surprised that Bluebeard had allowed this child to remain during their meeting.

And then he felt it. It was delicate and sweet and barely noticeable. But Kilian felt it. She was controlling the tenor of the conversation.

"We will dispatch an invitation for her to join us," Bluebeard finally said.

Kilian nodded and then said, "I want to see it dispatched, Bluebeard."

The older man smiled and said, "Of course. The dispatch shouldn't take more than three days to reach her."

Realization dawned on Kilian as he listened to Bluebeard speak. "Wait, you know where she is?" Anger seared through him at a rapid pace.

"'Course I do. She's been sending me progress updates since she left," Bluebeard responded.

"Progress reports?" Kilian asked.

Bluebeard laughed. "You didn't think she left without having another mission to accomplish, did you?" He twisted his beard in his fingers as he spoke.

"I...well... yes," Kilian stammered. Alex smirked at Kilian. A wave of insecurity passed through Kilian as he realized what a fool he'd been.

"It's alright, Kilian," Cordelia chimed in. "I know she'll be happy to see you. You're very special to her just like she is to you."

Kilian stared at the little girl incredulously. *She can't possibly know how Tavia feels*, Kilian thought.

"Enough," Bluebeard said, clapping his hands together. "Tavia will come or she won't. Just like any other mission, the decision is hers."

Kilian sunk deep into his seat. He couldn't decide if he was anxious to see Tavia again or afraid.

"Now, Kilian, it is high time we discuss that sword," Bluebeard said.

"What?" Kilian asked as he reached his hand over his shoulder to feel the hilt of the blade.

"You best be givin' that blade to me, son," Bluebeard said as he scraped dirt from his nails. "I gave you the ax. The sword is recompense for the weapon."

"No!" Kilian shouted as he stood and slammed his fists upon the table. "That ax never belonged to you. I…"

"You have accepted much from me, boy," Bluebeard nonchalantly stood and looked into Kilian's eyes with a cold, hard stare. "Consider this a gift on the eve of my coronation."

Kilian's hands were clammy and he found it difficult to think as he considered Bluebeard's words. A thought clicked into place. "You planned this," he said. Then, as if realizing something for the first time, "Was obtaining this sword even part of my prophecy, Bluebeard, or did you just use me to do something you couldn't do for yourself?"

A wave of magic washed over Kilian as he spoke. He glanced at Cordelia. Her cheeks were flushed and she had a concentrated look on her face. Gripping his ax more tightly in his hand, Kilian leaned towards Bluebeard. "Tell me, Bluebeard, why did you really bring me on this quest."

"You're meant for greatness, Kilian," Bluebeard began.

"Don't give me that. I want a straight answer for once!" Kilian's voice was jarring, even to his own ears.

Sighing loudly, Bluebeard said, "Retrieving the sword was just a way for me to ensure that you're ready for your true destiny, Kilian. Now that you've defeated Malmadi, I know that you are. So what if I chose a task that would also benefit me in the end?" Bluebeard shrugged. "That sword belongs in the hands of the merfolk, Kilian. Not you."

"I think it actually belongs to Clara," Kilian responded snidely.

"Yes," Bluebeard said in an exasperated tone. "And I'm sure I'll see her again." He smirked at Kilian as he held out his hand. "Now, the sword please."

Kilian hesitated. His ax hummed in his hand and he felt its power begin to seep into his veins. Feeling emboldened, Kilian said, "Seems to me that I was the one who earned this weapon, Bluebeard. Not you," he threw the words Bluebeard had just spoken back at him.

Bluebeard stroked his beard, an amused expression on his face. It glowed faintly. Kilian felt the urge to step away from Bluebeard, but he resisted it. Finally, the older man said, "Consider this, Kilian. You can only use one of these weapons at a time. If we are to beat the Shadow King and his knights, then we must be as prepared as possible. You're bonded to the ax. My people bear the same magic as is what's in that sword. Together, we can win."

"Bluebeard has a point, Kilian," Alex chimed in. Kilian shot a glance at him that he hoped conveyed just how much he valued his opinion. Kilian traced his fingers over the smooth steel of the sword's hilt. He sensed its power. He knew what his ax could do; he could only imagine what two weapons forged by the Creators could do in upcoming battle.

Making his decision, Kilian unsheathed the blade and handed it hilt-first to Bluebeard.

"Consider this your coronation gift," Kilian said begrudgingly.

Chapter Twenty-One

Kilian was surprised by the lack of fanfare at Bluebeard's coronation. The throne room had not been decorated for the occasion. The only difference to the throne room that was of any note to Kilian was the throne itself. Unlike the gilded throne Trithium had sat upon, a rough worked, drift wood chair had been placed on the dais. Glimmering coral adorned the otherwise simple chair. The savage merfolk who had joined them in their quest to secure the sword formed a row before the raised dais. Their weapons gleamed in the candle light and from the soft green glow emanating from within the ocean's depths. Aside from the guard, only a handful of guests filled the room. Kilian found himself wondering if this was because the people were protesting Bluebeard or because Bluebeard had not invited his people. In some ways it didn't matter. The whole ordeal had a militaristic minimalism to it that did not match Bluebeard's personality.

He was even more surprised when Trithium and Saraphina entered the throne room and took their places before the dais. Trithium, his face still bruised from the beating Kilian had administered, was carried into the throne room on a wooden cot. His eyes were glazed and he looked as if he would vomit at any moment. Saraphina gripped him beneath the shoulders when he stood to renounce the throne. A sour taste filled Kilian's mouth as he listened to the once elegant king stumble over his words. *She had wanted this*, he chided himself when he remembered that Clara had told him he had done a good job. He still wasn't sure how he felt about what he had done to the boyish king or how he had forgotten about Tavia so quickly. A barrage of boos and yelps of celebration filled the room as Trithium uttered his last words as Ula Una's king. Kilian glanced around the room, trying to determine where the boos had come from. He wondered how many of those who protested

Bluebeard would be exiled along with their king. Knowing Bluebeard, it would be many.

Kilian's eyes strayed from Trithium and fell on his cousin. Saraphina was radiant. She wore a midnight blue dress with a plunging neckline and back that accentuated her curves. The dress was so dark it could almost have been considered black except for the sparkling gems that had been hand-stitched into its fabric. Unlike Trithium, her eyes were clear and calculating as she glared at Kilian. They contained a hungry look that made Kilian's stomach squirm as he tried to ignore her gaze. It didn't work as well as he had hoped. He found himself glancing at her throughout the duration of the ceremony. She smiled slyly at him each time she caught his gaze. It was as if they were playing some secret game of cat and mouse. Kilian did not want to play this game with her.

Shadowy figures pressed against the translucent barrier between water and air. Their bodies moved with the waves as they parted to let a lone person swim between them. Notes from an instrument Kilian had never heard before filled the air. They were powerful and menacing and yet also sorrowful in a way Kilian could not describe. He closed his eyes to listen.

Kilian. The voice was low and familiar. It startled him and yet he kept his eyes shut. He somehow knew that if he were to open his eyes the voice would fade away. It was so familiar to him. It was like waking from a vibrant dream and desperately grasping the threads of memory as they disappear into morning sunlight. Although he wasn't sure why, Kilian did not want to lose this thread.

Kilian, it said more urgently this time. Kilian furrowed his brow as he tried to recognize that voice.

Who are you? He thought. He didn't dare speak out loud, not while the sorrowful music still played in the background and the shadowy figure of Bluebeard swam towards the throne where he would be crowned king of Ula Una.

You know me, son.

Kilian's eyelids fluttered and he almost opened them fully. He knew better. He knew that if he broke contact with this... he wasn't sure what to call it, that it might be years before he heard from him again.

Father? he questioned, although he already knew the answer.

A flash memory answered. It was a hot a day and the sun beat down upon them as they crossed the pasture towards the village on the far side of the clearing. May was nothing but a small child, barely able to walk and their father had swung her up onto his shoulders. He'd laughed. Kilian smiled at that laugh. Kilian missed that laugh.

The memory faded in a haze of color. Kilian hadn't had time to see his father's face. He couldn't remember what it looked like anymore. At times, he thought he could recreate an expression—an imprint—of what his father's face might have looked like, but it was a cheap imitation of the real thing.

We don't have much time, Kilian. His father's voice was urgent. It pressed against his mind with a force he had never witnessed from his father in real life.

Confused, Kilian asked, *Where have you been? All this time, Father, where have you been?*

Anger flooded Kilian's emotions. He felt the ax strapped to his side flood with hot magic and had the aching need to grasp its handle. *No time.* The thought filled his mind as the anger receded along with Kilian's desire to take his ax in hand.

What's wrong? He asked plaintively. He searched his mind for traces of his father but found nothing.

Father? he sent out tentatively.

A swirl of light filled his mind's eye. Kilian shivered as a rush of cold wind brushed the bare skin of his arms and face. *A boy born of the blessed. One of the Light, the other of*

Darkness. He alone shall determine the outcome of the Great War.

The words didn't make any sense to Kilian. And then it dawned on him. *The prophecy?* he asked, cutting over the flow of his father's voice through his mind.

Silence.

Kilian prodded the recesses of his mind, searching for his father. All that was left were memories.

Cold water splashed against him. Kilian's eyes flew open as he heaved in a gasp of surprise. Before him stood the towering figure of Bluebeard as he emerged from the water. Blue smoke swirled around the beast of a man as his tail transformed into legs. Instead of his usual traveling attire, Bluebeard wore a military jacket adorned with medals Kilian wasn't sure the captain had earned. Clara's sword hung on Bluebeard's hip. It glowed faintly in the dim room. Bluebeard winked at Kilian as he passed.

Throughout the procession of Bluebeard speaking the words to claim the Ula Unan throne, Kilian thought about the words his father had spoken to him. It had been nearly two and a half years since he'd heard his father speak to him like that. He knew it couldn't be a coincidence that his father had appeared to him on the eve of his departure to the Forgotten Isles and Beyond. And yet, from what he'd heard his father say, he couldn't find any reason for his father to keep this prophecy from him. *Why did my father steal me away from Kaldeena? Why didn't he ever teach me about my destiny?* None of it made sense to him. His father should have known, just as Kilian did, that he would follow the Light no matter what the cost. He would follow the Light. It was the only thing he knew how to do. No war could change that.

Clapping jarred him from his thoughts. He caught Saraphina smiling at him and realized that he had not joined in on the celebration of Bluebeard's coronation. He quickly clapped his hands together. Her smile broadened and Kilian realized his mistake. Now she knew that he had been caught ignoring the ceremony. He blushed profusely before he realized that it didn't matter what Saraphina saw—or thought she saw. Bluebeard would believe him over that weakling of a woman.

A small hand slipped into his, startling him. Kilian looked down to see that Cordelia had joined him. Her small hand felt like ice in his overly warm one. She smiled up at him, her eyes swimming with mischief. He winked at her before jerking his head up to the dais where Bluebeard knelt so that a surly looking man with a long gray beard could lay a knotted crown upon his head. He stole a quick glance at Saraphina as the crown crested the new king's brow. Her smile had vanished and a cold, almost lifeless look, filled her eyes. For a moment—and only a moment—Kilian felt, almost felt, sorry for her. The emotion fled as soon as it registered as a thought within Kilian's mind.

Cordelia squeezed his hand tightly when her uncle spoke the final words to accept responsibility for the whole of the merfolk. Kilian looked down at her, smiling. Although he couldn't sense it, not yet anyway, Kilian was almost certain that Cordelia was using her abilities to manipulate the emotions of everyone standing in the crowd. No doubt Bluebeard had cajoled her into forcing his protesters to believe that Bluebeard was the correct choice for role of king.

"I'm glad you have reconciled with my uncle," she whispered.

"As am I," Kilian responded, though he wasn't sure how much he believed his own words.

She smiled brightly up at him. "I wish I could go with you."

The plea lingered in the air between them as a different noble stepped forward and placed the driftwood crown upon Bluebeard's brow. More clapping erupted from the crowd.

"You cannot, little one. This battle has no place for you."

She pouted and Kilian's heart sank.

"I'm more capable than you think," she nearly growled. It was the first time Kilian had heard such vehemence in her voice. It saddened him to know that he had created this strife.

"I know you are, dear one," he whispered as Bluebeard began to walk down the middle of the crowd. The strange music had returned and he found his eyes drawn to the newly crowned king. For all of Bluebeard's roguish ways, he did look stately at that moment.

Cordelia tugged on Kilian's hand, clearly impatient with him.

Kilian shrugged as he said, "There's not much I can really do, Cordelia. Your uncle is the one who decides who goes and who stays."

"But you convinced him to reach out to members of your old crew. Surely you could..."

"That was a different circumstance," Kilian said, cutting Cordelia off. "I'm sorry, Cordelia, but the answer is no."

She ripped her hand out of his and crossed her tiny arms over her small body.

"Don't be like that," Kilian said as he gently tugged on her arm.

"All I wanted was to prove that I could be a hero," she said in a dejected tone.

"You will one day," Kilian said as he grasped her small hands in his. "I promise."

Bluebeard walked past them. He did not glance their way as his large body strode by. Members of the nobility and the guard followed behind, including Saraphina and Trithium, who still lay on a cot. Saraphina smirked at him as she strolled past and Kilian had the unsettling feeling that he would see her again. He hoped that his intuition was wrong, but he doubted that it was.

"I hope you're right," Cordelia murmured as she took her place in the procession. Kilian followed behind her.

"I will be," he muttered, though he doubted she had heard.

The massive doors to the throne room closed behind Kilian with a resounding thud. It was done. Kilian had secured the sword from Malmadi. Bluebeard had been crowned king of Ula Una. Cold reality set in upon Kilian. There was no more time left. If the battle mentioned in the prophecy was about the fight against the Shadow Knights, then Kilian was about to face this battle head-on. His ax hummed as his mind cleared and he knew what he had to do.

It's high time I gave this ax a name, Kilian thought as he rounded the corner and made his way back to his room.

Part Three
Chapter Twenty-Two

We don't know when it began. 'Twas but a whisper in the night. The Darkness that rose and swept through the Creators like a plague. Even as I write this now, the Darkness continues to grow. It taints all that it touches. It makes what was once whole nothing but a shattered remnant of what it once was. I know not when or how or even if we can survive. But we must continue to try. We must…

-From the personal journal of Navalara the Bard, Oracle of the Second Order

Dragon's Breath rocked on the roaring seas. Kilian felt queasy for the first time since he'd received his 'sea legs', as Bluebeard had called them. Each time the ship pitched to one side, the burning, acid-filled taste of vomit filled his mouth. So far, Kilian had been able to swallow it back down. Kilian lay in the hammock of his old cabin. Despite having sat in Port Naumesi's harbor for two years, it was in surprisingly good condition. Despite the musty, slightly decayed smell permeating this air now, Kilian felt as if he were ending his journey in exactly the same way he had begun it.

The ship rolled on a massive wave and Kilian squeezed his eyes shut, breathing heavily. A cold hand on his shoulder startled him. In one fluid motion Kilian pulled his dagger from his belt and swung the blade upwards. Opening his eyes, Kilian blinked into the blaring glow of an orb of light.

"Wuh?" he mouthed as a hooded figure stepped into the shadows. The orb of light remained suspended in the air. Tiny sparkles of light flamed within its confines. It seemed to be churning with the rattle of the storm. Kilian blinked again as his eyes slowly adjusted to the brightness of the orb.

"There is much to discuss," the figure said.

A woman, Kilian thought as he held his dagger out before him and reached for his ax. He still had not named the thing, despite his multiple attempts to come up with a suitable one.

"Who are you?" Kilian asked, followed by, "Step into the light."

The figure pulled her hood further down, completely hiding her face. She wore long, dark gloves that covered her skin. Her dress had a high neck and stopped midway down her knee-high boots.

"You are in danger, Kilian," the woman said.

"Of course I am," Kilian nearly shouted. "I'm headed into the biggest battle of my life." He clamped his hand over his mouth as he spoke. *I shouldn't have said that*, he realized. *She might not have known where we were heading.*

"What if I told you there was a way to save you?" she asked, her voice soft. "What if I told you that there was a way to escape your prophecy?"

"Escape my..." Kilian stopped speaking. His heart hammered. *What if I could find a way to break my ties to the prophecy? What would it be like to no longer be in training. To just be myself?*

He shook his head, "There's no reason to even consider these possibilities," he said. "It cannot be done."

"But what if it could? What if your father had discovered a way?"

Warning bells rang in Kilian's mind. "Why are you here, Kaldeena?" he asked, his voice full of venom. She was, quite possibly, the last person Kilian ever wanted to see.

She barked a harsh laugh. "You really don't know?"

Bewildered, Kilian shook his head. His body felt numb, as if he had spent an entire day without water. Reaching for his water skin, Kilian drained the remains of its contents before looking back at Kaldeena. The water had done nothing to relieve his sense of numbness.

"Just tell me why you're here," he said. He looked down at his hands as he spoke. He couldn't face her.

She sighed loudly, drawing his attention back to her. "Can't a mother wish to save her child?" she asked. Her voice remained in its cold, aloof tenor. Kilian winced as he realized that he had expected—desired—something more.

He scoffed at her. It was a reflexive response that he instantly regretted. Yet, he couldn't bring himself to answer her question or apologize.

The twinkling orb floated closer to Kilian's face. He could see thousands of minuscule lights rotating in the orb. Some of the lights were larger than others, yet they all swirled in the same pattern. Hues of purple, blue, and pink swam through the orb as if in water. Their luminescent light filled Kilian with a sense of awe.

Kaldeena cleared her throat, bringing Kilian back to the present moment. "I think it's time that we set the record straight, Kilian. Your father wasn't who you think he was. He..." she paused. With her face still hidden in shadow, Kilian found it difficult to determine what she thinking or feeling. "He didn't take you away from me to save you. He stole you from me to destroy you."

"That's a lie!" Kilian shouted. He lifted his ax and swung at her. In the small space of his cabin, the ax should have passed through her stomach with absolutely no problem at all. And it did. Sort of. The blade swept through the image of her like a hand passes through a flame. Smoke billowed in the ax's wake.

"Oh, Kilian," Kaldeena said, her voice sad, "did you really think that I would risk boarding Dragon's Breath for a second time without the explicit permission of its captain," she chuckled, "I mean, look at what happened the last time."

"Don't you dare," Kilian began.

"That poor… well… person didn't have to die."

The smoke version of Kaldeena threaded a dagger though her fingers. Its sharp blade seemed to never touch her hand as she flicked it from one finger to the next.

"You killed him!" Kilian shouted again. "You… you… severed his soul." Kilian's voice caught on that last word. Adrienne's soul had been stripped away from him by one of the Creator's daggers. It hadn't been necessary; Kaldeena had wanted it.

"You are a disappointment, aren't you?" Kaldeena cackled. "No wonder your father…"

"You don't know anything about my father," Kilian said coldly.

She blinked at him. "I know more about your father than you could ever dream to."

Kilian scoffed at her. "All you do is lie. It's no wonder he didn't want me to be raised by you. You would have tried to turn me to the darkness."

The tittering sound of her laughter filled the small room. "Your father took you away from me for self-preservation, Kilian. He wanted to survive." Her voice trembled slightly as she spoke and Kilian realized that the woman before him might actually feel grief at the loss of Nathanial Clearwater.

A sliver of ice sank into Kilian's gut. All the fears and worries he had developed since meeting Bluebeard seemed to simmer within him. *What if she's telling the truth?* The thought did not comfort him.

"What do you want, Kaldeena?" His voice was cold and harsh.

There was a long pause and then the shadowy figure before him slowly pulled back her hood. Her long, raven hair fell in curls around her pale blue skin. She glowed slightly, but

Kilian instinctively knew that, as a figment, she wouldn't be able to harm him.

"What I want is for you to understand your true destiny."

"Alright," Kilian said, "What is my true destiny?"

Her face darkened. "Are you certain you truly want to know?" she asked.

Kilian hesitated for half a heartbeat before whispering, "I'm certain."

She smiled sorrowfully at him. Her misty hands clapped together. A wave of cool air burst from where her hands appeared to have met, sweeping over Kilian with such force that he bowed backwards. His cabin seemed to swirl around him, everything mixing as it went until Kilian had the sensation of falling. He flailed his arms in a futile attempt to stop himself from plummeting through the air. Consciously, he knew it wouldn't work, yet his still his arms desperately swatted through the air.

The sensation of falling ceased and was replaced by the feeling of being suspended midair. It was cold yet there was no breeze. Kilian's skin prickled with gooseflesh and his teeth chattered slightly. The world around him swirled with a myriad of sparkling lights. Kilian breathed in deeply as one of the lights zipped past him with a sudden warmth. The air smelled of dewing grass on a cool, clear night. The smell reminded him of his father.

"Where are we?" Kilian asked, remembering how he'd gotten to this place.

Kaldeena did not respond immediately. Instead, she slowly floated out of a sliver of darkness to Kilian's side. He spun around to face her, his blue eyes focused on her shadowy figure.

"Your father stole you from me because he didn't want you to fulfill your destiny."

"But I listened…" Kilian began.

"You listened to only part of the prophecy, my son. The rest is not as grand as the first."

Kilian glowered at her as he crossed his arms over his chest. When she did not continue, Kilian waved his arm at her in a gesture that said, 'please continue.' Kaldeena, of course, complied.

"Your life is the sacrifice needed to restore balance to the world, Kilian."

"What?" Kilian asked. "That can't possibly be true. Bluebeard wouldn't have sought me out and trained me this way if I were meant to die in the end."

His mother looked down at her hands and Kilian knew the truth. All these quests, all this time, had been nothing more than a setup for the final battle. Kilian gulped. There was no turning back now.

"Why?" Kilian demanded. "Why put me through all of this? Why force me to train this way if they knew that I would die in the end?" Anger boiled within him. All this time, they had given him hope of being a truly great hero and being able to return home to Lunameed. "I've been a fool," he murmured softly.

"Perhaps."

The word hung like a wall separating them. Kilian had never felt so alone. A thought suddenly occurred to him.

"What did taking me away from you have to do with self-preservation?" Kilian asked. His voice pitched as he spoke. Hearing his father's voice and then being, essentially, kidnapped by his birth mother all in the same week was not only confusing but also overwhelming. *So much for being a great hero*, he thought.

"In order to answer that question, I will first have to explain something to you. The day you were born was the happiest day of my life. I had longed for a child." At this point, a single tear ran down her cheeks. Kilian thought that she was being overly dramatic but said nothing as she continued, "When Bluebeard told me about the Light's Hero prophecy—about your prophecy—I knew that I had birthed you for a greater purpose than my own happiness." She looked Kilian straight in the eyes as she spoke. "Your father did not feel the same."

The force of her anger surprised Kilian. He clenched his jaw in frustration at her, but waited for her to continue.

"He didn't want to raise you to be the hero you were meant to be. He didn't want you to fulfill your destiny. He said that no child should have to bear that burden."

She smiled at him, "We cannot escape our destinies, Kilian. No matter how hard we try, they always have a way of coming back to haunt us in the end."

Kilian stared at her blankly. *She was willing to let me die, he thought. She was willing to sacrifice me. But not my father. Not him.*

"One night, Nathanial told me I was too much of a risk to the baby," she began speaking as if Kilian weren't there at all. "I tried to keep him. I tried. But Nathanial wouldn't listen. He told me that if the babe was going to live a normal life, he would have to do it without me. I thought Nathanial was just in one of his moods. He wasn't." Her voice quivered slightly at this and Kilian, for a moment, almost believed that she was remorseful. "He and the baby disappeared the very next day. I have sought vengeance ever since."

She looked him straight in the eyes and smiled, "But now you're here and it is time for you to fulfill the prophecy. It's time for you to become the Light's Hero. It's time for you to die."

A shiver ran down Kilian's spine as he listened to Kaldeena speak.

"You're even crazier than I thought!" he murmured.

She blinked at him. And then she cackled at him. Kilian couldn't believe his ears. He hadn't heard cackling like that since he'd met with the Queen Khaela of Siguila.

"My poor, dear boy. You honestly thought that you would have a happy ending, didn't you?"

Kilian stared at her, dumbfounded. He struggled to find the words to express the torrent of emotions coursing through him. Mostly, he felt betrayed. Betrayed by his father. Betrayed by this woman standing before him. Betrayed by Bluebeard.

"Why are you here?" he finally hissed.

She stopped laughing and turned her cold, golden eyes towards him. "I'm here to watch you fulfill your destiny, Kilian. Surely you have figured that out already." She smirked at him as she spoke and Kilian had the distinct impression that she was simply toying with him.

"Why are you doing this?" he asked. His voice cracked as he spoke.

"Tsk, tsk, Kilian. I thought you would have figured that out by now." She floated closer to him through the seemingly endless abyss. Cupping his cheek in her icy hand, Kaldeena stroked his cheek with her thumb as she said, "The Darkness is rising, Son, and there is nothing you can do to stop it. It is all-consuming. It is the next great power of the realm. Embrace this ending, Kilian. Your sacrifice shall not be in vain."

He jerked away from her, more to hide the tears that stung his eyes than out of anger. With a powerful flick of her wrist, she whipped his face back towards her.

"This is what you were born for. Don't try to fight it," she leaned her forehead against his. He could smell her sickly-sweet breath mixing with his own. The smell disgusted him. He tried to lean away from her, but her grasp on his jaw was so tight that he could feel the bruises forming on his skin.

"My sweet, sweet child," she whispered as she closed her eyes.

It was too much for Kilian. With a mighty cry, he brought his arms up and boxed her on the ears. She instantly released her hold on him and clapped her hands over her ears, a look of immense pain covered her face. Kilian tried to move through the air but found that he was stuck where he was. In a grunt of frustration, he swung his arm out and hooked it around Kaldeena's neck. He drew her towards him as she squirmed against his grip.

"Take me back to the ship," he growled at her. She shivered against him, her entire body shaking. Kilian momentarily felt pity for her. She was his birth mother, after all. But then, as if sensing his lingering guilt, Kaldeena pulled a slim dagger from her belt and held it against Kilian's hand.

"Don't tempt me, boy," she hissed through a swollen throat. Kilian's elbow still pressed firmly into her neck.

"Do you honestly think a little dagger scares me, Kaldeena?" Kilian sneered. "I've faced much worse and survived."

"This isn't for you," she whispered in a hoarse voice. She clawed at his arm with her free hand. Kilian pressed his elbow more firmly into her throat.

"Who is for then?" he asked, genuinely curious.

"For me," she said as she shifted the blade from his hand and thrust it into her own abdomen. "I see now what I must do," she whispered.

"What are you doing!" Kilian screamed as he released his hold on her neck and pressed his hand to her wound in one continuous motion.

Blood trailed from Kaldeena's mouth, staining her teeth a dark, crimson red as she reached up and stroked his face again.

"This is what you need to make the right choice. I've seen it."

He tried, to no avail, to transfer some of his strength into her. He felt the familiar warmth of his magic flare to life only to be snuffed out like a candle at dawn.

"Let me go, Kilian. It's what was meant to be."

"Hush," Kilian said, pressing more firmly on her wound. "Don't talk like that. Please, Kaldeena, just take us back to the ship. I can heal you there." In truth, Kilian wasn't sure that he would be able to heal her back on the ship either. He just knew that he needed to try.

"You'll be taken back once I'm gone," she whispered. She cupped his cheek again. This time, Kilian leaned into her cold, blood-covered palm.

"This was not but a dream." She smiled up at him as she spoke. "The best dream I've ever had."

"Hold on," Kilian pleaded. Despite his earlier anger and unyielding desire for Kaldeena to be honest with him, he felt the familiar twang of despair as he realized that she was going to die. Panic made his mind flip from one thought to the next, barely pausing between them. His breathing became ragged. A memory of a cold, gray sky filled his mind. He tried to block it out. Tried to stop it from taking control. His father's face, blurred by lost memory, filtered into his mind's eye. "You can't do this," Kilian yelped. "Not again." His father's face faded into darkness and Kilian was left with a sense of emptiness so profound that it was all he could do to clutch Kaldeena closer to him.

His hand slipped on her blood-slick stomach. Cursing under his breath, Kilian tried to staunch the blood flow with a swatch of cloth he tore from his linen undershirt.

"Kaldeena, I forbid you to die like this!" he shouted.

She blinked up at him in response. He couldn't understand how she could do this to herself. After everything she had done to see him once more, it didn't make sense. A single, fat tear plopped onto her face. Kilian quickly wiped it away.

"This is right," she whispered so quietly that Kilian had to lean in closer towards her to understand what she was saying. "Nathanial was a fool," she said vehemently.

Kilian shook his head slightly. Even in the shadow of death, she hated his father enough to curse him. Kilian wondered what had truly passed between them. He couldn't believe that Kaldeena's version of the story was completely the truth.

"You're mine," she whispered. "You have always been mine."

"I am no one's but my own," Kilian said resolutely. He wasn't sure why he said it, other than that he knew it to be true. *No one will control me*, he thought as he watched her lips pull into a thin smile.

"You belong to the Darkness, Kilian. Never forget that."

Kilian opened his mouth to respond, but when he peered into her eyes, he was confronted by the cold, blank stare of someone who can no longer see. He stroked her hair as he cradled her in his arms. He couldn't understand how their conversation had escalated so quickly. They had gone from discussing what the prophecy meant to her...

Kilian couldn't even think the word much less say it out loud. He stared down into her expressionless face, a cold dread settling in the pit of his stomach. He felt a yank at his navel and the sickening sensation of being pulled through time and space.

***

His hammock rocked gently with the ship, lulling Kilian and soothing his concerns. Sweat soaked his linen shirt—once again whole—making him shiver from the cool breeze wafting through his cracked door. Kilian breathed in deeply and exhaled slowly. *Did that actually happen?* He thought. He examined his shirt and hands. No blood covered them. *Perhaps it was only a dream*, he thought, though it seemed too real to be but a dream.

A gentle knock on his door startled him. He leaped from the hammock so quickly that he skinned his knee on the wall as he slammed into it. He yelped in pain, and the door lurched open, revealing Alex standing in the doorway. He smirked at Kilian when he saw how Kilian favored his newly injured leg.

"We're almost there," he said in a smooth, monotone voice. "Bluebeard requested that you join him on deck, Hero." He said that last word with so much sarcasm that Kilian was tempted to respond back with the same amount of angst. He stopped himself just as the words were about to come tumbling out.

"Let me change first," he said quickly to cover up his almost tirade. Alex eyed him suspiciously but turned his back to Kilian's door as he pulled it shut behind him.

Kilian sighed in relief. It was becoming more and more difficult to stop himself from pummeling Alex in his smug face. Kilian's hand itched. He knew it was nothing more than a psychological response to his pent-up anger, but he still scratched at his hand until he drew a thin line of blood with his sharpened fingernail. Wiping his hand on the back of his trousers, Kilian pulled on one of the shirts he'd been issued by Bluebeard's steward.

Unlike their first voyage across the Paralosa Ocean, the Dragon Breath's bustled with servants and warriors. Bluebeard had delivered when it came to merfolk warriors. Altogether, Bluebeard had raised an army of nearly three hundred merfolk. The savage merfolk who had remained loyal to Bluebeard throughout the years were also traveling with the party, yet they refused to take on legs.

"Removes us from our true selves," they had said when Kilian had asked them why they chose to face the perils of the sea instead of taking the safer route on the ship. They had been joined by a force of other barbaric merfolk in groves as they had journeyed across the open water. Kilian was surprised at the number of merfolk who had joined them for this battle.

Surely Bluebeard wants me to succeed in my fight against the Shadow Knights. He wouldn't risk this many of his own people's lives. The thought did not comfort Kilian. Instead, it brought on more anxiety as he tried to process Kaldeena's death. Despite barely knowing her, her death seemed insurmountable to move beyond.

Alex whistled at the door, and Kilian knew he was taking too long. Pulling his trousers up quickly, Kilian followed Alex up the steep ladder to the ship's main deck. Sunlight temporarily blinded him as he stepped onto the slick wood of the main deck. His heart hammered in his chest wildly as he stared up at where Bluebeard stood.

It can't be, he thought. *It simply cannot be.*

Chapter Twenty-Three

Kaldeena stood on deck, her dark-as-night cape fluttering behind her. Her braided raven hair hung to one side. Even from the distance between them, Kilian could see the smug expression spread across her face.

"Kilian," Bluebeard bellowed, "it's about time you came on deck."

Kilian remained locked in place. Sweat dripped from his hands as he clenched them. Already he could feel the heat rising within him, masking the confusion. *I saw her die.* The thought reverberated through him. *I know I saw her die.*

"What is she doing here?" Alex asked, jarring Kilian from his thoughts. His voice was a practiced tone of indifference, but Kilian saw the throbbing vein in Alex's jaw as he waited for a response from Bluebeard.

"Kaldeena is here to make amends with her son," Bluebeard stated unsympathetically. "And you," he added with a pointed look at Alex, "if you will accept it."

Kilian shot a sideways glance at the man standing beside him. Alex tightened his grip firmly around the hilt of his sword. Kilian could tell that Alex was battling between his loyalty to Bluebeard and his desire for revenge against Kaldeena. He listened to the other man's ragged breathing and waited.

"Fine," Alex spat after a tense moment. Kilian could hear the venom in Alex's voice. Alex slid the sword back into his scabbard without looking up at Kaldeena or Bluebeard. From the corner of his mouth, he whispered, "Trust no one, Kilian." With that, he disappeared into the throng of crew members who had formed a circle around them. Even with so many people surrounding him, Kilian was left with the sense of real loneliness as he stared up at the mother he never knew. He couldn't believe that she was standing before him once more, not after the terrors he had faced the previous night when he'd watched her die in his arms. He'd been powerless to save her. The guilt of knowing that he could do nothing for her filled him with a sense of urgency. Without pausing to consider the consequences, Kilian stepped forward and let Bluebeard take charge of their conversation.

"Kilian, me boy," Bluebeard said as he placed a massive hand upon Kilian's shoulder, "it is time for you to form a bond with your birth mother."

Kilian shivered and glanced back at where Alex had disappeared beneath deck. To him, Kaldeena represented the death of his friend. She was not his mother. That title was reserved for the woman back in Lunameed who had given everything she could to ensure Kilian's happiness.

"I thought you were dead," he muttered as he allowed Bluebeard to guide him towards Kaldeena.

Bluebeard's grip tightened on Kilian's shoulder. Briefly, as if it were a warning, though Kilian wasn't sure why.

"Not just yet," Kaldeena responded as she stepped forward and looped her arm through Kilian's. "Let's take a tour about the deck, shall we? There is much for us to discuss."

She tugged on his arm and they walked away from Bluebeard. The rest of the ship's crew gave them leeway as they traveled around the main deck at a slow pace.

"I'm sure you have many questions," she said. Her voice was cold, almost harsh. Kilian looked sideways at her as she spoke, trying to gauge the change in her tone and expression. Her face was void of all expression and Kilian could decipher nothing from her.

"I do, actually," he said. "About last night," he began.

"Oh that," Kaldeena replied, "That was nothing. Honestly, Kilian, I thought you would have recognized that by now."

Her words did nothing to quell Kilian's distrust of her.

"Why did you do that to me?" Kilian asked in a tightly controlled voice. "Why did you let me think that you were dead? I'm sorry, but you're going to have to explain this because I truly do not understand."

She dug her nails so deeply and so quickly into Kilian's arm that he let a yelp of pain escape his lips before he could gain control of himself again. He tried to pull his arm out of her grasp, but she only clenched her hand more tightly around his flesh.

"Let me go!" Kilian hissed. For some, unexplainable reason Kilian did not want the rest of the crew to hear this conversation with Kaldeena.

She did not release him entirely, but when she turned her gaze towards him Kilian could see that her eyes had become more alert. It wasn't that they had looked glazed over before; it was just that her eyes seemed more focused. It was as if she were seeing him for the first time. She blinked at him and her expression of clarity disappeared.

"I'm sorry, Kilian. It appears as if we have gotten off on the incorrect footing. For that I am sorry." She did not sound genuine to Kilian, but he nodded at her. She flashed a brilliant smile at him, and Kilian grimaced internally. He did—could—not accept her apology.

"Let me explain more clearly," she said. "When we met again two years ago I had been searching for you for nearly fifteen years." Her lips trembled as she spoke and Kilian had the distinct impression that she was an actress in a one-act play. "I didn't know how I was supposed to reenter your life. I didn't know what Bluebeard's plan was." She paused and Kilian leaned into her with baited breath. She smiled at him. It was the type of smile Kilian imagined a mermaid would give before biting a human head off. His innards tightened.

"I'm sorry you didn't know how to talk to me," Kilian retorted snidely. Kaldeena blinked at him; Kilian shrugged his shoulders nonchalantly. "I'm sorry, Kaldeena, but all those years you weren't part of my life I had a mother. A good one, actually," he yanked his arm out of her grasp and took a step away from her. "All of this," he said as he gestured at the ship around them, "all of your apologies, they mean nothing to me. All I want is to do the task I signed on for when I left Lunameed. That's it, Kaldeena. I don't want or need you."

Kaldeena puffed out her cheeks that had turned a ruddy red color before exhaling in a cloud of mist. Her eyes narrowed in on Kilian and, for a short moment, Kilian thought that she might let a chip of her sour self slip through the cracks of her mask. Instead, she clutched at his hand. With an elaborate sweep of her hand, she brought Kilian's hand up to her breast held it against her heart. Kilian could feel the warmth of his birth mother's skin through the thin fabric of her gown and feel the rhythmic drumming of her heart. In a way, it was comforting. In another way, it was unnerving.

"Kilian, this is your one chance to gain favor with the Creators and reset the balance in our world. If you succeed, you will save us all. If you fail, well…" she trailed off.

Kilian took a moment to scan the rest of the deck. Every set of eyes stared back at him and Kaldeena. Kilian gritted his teeth and felt the hum of his ax vibrate in his hand. Heaving in a giant breath he opened his mouth to respond to Kaldeena.

"I'm only here to offer my services to the cause," she said quickly, stopping him in his tracks. Kilian stared at her blankly.

"No," he said smoothly, "thank you, but no."

The deck went still. Even the wind ceased its near constant whipping as Kaldeena's jaw slowly dropped. She snapped her maw shut, her ruby-red lips turning a near violet color as she stared Kilian down.

"No?" she asked slowly.

"No," Kilian repeated firmly.

A blistering wind swept over the ship at Kilian's singular word. He shivered uncontrollably as the wind bit into his exposed skin. Kaldeena's cloak fluttered behind her. The skies darkened and Kilian smelled the dampness in the air that spoke of a torrential storm.

"You dare deny me that which is my right?" Kaldeena's said softly, her voice no more than the gentlest of a lover's caress.

Kilian gripped his ax more firmly in his hand and set his feet apart. Puffing his chest out in a show of courage he wasn't sure he felt, Kilian said, "Yes. I would deny you that right for I do not believe it to be your right at all."

Kaldeena screamed.

Kilian fell to the ground, clutching at his ears as her ear-splitting screech filled the air. His head pounded and he felt as if it would explode. Closing his eyes, Kilian began to count the way his father had taught him to all those years ago. Slowly, the scream began to subside and Kilian was left with the faintest ringing in his ears.

"You're just like your father," Kaldeena hissed when Kilian finally looked up at her following the scream.

"That's a compliment," Kilian said groggily. The ringing in his ear made it difficult to concentrate. He tried to focus on her eyes. They darkened to obsidian the longer Kilian stared into them. Kilian gulped slightly as the chilled wind picked up. Flicking his eyes around the deck, he realized that her scream had brought everyone to their knees. Even Bluebeard kneeled on the deck with his hands held over his ears. Everyone looked dazed.

Without warning Kaldeena dropped to her knees before Kilian and clutched his chin in a vice-like grip. Her fingers were icy cold as they slithered across his skin. Gritting his teeth,

Kilian forced himself to stare straight into her now entirely black eyes.

His lips twitched slightly as she whispered, "I will crush you, just like I crushed your father."

Kilian's innards roiled. He felt a surge of red anger course through his flesh, heating him from where his hand grasped the ax. Through tightly clenched teeth Kilian said, "My father died in an accident."

Kaldeena gazed into Kilian's eyes unblinkingly. Her cheeks hand sunken deep into her face and there were now dark circles under her eyes. She looked tired, almost bedraggled. As if in defiance of this thought, tiny flecks of glitter swam on her skin as the dying rays of sunlight struck her. Her black lips pulled into a thin smile. "It's adorable that you still believe your father's death was an accident."

The ringing in Kilian's ears ceased as he jerked his chin from Kaldeena's grasp and stood. The heat from his ax coursed through his veins, empowering—more like urging—him to fight. He quelled his desire to strike the first blow with difficulty.

"Kaldeena," Bluebeard grumbled from a distance. His voice carried the hard notes of warning within it. She did not remove her gaze from Kilian's face as she slowly stood. She smirked at Kilian when she finally stood at eye level.

"Yes, Captain?" she said, her voice of a mixture of mockery and amusement.

Bluebeard gripped the hilt of the Labrys Sword as he cleared his throat. "You'll not be harming that boy," he said.

She raised one eyebrow disdainfully at Bluebeard's comment before quickly whipping around to face the newly crowned king. Kilian watched in horror as sharp fangs formed beneath her upper lip. Her skin turned into a blue pallor.

"You dare attempt to command me?" she hissed, her teeth clanging with each syllable. "I am the boy's mother. You are nothing more than a stand-in coach."

Bluebeard hefted one of his side daggers at Kaldeena so quickly that, if Kilian had blinked, he would have missed seeing the glint of the dagger's metal as it rotated in the air. Kaldeena, who had been standing between Kilian and Bluebeard disappeared in a puff of black smoke just as the dagger was about to pierce her heart. The knife grazed Kilian's cheek as it flew past him and dug into the railing behind him. Hot blood trickled down his cheek from the small wound.

Loud laughter filled the open air. Kilian crouched in a defensive posture as he waited for Kaldeena to reveal herself. Gripping his ax, Kilian felt its magic course through him. He instantly felt more alert and energized. He breathed in deeply and let his mind still.

"You're still such a small boy," Kaldeena giggled from somewhere above them. Kilian lifted his head and saw her shadowy figure shrouded by the fluttering cloth of the sails. "I see now that we will never be able to reconcile." Her voice had taken on a sad, almost mournful tone.

"What did you do to my father?" Kilian growled. He could barely hear his voice over the whoosh of the wind.

"Me?" Kaldeena asked in a sing-song voice. "Oh, Kilian, there is so much for you to learn."

"Then teach me," Kilian said, standing. "Tell me everything you want me to know. I promise I will listen." His ax hummed in his hand as he spoke and Kilian felt a moment of hesitation as he recognized the warning emanating from the ax's magic.

Kaldeena opened her mouth to speak just as an arrow laced with black feathers dug into her shoulder. She cried out in pain. Kilian shot a glance towards Bluebeard, who was notching a second arrow.

Kaldeena yanked the arrow from her wound with a single, bloody thrust. Dark liquid sprayed across all who stood beneath her. Her dark gaze fell on Bluebeard. Even from the distance separating them, Kilian could see the blood-lust in her eyes.

Without pausing to consider, Kilian ran at Bluebeard and knocked him to the ground as a ball of glittering black flames struck the spot where Bluebeard had just been standing. Grunting Kilian hoisted the other man from the ground and raised his ax in a defensive stance once more. Bluebeard lumbered to his feet, the now glowing sword clutched tightly in his hand. Kilian peered up into the masts, searching for signs of Kaldeena, but quickly realized that she had once again disappeared.

"Why is she toying with us?" Kilian asked Bluebeard as he pressed his back against his mentor's. He felt Bluebeard shrug but heard no response from the older man.

"Kilian, my dear, sweet son, don't you fret. We will meet again very soon. I look forward to witnessing the fulfillment of your prophecy," her cold lips pressed into his check as she spoke and Kilian saw the flash of black smoke as she briefly appeared before him. He swung out with his ax. Too late.

Breathing heavily, Kilian waited for his heart to stop hammering in his chest. He felt Bluebeard momentarily sag behind him before he felt the giant man stand tall once more. The howling wind died as suddenly as it had begun. Slowly, the rest of the ship's crew began to mill about the ship once more. Kilian sank to the deck, cold tears streaming down his cheeks. He didn't care if the rest of the crew saw his tears. After the next battle he would be dead and it wouldn't matter what they thought of him then.

A warm hand rested upon Kilian's shoulder as he continued to cry. Sniveling slightly, Kilian glanced up to see that Bluebeard stood above him. His face was kind as he looked down at his protégé.

"I'm sorry for bringing you into this, Kilian. It had to be   done."

"Bringing me into what?" Kilian asked with venom laced in his voice. "My destiny? The thing my father died trying to protect me against? There are so many things that I do not know." Kilian shook with anger as he spoke. "Or are you sorry for lying to me this entire time? I guess I'll never know."

He shook Bluebeard's hand from his shoulder as he wiped away the tears from his face. His skin felt dry and cracked as the gentle sea breeze swept across it. Kilian glowered at Bluebeard. "I don't want any more lies, Bluebeard. I thought I wanted to know the truth, the games you and my parents used to play. But now I realize that I don't. I don't want to know the secrets of my father's past. I don't want to know anything about it!" he shouted.

With that, Kilian spun and walked away from Bluebeard. *At least now I have something in common with Alex,* he realized. *We have both lost a piece of our innocence that we can never get back.* Kilian brooded over this thought as he descended the steps to the lower deck and his quarters once more.

Chapter Twenty-Four

The ship jerked, causing Kilian to fall to his knees as he stood on the forward most part of the deck. The entire vessel lurched as it struck another chunk of ice floating in the water. Kilian leaned over the railing and peered into the ocean's depths. What had once been a tranquil turquoise blue color was now a midnight black. Waves lapped against the ship in a crest of white foam. Icebergs, varying in size, dotted the seas. In the distance, Kilian saw the rise of a misty mountain cast in shadow. A thunderous roar filled the air and a massive spray of icy water splashed onto the deck. Kilian, drenched by the cold water, shivered as he heaved a rope taunt to set it in the correct position.

"Why are we sailing so far north?" Kilian asked through chattering teeth. One of Bluebeard's soldiers, a woman with white and bronze dreadlocks and a deep scar that stretched from her left eyebrow to her chin, scowled at him in response.

"It's t-t-too cold," Kilian grumbled as the soldier turned her back on him.

She whipped around to face him, "Humans are weak," she snarled. "You think this is cold? Try swimming through the Fanghold Sea. That," she said pointedly, "is cold. This is nothing more than a little ice."

The ship shook slightly as it struck yet another hunk of ice. "I don't even know where the Fanghold Sea is," Kilian mumbled as a wave of ice water washed over him once more. He heard the soldier snicker at him, but she did not return to discuss the matter further.

It had been ten days since Kaldeena had interrupted Kilian's travels to Beyond the Forgotten Isles. During that time, Bluebeard and Alex had successfully avoided speaking with Kilian at every turn. Kilian suspected that Bluebeard had ordered his soldiers to answer only the most basic of inquiries. Although Kilian had decided that he no longer wished to know his father's secrets, he couldn't help but be angry at Bluebeard's treatment of him over the past ten days.

He had thought it strange that Bluebeard had changed their course from a straight shot to the Forgotten Isles to a northward drive. He had even ordered some of the merfolk to row against the waves to speed their progress towards the north. Within two days' time, the air had turned frosty and Kilian had taken to wearing his heavy cloak on deck. In contrast, the merfolk seemed to relish the near-freezing temperatures. They continued to parade around the ship in barely any clothing. At some points, Kilian had found himself blushing at the obvious display of skin from some of the female soldiers Bluebeard had brought with them. Now, he could barely see anything. His eyelashes were frozen together and his entire body shivered as he tried to keep warm.

"You look like death," Alex said as he sauntered over to where Kilian toiled with the rope. His stiff fingers barely curled around the rope as he struggled to keep ahold of it.

Kilian gave no response. His face stung from the icy air and the sound of yet another sliver of ice falling into the sea made his bones ache. His head pounded as he forced himself to cling to the rope.

"Honestly, Kilian. I can't see how everyone still thinks you're the hero spoken of in prophecy," Alex picked at a rough spot on the back of his hand as he spoke. "Look at you," he smirked as Kilian's lips cracked from the cold and began to bleed. "You're nothing more than a weak child."

Kilian gritted his teeth. "We'll see who the real hero is when we travel beyond the Forgotten Isles, Alex."

"Yes, we will."

They stood in silence for a moment as icy cold water doused them. "Do you know why we are traveling this far north?" Kilian asked.

Alex cleared his throat. Kilian waited for a response that didn't come.

"Ah, good, you're both here," Bluebeard bellowed as he strode towards them through the spray of yet another chunk of ice cascading into the water from the larger, more robust iceberg in the distance. "It is time."

Kilian raised an eyebrow at Bluebeard and stole a glance at Alex. He appeared just as perplexed as Kilian felt.

"Time for what, exactly, Bluebeard?" Kilian asked. Salt water dripped from his nose as he spoke. Kilian's entire face felt numb from the cold, but he forced himself to continue holding onto the rope. Thankfully, he wore thick leather gloves that helped keep his hands from becoming raw. Still, he felt his hand muscles cramping as he clenched the rope tightly in his fist.

"Just time," Bluebeard said mysteriously.

Grunting, Kilian heaved the rope towards him and tied it off to the railing of the ship. It lurched slightly as the small amount of slack gave way, but the knot held. Kilian sighed in relief as he noticed that Bluebeard was smiling in approval at him. Alex, on the other hand, only sneered.

"Follow me," Bluebeard commanded as he walked towards the aft of the ship.

Alex and Kilian jockeyed for position as they followed Bluebeard the way race-horses do on a track. Each time Kilian edged Alex out for being the first in line behind Bluebeard, Alex would shove himself into Kilian's path. Bluebeard did not seem to notice the silent battle happening behind him. Instead, he continued towards the back of the ship with long, powerful strides.

A figure, clad in a tan leather cloak and pantaloons stood at the railing. Even from the distance between them, Kilian could see that her hands were encased in fur-lined fingerless gloves that had a delicately embroidered dragonfly stitched into their backs. Although her back was turned to them, Kilian instantly knew who the figure was.

"Tavia," he whispered.

As if she could hear his muffled response, Tavia turned to face them as they approached her. Her face had become leaner during their time apart and her cheeks were not the same rosy color Kilian had come to adore. Her hair, once luscious, had turned into a dull, limp mess that was braided down her back. Aghast, Kilian audibly sucked in a sharp breath at the sight of her. Alex glanced at him with a strange expression on his face, but said nothing as they continued to approach Tavia.

Her eyes flicked over Kilian as if he were a plaything she had known as a child but now regretted ever purchasing. With a sinking sensation, Kilian watched as Tavia embraced first Bluebeard and then Alex. She did not offer to embrace Kilian. Instead, she merely nodded at him curtly. This was all the acknowledgment that she afforded him.

"It is good to see you, Tavia," Alex said. He smiled broadly at her.

"You as well, Alex," she smiled warmly at him and grasped his forearm in her hand. "It has been too long. You must tell me everything that has transpired since you left us after the Forgotten Isles."

Alex's eyes misted at the unspoken reference to Adrienne. He wiped at his eyes with the back of his hand. "Ach, this cold," he grumbled. "It's always making my eyes water."

Kilian hadn't noticed anything of the sort before, but he did not contradict Alex as he continued to wipe at his eyes.

"It is frigid here, isn't it?" Tavia said.

"Tis," Bluebeard said. "What in the blazes are you doing this far north, Tavia? Bout blew me mind when ya asked me ta travel this way for ya."

"I had business," Tavia said coyly. Bluebeard gave her a penetrating look as he waited for her to continue, but Tavia did not elaborate.

"I see," Bluebeard finally said. "Well, I'm mighty glad that we were able to rendezvous at this point. My how I have missed you."

They stood in awkward silence for a moment before Tavia asked, "I assume that my old cabin is still available?"

Bluebeard mumbled something about needing to kick out one of the soldiers he'd brought with him from Ula Una and wandered off. Alex, who had continued to wipe at his eyes for several moments, said something vague about needing to check on the rest of the crew. His boots squeaked on the water-slick deck of the ship as he left Tavia and Kilian alone.

Tavia looked out at the water. Bitter cold wind whipped through her tendrils of hair, causing them to flutter around her face. Even with her lines and graying hair, she looked more beautiful to him than any other woman he had ever met. Her back was turned to him, but he could see her profile among the rays of sunshine filtering through the overcast sky.

Stepping up towards her, Kilian stroked her back with the palm of his hand. Even through her layers of clothing, he could feel her warmth radiating outwards. To him, she would always be like the sun. She shivered slightly as his fingers grazed the soft spot between her neck and her right ear.

"I've missed you," he whispered as he leaned down to nuzzle at her neck.

She jerked away from him and the warmth he had felt only a second before fleeted away as if it had never been.

"It is good to see you, Kilian," she said flatly.

Gooseflesh covered Kilian's arms at the sound of his name on her lips. Though, he felt a twinge of fear sweep over him at the coldness of her voice.

"And you?" he responded. "Have you not missed me?"

"No," she barked quickly. Her voice was stern and emotionless as she spoke.

"Tavia," he whispered gently as he placed his hands on both of her shoulders and turned her body to face him. "Please, just talk to me." His voice cracked as he spoke. "Please," he pleaded.

She stepped away from him, extracting herself from his grasp in the process. "I'm glad you've made it to the final battle, Kilian. I'm certain you will be successful." she smiled at him for the first time since her arrival on-board.

She began to walk away from him, but Kilian clutched her hand in his own. Butterflies fluttered in his tummy as he clung to her.

"What happened to you?" he asked.

She tried to pull her hand out of his grasp, but he maintained a firm grip on her hand.

"Let me go," Tavia demanded as she struggled to pull her hand free from his grasp. "I mean it, Kilian."

"No," he said, taking a step towards her. "Not until you tell me why you left me."

She exhaled sharply and Kilian could smell the scent of sweet wine and dates on her breath. It was intoxicating. He leaned in to kiss her. She slapped him with her other hand. Surprised, Kilian loosened his grip on her hand just long enough for her to slip her hand out of his.

"Don't ever do that again," she said as she stalked away from him. Cursing beneath his breath, Kilian began to follow her but his boot slid across the wet deck and he thudded to the planks. He winced in pain as his knee slammed into the hard wood.

"Serves you right," Tavia said as she looked down on him. Then, more gently, she said, "You'll see that this is for the best."

Kilian shivered on the floor as he watched her walk away from him. *It can't be for the best*, he told himself. *It can't be*. He lay on the cold deck until his fingers turned a grayish-blue color. Only then did he push himself up and wandered to his cabin. No one stopped him as he went.

***

They traveled for two more weeks before finally reaching the shadows of the Forgotten Isles. Unlike the southern edge of the isles that they had traveled across during their first visit, the channels in the northern tip were too narrow and shallow for even a rowboat to pass through. Instead, they had to travel the entire length of the isles by foot. Kilian's boots sunk into deep mud as he followed the trail of merfolk through the shallows. They had abandoned the Dragon's Breath at the rocky beach separating the northern shore of the Forgotten Isles and the Paralosa Ocean.

The pillars were just as eerie as Kilian remembered them. They rose from murky water to touch the gray, clouded skies above. Only this time, there was a putrid smell wafting through the air that Kilian did not remember from before. The small golden key he'd retrieved from one of the statues hummed slightly against his leg. He kept it hidden, deep inside his pocket, but he still wasn't sure what he needed the key for. He trusted that Bluebeard would let him know when the time was right.

During their two-week journey, Tavia had kept her distance from him. Even when they'd disembarked from the Dragon's Breath, Tavia had remained far away from him. She had clung to Alex's side as they traveled across the muddy land. Whenever Kilian drew near, Alex would place his hand on the hilt of his sword and look at Kilian through narrowed eyes.

Now, as they crossed the muddy terrain towards the clearing where Kilian had secured the golden key, Tavia could avoid him by traveling at the head of the pack with Bluebeard. Kilian had been assigned guard duty at the end of the line. At the onset of their journey, he had contemplated arguing with Bluebeard about this assignment, but had thought better of it when he'd seen the hard look in Tavia's eyes.

Maybe she doesn't love me anymore, Kilian thought bitterly to himself as he squished through the mud. Kilian shivered slightly. *Maybe she hates me. It's my fault that Adrienne died*, he reminded himself. These thoughts plagued him the further they progressed into the Forgotten Isles.

The sound of a trumpet's call pulled Kilian from his thoughts. His first reaction to the sound was to tighten his grip on his ax. He remembered the last time he'd heard a sound like that. The memory of the pus-ridden creatures filled his mind as he listened for any sound coming from behind the misty pillars lining their path. The horn trumpeted again; this time it was louder. Kilian cocked his head toward the sound as he tried to determine how far away it was.

The scent of jasmine and rose water filled the otherwise putrid air just as a wall of shadowy figures moved beyond the line of pillars ahead of them. The trumpet blasted a single, ringing note that hung in the air long after the horn had been laid to rest. It was a forlorn, empty note that filled Kilian with a great sense of sadness at its sound. A shiver ran up his spine when the note finally faded into the wind.

Some of the younger soldiers shrieked as the first of the shadows shambled into the light. Just as Kilian had feared, they were the same pus-ridden monsters he had faced during his first journey to the Forgotten Isles.

"Stand back," he shouted as he raced towards the front of the army. "Don't let their blood or the pus touch you!"

He skidded to a halt as he neared Bluebeard and Tavia. The former had already drawn the Labrys Sword and his beard glowed a brilliant blue as he squinted his eyes at the monsters before them. They stopped their approach mere inches before the creatures. Kilian could smell their rotting bodies and heard their gurgled breathing as they piled into disorganized lines in front of them. A lone rider galloped between the monsters without opposition. If anything, the creatures bowed their heads in reverence to the man riding atop a massive midnight stallion.

"Kha-ael-ido," Kilian whispered. He held his ax firmly in his hand as the other man approached. Its haft sizzled in his grasp as the ax's heat mixed with Kilian's sweaty palms. His shoulders tensed as he remembered the promise he had made to the Kha-ael-ido the first time he'd visited the Forgotten Isles. He stole a glance at Tavia as he remembered another part of that night that was much more enjoyable.

"You have returned," Kha-ael-ido proclaimed as he drew near. His voice was as regal as ever. "I am so pleased to see you again, Kilian Clearwater." His face darkened as he looked beyond Kilian to where Tavia and Bluebeard stood. He raised an eyebrow at them, but quickly turned his attention back to Kilian.

"It is time, is it not, for you to accomplish your third and final task?" Kha-ael-ido asked as he turned in his saddle and waved his arm at the pus-covered monsters. They crawled back into the shadows at a slow pace. Their eyes never seemed to waver from the soldiers in Kilian's army.

"It is," Bluebeard chimed in. "As the gatekeeper to The Beyond, you know that Kilian cannot achieve his third task without your help."

"I see," Kha-ael-ido said absentmindedly. He was stroking his chin and staring out at the army. His eyes flicked to Bluebeard and Tavia, an amused expression on his face.

"Do you believe you're ready for this task, Kilian Clearwater?" he asked.

Kilian paused. In all the time it had taken them to travel to the Forgotten Isles, not once had someone asked him if he felt ready to face the Shadow King. "I suppose it doesn't matter," Kilian stated. "I'm here now and I have to face him if I am ever to be rid of the weight of the prophecy."

"The Shadow King is not easy to defeat," Kha-ael-ido pushed.

"Don't you mean, Rhymaldis?" Kilian asked sardonically. The slight smirk that had formed on Kilian's face as he'd uttered the Shadow's King's name vanished as a gust of blistering cold wind racked his body.

"We do not speak his name," Kha-ael-ido hissed. He tilted his head to the wind as he if he were listening for a response.

"Why not?" Kilian asked. He glanced at Tavia. Her face was shielded by the billowing fabric of her hood. *She doesn't care about me*, he reminded himself. Feeling emboldened, Kilian took a step towards Kha-ael-ido and said, "It's his name, isn't it? Rhymaldis." He said the Shadow King's name slowly, deliberately savoring each syllable as he spoke. The wind continued to bluster.

Kha-ael-ido slapped him. "You fool," he shouted over the wind. "You impotent little fool!"

The sky grew dark. The wind howled through the trees and between the spaces of the stone pillars. Kilian instinctively grasped his ax firmly in his hand. Its warmth comforted him as he scanned his surroundings. It was too dark to see much; however, in the distance he could see the reflection of a hundred glowing eyes. Gulping loudly, Kilian turned to face Kha-ael-ido once more, but the other man had disappeared.

"To me!" Bluebeard commanded. His voice was hoarse and Kilian thought he detected a note of panic in the captain's tenor. The rest of the guards formed a tight circle around Bluebeard.

Kilian did not join them. Instead, he peered into the dark depths before him. Even the sister moons had been blocked by the cloud cover as the wind continued to rush through the trees.

"Kilian," he heard Tavia shout behind him. "Please come back!"

Kilian could hear the tremble in her voice as she spoke, but paid it no heed. The glowing eyes seemed to grow the longer Kilian stood on the precipice between the shadowy woods and the swamp-like water. Within the howling wind Kilian thought he heard the anguished cries of men.

A firm hand clasped Kilian's shoulder and yanked him backwards. He stumbled from the shock and nearly fell to the ground. Tavia threw her weight under his and kept him from slipping into the murky water of the Forgotten Isles.

"What were you thinking?" Tavia muttered as she peered into his face. Her cheeks were flushed and sweat ran in droplets down her brow.

He looked past her without answering. The reflective eyes had moved closer. They were just beyond the dim light of the torches the soldiers carried. Kilian raised one trembling hand and pointed at the eyes. Tavia turned quickly. Her hair smacked Kilian in the face as she turned, momentarily breaking his concentration.

When he looked again, the eyes had disappeared. Tavia turned back to him, one eyebrow raised, "Damnation, Kilian! You could have gotten us killed!" She shoved him in the chest with her right hand.

Her voice was shrill in his ear. Kilian jerked away from her as he continued to peer out into the wilderness. *I could have sworn*, he began to think, but then stopped himself as he looked again. There was nothing expect the trees.

"We do not speak his name this close to the Beyond, Kilian," Bluebeard said as he approached. His expression was grim and Kilian had the nagging sensation that he was about to receive a lecture. "How do you even know his name?" the captain grumbled as he shoved past him to examine the trees for himself.

"You're the one," Kilian began.

The sound of Bluebeard's laughter cut him off. "Damnation, Kilian. Do you have to repeat everything I say?"

Sweat slipping down his forehead, Kilian turned his attention back to Kha-ael-ido as he emerged from the treeline. The regal old man had summoned his creatures again. With a sigh, Kha-ael-ido said, "You are still young and foolish, Kilian Clearwater, but you are the best the Light has seen fit to provide us. Come. I will take you to the bridge between the Isles and the Beyond."

Kha-ael-ido led the army through a small forest before coming upon what appeared to be a solid wall of gray mist. Kilian couldn't see more than a fingertip into the dense haze.

"What is this?" he asked as Kha-ael-ido shoved his hand through the wall of mist.

"This, Kilian, is how the Creators ensured that the Shadow King would never be able to invade the rest of Mitier."

"But I thought…" Kilian began.

"Yes, the Shadow King has been gaining power. He has almost broken free from his prison on several occasions. If it were not for this, I would never allow you to cross the bridge to his realm. You're still not ready."

Annoyed at Kha-ael-ido's condescending tone, Kilian shoved his hand into the mist. He felt the hum of magic and then a great sense of confusion. Pulling his hand back out of the mist, he asked, "What are we doing here?"

Kha-ael-ido smirked. "This is a magical barrier forged by the Creators, Kilian. You cannot cross to the other side without my help." He smiled down at Kilian the way a grandfather does a small child. "Now, where is that golden key you procured from the statue?"

Digging deep into his pocket, Kilian retrieved the golden key. Lint and an old bit of string came with it. Kilian shoved the key into Kha-ael-ido's outstretched hand. His hands were clammy and he felt just a little lightheaded. *This is it*, he told himself. *The final battle.* He gulped as he stole a glance at Tavia. Since returning to the Dragon's Breath, the color had returned to her cheeks and her hair had regained its full lushness. The violet starbursts around her eyes seemed to sparkle as she stared into the mists. *She's even more beautiful now than she was when I first met her*, Kilian thought. She did not look at him as she strode forwards until she was parallel with Kha-ael-ido.

"Are you sure we can return once we've crossed the divide?"

Kha-ael-ido laughed. "Only if our young chosen one here survives."

Kilian felt the heat rise in his cheeks as he noticed several of the soldiers eyeing him with distrust.

"What do you mean I have to succeed? Are you saying that none of these warriors will be able to retreat if I fall?"

"That's exactly the letter of it, my friend," Kha-ael-ido responded, a faint smile on his lips. "But, of course, you will prevail. You are the Light's Hero, after all." His smile did not reach his eyes and Kilian felt his innards squirm as he realized that he might be condemning everyone in the army to death.

"Bah!" Bluebeard exclaimed. "We've come this far. We cannot turn back now." He winked at Kilian as he stepped towards Kha-ael-ido. "Do it," he commanded.

Kha-ael-ido shoved the key into the wall of mist. Instantly, the gray mist began to shimmer. It was if the entire wall of mist had turned into thousands of diamond shards. Kilian gasped as they reflected the starlight into millions of fractured light beams. It was one of the most beautiful things he had ever seen.

Kha-ael-ido stretched out a finger and lightly flicked the surface of the barrier. The diamond shards turned to glittering dust that fell heavily upon the army. Kilian coughed as he accidentally sucked in a mouthful of the powder. Where there had been only mist now stood a long causeway. Kilian could not see where it ended, but he knew where it must lead.

"The Beyond," he whispered out loud.

Kha-ael-ido clapped him on the shoulder. "So it is, my friend. So it is."

Kilian made the mistake of looking down one side of the bridge. There was nothing but a steep drop into darkness. Shivering slightly, Kilian waited for Bluebeard to give the command to cross the bridge. His heart hammered in his chest. *This is it*, he thought.

Bluebeard raised the Labrys Sword high into the air. Only the sound of the wind interrupted the silence that followed. Kilian watched in awe as Bluebeard's soldiers slowly raised their weapons in fidelity to their king. *And to me*, he realized as Bluebeard pointed his sword towards Kilian. *They also fight for me*. Bluebeard lowered his arm and the army began marching towards the bridge in tight, practiced lines.

"Wait," Kha-ael-ido said. Bluebeard instantly raised his fist and the army stopped their advance. "To honor the bravery of our new hero, I would like to make a tribute." He rubbed his hands together as he spoke. "Please, accept my army of Revanti to aid you in your quest."

"Revanti?" Kilian asked.

"My creatures," Kha-ael-ido responded as he motioned towards the pus-ridden creatures shambling from out of the shadows. "They cannot be controlled by the Shadow King for they belong to me."

"And here I had just been calling them pus-ridden creatures," Kilian said with a laugh. "It's good to know that they have a name."

"Uh, yes," Kha-ael-ido said slowly. He looked uncomfortable as he continued, "I hope they serve you well."

"Thank you," Kilian replied as more than seventy of the Revanti joined the armies' ranks. "They won't turn on anyone in our army, will they?" he asked suddenly as he remembered how the effects of their pus had nearly killed Tavia.

"They will not harm those who follow your lead, Kilian Clearwater," Kha-ael-ido responded mysteriously.

Kilian glanced back at the army. They were an interesting group. *Merfolk and pus-ridden creatures from the Forgotten Isles, who would have thought?* Kilian wondered as he turned back to thank Kha-ael-ido once more. However, the older man had completely disappeared. Shrugging, Kilian motioned for Bluebeard to lead the charge to battle.

Chapter Twenty-Five

At times, the winds that whipped across the bridge to the Beyond were so strong that Kilian felt like the entire army could be swept into the abyss. Bluebeard had ordered that the men tie ropes around their waists to ensure that if one warrior fell, the rest would be able to save them. Despite the wind, the world around them was completely silent, save for an occasional moan from somewhere always ahead of them. The sounds of despair made the hair on Kilian's arms stand-on-end and his mind create images of death and destruction—mainly his own. During these moments, Kilian would grip his ax and let the surge of power therein sustain him. The ax's power was like a drug of which he constantly needed. It unsettled Kilian how much he relied upon its strength.

Although the journey across the bridge seemed to take days, Kilian never felt thirst nor hunger. All he felt was an intense desire to keep going. He had tried to speak to Bluebeard on several occasions, but the older man only grunted and continued forward in silence. During these times, Kilian would turn his attention to Tavia. Although there had been a moment on the Forgotten Isles where she had shown concern for his safety, it had been a fleeting one. She, too, traveled in silence and steadfastly ignored him as they traveled across the bridge. Kilian prayed to the Light that they would reach the Beyond soon and end their days of silent darkness.

His prayer came true in the form of a gust of a hot, dusty whirlwind that pushed against them. Rough sand swept across their faces, ripping away flesh and leaving behind screams of agony. Through the torrent of sandstorm, Kilian could see mountainous hills looming ahead of them. The army of merfolk and Revanti pushed onwards. Through the wind, Kilian saw the soft glow of Bluebeard's beard as he tried to soften the wind's effects. Gritty sand filled Kilian's mouth, nose, and ears. He couldn't cough. He could barely see without the sand scraping across his eyes. Just when he thought he couldn't stand the sand blast a moment longer, he stepped through to the other side.

The orange sun hurt Kilian's eyes. The journey through darkness had been too long and now the light was too bright. He quickly pulled his hood up and over his face, blocking out the sun's brilliance. Slowly, his eyes adjusted to the light. Stubby shrubs sprouted across the terrain. There were no birds or animals that Kilian could see. Unlike in the forests back in Lunameed and Siguila, there was no sound in this place. Not even the wind blew hard enough to cause even the slightest rattle. The silence unnerved him.

"Well, me boy, we're finally here," Bluebeard said roughly as he pulled out his pipe and stuffed it full of mureechi. The familiar, pungent odor swept over Kilian. He coughed, slightly, from the mixture of dry air and smoke. Bluebeard blew a ring of smoke that deftly turned into the shape of a flying dragon as he stared out in the wasteland. Kilian knew that the mureechi pipe meant that Bluebeard was locked in deep thought about his next move.

As he waited for Bluebeard to finish thinking, Kilian turned back to face the army they had rallied to join them in their fight against the Shadow King. They were not a large force. With the addition of Kha-ael-ido's Revanti, Kilian estimated that they now had only four-hundred soldiers.

"I'm not sure we'll win in the end, Kilian," Bluebeard said. Kilian's ax hummed violently in his hand. *I still haven't given this a name yet*, he thought as he peered into Bluebeard's eyes.

"Why do you say that?" he asked.

Bluebeard puffed on his pipe several times before responding. His eyes were pensive and Kilian had the distinct impression that he was seeing a different side to the captain than he had since Kaldeena had murdered Adrienne. He waited for Bluebeard to reply.

"I'm not sure you're ready," the captain responded.

Kilian balked at that. "I've been training for the past two years, Bluebeard. I know this is the final task that you've been preparing me for, but you can't let your worry stop us now. We've come too far."

Bluebeard chuckled to himself. "It's not that son," he said softly. He looked away from Kilian before saying, "It's just that I'm not sure…" he trailed off.

"You're not sure about what, Bluebeard? That I'll survive?" Kilian shrugged. "You know, ever since you basically kidnapped me from my family, I've had the unnerving feeling that I wouldn't see them again, or that, if I did, that I would do terrible things to them. I've dreamt about it."

Bluebeard perked up at Kilian's words. "You've dreamt about it?" Bluebeard searched Kilian's face as he spoke.

"Yes," Kilian said uncertainly. He had never spoken with Bluebeard about his fears before.

Bluebeard paled slightly as he puffed on his pipe and stared past Kilian into the sandy desert.

"Do you care to explain your concern?" Kilian asked as he grasped Bluebeard's arm and slowly pulled the pipe away from the other man's mouth. "I can tell that you know more than what you're letting on."

Bluebeard sighed heavily. He opened his mouth to speak but before a single word was uttered a spinning pile of dust swept over them. The sand clung to every crevice of Kilian's body. He could feel the sharp particles scraping across his skin as they rushed past him. He tried to breath but was met with a mouthful of grainy filth. His eyes burned as sand darted into them. His throat raw from being scraped clean from the copious amount of grit he'd swallowed, Kilian cough profusely as the whirlwind subsided.

His vision clearing, Kilian peered into the desert. He sucked a breath in sharply at what he saw. Knights clad in black armor ranged in the desert in rows that were seemingly unending. They did not move, even as the funnel of wind and sand passed over them. Kilian shivered as a coldness crept over him. Not even the warmth of his ax made the ice coursing through his veins subside. His locked on a figure at the front of the army.

Clad in red robes and armor so dark that it barely shimmered in the bright sunlight, a lone figure silently drifted forward. He carried a glowing hammer. Kilian's heart skipped as recognition set in.

"Rhymaldis," he whispered into the wind.

The figure paused and seemed to stare straight at Kilian. In a slow, deliberate manner, the Shadow King raised his massive hammer. Kilian gulped and his sweaty hands slipped on the smooth handle of his ax. *I never did name you*, he thought as he waited for what he knew was coming. *Hopefully your next bearer will.* As if in slow motion the knights behind Rhymaldis began to charge.

"To arms!" Bluebeard shouted in a raspy voice that Kilian barely recognized. He shoved past Kilian as a cloud of dust rose from behind the charging army.

The Revanti rushed forward, leaving the merfolk and the rest of the army behind. Although they carried no weapons with them, they fell upon the first wave of Shadow Knights in an explosion of black pus and cracking bones. Kilian couldn't tell if it were the Shadow Knights or the Revanti being broken apart, but he was thankful for the distraction.

The sun was blotted out as arrows rained down upon them from above. Kilian had just enough time to lift his shield before the arrows lodged themselves into the ground around him. One arrow sank into his shield and grazed the tip of his nose. A thin trickle of blood ran down his face as Kilian let his shield fall and began charging towards the army with his ax raised.

Kilian saw a barrage of blue fire shoot through the sky and land on the hills before him. Each blast erupted in a tower of flame before quickly receding. Scorched knights, their capes on fire fell to the ground wordlessly. The merfolk pressed forwards, their curved blades and crossbows ready. *We just might win this*, Kilian thought as he cut through a group of three shadow knights. Their heads rolled as his glowing red ax severed them from their bodies.

He cut the legs out from under another knight before turning to see how Tavia was faring. She was nowhere to be found. Kilian's heart beat rapidly in his chest and he searched for her in the fray. That's when he noticed the bones of the Shadow Knights reforming.

Pointing his hand at the reanimating Shadow Knights, Kilian called towards Bluebeard, "Watch out!" just as one of the knights grasped Bluebeard around the neck. Kilian watched in horror as Bluebeard's face turned puce and he dropped his sword as he tried to pry the knight's fingers off his neck. Alex unexpectedly retrieved Bluebeard's sword and slashed it through the knight's arm. Bluebeard dropped to the ground heavily, but he was alive.

Kilian breathed a sigh of relief just as a piercing pain shot through the back of his head. It felt the way he imagined a knife sinking into his brain would. The world spun in an array of colors and dust. Debilitated by the pain, Kilian sank to one knee. His ax slipped from his fingers as he clutched his head between his open palms. The thudding of his own heart blocked out the sounds of battle he knew must be happening all around him. His body jolted as he felt the familiar pressure of someone—something—trying to break through the barriers he'd placed as protection around his mind.

NO! Kilian screamed, if only in his mind. The presence pushed against Kilian's resolve. It battered him. It made him cringe each time he felt it rage against Kilian's barriers.

"At last, you have come."

The voice reverberated through Kilian's dulled mind. He shook as the words consumed every bit of him. A single word repeated in his mind until at last he shouted, "Rhymaldis!"

The ringing in Kilian's ears ceased.

Kilian stood in a dark, misty abyss, like the dream world Kaldeena had taken him. Black water covered his bare feet. It sloshed as he spun in a circle, desperately trying to figure out where he was. The air was cool and carried not a hint of a breeze. Twinkling yellow lights fluttered around him. It reminded him of the starbugs his sister, May, had always insisted that they catch during the summer months back in Lunameed.

The sound of splashing water drew his attention. She was there. He saw her small frame silhouetted by the twinkling lights.

"May," he called out. Her narrow shoulders shook as she inhaled a breath. "May!" he said again. He took a step towards her.

Her shadow shuddered and she took a shambling step towards him.

Kilian breathed in sharply. May's cheeks were pale and sunken. Her once lively eyes appeared dull. A cut above her eyebrow had been poorly patched and the black threads of her stitches puckered as a thin trail of black pus seeped from between their gaps.

"Oh, May," Kilian stammered as he reached out to her. "What happened to you? What…"

"You should have never left us, Kilian." Her voice came in a whimper. She bowed her head and Kilian saw what he had not before. She carried a limp body in her arms.

"No," Kilian whispered as he staggered towards his younger sibling. May's expression darkened the closer he got to them.

"You did this," she said flatly.

Willis's eyes were still open. They were opaque, the way a porcelain doll's turn when they've been left in the rain for too long. *Except*, Kilian reminded himself, *Willis isn't a doll.* He reached out towards his little brother, his entire hand quivering.

"What happened?" he found himself asking. He couldn't bring himself to touch his brother's face. He knew what he would feel: cold, rotting flesh.

"Not sure. Ma took sick with it first. She didn't last too long after Willis caught it."

Black boils covered one side of his little brother's face. They were crusted over with a yellow-white film. Kilian smelled his brother's decay. Even as he looked on a maggot squirmed out of one of the pustules in a small spray of dark discharge.

"You did this," May repeated. Her voice sounded hollow and distant. Kilian tore his gaze from his brother and peered into his sister's eyes. They carried a fury in them that Kilian couldn't believe was real.

"I'm sorry," he began, but stopped when he noticed that the air around his sister had begun to shimmer.

"You're not real," he found himself whispering as he cupped her cheek. The shimmering air engulfed them and Kilian had the sensation of being pulled through dense water. His sister's face faded into the shadows, his hand slipping through the still-shimmering mist.

He landed, with a bone-shattering thud upon the hard, familiar ground of his home's farm. It didn't look the way he remembered. Gray skies clouded out all traces of the sun and long shadows stretched across the muddy, unkempt land. His heart beat loudly in his chest and his breathing came in ragged bursts. *I can't be here*, Kilian thought. His mind raced. *Has this all been some sort of terrible dream?* He pinched himself and felt the tingling pain of his short nails digging into his skin. Condensation from the air pooled on his arms and shoulders. It was cold to the touch and Kilian wished that he were wearing something more than the old, tattered clothes he'd had following his father's death.

"Kilian, me boy, I'm so glad that we get to have this one last chance to talk."

Kilian spun around in the direction of his father's voice. "I'm here, Father!" he shouted.

There was no one there.

Tendrils of fear wound themselves around his gut. Breathing shakily, Kilian called out, "Father?"

"It's not too late, son. You can still turn back."

His father materialized out of the gray mist swirling across the land. Kilian took an involuntary step backwards. He had seen a lot of things during his time traveling with Bluebeard, but never had he seen someone materialize from the mists the way his father just had.

"You can still be free," his father's incorporeal form said as he floated closer to Kilian.

This isn't real, Kilian reminded himself. *This is just the dreamland, like the place Kaldeena took me. This can't be real.* Still, he couldn't help but feel joy at being able to speak to his father again, even if it was only in his mind.

"I know you were just trying to protect me," Kilian said. "I understand why you stole me away from Kaldeena, why you married Ma. I get it now," Kilian paused. "I forgive you, Father." A tear slipped from the corner of Kilian's eye as he spoke. "I forgive you."

"You have nothing to forgive, Kilian. I saved your life. I had hoped that I would have been able to train you before this time came, but it wasn't meant to be."

"You should have taught me all those years..." Kilian trailed off as his father placed a ghostly hand upon his shoulder. Really, his hand hovered inches above Kilian's skin. He knew his father couldn't touch him. Still, a shiver ran up his spine as his father's hand lingered above his body.

"You deserved to have a chance at a normal life, Kilian," his father's voice wavered as he spoke and his smoky silhouette shimmered slightly. "All I ever wanted was to protect you."

"Yeah," Kilian grumbled as he swatted at his father's incorporeal hand. "You really protected me." His voice was mocking and cold, but Kilian didn't care. Even his bones felt tired as he regarded his father. "You died, we were thrust into poverty, and I had to make a choice." Despite his best efforts to contain his emotions, Kilian's voice cracked as he spoke. "There was a prophecy, Father. I never had a chance. Kaldeena..."

"I see you've met your birth mother," Nathanial said sardonically as he cut into Kilian's tirade.

"I have," Kilian responded. Despite his heavy breathing, he kept his voice as neutral as possible.

"And how did that go?" his father asked as he stole a quick glance at Kilian.

Kilian picked at a scab on his thumb to avoid speaking to his father. It stung slightly as the hard layer of skin peeled away from his hand. Blood sprang to the surface and he sucked on it to take the pain away.

"Ah," Nathanial sighed, startling Kilian.

Kilian glared up at his father. "None of this would have happened if you had only been honest with me!" He pulled his thumb out of his mouth as he spoke. "Kaldeena told me that it was her fault you died." Hot tears pooled in his eyes. The frustration and fear he had felt following his father's death swelled within him as he continued to speak. "If only you had just told me about her, maybe you'd still be alive. Maybe I would be more prepared for this." He sank to his knees. He cried in a way he hadn't since the day they'd buried what remained of his father's charred bones. All the pain he'd kept locked away spilled out of him. *Stupid*, Kilian thought as he angrily wiped at his face. *I'm about to battle against the greatest warrior Mitier has ever known and I'm bawling like a child. Snap out of it Kilian!* He commanded himself to quit acting like the blubbering baby he knew he must seem.

He sprang to his feet.

"I wanted to give you your best chance, Kilian," Nathanial said softly. His shadowy figure seemed to be fading into the dimness all around them. "I'm so sorry I couldn't save you."

Pain shot through Kilian's shoulder. He imagined his arm being ripped away from his body as he skid backwards from the force of whatever—or whoever—had hit him. He released a howl of pain as his back slammed into a large boulder. Whirling lights danced around his eyes as his head whipped backwards and then forwards again. The crash of metal against metal resounded in his ears, causing his head to ache. He smelled the mixture of piss and sweat as he rolled over and his face pressed into the damp earth.

Blinking through the mud, Kilian slowly pushed himself up. His head pounded as he stared up into the harsh light of the orange sun. His ears rang as he sat up. A spasm passed through his body and he retched as he realized his left shoulder had popped out of its socket. Tenderly, Kilian prodded at his arm. His skin burned and he could already see his flesh swelling. Even the lightest of touches was agony.

Without thinking, Kilian bit his bottom lip and shoved his arm upwards. Tears leaked from his eyes until he heard the faint pop of his shoulder sliding back into place. Instantly, the pain subsided. His body still ached and he could feel how tender his flesh was, but his mind slowly began to clear. Much to his chagrin, Kilian tasted the copper of his blood as he stopped biting his lower lip. *Well, that's just great*, he chided himself as the initial flow of blood subsided. *Just what I needed: another injury. No wonder this venture is going to kill me.* He sighed loudly at the thought.

One of Bluebeard's soldiers fell to Kilian's right side. The merman's blue skin turned an ashen gray as Kilian watched the light leave the man's eyes. He shivered as he realized that he was still in the midst of battle. *How long have I been out of it?* he thought as he grasped for his ax. His fingers went through air. Try as he might, he couldn't remember the last time he'd felt the ax's magic flow through him.

Frantically, Kilian scrambled around the fallen soldiers in his search for his weapon. He slipped on a river of blood and slid into a mound of dead bodies. He landed face-to-face with another one of Bluebeard's warriors. Her cheeks were sunken and her eyes burned out. Kilian jerked backwards as she stared sightlessly at him. From the recesses of his mind he remembered how Adrienne looked the night Kaldeena killed him. Instinctively, he knew Rhymaldis's army had the power to doom those they killed to be separated from their souls.

"So, this is the great hero whispered about through the ages," a voice said gravelly.

Kilian snapped his head up. There, not ten feet away from him, stood the Shadow King himself. Rhymaldis seemed to float over the rocky terrain. Despite the lack of wind, Rhymaldis' red cape fluttered behind him.

"You are not what I was expecting," the same voice said.

Kilian tried to stand, but his knees gave out as soon as he put pressure on them. His hand slipped on a sword's blade, slicing his palm wide open. Fumbling, Kilian gripped the sword's hilt. It felt heavy in his hand. Still, Kilian swung the sword towards the Shadow King. It slipped from his hand and fell to the ground with a muffled thump. Cursing beneath his breath, Kilian crawled towards a large boulder that stood between them.

Rhymaldis stopped advancing on Kilian. It was difficult to tell, but Kilian was certain that the wraith-like Creator was watching Kilian struggle through the slits in his helmet. A shiver ran up Kilian's back and he felt the force from earlier sweep through his mind.

"How weak you are, Kilian," Rhymaldis hissed in Kilian's mind.

Kilian threw up a weak barrier to protect himself. Rhymaldis pushed through it as if it were nothing more than a gossamer spider web. Kilian's head whipped backwards as the force of Rhymaldis's presence pressed upon him. Although it was not a physical assault, Kilian felt as if he were being gnawed down to the bone. Grimacing, he turned to face the Shadow King once more.

A glimmer of red caught Kilian's eye. *My ax,* he thought groggily. The blade was dug deep into the orange earth, but not enough to mask its glow. Kilian breathed in deeply. All thoughts of his pain and the impending doom he knew he would have to face faded. Even from the distance between them, Kilian could feel the call of his ax.

Kilian leapt to his feet. Pain shot through his back in the places he knew he must be bruised. Deftly, Kilian pulled out the small knife he kept in his boot and feigned a lung at Rhymaldis. He could hear the Shadow King laugh as he thrust his massive hammer at Kilian. Twisting to the left, Kilian managed to miss being struck by the hammer by mere inches; however, Kilian did not have enough time to get his feet beneath him.

He rolled uncontrollably across the rocky terrain. Multiple rocks ripped through his skin, leaving flesh wounds in their wake. When he finally stopped rolling, Kilian felt nauseous and out of breath. Panting, Kilian assumed one of the crouching stances that Narcon had taught him all those years ago and examined the new layout of the battle.

He was now only about three arms' lengths away from his ax. The clash of armies rang through the air. Kilian searched the battle for any sign of Tavia. He couldn't find her in the fray, but he did see Alex slice through a group of four wraiths before falling back to Bluebeard's banner. The fallen Shadow Knights lumbered back to their feet and began advancing on Alex once more. *There's no way we can win this battle*, Kilian realized, *not unless I'm able to defeat Rhymaldis*. He turned his attention back to the Shadow King.

Rhymaldis loomed above him. He seemed to be waiting for Kilian to act. While Kilian had been distracted in his search to find Tavia in the battle, Rhymaldis had claimed his hammer once more. *She'll die if I don't do this*, Kilian thought. Then, as if believing in himself for the first time, Kilian thought, *I was born for this*. Scrambling to his feet, Kilian flung himself towards his ax. His fingers wrapped around the hilt of the ax just as Kilian felt the hammer slam into the back of his calf.

He felt his bones snap.

Kilian screamed in pain and nearly dropped his ax once more. He fell forwards with his hand still wrapped around the leather handle. *I can't give up*, he told himself as he felt the ax's power begin to creep through his veins. Heat coursed through his body, leaving the sensation of blisters trailing behind. His entire body was alight with energy. It felt as if his muscles were strengthening and pulsing with a newfound force. All he saw was red.

Snarling, Kilian heaved his ax upwards and flung himself at Rhymaldis. The ax's power yielded strength to his shattered body. Putting all his weight into his weapon, Kilian lodged the ax's blade into the Shadow King's chest. He felt hot, sticky blood flow over his hand as he yanked the ax free from Rhymaldis's chest. It was coated in black slime that smelled like sulfur.

"Did you really think that little toy of yours would be enough to kill me?" Rhymaldis sneered. Kilian watched in horror as the deep gash in the Shadow King's chest mended itself completely. Even the blackened armor fused itself back together. "I am a Creator, Kilian. Who do you think you are?" Rhymaldis laughed as he waved his hand in front of him. His hammer zipped through the air and landed in the palm of his hand. "You are nothing but a bug that I intend to squash."

Kilian's knee began to buckle from the strain of holding him upright. Kilian tottered before ducking into a low crouch just as Rhymaldis swung his hammer in the spot where Kilian's head had been only seconds before. Tucking his injured leg to his chest, Kilian rolled towards Rhymaldis and dug his ax into his opponent's ankle. A puff of black smoke escaped the wound, but there was no other indication that Kilian had injured the Shadow King.

Kilian was about to roll away from Rhymaldis when the wraith stomped on Kilian's shoulder with surprising speed. Kilian tried to pull himself out of Rhymaldis's hold, but not even the added strength his ax provided him could help him break free. Kilian's eyes widened as Rhymaldis raised his hammer high above his head.

So, this is it, Kilian thought as he closed his eyes and waited for the blow. *I failed*. Tavia's face filled his mind as he sucked in one last breath.

Chapter Twenty-Six

"What does it mean to be a hero? Many have pondered on this topic and yet so very few have found a suitable response. I have found that the truest hero is the one who, despite all the odds, remains true to their cause. Even now, the prophecies of old have begun to fracture. Those who were raised to believe in their destiny have failed. It is the world shattering. It is the remaking of a realm long overdue. So many of our 'heroes' lose faith in the Light. They destroy that which they are meant to save. They perish in their pursuit to fulfill their own desires instead of those of the Light.

I fear for the future. For I have seen what is to come and none of us shall survive.

-From the personal journal of Navalara the Bard,

Oracle of the Second Order

***

The impact of the hammer was not what Kilian had been expecting. It was heavy, yet somehow soft. Warm liquid spilled over his face in what Kilian assumed to be the mashing of his own flesh and bones. *This is what it feels like to die?* Kilian thought as he waited for the pain that didn't come.

Opening his eyes, Kilian stared straight into an unblinking eyeball. Shouting slightly, Kilian squirmed away from the face. Her blue skin slid over him, covered in her still warm blood. *Kaldeena,* Kilian realized as he pulled himself out from beneath her. Her head lulled to one side and her eyes remained open. Kilian grimaced as he noticed the deep crevasse in her chest.

"No," he whispered. His mind raced as he tried to come up with all the possible solutions for why Kaldeena was here. He thought for a moment that perhaps Rhymaldis was once again forcing images into his mind that weren't real. Yet, the longer he stared at his mother, the more he realized just how real she was. Blood spilled from her sunken chest like an overflowing water bucket. It seemed to never stop.

Leaning down, Kilian stroked Kaldeena's raven-black hair away from her face. Her eyelids fluttered slightly, but her eyes stared blankly ahead. Kilian wondered if his mother had taken refuge in her dream world when Rhymaldis struck her. Anger boiled within him.

"That blow was meant for me!" he cried. He pulled Kaldeena's lifeless body into his arms. Blue blood coated his hands as he tried to staunch the bleeding. A thin trail of blood slowly ran from her mouth. Leaning down, Kilian willed himself to feel her breath upon his ear. There was nothing.

"What are you doing here?" he found himself asking her. The last time they had met, he was certain she would leave him to his fate—his death. *Why did you save me*? he thought as he stroked her face. *You should have just let me die*. Although Kilian had every reason to despise her, he knew that he would always regret not having a true opportunity to know the woman who had given birth to him. "I'm so sorry, Kaldeena," he whispered as he held her to his chest.

"Her sacrifice will not save you," Rhymaldis whispered from above him.

Kilian glared at the Shadow King. "You killed her," he shouted.

Rhymaldis laughed. "Yes, and now I shall kill you," he said as he lifted the visor of his helmet.

Kilian gasped. The face beneath the helmet was shriveled and gray. The eyes were hollowed out empty pits. He glanced back down at Kaldeena. He didn't know how she had gotten to the Beyond, but he knew that if she had sacrificed herself now that he had to take a final stand.

Gripping his ax as tightly as he could, Kilian forced himself to rise. Kaldeena's body slid to the ground between Kilian and Rhymaldis. He let loose a wordless cry of rage and charged at his foe.

He couldn't be sure, but Kilian thought he saw a look of surprise cross Rhymaldis's face. The expression only spurred him onwards. Rhymaldis blocked Kilian's initial blow with his vambrace. His ax slid on the hardened armor. *It must be magicked*, Kilian thought as sparks flew in his face. He landed on his injured leg and fell to the ground. Growling, Kilian spun around just as Rhymaldis was bringing his hammer down to crush Kilian's skull from the back. Using the ax, Kilian blocked the assault.

"I will never give up," Kilian grimaced as his muscles strained against Rhymaldis's attack.

"You should prepare yourself, Kilian. None survive against me," Rhymaldis hissed.

Yelling, Kilian used the last reserves of his strength to force Rhymaldis backwards. He felt the full force of his ax's powers course through his body. The Shadow King stumbled as he was thrust backwards.

Kilian saw him smirk. He knelt on his good knee. Blood continued to trail from Kilian's crushed calf. His ax could do many things, but it could not heal his wounds. Breathing heavily, Kilian forced himself to stand once more.

"I. Will. Never. Give. Up!" Kilian screamed as he flung himself on Rhymaldis at the same time the Shadow King lifted his hammer to swing.

Two things happened at once. Kilian lodged his ax, glowing the most brilliant red it ever had before, into Rhymaldis's neck. And Rhymaldis's hammer slammed into Kilian's chest.

Kilian landed on his back with the hammer still wedged into his chest. He didn't feel the pain. He had heard the twins discuss battle shock before, but he had never truly understood what the expression meant. Now he did. He knew that if it hadn't been for the ax's power that he would have been instantly killed from the blow. He wheezed as he groped at his chest. His hands came back coated in blood.

Rhymaldis's shadow fell across Kilian's face.

"You fight bravely, hero."

Kilian spat. "I've been taught by the best," he managed to rasp through his crushed chest.

Rhymaldis laughed. "None are better than I," he said. The roar of the battle almost drowned out the Shadow Knight's voice. Yet, Kilian somehow heard him as he continued, "You have a choice, Kilian Clearwater."

"I've never had a choice," Kilian began.

Rhymaldis snarled at this. "This is what my brethren would have you believe." He said as he crouched down next to Kilian. "There is always a choice, Kilian, if you are brave enough to make it."

"I'm sure my fellow Creators have fed you with lies," he continued. "Did they tell you that I betrayed them? Did they align me with the Darkness?"

When Kilian didn't answer, Rhymaldis pressed his icy cold hand upon Kilian's brow. "I represent the free world, Kilian, and I offer you the following choice. Join me as one of my knights in the impending war or I will kill you."

"That doesn't seem like much of a choice," Kilian managed to croak.

"It's the only choice you have. Either way, you will achieve freedom."

Kilian shivered. He felt colder than he ever had before. He thought about everything he had faced to get to this point. All the lies. All the adventures. Everything had led him to this point. The smell of Tavia filled him. He saw the curve of her smile and the way her eyes brightened whenever he was near. *If I fail*, Kilian realized, *she'll die*.

Cordelia's words came back to him. He remembered what she had said about Clara. He remembered how the other six Creators had used her sword to trap her in sea serpent form. In that moment, Kilian knew how he could defeat the Shadow King.

Without pausing to think about the consequences, Kilian wrenched the hammer out of his sternum. Blood sprayed Rhymaldis's face. Like the ax and the sword, Kilian felt a burst of energy as he wielded the hammer. Although he felt weaker than he ever had before, Kilian exerted what little life was left in him to slam the hammer into Rhymaldis's temple.

The Shadow King's skull burst into black dust as his own weapon was used against him. The rest of Rhymaldis's body disintegrated. The black powder swirled in the air before Kilian. The hammer felt hot in his hand. It glowed a fiery yellow as the dust swelled. The black dust surged towards Kilian and funneled into the hammer. The air felt thick and hot. Kilian's ears popped as the air pressure increased. In an instant, the black dust disappeared into the hammer. Exhausted, Kilian collapsed to the ground.

Chapter Twenty-Seven

Kilian felt weightless. He wondered if this was how people felt when they were dying. The only thing holding him to his body was the weight of Rhymaldis's hammer in his hand. It was excruciatingly hot and vibrated softly. The sound of battle faded into silence. Kilian allowed himself to fall backwards onto the ground. Orange dust billowed in the air, causing him to cough slightly. The yellow sun was too bright in his eyes. *I've done it*, he thought. *I've fulfilled my destiny*. The thought comforted him as he allowed the sense of warmth to overtake him.

A force swept through his body. Kilian felt his bones mending and his skin stretching across his wounds. He felt strong, stronger than he ever had before. The hammer shook violently as the last of Kilian's wounds healed. With a jolt, the hammer went completely still. He rose from the ground.

Dropping his ax, Kilian held the hammer with both hands. He glowed a brilliant gold as he stepped forwards. The entirety of Rhymaldis's army bowed before him. Bluebeard stood alone amid the crouching figures. His beard glowed blue and Clara's purple sword was held before him.

"A challenge?" Kilian asked in a booming voice. He was powerful. He alone could control what remained of the undead army.

"Aye," Bluebeard said as he took a step towards Kilian. "If that be what you want." He showed no signs of backing down.

"I have done what you asked, Bluebeard," Kilian said. "I have achieved the three tasks. I have conquered a Creator. You will bow before me." Kilian wasn't sure where these words were coming from, but the moment he spoke them he knew they were true. He was meant to rule.

"Kilian," Bluebeard said firmly, "this isn't what you want, son."

"How would you know what I want, Bluebeard?" Kilian responded imperiously. "You tricked me into coming here. You knew my father never wanted this life for me. You knew that this task would most likely end in my death." He lifted the hammer. "You took the Ula Unan throne because of me. You have one of the Creator's weapons because of me." He pointed the hammer in Bluebeard's direction. "You exist because of me."

Bluebeard took a step towards Kilian. His beard glowed even more brilliantly. Kilian felt the tendrils of Bluebeard's magic pressing in upon him, but he whisked it away as if it were nothing but an annoying gnat in the breeze.

"I'm sorry, son," Bluebeard whispered as he charged at Kilian.

By instinct Kilian thrust the hammer straight at Bluebeard's chest. The glowing weapon twirled in the air before slamming into Bluebeard's breast plate with a resounding thud. Bluebeard stumbled backwards, but his armor displayed no signs of damage. Whispered words, barely distinct echoed in Kilian's mind. They called to him to destroy. To conquer. To control.

Lifting his hand, Kilian called the hammer back to him. It obeyed as easily as it had when Rhymaldis was its bearer. A knife pierced Kilian's left greave. Twirling around Kilian swung the hammer in a large arch towards his attacker. Sparks flared in the sky as a chunk of Alex's helmet flew into the air. A long gash stretched across Alex's forehead where the broken metal of his helmet had bit into his skin as it was ripped away.

"You dare defy me?" Kilian asked. "You are nothing more…"

He stopped talking as an arrow lodged itself in the space between Kilian's vambrace and rerebrace. Growling,

Kilian spun to see Bluebeard notching another arrow into a bow. Dark blood seeped from the wound as Kilian plucked it from his arm. The pain only lasted a moment before the hammer's magic healed his wound. He threw the hammer in Bluebeard's direction once more. This time the hammer struck Bluebeard's breast plate with such force that the armor shattered into dozens of shards. Bluebeard fell to the ground, clutching at his chest. Kilian summoned the hammer back to him and prepared to launch it at Bluebeard for a final blow.

A rock clinked off Kilian's armor. He released a loud roar as he spun around to see Tavia holding a slingshot in her hand. Rage filled him.

"Kilian," she called out.

He turned his back on her and advanced on Bluebeard. Raising the hammer high, Kilian prepared to bring his weapon down upon Bluebeard's head. Bluebeard stared up at him, his expression resigned.

"I forgive you, Kilian," he rasped as he held his hands to his chest. "I forgive you."

"There is nothing to forgive," Kilian snarled. His muscles strained as he brought the hammer down.

Tavia shoved Bluebeard out of the way. Kilian stilled his swing just as the hammer's tip landed on Tavia's forehead. Tears filled her eyes as she stared up at him.

"Please, Kilian," she whispered. "Don't do this."

Kilian paused as he heaved the hammer up once more. He peered into her eyes, those stormy, blue with their violet starbursts eyes. Her lips trembled as she bit her bottom lip and looked up at him. Kilian battled within himself. In his mind the word "kill" repeated. Yet, the longer he stared into Tavia's eyes the more at ease he felt.

"I love you," he whispered as his muscles responded to the hammer's command.

The world turned to night. Kilian stumbled as Tavia disappeared and his swing swept through empty air. Cursing, Kilian spun around like a wild animal. He swung uncontrollably as he growled.

A cool breeze swept over him. He was standing in the field outside his family's cottage again. Smoke curled from the chimney the way it had in his youth. Kilian smiled as he remembered his mother's cooking and the smell of his father's pipe in the evening. He heard his siblings laughing as they caught starbugs in their outstretched hands.

"May! Willis!" he called.

The laughter faded into memory and with it the image of his family's cottage. The charred remains of the cottage smoldered as Kilian stepped towards it.

"No," he whispered.

Yes, a voice said in his mind. *This is your destiny, Kilian Clearwater. This is what you were born for.*

The world around him swirled in an array of color. Kilian clenched the hammer tightly in his fist.

"I will destroy them!" he shouted. "I will destroy them all." He writhed in anger. "Who did this?" he asked, although he did not expect an answer.

You did, the voice said in response. *You did this all.*

As Kilian watched, he saw an army of wraiths spill across the land. They left nothing but the dead in their wake. The land withered and turned to dust. Entire towns were destroyed. At their lead was Kilian.

Kilian sank to his knees as tears spilled from his eyes.

"No!" he howled.

Yes! The voice said in response. *Do not look away, Kilian. Do not shy away from what you will do. This is the power of the hammer. This is what you will achieve.*

The hammer glowed a brilliant golden color and vibrated within his clenched fist. He felt its power swell within him. He would be invincible. He would rule the world and there would be none who could defeat him.

"I make my own destiny," Kilian shouted as he held out the hammer and let it drop to the ground.

Sweat dripped down Kilian's brow as the hot sun beat upon him. The hammer rested on the ground by his feet. It seemed to call to him the longer he stared at it. Although it no longer glowed, Kilian could feel its power. He searched for Tavia, but she was nowhere to be found.

"Kilian?" Bluebeard croaked from behind him. Kilian whirled around. The older man held the glowing purple sword before him. His arms trembled from its weight and his cheeks were sunken.

"I'm so sorry, Bluebeard," Kilian said. He remembered the power he'd felt when bearing the hammer. His body ached from battle and he felt cold and weak. The hammer hummed at his feet. Kilian's fingers itched to wrap around its handle. He envisioned how he could control the armies. He saw himself leading the charge to victory in every battle. He would be invincible.

It was then that Kilian realized he would never be free from his desire to wield the hammer. It would always call to him. It would always seek to control him. Kilian peered into Bluebeard's eyes. He had never been able to read those eyes. Sighing, Kilian rushed towards Bluebeard's outstretched sword.

The blade slipped through the gap in what remained of Kilian's leather armor. He pushed himself forward until he felt the tip of the blade break through his back. Tears swelled in his eyes and he gurgled on blood as he whispered Tavia's name.

Bluebeard withdrew the sword almost as quickly as Kilian had impaled himself on it.

"No, no, no," he said as he knelt over Kilian. Kilian had never seen so much concern in the pirate's eyes before.

"Hold on, Kilian," Bluebeard was saying. "Just hold on."

Kilian reached one bloodied hand up and stroked Bluebeard's cheek before closing his eyes and allowing the darkness to consume him.

Chapter Twenty-Eight

Birds chirped above him and the sound of babbling water roared in his head. Kilian could smell the fresh scent of damp earth and feel soft grass beneath his fingertips.

"Where am I?" he asked as he opened his eyes to see sunlight filtering through trees. A stone well stood mere inches away from his head. It was etched with the runes of the Creators. Kilian ran his fingertips over the smooth stone of the alter. It was so like the one his family had prayed at during his youth—the one where Bluebeard had made his blood oath. Kilian breathed in deeply. It had been a long time since he'd felt this at peace.

"Kilian."

Tavia's voice startled Kilian out of his thoughts. Particles of light swirled around him. At first, they took on the transparent shapes of figures cloaked in shimmering robes. Then, as Kilian watched, the figures solidified and morphed into corporeal bodies. Astonished, Kilian took a step back.

"What are you doing here?" Kilian asked, confused. He had been certain impaling himself on Clara's sword had killed him. Yet, here he was.

Glancing at the faces before him, Kilian realized that he recognized one other person other than Tavia.

"Kha-ael-ido?" Kilian asked in surprise. "What's going on? How did you get here? Where are we?" He looked from Kha-ael-ido to Tavia. Neither of them said a word as Kilian desperately tried to piece together what was happening.

"Tell me what's going on!" he demanded.

"Hush now," one of figures commanded. She was tall and stately with long silver hair and pointed ears. A circlet of silver and emeralds adorned her brow. Like Tavia, her eyes were a tumultuous mixture of blues and greens. A starburst of silver outlined her pupils.

Kilian did as he was told.

"Do you know who we are, Kilian?" the woman asked.

"I can guess," Kilian responded quickly. When the woman raised an eyebrow and continued to peer at him without speaking, Kilian uttered in the faintest of whispers, "the Creators."

"Well of course we are," Kha-ael-ido retorted. "I told you that the first time we met."

Kilian barely heard Kha-ael-ido's remarks as he turned all his attention on Tavia. *This can't be true*, he thought. *She would have told me. I would have known.*

"Why didn't you tell me?" Kilian asked as he stepped towards her. His voice was accusatory and harsh, even to his own ears.

Her shoulders sank and she peered down at her clasped hands. "It wasn't part of the plan," she finally said.

"Wasn't part of the plan!" Kilian exclaimed. "What do you mean it wasn't part of the plan?" his voice rose as he spoke and his breathing became ragged as he tried to control his anger.

"Now is not the time to argue over the past. What's done is done," another one of the Creator's said. This one, a man, had long black hair and pointed nose that looked like a hawk's beak. His eyes were hard and dark. Kilian felt a chill pass over him as the man stared him straight in the eyes.

"Kilian," Tavia said, her voice smooth and plaintive, "we've brought you here to offer you a choice."

"A choice?" Kilian asked. He rubbed his hand on his chin. "You mean like the choice of having a prophecy written about me? You mean a choice like being lied to my entire life? You mean a choice like dying!" He strode towards her. "I'm dead, Tavia. There are no more choices for me."

"What if there were?" The woman to Tavia's right with the silver-starburst eyes asked. "What if you could live, Kilian?"

Kilian's heart hammered in his chest. *Weird*, he thought, *I didn't know dead people could feel their heartbeats*. He decided he wouldn't think about that now. Besides, it was more of a sense of panic than anything else. He couldn't go back, not if the hammer still existed. He remembered the power he'd felt in wielding it, but he also remembered the terrible things he saw himself doing.

"I can't," he said. "I'm sorry, but I must decline whatever offer you had in mind."

A collective gasp circled around the clearing.

"No one declines us, Kilian," he heard one of them say.

"You're making a mistake, my friend," Kha-ael-ido remarked.

"He's nothing but a child, Tavia. How could you think he was ready?" the man with the hawk eyes barked. He glared at Tavia as he traced his finger over the edge of a knife belted to his side.

"Kilian," Tavia's voice cut through the clamor. "Before you make your final decision, there is much that we…I… would like to say to you."

Kilian stared at her, dumbfounded. Folding his arms across his chest Kilian nodded for her to continue. She did.

"I saw Kaldeena die tonight. She sacrificed herself to save you," her voice stammered as she spoke. "Surely you must recognize what this means." She paused as she licked her dry lips. Kilian tried to remain as stoic as possible. His hands still carried the stain of his mother's blood upon them.

"I was surprised to see her here, after your encounter with her on the Dragon's Breath. So, I… examined her mind."

"You did what!" Kilian shouted.

"I needed to know that she wouldn't try to harm you or try to stop what we all knew must occur." Her eyes filled with tears.

She's so beautiful, Kilian caught himself thinking as he stared into those eyes. *No!* he nearly screamed at himself. *Pull yourself together, Kilian. She's a Creator. She's been lying to you this whole time. She probably doesn't even...*

"In the end, she gave up everything for you. Don't waste her sacrifice now."

"Trust me, I'm not," Kilian responded as he remembered the smell of burning flesh and decay from the havoc he wrecked upon the whole of Mitier.

Tavia floated towards him. Her feet never touched the ground as she hovered before him. Gently, she took his hands in her own. "Please, Kilian. At least listen to what we have to offer. You may find that it is exactly what you have always wanted."

Kilian balked at her. "There's nothing that you could offer me..."

"I love you, Kilian Clearwater," Tavia said, cutting him off. She leaned towards him and kissed him. A jolt of energy passed between them and Kilian found himself responding to her touch. Her soft lips caressed his own and her fingers found their way into his hair. "We could be together," she whispered huskily as she kissed him again.

Kilian let himself succumb to her kisses. He traced his fingers up and down her back. He felt her shiver as his hands landed on her hips and pulled her in tight against him. He smothered her in caresses.

"I've missed you," he whispered, all thoughts of his mother, the hammer, and their onlookers slipped from his mind as he breathed in her familiar chocolate and pine needle scent.

"Then choose to stay with me," she murmured into his ear as she nuzzled his neck.

Kilian pulled back just enough to peer into her eyes. Despite everything that had happened between them, he loved her. Tilting his head towards her, Kilian kissed her. He felt her heat—her magic—course through his veins.

So, this is what it's like to be alive.

Epilogue

Tree branches scraped across Kilian's flesh as he raced through the forest. The Arcadi River flowed to his right as he followed the path left behind by his prey. Breathing in deeply, Kilian let himself remember how his father had taught him to track animals in the forest. He had been six years old when his father had first shown him how to set a trap. Kilian had cried when his father had made him skin the rabbit they'd caught and roast it over an open fire. Now, the memory made him laugh.

Dim starlight and the faint glow of the sister moons filtered through treetops as he wound his way through the trees. He heard horses neighing ahead and the sound of hushed conversations. Crouching low, Kilian pulled his ax, Wraith-Killer, from his belt. Its familiar warmth rushed through him. Smirking, Kilian watched as a group of soldiers clad in the red banners of Szarmi set up camp by the river.

Taking a step backwards, Kilian heard a loud snapping noise as his foot broke a small twig. *Damnation*! Kilian thought as he heard shouts rise from camp. *And I thought this would be a silent mission.* Shrugging, Kilian charged into the band of soldiers at the perimeter of the clearing.

He cut through one of the soldier's legs as easily as he cut his morning toast. The soldier cried out in pain as blood spurted from his severed arteries. Twisting his body around, Kilian slammed Wraith-Killer through another soldier's helmet and deep into his skull. The soldier's eyes bulged as Kilian yanked his ax free. Gray particles slid from the smooth blade as Kilian twirled it around as he chose his next victim.

The soldiers fell back, their shields held before them. The man with the severed leg whimpered as Kilian stepped on his gut as he advanced to the remaining twelve soldiers. One of them, a younger lad with a mop of blonde hair who had forgotten to put on his helmet, launched an arrow at Kilian's head. The arrow pierced Kilian's skin. Flecks of blood sprayed into Kilian's eyes. He flicked them away with the back of his hand as he pulled the arrow from his flesh. The wound instantly healed.

Kilian dropped the arrow to the ground. The Szarmian soldier shot another arrow at Kilian. This time, it slammed into his chest, just above Kilian's heart. Kilian jerked in pain at the initial impact. The powers She and the rest of the Creators had imbued him with had not taken away his ability to feel. They had only given him the power to heal.

Gripping the arrow tightly in his fist, Kilian slowly pulled it from his wound. He stared at the young soldier who had injured him the entire time he was removing the arrow. The soldier's lower lip quivered as Kilian rushed forwards and slammed the arrow through the soft spot between the soldier's neck and chin. Warm blood spilled onto his hands as Kilian ripped the arrow out of the soldier's neck and impaled him through the eye. Three of the soldiers whacked Kilian in the back with their swords. Deftly, Kilian swung his ax at their legs, chopping them down as he did so. He left them to die of their own accord as he turned to face the remaining eight soldiers.

Four of them dropped their weapons and bolted into the wilderness. Although his instincts told him to chase them down, Kilian ignored their cowardice. He was here for a single task. Turning his back on the fleeing soldiers, Kilian lunged at the soldier closest to him. Using both hands to wield Wraith-Killer, Kilian cleaved the man's skull in half as he slammed his weapon down.

The final three soldiers crowded around an ornately decorated tent. Fear danced in their eyes as they watched Kilian lift his ax from the remains of their comrade.

"Leave now and I will let you live," Kilian offered. His muscles flexed as he tossed his ax from one hand to the other.

"We cannot," one of the soldiers—the captain from his insignia—responded. His voice quavered as he spoke.

Kilian did not hesitate. Charging forwards, Kilian nearly severed the head of one of the soldiers before quickly jamming his knife into the gut of another. For the captain, the one who had refused him, Kilian slammed his ax into the man's belly and then wrenched it free in a spray of intestines.

Pulling back the flap of the tent, Kilian stared down into the face of a boy no older than ten years of age. He wore a golden crown upon his head. Clutched in the boy's hands was a slender sword. The boy dropped the sword to the ground as he slowly backed away from Kilian as he entered the tent.

"Who are you?" the boy stammered.

"The Light's Hero," Kilian responded imperiously. "I have come to seek recompense for the terrors your people have inflicted upon the magical folk of Mitier."

The boy interrupted, "Do you know who I am?" Although his voice still quivered, the boy stood a little taller as he asked.

"The Crown Prince of Szarmi," Kilian said without emotion.

"Then you know you should take me home," the princeling pouted. "Father doesn't like it when I've been delayed."

Kilian laughed. "You're not going home, Princeling."

"What?" the little boy asked.

Kilian raised Wraith-Killer. He saw the princeling's eyes widen as he realized what Kilian was about to do. For a moment, Kilian thought he heard his father's voice in the recesses of his mind. Then it was gone and all he could think about was what She had asked him to do.

The boy fell to the ground, blood seeping from the wound in his forehead. Kilian's shoulders sagged slightly as he watched the light leave the child's eyes. *It's for my people*, Kilian reminded himself. *This will set them free.*

Find the Other Works of S.A. McClure

Keepers of the Light
The Search

Explore the World of the Broken Prophecies at
www.samcclure.com

Did you enjoy Kilian: A Broken Prophecies Story?

Leave a review on Amazon and Goodreads!

Join Kilian Clearwater as his story continues in the Broken Prophecies Series.

Made in the USA
Lexington, KY
07 August 2017